FIRST AND ONLY

Dan Abnett

BLACK LIBRARY CLASSICS

A WARHAMMER 40,000 NOVEL

BLACK LIBRARY CLASSICS

FIRST AND ONLY

Dan Abnett

BLACK LIBRARY

For Nik, first & only.

A Black Library Publication

First published in 1999 by Games Workshop Ltd.

This edition published in Great Britain in 2013 by
Black Library,
Games Workshop Ltd.,
Willow Road,
Nottingham, NG7 2WS, UK.

10 9 8 7 6 5 4 3 2 1

Cover illustration by Nicolas Delort.

A CIP record for this book is available from the British Library.

UK ISBN 13: 978 1 84970 504 2
US ISBN 13: 978 1 84970 505 9

See Black Library on the internet at

www.blacklibrary.com

Find out more about Games Workshop
and the world of Warhammer 40,000 at

www.games-workshop.com

Printed and bound by CPI Group (UK) Ltd, Croydon, CR0 4YY

It is the 41st millennium. For more than a hundred centuries the Emperor has sat immobile on the Golden Throne of Earth. He is the master of mankind by the will of the gods, and master of a million worlds by the might of his inexhaustible armies. He is a rotting carcass writhing invisibly with power from the Dark Age of Technology. He is the Carrion Lord of the Imperium for whom a thousand souls are sacrificed every day, so that he may never truly die.

Yet even in his deathless state, the Emperor continues his eternal vigilance. Mighty battlefleets cross the daemon-infested miasma of the warp, the only route between distant stars, their way lit by the Astronomican, the psychic manifestation of the Emperor's will. Vast armies give battle in His name on uncounted worlds. Greatest amongst his soldiers are the Adeptus Astartes, the Space Marines, bioengineered super-warriors. Their comrades in arms are legion: the Imperial Guard and countless Planetary Defence Forces, the ever-vigilant Inquisition and the tech-priests of the Adeptus Mechanicus to name only a few. But for all their multitudes, they are barely enough to hold off the ever-present threat from aliens, heretics, mutants – and worse.

To be a man in such times is to be one amongst untold billions. It is to live in the cruellest and most bloody regime imaginable. These are the tales of those times. Forget the power of technology and science, for so much has been forgotten, never to be re-learned. Forget the promise of progress and understanding, for in the grim dark future there is only war. There is no peace amongst the stars, only an eternity of carnage and slaughter, and the laughter of thirsting gods.

AUTHOR
INTRODUCTION

As time has gone by (and it's now coming up on a shocking *decade and a half* since the book was published), *First and Only* has become an increasingly misleading title. It wasn't the first novel I ever wrote (first one published, maybe) and with forty-five other novels sitting on the shelf beside it these days, it's hardly the 'only' either.

Yes, before you say it, I *know* the title actually refers to the Tanith regiment's nickname, but when I chose it I was using it coyly, as a kind of plea for leniency. At that time, I'd been writing comics professionally for over a decade, and though I had ambitions to write novels, it was Black Library's offer to publish the Gaunt book that gave me my first commissioned opportunity. I'd written two novels before that during the nineties (and started *many* others), but they had been written as exercises, to see how I handled the demands of long-form fiction. Basically, I wrote them in my 'spare time' between comic jobs, and I never really pursued publication.

One of them, entirely rebuilt like Steve Austin from the ground up, eventually became my first novel for another publisher. The other still sits in a drawer somewhere, not getting any better with age.

So I was keen, but nervous. I didn't know how readers would take to my prose. I didn't know how I'd get on with the very different disciplines of writing long fiction. I imagined it would be an interesting opportunity, but that I'd soon be heading back to the comparative safety of comics, where evidence suggested that I knew what the hell I was doing. So I chose the title, I suppose, ironically. It was typically coy, diffident, self-deprecating and slightly sarcastic. In short, it was a shield against what I thought would be an inevitable torrent of criticism, a shield wrought from purest British-ness.

Incidentally, dear American readers, do not be flummoxed by my wilful use of the word 'ironically'. I am aware that irony can be a contentious concept. Try not to use the Alanis Morissette definitions, okay? A traffic jam when you're already late is not ironic. It's a good excuse for being late. A plane crash when you're afraid of flying isn't ironic, it's a bleak vindication of your phobia. A black fly in your Chardonnay isn't ironic, it's a bug in your drink, and a death row pardon two minutes too late isn't ironic, it's a searing human tragedy and a savage indictment of capital punishment and the judicial systems that uphold it, which, frankly, makes it your problem and nothing to do with British-ness at all.

Where was I? Oh yeah, so I was being coy. I admit it. I was getting the digs in first before anyone else could. Though I wanted it very much, I never expected a career writing novels, nor did I imagine that *First and Only* would be the basis of a long-running series, or that today I'd be writing an introduction to it as a 'Black Library Classic' just before starting work on the fourteenth in the series, *Flog A Dead Horse!* (NB – joke. Actually called *The Warmaster*).

First and Only was also Black Library's first fully commissioned original novel (before it, other books in the line had been reprints of pre-Black Library works, and fix-ups of stories from *Inferno!*), so I was referencing that landmark too. Again, neither I nor any of the staff at Black Library had any notion of what that landmark would come to represent.

The magazine *Inferno!* was where Gaunt and the Ghosts first began life. I wrote a couple of shorts there, and then expanded the premise of what would have been the next short into the novel. I frankly had very little idea what I was doing, but I loved doing it. I just wrote furiously.

I've said before, but I'll repeat here, that I chose to write an Imperial Guard novel because human characters gave me a way into the universe of Warhammer 40,000. I found the transhuman Space Marines too intimidating and remote to grapple with at first (though I got the hang of it later on). Gaunt and his rabble of regulars were as close to modern human as I could get, and thus gave me – and the readers – something to identify with.

I've also said before that *Necropolis* (the third novel in the series) was the one that really gave me the feeling I was getting the 'hang' of books in general and the Gaunt series in particular. But that does a disservice to *First and Only,* because it suggests that it's an apprentice piece. Looking back on it, I am surprised at how well-constructed it is. Even from the outset, the main ingredients are there: strong human characters, lots of personal interplay, tough action, the tragedy of war, honour in the face of injustice, the ruthless killing of likeable characters…

Also, right out of the gate, I notice how much in-universe vocab I was making up, words that are now fully integrated into the game as basic vernacular. Vox and vox-caster, data-slate, promethium… I was simply trying to find authentic-sounding terms for everyday objects that needed to feature. I had no idea I was helping to build the universe in any lasting way.

'Authentic' is an important word, actually. As time has gone by, people have told me how much they've loved the Gaunt series, and that's always very gratifying (little by little, the coyness slips away), but I think the greatest compliments I've been paid about the Gaunt series, and about related parts of my Warhammer 40,000 output, have been from serving or veteran members of the military all around the world, who seem to recognise and identify with something in the books. It's not simply a case of the subject matter, apparently (I know, because I've asked the question whenever it's come up), it's something to do with the way the Ghosts interrelate as a body of soldiers, both in frontline war and down-time. I'm told they feel exactly like real soldiers, in terms of their humours, their comradeship, their rivalries, their boredoms, their tricks. I'm extraordinarily glad about that. I do a lot of research, of course, reading about aspects of war through the ages, but I am not (though I have been asked many times) a veteran myself. I think the best SF and Fantasy comes from finding the closest real-world analogue to what you're writing about, researching that to gather an authentic feel, and then translating it sideways into the fictional universe. *First and Only* is where I began to learn how to do that.

This is an unusually sentimental introduction by my standards, so forgive me if it ends like an Oscar ceremony speech. I've been writing the Ghosts for long enough to feel they're real, and I enjoy their company, so I'd like to thank them – Ibram, Tona, Larks, Rawne and the rest – for putting up with my murderous and capricious whimsies. I'd like to thank Marc Gascoigne and Andy Jones for their original faith in me, back when Black Library was all fields, and I'd like to thank all the editors, staffers and fellow authors I've had the pleasure of working with since. I've come a long way, and so has Black Library (fifth largest SF publisher in *the world*, don't cha know!?). I need to thank Nik for believing that I could write novels, for adjusting our lifestyle accordingly, and for being my beta-reader and editor ever since, and Lily and Jess who had to put up with seeing a great deal less of me while I was writing *First and Only*… and who have had to put up with seeing less of me ever since. I tell you, writing novels, it ain't like dusting crops, boy…

And, of course, I want to thank you, the readers, without whose enthusiasm, support, passion and, well, *reading*, all the rest would be rather pointless. *First and Only* is where you got on board. I hope you've enjoyed the ride so far. Are we there yet? Feth, no, we are most certainly not. *Hold tight!*

Dan Abnett
Maidstone, March 2013.

'The High Lords of Terra, lauding the great Warmaster Slaydo's efforts on Khulen, tasked him with raising a crusade force to liberate the Sabbat Worlds, a cluster of nearly one hundred inhabited systems along the edge of the Segmentum Pacificus. From a massive fleet deployment, nearly a billion Imperial Guard advanced into the Sabbat Worlds, supported by forces of the Adeptus Astartes and the Adeptus Mechanicus, with whom Slaydo had formed cooperative pacts.

'After ten hard-fought years of dogged advance, Slaydo's great victory came at Balhaut, where he opened the way to drive a wedge into the heart of the Sabbat Worlds.

'But there Slaydo fell. Bickering and rivalry then beset his officers as they vied to take his place. Lord High Militant General Hechtor Dravere was an obvious successor, but Slaydo himself had chosen the younger commander, Macaroth.

'With Macaroth as warmaster, the Crusade force pushed on, into its second decade, and deeper into the Sabbat Worlds, facing theatres of war that began to make Balhaut seem like a mere opening skirmish…'

— from *A History of the Later Imperial Crusades*

PART ONE

Nubila Reach

The two Faustus-class Interceptors swept in low over a thousand slowly spinning tonnes of jade asteroid and decelerated to coasting velocity. Striated blurs of shift-speed light flickered off their gunmetal hulls. The saffron haze of the nebula called the Nubila Reach hung as a spread backdrop for them, a thousand light years wide, a hazy curtain which enfolded the edges of the Sabbat Worlds.

Each of these patrol Interceptors was an elegant barb about one hundred paces from jutting nose to raked tail. The Faustus were lean, powerful warships that looked like serrated cathedral spires with splayed flying buttresses at the rear to house the main thrusters. Their armoured flanks bore the Imperial eagle, together with the green markings and insignia of the Segmentum Pacificus Fleet.

Locked in the hydraulic arrestor struts of the command seat in the lead ship, Wing Captain Torten LaHain forced down his heart rate as the ship decelerated. Synchronous mind-impulse links bequeathed by the Adeptus Mechanicus hooked his metabolism to the ship's ancient systems, and he lived and breathed every nuance of its motion, power-output and response.

LaHain was a twenty-year veteran. He'd piloted Faustus Interceptors for so long, they seemed an extension of his body. He glanced down into the flight annex directly below and behind the command seat, where his observation officer was at work at the navigation station.

'Well?' he asked over the intercom.

The observer checked off his calculations against several glowing runes on the board. 'Steer five points starboard. The astropath's instructions are to sweep down the edge of the gas clouds for a final look, and then it's back to the fleet.'

Behind him, there was a murmur. The astropath, hunched in his small throne-cradle, stirred. Hundreds of filament leads linked the astropath's socket-encrusted skull to the massive sensory apparatus in the Faustus's belly. Each one was marked with a small, yellowing parchment label, inscribed with words LaHain didn't want to have to read. There was the cloying smell of incense and unguents.

'What did he say?' LaHain asked.

The observer shrugged. 'Who knows? Who wants to?' he said.

The astropath's brain was constantly surveying and processing the vast wave of astronomical data which the ship's sensors pumped into it, and psychically probing the warp beyond. Small patrol ships like this, with their astropathic cargo, were the early warning arm of the fleet. The work was hard on the psyker's mind, and the odd moan or grimace was commonplace. There had been worse. They'd gone through a nickel-rich asteroid field the previous week and the psyker had gone into spasms.

'Flight check,' LaHain said into the intercom.

'Tail turret, aye!' crackled back the servitor at the rear of the ship.

'Flight engineer ready, by the Emperor!' fuzzed the voice of the engine chamber.

LaHain signalled his wingman. 'Moselle… you run forward and begin the sweep. We'll lag a way behind you as a double-check. Then we'll pull for home.'

'Mark that,' the pilot of the other ship replied and his craft gunned forward, a sudden blur that left twinkling pearls in its wake.

LaHain was about to kick in behind when the voice of the astropath came over the link. It was rare for the man to speak to the rest of the crew.

'Captain… move to the following co-ordinates and hold. I am receiving a signal. A message… source unknown.'

LaHain did as he was instructed and the ship banked around, motors flaring in quick, white bursts. The observer swung all the sensor arrays to bear.

'What is this?' LaHain asked, impatient. Unscheduled manoeuvres off a carefully set patrol sweep did not sit comfortably with him.

The astropath took a moment to respond, clearing his throat.

'It is an astropathic communiqué, struggling to get through the warp. It is coming from extreme long range. I must gather it and relay it to Fleet Command.'

'Why?' LaHain asked. This was all too irregular.

'I sense it is secret. It is primary level intelligence. It is Vermilion level.'

There was a long pause, a silence aboard the small, slim craft broken only by the hum of the drive, the chatter of the displays and the whirr of the air-scrubbers.

'Vermilion...' LaHain breathed.

Vermilion was the highest clearance level used by the Crusade's cryptographers. It was unheard of, mythical. Even main battle schemes usually only warranted a Magenta. He felt an icy tightness in his wrists, a tremor in his heart.

Sympathetically, the Interceptor's reactor fibrillated. LaHain swallowed.

A routine day had just become very un-routine. He knew he had to commit everything to the correct and efficient recovery of this data.

'How long do you need?' he asked over the link.

Another pause. 'The ritual will take a few moments. Do not disturb me as I concentrate. I need as long as possible,' the astropath said. There was a phlegmy, strained edge to his voice. In a moment, that voice was murmuring a prayer. The air temperature in the cabin dropped perceptibly. Something, somewhere, sighed.

LaHain flexed his grip on the rudder stick, his skin turning to gooseflesh. He hated the witchcraft of the psykers. He could taste it in his mouth, bitter, sharp. Cold sweat beaded under his flight-mask. Hurry up! he thought... It was taking too long, they were idling and vulnerable; and he wanted his skin to stop crawling.

The astropath's murmured prayer continued. LaHain looked out of the canopy at the swathe of pinkish mist that folded away from him into the heart of the nebula a billion kilometres away. The cold, stabbing light of ancient suns slanted and shafted through it like dawn light on gossamer. Dark-bellied clouds swirled in slow, silent blossoms.

'Contacts!' the observer yelled suddenly. 'Three! No, four! Fast as hell and coming straight in!'

LaHain snapped to attention. 'Angle and lead time?'

The observer rattled out a set of co-ordinates and LaHain steered the nose towards them. 'They're coming in fast!' the observer repeated. 'Throne of Earth, but they're moving!'

LaHain looked across his over-sweep board and saw the runic cursors flashing as they edged into the tactical grid.

'Defence system activated! Weapons to ready!' he barked. Drum autoloaders chattered in the chin turret forward of him as he armed the autocannons, and energy reservoirs whined as they powered up the main forward-firing plasma guns.

'Wing Two to Wing One!' Moselle's voice rasped over the long-range vox-caster. 'They're all over me! Break and run! Break and run in the name of the Emperor!'

The other Interceptor was coming at him at close to full thrust. LaHain's enhanced optics, amplified and linked via the canopy's systems, saw Moselle's ship while it was still a thousand kilometres away. Behind it, lazy and slow, came the vampiric shapes, the predatory ships of Chaos. Fire patterns winked in the russet darkness. Yellow traceries of venomous death.

Moselle's scream, abruptly ended, tore through the vox-cast.

The racing Interceptor disappeared in a rapidly expanding, superheated fireball. The three attackers thundered on through the fire wash.

'They're coming for us! Bring her about!' LaHain yelled and threw the Faustus round, gunning the engines. 'How much longer?' he bellowed at the astropath.

'The communiqué is received. I am now… relaying…' the astropath gasped, at the edge of his limits.

'Fast as you can! We have no time!' LaHain said.

The sleek fighting ship blinked forward, thrust-drive roaring blue heat. LaHain rejoiced at the singing of the engine in his blood. He was pushing the threshold tolerances of the ship. Amber alert sigils were lighting his display. LaHain was slowly being crushed into the cracked, ancient leather of his command chair.

In the tail turret, the gunner servitor traversed the twin auto-cannons, hunting for a target. He didn't see the attackers, but he saw their absence – the flickering darkness against the stars.

The turret guns screamed into life, blitzing out a scarlet-tinged, boiling stream of hypervelocity fire.

Indicators screamed shrill warnings in the cockpit. The enemy had obtained multiple target lock. Down below, the observer was bawling up at LaHain, demanding evasion procedures. Over the link, Flight Engineer Manus was yelling something about a stress-injection leak.

LaHain was serene. 'Is it done?' he asked the astropath calmly.

There was another long pause. The astropath was lolling weakly in his cradle. Near to death, his brain ruined by the trauma of the act, he murmured, 'It is finished.'

LaHain wrenched the Interceptor in a savage loop and presented himself to the pursuers with the massive forward plasma array and the nose guns blasting. He couldn't outrun them or outfight them, but by the Emperor he'd take at least one with him before he went.

The chin turret spat a thousand heavy bolter rounds a second. The plasma guns howled phosphorescent death into the void. One of the shadow-shapes exploded in a bright blister of flame, its shredded fuselage and mainframe splitting out, carried along by the burning, incandescent bow-wave of igniting propellant.

LaHain scored a second kill too. He ripped open the belly of another attacker, spilling its pressurised guts into the void. It burst like a swollen balloon, spinning round under the shuddering impact and spewing its contents in a fire trail behind itself.

A second later, a rain of toxic and corrosive warheads, each a sliver of metal like a dirty needle, raked the Faustus end to end. They detonated the astropath's head and explosively atomised the observer out through the punctured hull. Another killed the flight engineer outright and destroyed the reactor interlock.

Two billiseconds after that, stress fractures shattered the Faustus class Interceptor like a glass bottle. A super-dense explosion boiled out from the core, vaporising the ship and LaHain with it.

The corona of the blast rippled out for eighty kilometres until it vanished in the nebula's haze.

A MEMORY

Darendara, Twenty Years Earlier

The winter palace was besieged. In the woods on the north shore of the frozen lake, the field guns of the Imperial Guard thumped and rumbled. Snow fluttered down on them, and each shuddering retort brought heavier falls slumping down from the tree limbs. Brass shell-cases clanked as they spun out of the returning breeches and fell, smoking, into snow cover that was quickly becoming trampled slush.

Over the lake, the palace crumbled. One wing was now ablaze, and shell holes were appearing in the high walls or impacting in the vast arches of the steep roofs beyond them. Each blast threw up tiles and fragments of beams, and puffs of snow like icing sugar. Some shots fell short, bursting the ice skin of the lake and sending up cold geysers of water, mud, and sharp chunks that looked like broken glass.

Commissar-General Delane Oktar, chief political officer of the Hyrkan Regiments, stood in the back of his winter-camouflage painted halftrack and watched the demolition through his field scope. When Fleet Command had sent the Hyrkans in to quell the uprising on Darendara, he had known it would come to this. A bloody, bitter end. How many opportunities had they given the Secessionists to surrender?

Too many, according to that rat-turd Colonel Dravere, who commanded the armoured brigades in support of the Hyrkan infantry. That would be a matter Dravere would gleefully report in his despatches, Oktar knew. Dravere was a career soldier with the pedigree of noble blood who was gripping the ladder of advancement so tightly with both hands that his feet were free to kick out at those on lower rungs.

Oktar didn't care. The victory mattered, not the glory. As a commissar-general, his authority was well liked, and no one doubted his loyalty to the Imperium, his resolute adherence to the primary dictates, or the rousing fury of his speeches to the men. But he believed war was a simple thing, where caution and restraint could win far more for less cost.

He had seen the reverse too many times before. The command echelons generally believed in the theory of attrition when it came to the Imperial Guard. Any foe could be ground into pulp if you threw enough at them, and the Guard was, to them, a limitless supply of cannon fodder for just such a purpose.

That was not Oktar's way. He had schooled the officer cadre of the Hyrkans to believe it too. He had taught General Caernavar and his staff to value every man, and knew the majority of the six thousand Hyrkans, many by name. Oktar had been with them from the start, from the First Founding on the high plateaux of Hyrkan, those vast, gale-wracked industrial deserts of granite and grassland. Six regiments they had founded there, six proud regiments, and just the first of what Oktar hoped would be a long line of Hyrkan soldiers, who would set the name of their planet high on the honour roll of the Imperial Guard, from Founding to Founding.

They were brave boys. He would not waste them, and he would not have the officers waste them. He glanced down from his half-track into the tree-lines where the gun teams serviced their thumping limbers. The Hyrkan were a strong breed, drawn and pale, with almost colourless hair which they preferred to wear short and severe. They wore dark grey battledress with beige webbing and short-billed forage caps of the same pale hue. In this cold theatre, they also had woven gloves and long great-coats. Those labouring at the guns, though, were stripped down to their beige undershirts, their webbing hanging loosely around their hips as they bent and carried shells, and braced for firing in the close heat of the concussions. It looked odd, in these snowy wastes, with breath steaming the air, to see men moving through gunsmoke in thin shirts, hot and ruddy with sweat.

He knew their strengths and weaknesses to a man, knew exactly who best to send forward to reconnoitre, to snipe, to lead a charge offensive, to scout for mines, to cut wire, to inter-rogate prisoners. He valued each and every man for his abilities in the field of war. He would not waste them. He and General Caernavar would use them, each one in his particular way, and they would win and win and win again, a hundred times more than any who used his regiments like bullet-soaks in the bloody frontline.

Men like Dravere. Oktar dreaded to think what that beast might do when finally given field command of an action like this. Let the little piping runt in his starched collar sound off to the high brass about him. Let him make a fool of himself. This wasn't his victory to win.

Oktar jumped down from the vehicle's flatbed and handed his scope to his sergeant. 'Where's the Boy?' he asked, in his soft, penetrating tones.

The sergeant smiled to himself, knowing the Boy hated to be known as 'The Boy'.

'Supervising the batteries on the rise, commissar-general,' he said in a faultless Low Gothic, flavoured with the clipped, guttural intonations of the Hyrkan home world accent.

'Send him to me,' Oktar said, rubbing his hands gently to encourage circulation. 'I think it's time he got a chance to advance himself.'

The sergeant turned to go, then paused. 'Advance himself, commissar – or advance, himself?'

Oktar grinned like a wolf. 'Both, naturally.'

The Hyrkan sergeant bounded up the ridge to the field guns at the top, where the trees had been stripped a week before by a Secessionist airstrike. The splintered trunks were denuded back to their pale bark, and the ground under the snow was thick with wood pulp, twigs and uncountable fragrant needles.

There would be no more airstrikes, of course. Not now. The Secessionist airforce had been operating out of two airstrips south of the winter palace which had been rendered useless by Colonel Dravere's armoured units. Not that they'd had much to begin with – maybe sixty ancient-pattern slamjets with cycling cannons in the armpits of the wings and struts on the wingtips for the few bombs they could muster.

The sergeant had cherished a sneaking admiration for the Secessionist fliers, though. They'd tried damn hard, taking huge risks to drop their payloads where it counted, and without the advantage of good air-to-ground instrumentation. He would never forget the slamjet which took out their communication bunker in the snow lines of the mountain a fortnight before. It had passed low twice to get a fix, bouncing through the frag-bursts which the anti-air batteries threw up all around it. He could still see the faces of the pilot and the gunner as they passed, plainly visible because the canopy was hauled back so they could get a target by sight alone.

Brave... desperate. Not a whole lot of difference in the sergeant's book. Determined, too – that was the commissar-general's view. They knew they were going to lose this war before it even started, but still they tried to break loose from the Imperium. The sergeant knew that Oktar admired them; and, in turn, he admired the way Oktar had urged the chief of staff to give the rebels every chance to surrender. What was the point of killing for no purpose?

Still, the sergeant had shuddered when the three thousand pounder had fishtailed down into the communications bunker and flattened it. Just as he had cheered when the thumping, traversing quad-barrels of the Hydra anti-air batteries had pegged the slamjet as it pulled away. It looked like it had been kicked from behind, jerking up at the tail and then tumbling, end over end, as it exploded and burned in a long, dying fall into the distant trees.

The sergeant reached the hilltop and caught sight of the Boy. He was standing amidst the batteries, hefting fresh shells into the arms of the gunners from the stockpiles half-buried under blast curtains. Tall, pale, lean and powerful, the Boy intimidated the sergeant. Unless death claimed him first, the Boy would one day become a commissar in his own right. Until then, he enjoyed the rank of cadet commissar, and served his tutor Oktar with enthusiasm and boundless energy. Like the commissar-general, the Boy wasn't Hyrkan. The sergeant thought then, for the first time, that he didn't even know where the Boy was from – and the Boy probably didn't know either.

'The commissar-general wants you,' he told the Boy as he reached him.

The Boy grabbed another shell from the pile and swung it round to the waiting gunner.

'Did you hear me?' the sergeant asked.

'I heard,' said Cadet Commissar Ibram Gaunt.

He knew he was being tested. He knew that this was responsibility and that he'd better not mess it up. Gaunt also knew that it was his moment to prove to his mentor Oktar that he had the makings of a commissar.

There was no set duration for the training of a cadet. After education at the Schola Progenium and Guard basic training, a cadet received the rest of his training in the field, and the promotion to full commissarial level was a judgement matter for his commanding officer. Oktar, and Oktar alone, could make him or break him. His career as an Imperial commissar, to dispense discipline, inspiration and the love of the God-Emperor of Terra to the greatest fighting force in creation, hinged upon his performance.

Gaunt was an intense, quiet young man, and a commissarial post had been his dearest ambition since his earliest days in the Schola Progenium. But he trusted Oktar to be fair. The commissar-general had personally selected him for service from the cadet honour class, and had become in the last eighteen months almost a father to Gaunt. A stern, ruthless father, perhaps. The father he had never really known.

'See that burning wing?' Oktar had said. 'That's a way in. The Secessionists must be falling back into their inner chambers by now. General Caernavar and I propose putting a few squads in through that hole and cutting out their centre. Are you up to it?'

Gaunt had paused, his heart in his throat. 'Sir... you want me to...'

'Lead them in. Yes. Don't look so shocked, Ibram. You're always asking me for a chance to prove your leadership. Who do you want?'

'My choice?'

'Your choice.'

'Men from the fourth brigade. Tanhause is a good squad

leader and his men are specialists in room to room fighting. Give me them, and Rychlind's heavy weapons team.'

'Good choices, Ibram. Prove me right.'

They moved past the fire and into long halls decorated with tapestries where the wind moaned and light fell slantwise from the high windows. Cadet Gaunt led the men personally, as Oktar would have done, the lasgun held tightly in his hands, his blue-trimmed cadet commissar uniform perfectly turned out.

In the fifth hallway, the Secessionists began their last-ditch counter-attack.

Las-fire cracked and blasted at them. Cadet Gaunt ducked behind an antique sofa that swiftly became a pile of antique matchwood. Tanhause moved up behind him.

'What now?' the lean, corded Hyrkan major asked.

'Give me grenades,' Gaunt said.

They were provided. Gaunt took the webbing belt and set the timers on all twenty grenades. 'Call up Walthem,' he told Tanhause.

Trooper Walthem moved up. Gaunt knew he was famous in the regiment for the power of his throw. He'd been a javelin champion back home on Hyrkan.

'Put this where it counts,' Gaunt said.

Walthem hefted the belt of grenades with a tiny grunt. Sixty paces down, the corridor disintegrated.

They moved in, through the drifting smoke and masonry dust. The spirit had left the Secessionist defence. They found

Degredd, the rebel leader, lying dead with his mouth fused around the barrel of his lasgun.

Gaunt signalled to General Caernavar and Commissar-General Oktar that the fight was over. He marshalled the prisoners out with their hands on their heads as Hyrkan troops set about disabling gun emplacements and munitions stores.

'What do we do with her?' Tanhause asked him.

Gaunt turned from the assault cannon he had been stripping of its firing pin.

The girl was lovely, white-skinned and black haired, as was the pedigree of the Darendarans. She clawed at the clenching hands of the Hyrkan troops hustling her and other prisoners down the draughty hallway.

When she saw Gaunt, she stopped dead. He expected vitriol, anger, the verbal abuse so common in the defeated and imprisoned whose beliefs and cause had been crushed. But what he saw in her face froze him in surprise. Her eyes were glassy, deep, like polished marble. There was a look in her face as she stared back at him. Gaunt shivered when he realised the look was recognition.

'There will be seven,' she said suddenly, speaking surprisingly perfect High Gothic with no trace of the local accent. The voice didn't seem to be her own. It was guttural, and its words did not match the movement of her lips. 'Seven stones of power. Cut them and you will be free. Do not kill them. But first you must find your ghosts.'

'Enough of your madness!' Tanhause snapped, then ordered

the men to take her away. The girl was vacant-eyed by now and froth dribbled down her chin. She was plainly sliding into the throes of a trance. The men were wary of her, and pushed her along at arm's length, scared of her magic. The temperature in the hallway itself seemed to drop. At once, the breaths of all of the men steamed the air. It smelled heavy, burnt and metallic, the way it did before a storm. Gaunt felt the hairs on the back of his neck rise. He could not take his eyes off the murmuring girl as the men bustled her away gingerly.

'The Inquisition will deal with her,' Tanhause shivered. 'Another untrained psyker witch working for the enemy.'

'Wait!' Gaunt said and strode over to her. He tensed, scared of the supernaturally-touched being he confronted. 'What do you mean? "Seven stones"? "Ghosts"?'

Her eyes rolled back, pupilless. The cracked old voice bubbled out of her quivering lips. 'The warp knows you, Ibram.'

He stepped back as if he had been stung. 'How did you know my name?'

She didn't answer. Not coherently, anyway. She began to thrash, gibber and spit. Nonsense words and animal sounds issued from her shuddering throat.

'Take her away!' Tanhause barked.

One man stepped in, then spun to his knees, flailing, blood streaming from his nose. She had done nothing but glance at him. Snarling oaths and protective charms, the others laid in with the butts of their lasguns.

Gaunt watched the corridor for five full minutes after the girl had been dragged away. The air remained cold long after she had disappeared. He looked around at the drawn, anxious face of Tanhause.

'Pay it no heed,' the Hyrkan veteran said, trying to sound confident. He could see the cadet was spooked. Just inexperience, he was sure. Once the Boy had seen a few years, a few campaigns, he'd learn to shut out the mad ravings of the foe and their tainted, insane rants. It was the only way to sleep at night.

Gaunt was still tense. 'What was that about?' he asked, as if he hoped that Tanhause could explain the girl's words.

'Rubbish is what. Forget it, sir.'

'Right. Forget it. Right.'

But Gaunt never did.

PART TWO

Fortis Binary
Forge-world

One

The night sky was matt and dark, like the material of the fatigues they wore, day after day. The dawn stabbed in, as silent and sudden as a knife-wound, welling up a dull redness through the black cloth of the sky.

Eventually the sun rose, casting raw amber light down over the trench lines. The star was big, heavy and red, like a rotten, roasted fruit. Dawn lightning crackled a thousand kilometres away.

Colm Corbec woke, acknowledged briefly the thousand aches and snarls in his limbs and frame, and rolled out of his billet in the trench dugout. His great, booted feet kissed into the grey slime of the trench floor where the duckboards didn't meet.

Corbec was a large man on the wrong side of forty, built like an ox and going to fat. His broad and hairy forearms were decorated with blue spiral tattoos and his beard was thick and shaggy. He wore the black webbing and fatigues of the Tanith and also the ubiquitous camo-cloak which had become their trademark. He also shared the pale complexion, black hair and blue eyes of his people. He was the colonel of the Tanith First and Only, the so-called Gaunt's Ghosts.

He yawned. Down the trench, under the frag-sack and gabion breastwork and the spools of rusting razor wire, the Ghosts awoke too. There were coughs, gasps, soft yelps as nightmares became real in the light of waking. Matches struck under the low bevel of the parapet; firearms were un-swaddled and the damp cleaned off. Firing mechanisms were slammed in and out. Food parcels were unhooked from their vermin-proof positions up on the billet roofs.

Shuffling in the ooze, Corbec stretched and cast an eye down the long, zigzag traverses of the trench to see where the picket sentries were returning, pale and weary, asleep on their feet. The twinkling lights of the vast communication up-link masts flashed eleven kilometres behind them, rising between the rusting, shell-pocked roofs of the gargantuan shipyard silos and the vast Titan fabrication bunkers and foundry sheds of the Adeptus Mechanicus tech-priesthood.

The dark stealth capes of the picket sentries, the distinctive uniform of the Tanith First and Only, were lank and stiff with dried mud. Their replacements at the picket, bleary eyed and puffy, slapped them on the arms as they passed, exchanging jokes and cigarettes. The night sentries, though, were too weary to be forthcoming.

They were ghosts, returning to their graves, Corbec thought. As are we all.

In a hollow under the trench wall, Mad Larkin, the first squad's wiry sniper, was cooking up something that approximated caffeine in a battered tin tray over a fusion burner. The acrid stink hooked Corbec by the nostrils.

'Give me some of that, Larks,' the colonel said, squelching across the trench.

Larkin was a skinny, stringy, unhealthily pale man in his fifties with three silver hoops through his left ear and a purple-blue spiral-wyrm tattoo on his sunken right cheek. He offered up a misshapen metal cup. There was a fragile look, of fatigue and fear, in his wrinkled eyes. 'This morning, do you reckon? This morning?'

Corbec pursed his lips, enjoying the warmth of the cup in his hefty paw. 'Who knows…' His voice trailed off.

High in the orange troposphere, a matched pair of Imperial fighters shrieked over, curved around the lines and plumed away north. Fire smoke lifted from Adeptus Mechanicus work-temples on the horizon, great cathedrals of industry, now burning from within. A second later, the dry wind brought the *crump* of detonations.

Corbec watched the fighters go and sipped his drink. It was almost unbearably disgusting. 'Good stuff,' he muttered to Larkin.

A kilometre off, down the etched zigzag of the trench line, Trooper Fulke was busily going crazy. Major Rawne, the regiment's second officer, was woken by the sound of a lasgun firing at close range, the phosphorescent impacts ringing into frag-sacks and mud.

Rawne spun out of his cramped billet as his adjutant, Feygor, stumbled up nearby. There were shouts and oaths from the men around them. Fulke had seen vermin, the ever-present vermin, attacking his rations, chewing into the plastic seals with their snapping lizard mouths. As Rawne blundered down the trench, the animals skittered away past him, lopping on their big, rabbit-legs, their lice-ridden pelts smeared flat with ooze. Fulke was firing his lasgun on full auto into his sleeping cavity under the bulwark, screaming obscenities at the top of his fractured voice.

Feygor got there first, wrestling the weapon from the bawling trooper. Fulke turned his fists on the adjutant, mashing his nose, splashing up grey mud-water with his scrambling boots.

Rawne slid in past Feygor, and put Fulke out with a hook to the jaw.

There was a crack of bone and the trooper went down, whimpering, in the drainage gully.

'Assemble a firing squad detail,' Rawne spat at the bloody Feygor unceremoniously and stalked back to his dugout.

Trooper Bragg wove back to his bunk. A huge man, unarguably the largest of the Ghosts, he was a peaceable, simple soul. They called him 'Try Again' Bragg because of his terrible aim. He'd been on picket all night and now his bed was singing a lullaby he couldn't resist. He slammed into young Trooper Caffran at a turn in the dugout and almost knocked the smaller man flat.

Bragg hauled him up, his weariness clamming his apologies in his mouth.

'No harm done, Try,' Caffran said. 'Get to your billet.'

Bragg blundered on. Two paces more and he'd even forgotten what he'd done. He simply had an afterimage memory of an apology he should have made to a good friend. Fatigue was total.

Caffran ducked down into the crevice of the command dugout, just off the third communication trench. There was a thick polyfibre shield over the door, and layers of anti-gas curtaining. He knocked twice and then pulled back the heavy drapes and dropped into the deep cavity.

Two

The officer's dugout was deep, accessed only by an aluminium ladder lashed to the wall. Inside, the light was a frosty white from the sodium burners. The floor was well-made of duckboards and there were even such marks of civilisation as shelves, books, charts and an aroma of decent caffeine.

Sliding down into the command burrow, Caffran noticed first Brin Milo, the sixteen year-old mascot the Ghosts had acquired at their Founding. Word was, Milo had been rescued personally from the fires of their homeworld by the commissar himself, and this bond had led him to his status of regimental musician and adjutant to their senior officer. Caffran didn't like to be around the boy much. There was something about his youth and his brightness of eye that reminded him of the world they had lost. It was ironic – back on Tanith with only a year or two between them, they like as not would have been friends.

Milo was setting out breakfast on a small camp table. The smell was delicious: cooking eggs and ham and some toasted bread. Caffran envied the commissar, his position and his luxuries.

'Has the commissar slept well?' Caffran asked.

'He hasn't slept at all,' Milo replied. 'He's been up through the night reviewing reconnaissance transmissions from the orbital watch.'

Caffran hesitated in the entranceway to the burrow, clutching his sealed purse of communiqués. He was a small man, for a Tanith, and young, with shaved black hair and a blue dragon tattoo on his temple.

'Come in, sit yourself down.' At first, Caffran thought Milo had spoken, but it was the commissar himself. Ibram Gaunt emerged from the rear chamber of the dugout looking pale and drawn. He was dressed in his uniform trousers and a white singlet with regimental braces strapped tight in place. He gestured Caffran to the seat opposite him at the small camp table and then swung down onto the other stool.

Caffran hesitated again and then sat at the place indicated.

Gaunt was a tall, hard man in his forties, and his lean face utterly matched his name. Trooper Caffran admired the commissar enormously and had studied his previous actions at Balhaut, at Formal Prime, his service with the Hyrkan Eighth, even his majestic command of the disaster that was Tanith.

Gaunt seemed more tired than Caffran had ever seen, but he trusted this man to bring them through. If anyone could redeem the Ghosts it would be Ibram Gaunt. He was a rare beast, a political officer who had been granted full regimental command and the brevet rank of colonel.

'I'm sorry to interrupt your breakfast, commissar,' Caffran said, sitting uneasily at the camp table, fussing with the purse of communiqués.

'Not at all, Caffran. In fact, you're just in time to join me.' Caffran hesitated once more, not knowing if this was a joke.

'I'm serious,' Gaunt said. 'You look as hungry as I feel. And I'm sure Brin has cooked up more than enough for two.'

As if on cue, the boy produced two ceramic plates of food – mashed eggs and grilled ham with tough, toasted chunks of wheatbread. Caffran looked at the plate in front of him for a moment as Gaunt tucked into his with relish.

'Go on, eat up. It's not every day you get a chance to taste officers' rations,' Gaunt said, wolfing down a forkful of eggs.

Caffran nervously picked up his own fork and began to eat. It was the best meal he'd had in sixty days. It reminded him of his days as an apprentice engineer in the wood mills of lost Tanith, back before the Founding and the Loss, of the wholesome suppers served on the long tables of the refectory after last shift. Before long, he was consuming the breakfast with as much gusto as the commissar, who smiled at him appreciatively.

The boy Milo then produced a steaming pot of thick caffeine, and it was time to talk business.

'So, what do the dispatches tell us this morning?' Gaunt started.

'I don't know, sir,' Caffran said, pulling out the communiqué purse and dropping it onto the tabletop in front of him. 'I just carry these things. I never ask what's in them.'

Gaunt paused for a moment, chewing a mouthful of eggs and ham. He took a long sip of his steaming drink and then reached out for the purse.

Caffran thought to look away as Gaunt unsealed the plastic envelope and read the print-out strips contained within.

'I've been up all night at that thing,' Gaunt said, gesturing over his shoulder to the green glow of the tactical communication artificer, built into the muddy wall of the command burrow. 'And it's told me nothing.'

Gaunt reviewed the dispatches that spilled out of Caffran's purse. 'I bet you and the men are wondering how long we'll be dug into this hell-hole,' Gaunt said. 'The truth is, I can't tell you. This is a war of attrition. We could be here for months.'

Caffran was by now feeling so warm and satisfied by the good meal he had just eaten that the commissar could have told him his mother had been murdered by orks and he wouldn't have worried much.

'Sir?' Milo's voice was a sudden intruder into the gentle calm.

Gaunt looked up. 'What is it, Brin?' he said.

'I think… that is… I think there's an attack coming.'

Caffran chuckled. 'How could you know–' he began but the commissar cut him off.

'Somehow, Milo's sensed each attack so far before it's come. Each one. Seems he has a gift for anticipating shell-fall. Perhaps it's his young ears.' Gaunt crooked a wry grin at Caffran. 'Do you want to argue, eh?'

Caffran was about to answer when the first wail of shells howled in.

Three

Gaunt leapt to his feet, knocking the camp table over. It was the sudden motion rather than the scream of incoming shells which made Caffran leap up in shock. Gaunt was scrabbling for his side-arm, hanging in its holster on a hook by the steps. He grabbed the speech-horn of the vox-caster set, slung under the racks that held his books.

'Gaunt to all units! To arms! To arms! Prepare for maximum resistance!'

Caffran didn't wait for any further instruction. He was already up the steps and banging through the gas curtains as volleys of shells assaulted their trenches. Huge plumes of vaporised mud spat up from the trench head behind him and the narrow gully was full of the yells of suddenly animated guardsmen.

A shell whinnied down low across his position and dug a hole the size of a drop-ship behind the rear breastwork of the trench. Liquid mud drizzled down on him. Caffran pulled his lasgun from its sling and slithered up towards the top of the trench firestep. There was chaos, panic, troopers hurrying in every direction, screaming and shouting.

Was this it? Was this the final moment in the long, drawn-out conflict they had found themselves in? Caffran tried to slide up the side of the trench far enough to get a sight over the lip, across no-man's-land to the enemies' emplacements which they had been locked into for the last six months. All he could see was a mist of smoke and mud.

There was a crackle of lasweapons and several screams. More shells fell. One of them found the centre of a nearby communications trench. Then the screaming became real and immediate. The drizzle that fell on him was no longer water and mud. There were body parts in it.

Caffran cursed and wiped the sight-lens of his lasgun clean of filth. Behind him he heard a shout, a powerful voice that echoed along the traverses of the trench and seemed to shake the duckboards. He looked back to see Commissar Gaunt emerging from his dugout.

Gaunt was dressed now in his full dress uniform and cap, the camo-cloak of his adopted regiment swirling about his shoulders, his face a mask of bellowing rage. In one hand he held his bolt pistol and in the other his chainsword, which whined and sang in the early morning air.

'In the name of Tanith! Now they are on us we must fight! Hold the line and hold your fire until they come over the mud wall!'

Caffran felt a rejoicing in his soul. The commissar was with them and they would succeed, no matter the odds. Then something closed down his world with a vibratory shock that blew mud up into the air and seemed to separate his spirit from his body.

The section of trench had taken a direct hit. Dozens of men were dead. Caffran lay stunned in the broken line of duckboards and splattered mud. A hand grabbed him by the shoulder and hauled him up. Blinking, he looked up to see the face of Gaunt. Gaunt looked at him with a solemn, yet inspiring gaze.

'Sleeping after a good breakfast?' the commissar enquired of the bewildered trooper.

'No sir… I… I…'

The crack of lasguns and needle lasers began to whip around them from the armoured loopholes on the trench head. Gaunt wrenched Caffran back to his feet.

'I think the time has come,' Gaunt said, 'and I'd like all of my brave men to be in the line with me when we advance.'

Spitting out grey mud, Caffran laughed. 'I'm with you, sir,' he said, 'from Tanith to wherever we end up.'

Caffran heard the whine of Gaunt's chainsword as the commissar leapt up the scaling ladder nailed into the trench wall above the firestep and yelled to his men.

'Men of Tanith! Do you want to live forever?'

Their reply, loud and raucous, was lost in the barrage of shells. But Ibram Gaunt knew what they had said.

Weapons blazing, Gaunt's Ghosts went over the top and blasted their way towards glory, death or whatever else awaited them in the smoke.

Four

There was a sizzling thicket of las-fire a hundred paces deep and twenty kilometres long where the advancing legions of the enemy met the Imperial Guard regiments head on. It looked for all the world like squirming nests of colonial insects bursting forth from their mounds and meeting in a chaotic mess of seething forms, lit by the incessant and incandescent sparking crossfire of their weapons.

Lord High Militant General Hechtor Dravere turned away from his tripod-mounted scope. He smoothed the faultless breast of his tunic with well-manicured hands and sighed.

'Who would that be dying down there?' he asked in his disturbingly thin, reedy voice.

Colonel Flense, field commander of the Jantine Patricians, one of the oldest and most venerated Guard regiments, got off his couch and stood smartly to attention. Flense was a tall, powerful man, the tissue of his left cheek disfigured long ago by a splash of tyranid bio-acid.

'General?'

'Those... those ants down there...' Dravere gestured idly over his shoulder. 'I wondered who they were.'

Flense strode across the veranda to the chart table where a flat glass plate was illuminated from beneath with glowing indication runes. He traced a finger across the glass, assessing the four hundred kilometres of battlefield frontline which represented the focus of the war here on Fortis Binary, a vast and ragged pattern of opposing trench systems, facing each other across a mangled deadland of cratered mud and shattered factories.

'The western trenches,' he began. 'They are held by the Tanith First Regiment. You know them, sir – Gaunt's mob, what some of the men call "The Ghosts", I believe.'

Dravere wandered across to an ornate refreshment cart and poured himself a tiny cup of rich black caffeine from the gilt samovar. He sipped and for a moment sloshed the heavy fluid between his teeth.

Flense cringed. Colonel Draker Flense had seen things in his time that would have burned through the souls of most ordinary men. He had watched legions die on the wire, he had seen men eat their comrades in a frenzy of Chaos-induced madness, he had seen planets, whole planets, collapse and die and rot. There was something about General Dravere that touched him more deeply and more repugnantly than any of that. It was a pleasure to serve him.

Dravere swallowed at last and set aside his cup. 'So Gaunt's Ghosts get the wake-up call this morning,' he said.

Hechtor Dravere was a squat, bullish man in his sixties, balding and yet insistent upon lacquering the few remaining strands of hair across his scalp as if to prove a point. He was fleshy and ruddy, and his uniform seemed to require an entire regimental ration of starch and whitening to prepare each morning. There were medals on his chest which stuck out on a stiff brass pin. He always wore them. Flense was not entirely sure what they all represented. He had never asked. He knew that Dravere had seen at least as much as him and had taken every ounce of glory for it that he could. Sometimes Flense resented the fact that the lord general always wore his decorations. He supposed it was because the lord general had them and he did not. That was what it meant to be a lord general.

The ducal palace on whose veranda they now stood was miraculously intact after six months of serial bombardment and overlooked the wide rift valley of Diemos, once the hydro-electric industrial heartland of Fortis Binary, now the axis on which the war revolved. In all directions, as far as the eye could see, sprawled the gross architecture of the manufacturing zone: the towers and hangars, the vaults and bunkers, the storage tanks and chimney stacks. A great ziggurat rose to the north, the brilliant gold icon of the Adeptus Mechanicus displayed on its flank. It rivalled, perhaps even surpassed, the Temple of the Ecclesiarchy, dedicated to the God-Emperor. But then, the Tech-Priests of Mars would argue this entire world was a shrine to the God-Machine Incarnate.

The ziggurat had been the administrative heart of the tech-priests' industry on Fortis, from where they directed a workforce of nineteen billion in the production of armour and heavy weaponry for the Imperial war machine. It was a burned-out shell now. It had been the uprising's first target.

In the far hills of the valley, in fortified factories, worker habitats and material store yards, the enemy was dug in – a billion strong, a vast massed legion of daemonic cultists. Fortis Binary was a primary Imperial forge-world, muscular and energetic in its industrial production.

No one knew how the Ruinous Powers had come to corrupt it, or how a huge section of the massive labour force had been infected with the taint of the Fallen Gods. But it had happened. Eight months before, almost overnight, the vast manufactory arks and furnace-plants of the Adeptus Mechanicus had been overthrown by the Chaos-corrupted workforce, once bonded to serve the machine cult. Only a scarce few of the tech-priests had escaped the sudden onslaught and evacuated off-world.

Now the massed legions of the Imperial Guard were here to liberate this world, and the action was very much determined by the location. The master-factories and tech-plants of Fortis Binary were too valuable to be stamped flat by an orbital bombardment.

Whatever the cost, for the good of the Imperium, this world had to be retaken a pace at a time, by men on the ground: fighting men, Imperial Guard, soldiers who would, by the sweat of their backs, root out and destroy every last scrap of Chaos and leave the precious industries of the forge-world ready and waiting for re-population.

'Every few days they try us again, pushing at another line of our trenches, trying to find a weak link.' The lord general looked back into his scope at the carnage fifteen kilometres away.

'The Tanith First are strong fighters, general, so I have heard.' Flense approached Dravere and stood with his hands behind his back. The scar-tissue of his cheek pinched and twitched slightly, as it often did when he was tense. 'They have acquitted themselves well on a number of campaigns and Gaunt is said to be a resourceful leader.'

'You know him?' the general looked up from his eye-piece, questioningly.

Flense paused. 'I know *of* him, sir. In the main by reputation,' he said, swallowing many truths, 'but I have met him in passing. His philosophy of leadership is not in tune with mine.'

'You don't like him, do you, Flense?' Dravere asked pertinently. He could read Flense like a book, and could see some deep resentment lay in the colonel's heart when it came to the

DAN ABNETT   49 subject of the infamous and heroic Commissar Gaunt. He knew what it was. He'd read the reports. He also knew Flense would never actually mention it.

'Frankly? No, sir. He is a commissar. A political officer. But by a turn of fate, he has achieved a regimental command. Warmaster Slaydo granted him the command of the Tanith on his deathbed. I understand the role of commissars in this army, but I despise his officer status. He is sympathetic where he should be inspiring, inspirational where he should be dogmatic. But... still and all, he is a commander we can probably trust.'

Dravere smiled. Flense's outburst had been from the heart, and honest, but it still diplomatically skirted the real truth. 'I trust no other commander than myself, Flense,' the general said flatly. 'If I cannot see the victory, I will not trust it to other hands. Your Patricians are held in reserve, am I correct?'

'They are barracked in the work habitats to the west, ready to support a push on either flank.'

'Go to them and bring them to readiness,' the lord general said. He crossed to the chart table again and used a stylus to mark out several long sweeps of light on the glassy top. 'We have been held here long enough. I grow impatient. This war should have been over and done months ago. How many brigades have we committed to break the deadlock?'

Flense wasn't sure. Dravere was famously extravagant with manpower. It was his proud boast that he could choke even the Eye of Terror if he had enough bodies to march into it. Certainly in the last few weeks, Dravere had become increasingly frustrated at the lack of advance. Flense guessed that Dravere was anxious to please Warmaster Macaroth, the new overall commander of the Sabbat Worlds Crusade. Dravere and Macaroth had been rivals for Slaydo's succession. Having lost to Macaroth, Dravere probably had a lot to prove. Like his loyalty to the new warmaster.

Flense had also heard rumours that Inquisitor Heldane, one of Dravere's most trusted associates, had come to Fortis a week before to conduct private talks with the lord general. Now it was as if Dravere yearned to move on, to be somewhere, to achieve something even grander than the conquest of a world, even a world as vital as Fortis Binary.

Dravere was talking again. 'The Shriven have shown their hand this morning, in greater force than before, and it will take them eight or nine hours to withdraw and regroup from whatever advances they make now. Bring your regiments in from the east and cut them off. Use these Ghosts as a buffer and slice a hole into the heart of their main defences. With the will of the beloved Emperor, we may at last break this matter and press a victory.' The lord general tapped the screen with the point of the stylus as if to emphasise the non-negotiable quality of his instruction.

Flense was eager to comply. It was his determined ambition that his regiments should be fundamental in achieving the victory on Fortis Binary. The notion that Gaunt could somehow take that glory from him sickened him, made him think of–

He shook off the thought, and basked in the idea that Gaunt and his low-born scum would be used, expended, sacrificed on the enemy guns to affect his own glory. Still, Flense wavered for a second, about to leave. There was no harm in creating a little insurance. He crossed back to the chart table and pointed a leather-gloved finger at a curve of the contours on the map. 'There is a wide area to cover, sir,' he said, 'and if Gaunt's men were to… well, break with cowardice, my Patricians would be left vulnerable to both the dug-in forces of the Shriven and to the retreating elements.'

Dravere mused on this for a moment. Cowardice: what a loaded word for Flense to use in respect to Gaunt. Then he clapped his chubby hands together as gleefully as a young child at a birthday party. 'Signals! Signals officer in here now!'

The inner door of the lounge room opened and a weary soldier hurried in, snapping his worn, but clean and polished boots together as he saluted the two officers. Dravere was busy scribing orders onto a message slate. He reviewed them once and then handed them to the soldier.

'We will bring the Vitrian Dragoons in to support the Ghosts in the hope that they will drive the Shriven host back into the flood plains. In this way, we should ensure that the fighting is held along the western flank for as long as it takes your Patricians to engage the enemy. Signal to this effect, and signal also the Tanith commander, Gaunt. Instruct him to push on. His duty today is not merely to repel. It is to press on and use this opportunity to take the Shriven frontline trenches. Ensure that this instruction is clearly an order directly from me. There will be no faltering, tell him. No retreat. They will achieve or they will die.'

Flense allowed himself an inward smile of triumph. His own

back was now comfortably covered, and Gaunt had been forced into a push that would have him dead by nightfall. The soldier saluted again and made to exit.

'One last thing,' Dravere said.

The soldier skidded to a halt and turned, nervously.

Dravere tapped the samovar with a chunky signet ring. 'Ask them to send in some fresh caffeine. This is stale.' The soldier nodded and exited. From the clunk of the ring it was clear that the big, gilt vessel was still nearly full. A regiment could drink for several days on what the general clearly intended to throw away. He managed to wait until he was out of the double doors before he spat a silent curse at the man who was orchestrating this bloodbath.

Flense saluted too and walked towards the door. He picked up his peaked cap from the sideboard and carefully set it upon his head, the back of the brim first.

'Praise the Emperor, lord general,' he said.

'What? Oh, yes. Indeed,' Dravere said absently, as he sat back on his chaise and lit a cigar.

Five

Major Rawne threw himself flat into a foxhole and almost drowned in the milky water which had accumulated in its depths. Spluttering, he pulled himself up to the lip of the crater and took aim with his lasgun. The air all around was thick with smoke and the flashing streams of gunfire. Before he had time to fire, several more bodies crashed into the makeshift cover by his side: Trooper Neff and the platoon adjutant, Feygor, beside them Troopers Caffran, Varl and Lonegin.

There was Trooper Klay as well, but he was dead. The fierce crossfire had cauterised his face before he could reach cover. None of them looked twice at Klay's body in the water behind them. They had seen that sort of thing a thousand times too often.

Rawne used his scope to check over the rim of the foxhole. Somewhere out there the Shriven were using some heavy weapon to support their infantry. The thick and explosive fire was cutting a wedge out of the Ghosts as they advanced. Neff was fiddling with his weapon and Rawne glanced down at him.

'What's the matter, trooper?' he asked.

'There's mud in my firing mechanism, sir. I can't free it.'

Feygor snatched the lasgun from the younger man, ejected the magazine and slung back the oiled cover of the ignition chamber, so that it was open and the focus rings exposed.

Feygor spat into the open chamber and then slammed it shut with a clack. Then he shook it vigorously and jammed the energy magazine back into its slot. Neff watched as Feygor swung round again and lifted the gun above his head, firing it wholesale into the smoke beyond the foxhole.

Feygor tossed the weapon back to the trooper. 'See? It's working now.'

Neff clutched the returned weapon and wriggled up to the lip of the hole.

'We'll be dead before we go another metre,' Lonegin said from below them.

'For feth's sake!' Trooper Varl spat. 'We'll just get them ducking then.' He unhooked a clutch of grenades from his webbing and tossed them out to the other soldiers, sharing them like a schoolboy shares stolen fruit. A click of the thumb primed each weapon and Rawne smiled to his men as he prepared to heave his into the air.

'Varl's assessment is correct,' Rawne said. 'Let's blind them.'

They hefted the bombs into the sky. They were frag grenades, designed to deafen, blind and pepper those in range with needles of shrapnel.

There was the multiple *crump* of detonation.

'That's got them ducking at least,' Caffran said, then realised that the others were already scrambling up out of the foxhole to charge. He followed quickly.

Screaming, the Ghosts charged over a short stretch of grey ooze and then slithered down into a revetment, screened from them by the smoke. The blackened impacts of the grenades were all around them, as were the twisted bodies of several of their dead foe.

Rawne slammed onto his feet at the bottom of the slide and looked around. For the first time in six months on Fortis Binary, he saw the enemy face to face. The Shriven, the ground forces of the enemy he had been sent here to fight.

They were surprisingly human, but twisted and malformed. They wore combat armour cleverly adapted from the worksuits that they had used in the forges of the planet, the protective masks and gauntlets actually woven into their wasted, pallid flesh. Rawne tried not to linger on the dead. It made him think too much about those legions he had still to kill. In the smoke he found two more of the Shriven, crippled by the grenade blasts. He finished them quickly.

He found Caffran close behind him. The young trooper was shocked by what he saw.

'They have lasguns,' Caffran said, aghast, 'and body armour.'

Beside him, Neff turned one of the corpses over, with his toe. 'And look… they have grenades and munitions.' Neff and Caffran looked at the major.

Rawne shrugged. 'So they're tough bastards. What did you expect? They've held the Imperium off for six months.' Lonegin, Varl and Feygor hurried along to join them. Rawne waved them along, further into the enemy dugout. The space widened in front of them and they saw the metal-beamed, stone barns of an industrial silo.

Rawne quickly gestured them into cover. Almost at once lasfire started to sear down the trench towards them. Varl was hit and his shoulder vanished in a puff of red mist. He went down hard on his backside and then flopped over clutching with the one arm that would still work. The pain was so momentous he couldn't even scream.

'Feth!' spat Rawne. 'See to him, Neff!'

Neff was the squad medic. He pulled open his thigh pouch of field dressings as Feygor and Caffran tried to drag the whimpering Varl into cover. Gleaming lines of las-fire stitched the trench line and tried to pin them all. Neff quickly bound Varl's ghastly injury. 'We have to get him back, sir!' he shouted down the grey channel to Rawne.

Rawne was pushing himself into the cover of the defile, the grey ooze matting his hair as the las-bursts burned the air around him. 'Not now,' he said.

Six

Ibram Gaunt leapt down into the trench and broke the neck of the first Shriven he met with his descending boots. The chainsword screamed in his fist and as he reached the duckboards of the enemy emplacement he swung it left and right to cut two more apart in drizzles of blood. Another charged him, a great curved blade in his hand. Gaunt raised his bolt pistol and blew the masked head into vapour.

This was the thickest fighting Gaunt and his men had encountered on Fortis, caught in the frenzied narrows of the enemy trenches, sweeping this way and that to meet the incessant advance of the Shriven. Pinned behind the commissar, Brin Milo fired his own weapon, a compact automatic handgun that the commissar had given him some months before. He killed one – a bullet between the eyes – then another, winging him first and then putting a bullet into his upturned chin as he flailed backwards. Milo shivered. This was the horror of war that he had always dreamt of, yet never wished to see. Passionate men caught against each other in a dug out hole three metres wide and six deep. The Shriven were monsters, almost elephantine with the long, nozzled gas masks sewn into the flesh of their faces. Their body armour was a dull industrial green and rubberised. They had taken the protective garb of their workspace and made it their battledress, daubing everything with eye-aching symbols.

Slammed against the trench wall by a falling body, Milo looked down at the corpses which gathered around them. He saw for the first time, in detail, the nature of his foe... the twisted, corrupted human forms of the Chaos host, incised with twisted runes and sigils painted on the dull green rubber of their armour or carved into their raw flesh.

One of the Shriven ploughed in past Gaunt's shrieking sword and dove at Milo. The boy dropped and the cultist smashed into the trench wall. Scrabbling in the muddy wetness of the trench bed, Milo retrieved one of the lasguns that had fallen from the dying grasp of one of Gaunt's previous victims. The Shriven was on him as he hefted the weapon up and fired, point blank. The flaming round punched through his opponent's torso and the dead cultist fell across him, forcing him down by sheer weight into the sucking ooze of the trench floor. Foul water surged into his mouth, and mud and blood. A second later he was heaved, coughing, to his feet by Trooper Bragg, the most massive of the men of Tanith, who was somehow always there to watch over him.

'Get down,' Bragg said as he hoisted a rocket launcher onto his shoulder. Milo knelt and covered his ears, tight. Hopefully muttering the Litany of True Striking to himself, Bragg fired his huge weapon off down the companionway of the trench. A fountain of mud and other unnameable things were blown into fragments. He often missed what he was aiming at, but under these conditions that wasn't an option.

To their right, Gaunt was scything his way into the close-packed enemy. He began to laugh, coated with the rain of blood that he was loosing with his shrieking chainsword. Every now and then he would fire his pistol and explode another of the Shriven.

He was filled with fury. The signal from Lord General Dravere had been draconian and cruel. Gaunt would have wanted to take the enemy trenches if he could, but to be ordered to do so with no other option except death was, in his opinion, the decision of a flawed, brutal mind. He'd never liked Dravere, not at any time since their first meeting twenty years before, when Dravere had still been an ambitious armour colonel. Back on Darendara, back with Oktar and the Hyrkans...

Gaunt had kept the nature of the orders from his men. Unlike Dravere, he understood the mechanisms of morale and inspiration. Now they were taking the damned trenches, almost in spite of Dravere's orders rather than because of them. His laughter was the laughter of fury and resentment, and pride in his men for doing the impossible regardless.

Nearby, Milo stumbled to his feet, holding the lasgun.

We're there, Gaunt thought, we've broken them!

Ten metres down the line, Sergeant Blane leapt in with his platoon and sealed the event, blasting left and right with his lasgun as his men charged, bayonets first. There was a frenzy of las-fire and a flash of silver Tanith blades.

Milo was still holding the lasgun when Gaunt snatched it from him and threw it down onto the duckboards. 'Do you think you're a soldier, boy?'

'Yes, sir!'

'Really?'

'You know I am.'

Gaunt looked down at the sixteen year-old boy and smiled sadly.

'Maybe you are, but for now play up. Play a tune that will sing us to glory!'

Milo pulled his Tanith pipes from his pack and breathed into the chanter. For a moment it screamed like a dying man. Then he began playing. It was Waltrab's Wilde, an old tune that had always inspired the men in the taverns of Tanith to drink and cheer and make merry.

Sergeant Blane heard the tune and with a grimace he laid into the enemy. By his side, his adjutant, vox-officer Symber, started to sing along as he blasted with his lasgun. Trooper Bragg simply chuckled and loaded another rocket into the huge launcher that he carried. A moment later, another section of trench dissolved in a deluge of fire.

Trooper Caffran heard the music, a distant plaintive wail across the battlefield. It cheered him for a moment as he moved with the men under Major Rawne's direction up over the bodies of the Shriven, side by side with Neff, Lonegin, Larkin and the rest. Even now, poor Varl was being stretchered back to their lines, screaming as the drugs wore off.

That was the moment the bombardment started. Caffran found himself flying, lifted by a wall of air issued from a bomb blast that created a crater twelve metres wide. A huge slew of mud was thrown up in the sky with him.

He landed hard, broken, and his mind frayed. He lay for a

while in the mud, strangely peaceful. As far as he knew, Neff, Major Rawne, Feygor, Larkin, Lonegin, all the rest, were dead and vaporised.

As shells continued to fall, Caffran sank his head into the slime and silently begged for release from his nightmare.

A long way off, Lord High Militant General Dravere heard the vast emplacements of the Shriven artillery begin their onslaught. He realised that it would not be today, after all. Sighing angrily, he poured himself another cup from the freshly refilled samovar.

Seven

Colonel Corbec had three platoons with him and moved them forward into the traversed network of the enemy trenches. The bombardment had been howling over their heads for two hours now, obliterating the front edge of the Shriven emplacements and annihilating all those of the Guard who had not made it into the comparative cover of enemy positions. The tunnels and channels they moved through were empty and abandoned. Clearly the Shriven had pulled out as the bombardment began. The trenches were well-made and engineered, but at every turn or bend there was a blasphemous shrine to the Dark Powers that the enemy worshipped.

Corbec had Trooper Skulane turn his flamer on each shrine they found and burn it away before any of his men could fully appreciate the grim nature of the offerings laid before it.

By Curral's estimation, after consulting the tightly-scrolled fibre-light charts, they were advancing into support trenches behind the Shriven main line. Corbec felt cut off – not just by the savage bombardment that shook their very bones every other second, and he fervently prayed no shell would fall short into the midst of them – but more, he felt cut off from the rest of the regiment. The electro-magnetic aftershock of the ceaseless barrage was scrambling their communications, both the micro-bead intercoms that all the officers wore and the long range voxcaster radio sets. No orders were getting through, no urgings to regroup, to rendezvous with other units, to press forward for an objective, or even to retreat.

In such circumstances, the rulebook of Imperial Guard warfare was clear: if in doubt, move forward.

Corbec sent scouts ahead, men he knew were fast and able: Baru, Colmar and Scout-Sergeant Mkoll. They pulled their Tanith stealth cloaks around them and slipped away into the dusty darkness. Walls of smoke and powder were drifting back over the trench lines and visibility was dropping. Sergeant Blane gestured silently up at the billowing smoke banks that were descending.

Corbec knew his intent, and knew that he didn't wish to voice it for fear of spooking the unit. The Shriven had no qualms about the use of poison agents, foul airborne gases that would boil the blood and fester the lungs. Corbec pulled out a whistle and blew three short blasts. The men behind him put guns at ease and pulled respirators from their webbing. Colonel Corbec buckled his own respirator mask around his face. He hated the loss of visibility, the claustrophobia of the thick-lensed gas hoods, the shortness of breath that the tight rubber mouthpiece provoked. But poison clouds were not the half of it. The sea of mud that the bombardment was agitating and casting up into the wind as vapour droplets was full of other venoms – the airborne spores of disease incubated in the decaying bodies out there in the dead zone: typhus, gangrene, livestock anthrax bred in the corrupting husks of pack animals and cavalry steeds, and the vicious mycotoxins that hungrily devoured all organic matter, transforming it into a black, insidious mould.

As first officer to the Tanith First, Corbec had been privy to the dispatches circulated from the general staff. He knew that nearly eighty per cent of the fatalities amongst the Imperial Guard since the invasion began had been down to gas, disease and secondary infection. A Shriven soldier could face you point-blank with a charged lasgun and still your chances of survival would be better than if you took a stroll in no-man's-land.

Muffled and blinkered by the mask, Corbec edged his unit on. They reached a bifurcation in the support trenches and Corbec called up Sergeant Grell, officer of the fifth platoon, instructing him to take three fire-teams to the left and cleanse whatever they found. The men moved off and Corbec became aware of his increasing frustration. Nothing had come back from the scouts. He was moving as blind as he had been before he sent them out.

Advancing now at double-time, the colonel led his remaining hundred or so men along a wide communication trench. Two of his sharper-eyed vanguard moved in front, using magnetically sensitive wands attached to heavy backpacks to sweep for explosives and booby traps. It seemed that the Shriven had pulled back too rapidly to leave any surprises, but every few metres, the column stopped as one of the sweepers found something hot: a tin cup, a piece of armour, a canteen tray. Sometimes it was a strange idol made of smelt ore from the forge furnaces that the corrupted workers had carved into some bestial form. Corbec personally put his laspistol to each one and blew it into fragments.

The third time he did this, the wretched thing he was destroying blew up in sharp fragments as his round tore it open along some fault. Trooper Drayl, cowering a few paces away, was hit in the collarbone by a shard, which dug into the flesh. He winced and sat back in the mud, hard. Sergeant Curral called up the medic, who put on a field dressing.

Corbec cursed his own stupidity. He was so anxious to erase any trace of the Shriven cult he had hurt one of his own.

'It's nothing, sir,' Drayl said through his gas mask as Corbec helped him to his feet. 'At Voltis Watergate I took a bayonet in the thigh.'

'And back home on Tanith he got a broken bottle end in his cheek in a bar fight!' laughed Trooper Coll behind them. 'He's had worse.'

The men around them laughed, ugly, sucking sounds through their respirators. Corbec nodded to show he was in tune with them. Drayl was a handsome, popular soldier whose songs and good humour kept his platoon in decent spirits. Corbec also knew that Drayl's roguish exploits were a matter of regimental legend.

'My mistake, Drayl,' Corbec said, 'I owe you a drink.'

'At the very least, colonel,' Drayl said and deftly armed his lasgun to show he was ready to continue.

Eight

They moved on. They reached a section of trench where a monumental shell had fallen short and blown the thin cavity open in a huge crater wound nearly thirty metres across. Already, brackish ground water was welling up in its bowl. With only the sweepers ahead of him, Corbec waded in first to lead them across into the cover where the trench recommenced. The water came up to his mid-thigh and was acidic. He could feel it burning the flesh of his legs through his fatigues and there was a faint swirl of mist around the cloth of his uniform as the fabric began to burn. He ordered the men behind him back and scrambled up on the far side to join the sweepers. The three of them looked down at their legs, horrified by the way the water had already begun to eat into the tunic cloth. Corbec felt lesions forming on his thighs and shins.

He turned back to Sergeant Curral at the head of the column across the crater.

'Move the men up and round!' he cried. 'And bring the medic over in the first party.' Afraid by the exposure of moving around the lip of the crater against the sky, the men traversed quickly and timidly. Corbec had Curral regroup them on the far side in fire-team lines along each side of the trench. The medic came to him and the sweepers, and sprayed their legs with antiseptic mist from a flask. The pain eased and the fabric was damped so that it no longer smouldered.

Corbec was picking up his gun when Sergeant Grell called to him. He moved forward down the lines of waiting men and saw what Grell had found.

It was Colmar, one of the scouts he had sent forward. He was dead, hanging pendulously from the trench wall on a great, rusty iron spike which impaled his chest. It was the sort of spike that the workers of the forge-world would have used to wedge and manipulate the hoppers of molten ore in the Adeptus Mechanicus furnace works. His hands and feet were missing.

Corbec gazed at him for a minute and then looked away. Though they had met no serious resistance, it was sickeningly clear that they weren't alone in these trenches. Whatever the number of the Shriven still here, be it stragglers left behind or guerrilla units deliberately set to thwart them, a malicious presence was shadowing them in the gullies and channels of the support trenches.

Corbec took hold of the spike and pulled Colmar down. He took out the ground sheet from his own bedroll and rolled the pitiful corpse in it so that no one would see. He could not bring himself to incinerate the soldier, as he had done with the shrines.

'Move on,' he instructed and Grell led the men forward behind the sweepers.

Corbec suddenly stopped dead as if an insect had stung him. There was a rasping in his ear. He realised it was his micro-bead link. He registered an overwhelming sense of relief that the radio link should be live at all even as he realised it was a short range broadcast from Mkoll, sergeant of the scouting unit.

'Can you hear it, sir?' came Mkoll's voice.

'Feth! Hear what?' Corbec asked. All he could hear was the ceaseless thunder of the enemy guns and the shaking tremors of the falling shells.

'Drums,' Scout-Sergeant Mkoll said, 'I can hear drums.'

Nine

Brin Milo heard the drums before Gaunt did. Gaunt valued his musician's almost preternaturally sharp senses, but they sometimes disturbed him nonetheless. The insight reminded him of someone. The girl perhaps, years ago. The one with the sight. The one who had haunted his dreams for so many years afterwards.

'Drums!' the boy hissed – and a moment later Gaunt caught the sound too.

They were moving through the silos and shelled-out structures of the rising industrial manufactories just behind the Shriven lines, sooty shells of melted stone, rusted metal girderwork and fractured ceramite. Gargoyles, built to protect the buildings against contamination, had been defaced or toppled completely. Gaunt was exceptionally cautious. The action of the day had played out unexpectedly. They had advanced far further than he had anticipated from the starting point of a simple repulse of an enemy attack, thanks both to good fortune and Dravere's harsh directive. Reaching the front of the enemy lines they had found them generally abandoned after the initial fighting, as if the majority of the Shriven had withdrawn in haste. Though a curtain of enemy bombardment cut off their lines of retreat, Gaunt felt that the Shriven had made a great mistake and pulled back too far in their urgency to avoid both the Guard attack and their own answering artillery. Either that or they were planning something.

Gaunt didn't like that notion much. He had two hundred and thirty men with him in a long spearhead column, but he knew that if the Shriven counterattacked now he might as well be on his own.

As they progressed, they swept each blackened factory bunker, storehouse and forge-tower for signs of the enemy, moving beneath flapping, torn banners, crunching broken stained glass underfoot. Machinery had been stripped out and removed, or simply vandalised. There was nothing whole left here – apart from the Chaos shrines which the Shriven had erected at regular intervals. Like Colonel Corbec, the commissar had a flamer brought up to expunge any trace of these outrages. However, ironically, he was moving in exactly the opposite direction along the trench lines to Corbec's advance. Communication was lost and the breakthrough elements of the Tanith First and Only were wandering blind and undirected through what was by any estimation enemy territory.

The sound of the drums rolled in. Gaunt called up his vox-caster operator, Trooper Rafflan, and tersely barked into the speech-horn of the heavy backpack set, demanding to know if there was anyone out there.

The drums rolled.

There was a return across the radio link, an incomprehensible squawk of garbled words. At first, Gaunt thought the transmission was scrambled, but then he realised that it was another language. He repeated his demand and after a long painful silence a coherent message returned to him in clipped Low Gothic.

'This is Colonel Zoren of the Vitrian Dragoons. We are moving in to support you. Hold your fire.'

Gaunt acknowledged and then spread his men across the silo concourse in cover, watching and waiting. Ahead of them something flashed in the dull light and then Gaunt saw soldiers moving down towards them. They didn't see the Ghosts until the very last minute. With their tenacious ability to hide in anything, and their obscuring cloaks, Gaunt's Ghosts were masters of stealth camouflage.

The Dragoons approached in a long and carefully arranged formation of at least three hundred men. Gaunt could see that they were well-drilled, slim but powerful men in some kind of chain-armour that was strangely sheened and which caught the light like unpolished metal.

Gaunt shrugged off the Tanith stealth cloak that had been a habitual addition to his garb since he joined the First and Only, and moved out of concealment, signalling them openly as he rose to his feet from cover. He advanced to meet the commanding officer.

Close to, the Vitrians were impressive soldiers. Their unusual body armour was made from a toothed metallic mail which covered them in form-fitting sections. It glinted like obsidian. Their helmets were full face and grim with narrow eye slits, glazed with dark glass. Their weapons were polished and clean.

'Commissar Gaunt of the Tanith First and Only,' Gaunt said as he saluted a greeting.

'Zoren of the Vitrian Dragoons,' came the reply. 'Good to see that there are some of you left out here. We feared we were being called in to support a regiment already slaughtered.'

'The drums? Are they yours?'

Zoren slid back the visor of his helmet to reveal a handsome, dark-skinned face. He caught Gaunt with a quizzical stare. 'They are not... we were just wondering what in the name of the Emperor it was ourselves.'

Gaunt looked away into the smoke and the fractured buildings around them. The noise had grown. Now it sounded like hundreds of drums... thousands... from all around. For each drum, a drummer. They were surrounded and completely outnumbered.

Ten

Caffran dragged himself across the mud and slid into a crater. Around him the bombardment showed no signs of easing. He had lost his lasgun and most of his kit, but he still had his silver knife and an autopistol that had come his way as a trophy at some time or other.

Wriggling to the lip of the crater he caught sight of figures far away, soldiers who seemed to be dressed in glass. There was a full unit of them, caught in the crossfire of the serial bombardment. They were being slaughtered.

Shells fell close again and Caffran slid down to cover his head with his arms.

This was hell and there was no way out of it. Curse this, in the name of feth!

He looked up and grabbed his pistol as something fell into the shell-hole next to him. It was one of the glass-clad soldiers he had seen from a distance, presumably one who had fled in search of cover. The man held up his hands to avoid Caffran's potential wrath.

'Guard! I'm Guard, like you!' the man said hastily, pulling off his dark-lensed full-face helmet to reveal an attractive face with skin that was almost as dark and glossy as polished ebonwood. 'Trooper Zogat of the Vitrian Regiment. We were called in to support you and half our number were in the open when the artillery cranked up.'

'My sympathies,' Trooper Caffran said humourlessly, holstering his pistol. He held out a pale hand to shake and was aware of the way the man in the articulated metallic armour regarded the blue dragon tattoo over his right eye with disdain.

'Trooper Caffran, Tanith First,' he said. After a moment the Vitrian shook his hand.

A shell fell close and showered them in mud. Getting up from their knees they turned and looked out at the apocalyptic vista all around.

'Well, friend,' Caffran said, 'I think we're here for the duration.'

Eleven

To the west, the Jantine Patricians moved in under the command of Colonel Flense. They rode on Chimera personnel carriers that lurched and reeled across the slick and miry landscape. The Patricians were noble soldiers, tall men in deep purple uniforms dressed with chrome. Flense had been honoured when, six years before, he had become their commanding officer. They were haughty and resolute, and had won for him a great deal of praise. They had a regimental history that dated back fifteen generations to their first Founding in the castellated garrisons of Jant Normanidus Prime, generations of notable triumphs, and associations with illustrious generals and campaigns. There was just the one blemish on their honour roll, just the one, and it nagged at Flense day and night. He would rectify that. Here, on Fortis Binary.

He took his scope and looked at the battlefield ahead. He had two columns of vehicles with upwards of ten thousand men scissoring in to cut into the flank of the Shriven as the Tanith and the Vitrians drove them back. Both those regiments were fully deployed into the Shriven lines. But Flense had not counted on this bombardment from the Shriven artillery in the hills.

Two kilometres ahead the ground was volcanic with the pounding of the macro-shells and a drizzle of mud fogged back to splatter their vehicles. There was no way of going round and Flense didn't even wish to consider the chances of driving his column through the barrage. Lord General Dravere believed in acceptable losses, and had demonstrated this practicality on a fair few number of occasions without compunction, but Flense wasn't about to commit suicide. His scar twitched. He cursed. For all his manoeuvring with Dravere, this wasn't the way it was meant to go. He had been cheated of his victory.

'Pull back!' he ordered into the vox handset and felt the gears of his vehicle grind into reverse as the carrier pulled around.

His second officer, a big, older man called Brochuss, glared at him under the low brim of his helmet. 'We are to pull out, colonel?' he asked, as if obliteration by artillery shell was something he craved.

'Shut up!' spat Flense and repeated the order into the vox-caster.

'What about Gaunt?' Brochuss asked.

'What do you think?' Flense sneered, gesturing out of the Chimera's vision slit at the inferno that raged along the deadland. 'We may not get glory today, but at least we can content ourselves in the knowledge that the bastard is dead.'

Brochuss nodded, and a slow smile of consolation spread across his grizzled features. None of the veterans had forgotten Khedd 1173.

The Patrician armoured convoy snaked back on itself and thundered home towards friendly lines before the Shriven emplacements could range them. Victory would have to wait a while longer. The Tanith First and Only and the Vitrian support regiments were on their own. If there were indeed any of them left alive.

A MEMORY

Gylatus Decimus

Eighteen Years Earlier

Oktar died slowly. It took eight days.

The commander had once joked – on Darendara, or was it Folion? Gaunt forgot. But he remembered the joke: 'It won't be war that slays me, it'll be these damn victory celebrations!'

They had been in a smoke-filled hall, surrounded by cheering citizens and waving banners. Most of the Hyrkan officers were drunk on their feet. Sergeant Gurst had stripped to his underwear and climbed the statue of the two-headed Imperial eagle in the courtyard to string the Hyrkan colours from the crest. The streets were full of bellowing crowds, static, honking traffic and wild firecrackers.

Folion. Definitely Folion.

Cadet Gaunt had smiled. Laughed, probably.

But Oktar had a way of being right all the time, and he had

been right about this. The Instrumentality of the Gylatus World Flock had been delivered from the savage ork threat after ten months of sustained killing on the Gylatan moons. Oktar, Gaunt with him, had led the final assault on the ork war bunkers at Tropis Crater Nine, punching through the last stand resistance of the brutal huzkarl retinue of Warboss Elgoz. Oktar had personally planted the spike of the Imperial Standard into the soft grey soil of the crater bottom, through Elgoz's exploded skull.

Then here, in the Gylatan hive-city capital on Decimus, the victory parades, the hosts of jubilant citizenry, the endless festivities, the medal ceremonies, the drinking, the–

The poison.

Canny, for orks. As if realising their untenable position, the orks had tainted the food and drink reserves in the last few days of their occupation. Taster servitors had sniffed most of it out, but that one stray bottle. That one stray bottle.

Adjutant Broph had found the rack of antique wines on the second night of the liberation festivities, hidden in a longbox in the palace rooms which Oktar had commandeered as a playground for his officer cadre. No one had even thought–

Eight were dead, including Broph, by the time anyone realised. Dead in seconds, collapsed in convulsive wracks, frothing and gurgling. Oktar had only just sipped from his glass when someone sounded the alarm.

One sip. That, and Oktar's iron constitution, kept him alive for eight days.

Gaunt had been off in the barracks behind the hive central

palace, settling a drunken brawl, when Tanhause summoned him. Nothing could be done.

By the eighth day, Oktar was a skeletal husk of his old, robust self. The medics emerged from his chamber, shaking hopeless heads. The smell of decay and corruption was almost overpowering. Gaunt waited in the anteroom. Some of the men, some of the toughest Hyrkans he had come to know, were weeping openly.

'He wants the Boy,' one of the doctors said as he came out, trying not to retch.

Gaunt entered the warm, sickly atmosphere of the chamber. Locked in a life-prolonging suspension field, surrounded by glowing fire-lamps and burning bowls of incense, Oktar was plainly minutes from death.

'Ibram...' The voice was like a whisper, a thing of no substance, smoke.

'Commissar-general.'

'It is past time for this. Well past time. I should never have left it to a finality like this. I've kept you waiting too long.'

'Waiting?'

'Truth of it is, I couldn't bear to lose you... not you, Ibram... far too good a soldier to hand away to the ladder of promotion. Who are you?'

Gaunt shrugged. The stench was gagging his throat.

'Cadet Ibram Gaunt, sir.'

'No... from now you are Commissar Ibram Gaunt, appointed in the extremis of the field to the commissarial office, to watch over the Hyrkan regiments. Fetch a clerk. We must record my authority in this matter, and your oath.'

Oktar willed himself to live for seventeen minutes more, as an Administratum clerk was found and the proper oath ceremony observed. He died clutching Commissar Gaunt's hands in his bony, sweat-oiled claws.

Ibram Gaunt was stunned, empty. Something had been torn out of his insides, torn out and flung away. When he wandered out into the anteroom, he didn't even notice the soldiers saluting him.

PART THREE

Fortis Binary

Forge-world

One

It wasn't the drums that Corbec really detested, it was the rhythm. There was no sense to it. Though the notes were a regular drum sound, the beats came sporadically like a fluctuating heart, overlapping and syncopated. The bombardment was still ever-present but now, as they closed on the source of the beating, the drumming overrode even the roar of the explosions beyond the front trenches.

Corbec knew his men were spooked even before Sergeant Curral said it. Down the channel ahead, Scout-Sergeant Mkoll was returning towards them. He had missed the signal to put on his respirator and his face was pinched, tinged with green. As soon as he saw the masked men of his company, he anxiously pulled on his own gas-hood.

'Report!' Corbec demanded quickly.

'It opens up ahead,' Mkoll said through his mask, breathing hard. 'There are wide manufactory areas ahead of us. We've broken right through their lines into the heart of this section of the industrial belt. I saw no one. But I heard the drums. It sounds like there are... well, thousands of them out there. They're bound to attack soon. But what are they waiting for?'

Corbec nodded and moved forward, ushering his men on behind him. They hugged the walls of the trench and assumed fire pattern formation, crouching low and aiming in a sweep above the head of the man in front.

The trench opened out from its zigzag into a wide, stone-walled basin which overlooked a slope leading down into colossal factory sheds.

The thump of the drums, the incessant and irregular beat, was now all-pervading.

Corbec waved two fire-teams forward on either flank, Drayl taking the right and Lukas taking the left. He led the front prong himself. The slope was steep and watery-slick. By necessity, they became more concerned with keeping upright and descending than with raising their weapons defensively.

The concourse around the sheds was open and empty. Feeling exposed, Corbec beckoned his men on, the front prong of the attack spearheading out into a wide phalanx as men slipped down the slope and joined them. Drayl's team was now established to his right covering them, and soon Lukas's was also in position.

The drums now throbbed so loudly they vibrated the hard plastic lenses in their respirator masks and thudded against their chest walls.

Corbec scurried across the open space with eight men accompanying him and covering every quarter. Sergeant Grell moved another dozen in behind them as Corbec reached the first of the sheds. He looked back and saw the men were keeping the line well, although he was concerned to see Drayl lift his respirator for a moment to wipe his face with the back of his cuff. He knew the man was ill at ease following that unhappy injury, but he still disliked undisciplined activity.

'Get that fething mask in place!' he shouted at Trooper Drayl and then, with seven lasguns covering the angles, he entered the shed.

The gabled building throbbed with the sound of drums. Corbec could scarcely believe what he saw. Thousands of makeshift mechanisms had been set up in here, rotary engines and little spinning turbines, all in one way or another driving levers that beat drumsticks onto cylinders of every shape and size, all stretched with skin. Corbec didn't even want to think where that skin had come from. All that he was aware of was the syncopated and irregular thudding of the drum machines that the Shriven had left here. There was no pattern to their beat. Worse still, Corbec was more afraid that there was a pattern, and he was too sane to understand it.

A further sweep showed that the building was vacant, and scouting further they realised all of the sheds were filled with the makeshift drum machines… ten thousand drums, twenty thousand, of every size and shape, beating away like malformed, failing hearts.

Corbec's men closed in around the sheds to hold them and assumed close defensive file, but Corbec knew they were all scared and the rhythms throbbing through the air were more than most could stand.

He called up Skulane, his heavy flamer stinking of oil and dripping petroleum. He pointed to the first of the sheds. 'Sergeant Grell will block you with a fire-team,' he told the flame-thrower. 'You don't have to watch your back. Just burn each of these hell-holes in turn.'

Skulane nodded and paused to tighten a gasket on his fire-blackened weapon. He moved forward into the first doorway as Grell ordered up a tight company of men to guard him. Skulane raised his flamer, his finger whitening under the tin guard of the rubberised trigger.

There was a beat. A single beat. For one incredible moment all of the eccentric rhythms of the mechanical drums struck as one.

Skulane's head exploded. He dropped like a sack of vegetables onto the ground, the impact of his body and the spasm of his nervous system clenching the trigger on his flamer. The spike of fierce flame stabbed around in an unforgiving arc, burning first the portico of the blockhouse and then whipping back to incinerate three of the troopers guarding him. They shrieked and flailed as they were engulfed.

Panic hit the men and they spread out in scurrying bewildered patterns. Corbec howled a curse. Somehow, at the point of death, Skulane's finger had locked the trigger of the flamer and the weapon, slack on its cable beneath his dead form, whipped back and forth like a fire-breathing serpent. Two more soldiers were caught in its breath, three more. It scorched great conical scars across the muddy concrete of the concourse.

Corbec threw himself flat against the side wall of the shed as the flames ripped past him. His mind raced and thoughts formed slower than actions. A grenade was in his hand, armed with a flick of his thumb.

He leapt from cover, and screamed to any who could hear him to get down even as he flung the grenade at Skulane's corpse and the twisting flamer. The explosion was catastrophic, igniting the tanks on the back of the corpse. Fire, white hot, vomited up from the door of the shed and blew the front of the roof out. Sections of splintered stone collapsed down across the vestigial remains of Trooper Skulane.

Corbec, like many others, was knocked flat by the hot shockwave of the blast. Cowering in a ditch nearby, Scout-Sergeant Mkoll had avoided the worst of the blast. He had noticed something that Corbec had not, though with the continual beat of the drums, now irregular and unformed again, it was so difficult to concentrate. But he knew what he had seen.

Skulane had been hit from behind by a las-blast to the head. Cradling his own rifle, he scrambled around to try and detect the source of the attack. A sniper, he thought, one of the Shriven guerrillas lurking in this disputed territory.

All the men were on their bellies and covering their heads with their hands, all except Trooper Drayl, who stood with his lasgun held loosely and a smile on his face.

'Drayl!' Mkoll yelled, scrambling up from the trench. Drayl turned to face him across the concourse with a milky nothingness in his eyes. He raised his gun and fired.

* * *

Two

Mkoll threw himself flat, but the first shot seared down the length of his back and broke his belt. Slumping into the ditch, he felt dull pain from the bubbled flesh along his shoulder blade. There was no blood. Las-fire cauterised whatever it hit.

There was shouting and panic, more panic than before. Whooping in a strange and chilling tone, Drayl turned and killed the two Ghosts nearest to him with point blank shots to the back of the head. As others scrambled to get out of his way, he turned his gun to full auto and blazed at them, killing five more, six, seven.

Corbec leapt to his feet, horrified at what he saw. He swung his lasgun into his shoulder, took careful aim and shot Drayl in the middle of the chest. Drayl barked out a cough and flew backwards with his feet and hands pointing out, almost comically.

There was a pause. Corbec edged forward, as did Mkoll and most of the men, those that didn't stop to try and help those that Drayl had blasted who were still alive.

'For feth's sake…' Corbec breathed as he walked forward towards the corpse of the dead guardsman. 'What the hell is going on?'

Mkoll didn't answer. He crossed the concourse in several fierce bounds and slammed into Corbec to bring him crashing to the ground.

Drayl wasn't dead. Something insidious and appalling was blistering and seething inside the sack of his skin. He rose, first from the hips and then to his feet. By the time he was standing, he was twice human size, his uniform and skin splitting to accommodate the twisting, enlarging skeletal structure that was transmuting within him.

Corbec didn't want to look. He didn't want to see the bony thing which was erupting from Drayl's flesh. Watery blood and fluid spat from Drayl as the Chaos infection grew something within him, something that burst out and stepped free of the shredded carcass that it had once inhabited.

Drayl, or the thing that had once been Drayl, faced them across the yard. It stood four metres high, a vast and grotesque skeletal form whose bones seemed as if they had been welded from tarnished sections of steel. The head was huge, topped by polished horns that twisted irregularly. Oil and blood and other unnameable fluids dripped from its structure. It looked like it was smiling. It turned its head from left to right, as if anticipating the carnage to come.

Corbec saw that, despite the fact that all fabric and flesh of Drayl had been shed away, the obscenity still wore his dog-tags.

The beast reached up with great metallic claws and screamed at the sky.

'Get into cover!' Corbec screamed to his terrified men and they fled into every shadow and crevice they could find. Corbec and Mkoll dropped into a culvert; the scout was shaking. Along the damp drainage channel, Corbec could see Trooper Melyr, who carried the company's rocket launcher. The man was too terrified to move. Corbec slithered down to him through the foetid soup and tried to pull the rocket launcher from his shoulder. Melyr was too limp and too scared to let it go easily.

'Mkoll! Help me, for feth's sake!' Corbec shouted as he wrestled with the weapon.

It came free. He had it in his hands, the unruly weight of the heavy weapon unfamiliar to his shoulders. A quick check told him it was primed and armed. A shadow fell across him.

The beast that was no longer Drayl stood over him and hissed with glee through its blunt, equine teeth.

Corbec fell on his back and tried to aim the rocket launcher, but it was wet and slippery in his hands and he slid in the mud of the culvert. He began to mutter: 'Holy Emperor, deliver us from the Darkness of the Void, guide my weapon in your service… Holy Emperor, deliver us from the Darkness of the Void…' He squeezed the trigger. Nothing happened. Damp was choking the baffles of the firing mechanism.

The thing reached down towards him and hooked him by the tunic with its metal fingers. Corbec was lifted up out of the channel, dangling at arm's length from the abomination. But the baffles were now clear. He squeezed the trigger mechanism again and the blast took the beast's head off at point blank range.

The explosion somersaulted Corbec back twenty paces and dumped him on his back in a pile of mud and slag. The rocket launcher skittered clear.

Headless, the obscenity teetered for a moment and then collapsed into the culvert. Sergeant Grell was right behind with a dozen men that he had roused out of their panic with oathing taunts. They stood around the lip of the culvert and fired their lasguns down at the twitching skeleton. In a few moments, the sculptural, metallic form of the beast was reduced to shrapnel and slag.

Corbec looked on a moment longer, then flopped back and lay prostrate.

Now he had seen everything. He couldn't quite get over the idea that it had been his fault all along. Drayl had been contaminated by that fragment from the damned statuette. Get a grip, he hissed to himself. The men need you. His teeth chattered. Rebels, bandits, even the foul orks he could manage, but this...

The bombardment continued over and behind them. Close at hand the drum machines continued to patter out their staccato message. For the first time since the fall of Tanith, weary beyond measure, Corbec felt tears in his eyes.

Three

Evening fell. The Shriven bombardment continued as the light faded, a roaring forest of flames and mud-plumes three hundred kilometres wide. Gaunt believed he understood the enemy tactic. It was a double-headed win-win manoeuvre.

They had launched their offensive at dawn in the hope of breaking the Imperial frontline, but expecting stiff opposition which Gaunt and his men had provided. Failing to break the line, the Shriven had then countered by falling back far further than necessary, enticing the Imperial Guard forward to occupy the Shriven frontline... and place themselves in range of the Shriven's artillery batteries in the hills.

Lord Militant General Dravere had assured Gaunt and the other commanders that three weeks of carpet bombing from orbit by the Navy had pounded the enemy artillery positions into scrap metal, thus ensuring comparative safety for an infantry advance. True enough, the mobile field batteries used by the Shriven to harry the Imperial lines had taken a pasting. But they clearly had much longer range fixed batteries higher in the hills, dug in to bunker emplacements impervious even to orbital bombardment.

The weapons that were throwing the shells their way were leviathans, and Gaunt was not surprised. This was a forge-world after all, and though insane with the doctrines of Chaos, the Shriven were not stupid. They had been spawned among the engineers and artisans of Fortis Binary, trained and schooled by the Tech-Priests of Mars. They could make all the weapons they wanted and they had had months to prepare.

So here it was, a finely executed battlefield trap, drawing the Tanith First, the Vitrian Dragoons and Emperor knew who else across no-man's-land into abandoned trench lines and fortifications where a creeping curtain of shell-fire would slowly pull back, a metre at a time, and obliterate them all.

Already, the frontline of the Shriven's old emplacements had been destroyed. Only hours before, Gaunt and his men had fought hand to hand down those trenches to get into the Shriven lines. Now the futility of that fighting seemed bitter indeed.

The Ghosts with Gaunt, and the company of Vitrian Dragoons with whom they had joined up, were sheltering in some ruined manufactory spaces, a kilometre or so from the creeping barrage that was coming their way. They had no contact with any other Vitrian or Tanith unit. For all they knew, they were the only men to have made it this far. Certainly there was no sign or hope of a supporting manoeuvre from the main Imperial positions. Gaunt had hoped the wretched Jantine Patricians or perhaps even some of Dravere's elite storm troops might have been sent in to flank them, but the bombardment had put paid to that possibility.

The electro-magnetic and radio interference of the huge bombardment was also cutting their comm-lines. There was no possible contact with headquarters or their own frontline units, and even short range vox-cast traffic was chopped and distorted. Colonel Zoren was urging his communications officer to try to patch an uplink to any listening ship in orbit, in the hope that they might relay their location and plight. But the upper atmosphere of a world where war had raged for half a year was a thick blanket of petrochemical smog, ash, electrical anomalies and worse. Nothing was getting through.

The only sounds from the world around them were the concussive rumble of the shelling – and the background rhythm of the incessant drums.

Gaunt wandered through the dank shed where the men were holed up. They sat huddled in small groups, camo-cloaks pulled around them against the chilly night air. Gaunt had forbidden the use of stoves or heaters in case the enemy rangefinders were watching with heat-sensitive eyes. As it was, the plasteel-reinforced concrete of the manufactory would mask the slight traces of their body heat.

There were almost a hundred more Vitrian Dragoons than there were Ghosts, and they kept themselves pretty much to themselves, occupying the other end of the factory barn. Some slight interchange was taking place between the two regiments where their troops were in closer proximity, but it was a stilted exchange of greetings and questions.

The Vitrians were a well-drilled and austere unit, and Gaunt had heard much praise heaped upon their stoic demeanour and approach to war.

He wondered himself if this clinical attitude, as clean and sharp-edged as the famous glass-filament mesh armour they wore, might perhaps be lacking in the essential fire and soul that made a truly great fighting unit. With the shellfire falling ever closer, he doubted he would ever find out.

Colonel Zoren gave up on his radio efforts and walked between his men to confront Gaunt. In the shadows of the shed, his dark-skinned face was hollow and resigned.

'What do we do, commissar-colonel?' he asked, deferring to Gaunt's braid. 'Do we sit here and wait for death to claim us like old men?'

Gaunt's breath fogged the air as he surveyed the gloomy shed. He shook his head. 'If we're to die,' he said, 'then let us die usefully at least. We have nearly four hundred men between us, colonel. Our direction has been chosen for us.'

Zoren frowned as if perplexed. 'How so?'

'To go back walks us into the bombardment, to go either left or right along the line of the fortification will take us no further from that curtain of death. There is only one way to go: deeper into their lines, forcing ourselves back to their new front line and maybe doing whatever harm we can once we get there.'

Zoren was silent for a moment, then a grin split his face. Even white teeth glinted in the darkness. Clearly the idea appealed to him. It had a simple logic and an element of honourable glory that Gaunt had hoped would please the Vitrian mindset.

'When shall we begin to move?' Zoren asked, buckling his mesh gauntlets back in place.

'The Shriven's creeping bombardment will have obliterated this area in the next hour or two. Any time before then would probably be smart. As soon as we can, in fact.'

Gaunt and Zoren exchanged nods and quickly went to rouse their officers and form the men up.

In less than ten minutes, the fighting unit was ready to move. The Tanith had all put fresh power clips in their lasguns, checked and replaced where necessary their focusing barrels, and adjusted their charge settings to half power as per Gaunt's instruction. The silver blades of the Tanith war knives attached to the bayonet lugs of their weapons were blackened with soil to stop them flashing. Camo-cloaks were pulled in tight and the Ghosts divided into small units of around a dozen men, each containing at least one heavy weapons trooper.

Gaunt observed the preparations of the Vitrians. They were drilled into larger fighting units of about twenty men each, and had fewer heavy weapons. Where heavy weapons appeared, they seemed to prefer the plasma gun. None of them had meltaguns or flamers as far as Gaunt could see. The Ghosts would take point, he decided.

The Vitrians attached spike-bladed bayonets to their lasguns, ran a synchronised weapons check with almost choreographed grace, and adjusted the charge settings of their weapons to maximum. Then, again in unison, they altered a small control on the waistband of their armour. With a slight shimmer in the darkness, the finely meshed glass of their body suits flipped and closed, so that the interlocking teeth were no longer the shiny ablative surface, but showed instead the dark, matt reverse side. Gaunt was impressed. Their functional armour had an efficient stealth mode for movement after dark.

The bombardment still shuddered and roared behind them, and it had become such a permanent feature they were almost oblivious to it. Gaunt conferred with Zoren as they both adjusted their micro-bead intercoms.

'Use channel Kappa,' said Gaunt, 'with channel Sigma in reserve. I'll take point with the Ghosts. Don't lag too far behind.'

Zoren nodded that he understood.

'I see you have instructed your men to set charge at maximum,' Gaunt said as an afterthought.

'It is written in the *Vitrian Art of War*: "Make your first blow sure enough to kill and there will be no need for a second."'

Gaunt thought about this for a moment. Then he turned to lead the convoy off.

Four

There were just two realities: the blackness of the foxhole below and the brilliant inferno of the bombardment above.

Trooper Caffran and the Vitrian cowered in the darkness and the mud at the bottom of the shell-hole as the fury raged overhead, like a firestorm on the face of the sun.

'Sacred Feth! I don't think we'll be getting out of here alive...' Caffran said darkly.

The Vitrian didn't cast him a glance. 'Life is a means towards death, and our own death may be welcomed as much as that of our foe.'

Caffran thought about this for a moment and shook his head sadly. 'What are you, a philosopher?'

The Vitrian trooper, Zogat, turned and looked at Caffran disdainfully. He had the visor of his helmet pulled up and Caffran could see little warmth in his eyes.

'The Byhata, the *Vitrian Art of War*. It is our codex, the guiding philosophy of our warrior caste. I do not expect you to understand.'

Caffran shrugged, 'I'm not stupid. Go on... how is war an art?'

The Vitrian seemed unsure if he was being mocked, but the language they had in common, Low Gothic, was not the native tongue of either of them, and Caffran's grasp of it was better than Zogat's. Culturally, their worlds could not have been more different.

'The Byhata contains the practice and philosophy of warriorhood. All Vitrians study it and learn its principles, which then direct us in the arena of war. Its wisdom informs our tactics, its strength reinforces our arms, its clarity focuses our minds and its honour determines our victory.'

'It must be quite a book,' Caffran said, sardonically.

'It is,' Zogat replied with a dismissive shrug.

'So do you commit it to memory or carry it with you?'

The Vitrian unbuttoned his flak armour tunic and showed Caffran the top of a thin, grey pouch that was laced into its lining. 'It is carried over the heart, a work of eight million characters transcribed and encoded onto mono-filament paper.'

Caffran was almost impressed. 'Can I see it?' he asked.

Zogat shook his head and buttoned up his tunic again. 'The filament paper is gene-coded to the touch of the trooper it is issued to so that no one else may open it. It is also written in Vitrian, which I am certain you cannot read. And even if you could, it is a capital offence for a non-Vitrian to gain access to the great text.'

Caffran sat back. He was silent for a moment. 'We Tanith... we've got nothing like that. No grand art of war.'

The Vitrian looked round at him. 'Do you have no code? No philosophy of combat?'

'We do what we do...' Caffran began. 'We live by the principle, "Fight hard if you have to fight and don't let them see you coming." That's not much, I suppose.'

The Vitrian considered this. 'It certainly... lacks the subtle subtext and deeper doctrinal significances of the Vitrian Art of War,' he said at last.

There was a long pause.

Caffran sniggered. Then they both erupted in almost uncontrollable laughter.

It took some minutes for their hilarity to die down, easing the morbid tension that had built up through the horrors of the day.

Even with the bombardment thundering overhead and the constant expectation that a shell would fall into their shelter and vaporise them, the fear in them seemed to relax.

The Vitrian opened his canteen, took a swig and offered it to Caffran. 'You men of Tanith… there are very few of you, I understand?'

Caffran nodded. 'Barely two thousand, all that Commissar-Colonel Gaunt could salvage from our home world on the day of our Founding as a regiment. The day our home world died.'

'But you have quite a reputation,' the Vitrian said.

'Have we? Yes, the sort of reputation that gets us picked for all the stealth and dirty commando work going, the sort of reputation that gets us sent into enemy-held hives and death worlds that no one else has managed to crack. I often wonder who'll be left to do the dirty jobs when they use the last of us up.'

'I often dream of my home world,' Zogat said thoughtfully, 'I dream of the cities of glass, the crystal pavilions. Though I am sure I will never see it again, it heartens me that it is always there in my mind. It must be hard to have no home left.'

Caffran shrugged. 'How hard is anything? Harder than storming an enemy position? Harder than dying? Everything about life in the Emperor's army is hard. In some ways, not having a home is an asset.'

Zogat shot him a questioning look.

'I've nothing left to lose, nothing I can be threatened with, nothing that can be held over me to force my hand or make me submit. There's just me, Imperial Guardsman Dermon Caffran, servant of the Emperor, may he hold the Throne for ever.'

'So then you see, you do have a philosophy after all,' Zogat said.

There was a long break in their conversation as they both listened to the guns. 'How… how did your world die, man of Tanith?' the Vitrian asked.

Caffran closed his eyes and thought hard for a moment, as if he was dredging up from a deep part of his mind something he had deliberately discarded or blocked. At last he sighed. 'It was the day of our Founding…' he began.

Five

They couldn't stay put, not there. Even if it hadn't been for the shelling that slowly advanced towards them, the thing with Drayl had left them all sick and shaking, and eager to get out.

Corbec ordered Sergeants Curral and Grell to mine the factory sheds and silence the infernal drumming. They would move on into the enemy lines and do as much damage as they could until they were stopped or relieved.

As the company – less than a hundred and twenty men since Drayl's corruption – prepared to move out, the scout Baru, one of the trio Corbec had sent ahead as they first moved in the area, returned at last, and he was not alone. He'd been pinned by enemy fire for a good half an hour in a zigzag of trenches to the east, and then the shelling had taken out his most direct line of return. For a good while, Baru had been certain he'd never reunite with his company. Edging through the wire festoons and stake posts along the weaving trench, he had encountered to his surprise five more Tanith: Feygor, Larkin, Neff, Lonegin and Major Rawne. They'd made it to the trenches as the bombardment had begun and were now wandering like lost livestock looking for a plan.

Corbec was as glad to see them as they were to see the company. Larkin was the best marksman in the regiment, and would be invaluable for the kind of insidious advance that lay ahead of them. Feygor, too, was a fine shot and a good stealther. Lonegin was good with explosives, so Corbec sent him immediately to assist Curral and Grell's demolition detail. Neff was a medic, and they could use all the medical help they could get. Rawne's tactical brilliance was not in question, and Corbec swiftly put a portion of the men under his direct command.

In the flicker of the shellfire against the night, which flashed and burst in a crazy syncopation against the beat of the drums, Grell returned to Corbec and reported the charges were ready; fifteen-minute settings.

Corbec advanced the company down the main communication way of the factory space away from the mined sheds at double-time, in a paired column with a floating spearhead fireteam of six: Sergeant Grell, the sniper Larkin, Mkoll and Baru the scouts, Melyr with the rocket launcher and Domor with a sweeper set. Their job was to pull ahead of the fast moving column and secure the path, carrying enough mobile firepower to do more than just warn the main company.

The sheds they had mined began to explode behind them. Incandescent mushrooms of green and yellow flame punched up into the blackness, shredding the dark shapes of the buildings and silencing the nearest drums.

Other, more distant rhythms made themselves heard as the roar died back. The drum contraptions closest to them had masked the fact that others lay further away. The beating ripple tapped at them. Corbec spat sourly. The drums were grating at him, making his temper rise. It reminded him of nights back home in the nalwood forests of Tanith. Stamp on a chirruping cricket near your watchfire and a hundred more would take up the call beyond the firelight.

'Come on,' he growled at his men. 'We'll find them all. We'll stamp 'em all out. Every fething one of 'em.'

There was a heartfelt murmur of agreement from his company. They moved forward.

Milo grabbed Gaunt's sleeve and pulled him around just a heartbeat before greenish explosions lit the sky about six kilometres to their west.

'Closer shelling?' Milo asked. The commissar pulled his scope round and the milled edge of the automatic dial whirred and spun as he played the field of view over the distant buildings.

'What was that?' Zoren's voice rasped over the short range intercom. 'That was not shellfire.'

'Agreed,' Gaunt replied. He ordered his men to halt and hold the area they had reached, a damp and waterlogged section of low-lying storage bays. Then he dropped back with Milo and a couple of troopers to meet with Zoren who led his men up to meet them.

'Someone else is back here with us, on the wrong side of hell,' he told the Vitrian leader. 'Those buildings were taken out with krak charges, standard issue demolitions.'

Zoren nodded his agreement. 'I... I am afraid...' he began respectfully, '...that I doubt it is any of mine. Vitrian discipline is tight. Unless driven by some necessity unknown to us, Vitrian troops would not ignite explosions like that. It might as well act as a marker fire for the enemy guns. They'll soon be shelling that section, knowing someone was there.'

Gaunt scratched his chin. He had been pretty sure it was a Tanith action too: Rawne, Feygor, Curral… maybe even Corbec himself. All of them had a reputation of acting without thinking from time to time.

As they watched, another series of explosions went off. More sheds destroyed.

'At this rate,' Gaunt snapped, 'they might as well vox their position to the enemy!'

Zoren called his communications officer to join them and Gaunt wound the channel selector on the vox-set frantically as he repeated his call sign into the wire-framed microphone. The range was close. There was a chance.

They had just set and flattened the third series of drum-sheds and were moving into girder-framed tunnels and walkways when Lukas called over to Colonel Corbec. There was a signal.

Corbec hurried over across the wet concrete, ordering Curral to take his demolition squad to the next row of thumping, clattering drum-mills. He took the headphones and listened. A tinny voice was repeating a call sign, chopped and fuzzed by the atrocious radio conditions. There was no mistaking it – it was the Tanith regimental command call sign.

At his urgings, Lukas cranked the brass dial for boost and Corbec yelled his call sign hoarsely into the set.

'Corbec!... olonel!... peat is that you?... mining... peat s...
ive away p...'

'Say again! Commissar, I'm losing your signal! Say again!'

Zoren's communications officer looked up from the set and
shook his head. 'Nothing, commissar. Just white noise.'

Gaunt told him to try again. Here was a chance, so close, to
increase the size of their expeditionary force and move forward
in strength – if Corbec could be dissuaded from his suicidal
actions in the face of the guns.

'Corbec! This is Gaunt! Desist your demolition and move
sharp east at double time! Corbec, acknowledge!'

'Ready to blow,' Curral called, but stopped short as Corbec held
up his hand for quiet. By the set, Lukas craned to hear past the
roar of the shelling and the thunder of the drumming.

'W-we're to stop... he's ordering us to stop and move east
double-time... w-we're...'

Lukas looked up at the colonel with suddenly anxious eyes.

'He says we're going to draw the enemy guns down on us.'

Corbec turned slowly and looked up into the night, where
the shells streaking from the distant heavy emplacements tore
whistling furrows of light out of the ruddy blackness.

'Sacred Feth!' he breathed as he realised the foolhardy course
his anger had made them follow.

'Move! Move!' he yelled, and the men scrambled up in confusion.
At a run, he led them around, sending a signal ahead to pull his vanguard back around in their wake. He knew he had scarce seconds to

get his men clear of the target zone they had lit with their mines, an arrow of green fire virtually pointing to their advance.

He had to pull them east. East was what Gaunt had said. How close was the commissar's company? A kilometre? Two? How close was the enemy shelling? Were they already swinging three tonne deuterium macro-shells filled with oxy-phosphor gel into the gaping breeches of the vast Shriven guns, as range finders calibrated brass sights and the sweating thews of gunners cranked round the vast greasy gears that lowered the huge barrels a fractional amount?

Corbec led his men hard. There was barely time for running cover. He put his faith in the fact that the Shriven had pulled back and left the area.

The Vitrian communications officer played back the last signal they had received, and made adjustments to his set to try to wash the static out. Gaunt and Zoren watched intently.

'A response signal, I think,' the officer said. 'An acknowledgement.'

Gaunt nodded. 'Take up position here. We'll hold this area until we can form up with Corbec.'

At that moment, the area to their west where Corbec's mines had lit up the night, and the area around it, began to erupt. Lazily blossoming fountains of fire, ripple after ripple, annihilated the zone. Explosion overlaid explosion as the shells fell together. The Shriven had pulled a section of their overall barrage back by about three kilometres to target the signs of life they had seen.

Gaunt could do nothing but watch.

* * *

Colonel Flense was a man who'd modelled his career on the principle of opportunity. That was what he seized now, and he could taste victory.

Since the abortive Jantine advance in the late afternoon, he had withdrawn to the Imperium command post to consider an alternative. Nothing was possible while the enemy barrage was curtaining off the entire front. But Flense wanted to be ready to move the moment it stopped or the moment it faltered. The land out there after such a bombardment would be ash-waste and mud, as hard for the Shriven to hold as it was for the Imperials. The perfect opportunity for a surgical armoured strike.

By six that evening, as the light began to fail, Flense had a strike force ready in the splintered streets below a bend in the river. Eight Leman Russ siege tanks, the beloved Demolishers with their distinctive short thick barrels, four standard Phaethon-pattern Leman Russ battle tanks, three Griffon Armoured Weapons Carriers, and nineteen Chimeras carrying almost two hundred Jantine Patricians in full battledress.

He was at the ducal palace, discussing operational procedures with Dravere and several other senior officers, who were also trying to assess the losses in terms of Tanith and Vitrians sustained that day, when the vox-caster operator from the watchroom entered with a sheaf of transparencies that the cogitators of the orbital Navy had processed and sent down.

They were orbital shots of the barrage. The others studied them with passing interest, but Flense seized on them at once. One shot showed a series of explosions going off at least a kilometre inside the bombardment line.

Flense showed it to Dravere, taking the general to one side.

'Short fall shells,' was the general's comment.

'No sir, these are a chain of fires… the blast areas of set explosions. Someone's inside there.'

Dravere shrugged. 'So someone survived.'

Flense was stern. 'I have dedicated myself and my Patricians to taking this section of the front, and therein taking the world itself. I will not stand by and watch as vagabond survivors run interference behind the lines and ruin our strategies.'

'You take it so personally, Flense…' Dravere smiled.

Flense knew he did, but he also recognised an opportunity. 'General, if a break appears in the bombardment, do I have your signal permission to advance? I have an armoured force ready.'

Bemused, the lord general consented. It was dinner time and he was preoccupied. Even so, the prospect of victory charmed him. 'If you win this for me, Flense, I'll not forget it. There are great possibilities in my future, if I am not tied here. I would share them with you.'

'Your will be done, Lord Militant General.'

Flense's keen opportunistic mind had seen the possibility – that the Shriven might retarget their bombardment, or better still a section of it, to flatten the activity behind their old lines. And that would give him an opening.

Taking his lead from the navigation signals transmitted from the fleet to an astropath in his lead tank, Flense rumbled his column out of the west, along the river road and then out across a pontoon bridgehead as far as he dared into the wasteland. The

Shriven bombardment dropped like fury before his vehicles.

Flense almost missed his opportunity. He had barely got his vehicles into position when the break appeared. A half-kilometre stretch of the bombardment curtain abruptly ceased and then reappeared several kilometres further on, targeting the section that the orbital shots had shown.

There was a doorway through the destruction, a way in to get at the Shriven.

Flense ordered his vehicles on. At maximum thrust they tore and bounced and slithered over the mud and into the Shriven heartland.

Six

The voice of Trooper Caffran floated out of the fox-hole darkness, just audible over the shelling.

'Tanith was a glorious place, Zogat. A forest world, evergreen, dense and mysterious. The forests themselves were almost spiritual. There was a peace there... and they were strange too. What they call motile treegrowth, so I'm told. Basically, the trees, a kind we called nalwood, well... moved, replanted, repositioned themselves, following the sun, the rains, whatever tides and urges ran in their sap. I don't pretend to understand it. It was just the way things were.

'Essentially, the point is, there was no frame of reference for location on Tanith. A track or a pathway through the nal-forest might change or vanish or open anew overnight. So, over the generations, the people of Tanith got an instinct for direction. For tracking and scouting. We're good at it. I guess we can thank those moving forests of our homeworld for the reputation this regiment has for recon and stealth.'

'The great cities of Tanith were splendid. Our industries were agrarian, and our off-world trade was mainly fine, seasoned timbers and wood carving. The work of the Tanith craftsmen was something to behold. The cities were great, stone bastions that rose up out of the forest. You say you have glass palaces back home. This was nothing so fancy. Just simple stone, grey like the sea, raised up high and strong.'

Zogat said nothing. Caffran eased his position in the dark mud-hole to be more comfortable. Despite the bitterness in his voice and his soul, he felt a mournful sense of loss he had not experienced for a long while.

'Word came that Tanith was to raise three regiments for the Imperial Guard. It was the first time our world had been asked to perform such a duty, but we had a large number of able fighting men trained in the municipal militias. The process of the Founding took eight months, and the assembled troops were waiting on wide, cleared plains when the transport ships arrived in orbit. We were told we were to join the Imperial Forces engaged in the Sabbat Worlds campaign, driving out the forces of Chaos. We were also told we would probably never see our world again, for once a man had joined the service he tended to go on wherever the war took him until death claimed him or he was mustered out to start a new life wherever he had ended up. I'm sure they told you the same thing.'

Zogat nodded, his noble profile a sad motion of agreement in the wet dark of the crater. Explosions rippled above them in a long, wide series. The ground shook.

'So we were waiting there,' Caffran continued, 'thousands of us, itchy in our stiff new fatigues, watching the troop ships roll in and out. We were eager to be going, sad to be saying goodbye to Tanith. But the idea that it was always there, and would always be there, kept our spirits up. On that last morning we learned that Commissar Gaunt had been appointed to our regiment, to knock us into shape.' Caffran sighed, trying to resolve his darker feelings towards the loss of his world. He cleared his throat. 'Gaunt had a certain reputation, and a long and impressive history with the veteran Hyrkan regiments. We were new, of course, inexperienced and certainly full of rough edges. High Command clearly believed it would take an officer of Gaunt's mettle to make a fighting force out of us.'

Caffran paused. He lost the track of his voice for a moment as anger welled inside him. Anger – and the sense of absence. He realised with a twinge that this was the first time since the Loss that he had recounted the story aloud. His heart closed convulsively around threads of memory, and he felt his bitterness sharpen. 'It all went wrong on that very last night. Embarkation had already begun. Most of the troops were either aboard transports waiting for takeoff or were heading up into orbit already. The Navy's picket duty had not done its job, and a significantly-sized Chaos fleet, a splinter of a larger fleet running scared since the last defeat the Imperial Navy had inflicted, slipped into the Tanith system past the blockades. There was very little warning.

The forces of Darkness attacked my home world and erased it from the galactic records in the space of one night.'

Caffran paused again and cleared his throat. Zogat was looking at him in fierce wonder. 'Gaunt had a simple choice to deploy the troops at his disposal for a brave last stand, or to take all those he could save and get clear. He chose the latter. None of us liked that decision. We all wanted to give our lives fighting for our home world. I suppose if we'd stayed on Tanith, we would have achieved nothing except maybe a valiant footnote in history. Gaunt saved us. He took us from a destruction we would have been proud to be a part of so that we could enjoy a more significant destruction elsewhere.'

Zogat's eyes were bright in the darkness. 'You hate him.'

'No! Well, yes, I do, as I would hate anyone who had supervised the death of my home, anyone who had sacrificed it to some greater good.'

'Is this a greater good?'

'I've fought with the Ghosts on a dozen warfronts. I haven't seen a greater good yet.'

'You do hate him.'

'I admire him. I will follow him anywhere. That's all there is to say. I left my home world the night it died, and I've been fighting for its memory ever since. We Tanith are a dying breed. There are only about twenty hundred of us left. Gaunt only got away with enough for one regiment. The Tanith First. The First and Only. That's what makes us "ghosts", you see. The last few unquiet souls of a dead world. And I suppose we'll keep going until we're all done.'

Caffran fell silent and in the dimness of the shell-hole there was no sound except the fall of the bombardment outside. Zogat was silent for a long while, then he looked up at the paling sky. 'It will be dawn in two hours,' he said softly. 'Maybe we'll see our way out of this when it gets light.'

'You could be right,' Caffran replied, stretching his aching, mud-caked limbs. 'The bombardment does seem to be moving away. Who knows, we might live through this after all. Feth, I've lived through worse.'

Seven

Daylight rolled in with a wet stain of cloud, underlit by the continued bombardment. The lightening sky was streaked and cross-hatched by contrails, shell-wakes and arcs of fire from the massive Shriven emplacements in the distant shrouded hills. Lower, in the wide valley and the trench lines, the accumulated smoke of the onslaught, which had now been going on for just about twenty-one hours, dropping two or three shells a second, curdled like fog, thick, creamy and repellent with the stink of cordite and fyceline.

Gaunt brought his assembled company to a halt in a silo bay that had once held furnaces and bell kilns. They pulled off their rebreather masks. The floor, the air itself, was permeated with a greenish microdust that tasted of iron or blood. Shattered plastic crating was scattered all over the place. They were five kilometres from the bombardment line now, and the noise of the drum-mills, chattering away in barns and manufactories all around them, was even louder than the shells.

Corbec had got his men away from the fire zone just about intact, although everyone had been felled by the shockwave and eighteen had been deafened permanently by the air-burst. The Imperial Guard infirmaries over the lines would patch ruptured ear drums with plastene diaphragms or implant acoustic enhancers in a matter of moments. But that was over the lines. Out here, eighteen deaf men were a liability. When they formed up to move, Gaunt would station them in the midst of his column, where they could take maximum guidance and warning from the men around them. There were other injuries too, a number of broken arms, ribs and collarbones. However, everyone was walking and that was a mercy.

Gaunt took Corbec to one side. Gaunt knew a good soldier instinctively, and it worried him when confidence was misplaced. He'd chosen Corbec to offset Rawne. Both men commanded respect from the Tanith First and Only, one because he was liked and the other because he was feared.

'Not like you to make a tactical error of that magnitude...' Gaunt began.

Corbec started to say something and then cut himself short. The idea of making excuses to the commissar stuck in his throat.

Gaunt made them for him. 'I understand we're all in a tight spot. This circumstance is extreme, and your lot had suffered particularly. I heard about Drayl. I also think these drummills, which you decided to target with an almost suicidal determination, are meant to disorientate. Meant to make us act irrationally. Let's face it, they're insane. They are as much a weapon as the guns. They are meant to wear us down.'

Corbec nodded. The war had pooled bitterness in his great, hoary form. There was a touch of weariness to his look and manner.

'What's our plan? Do we wait for the barrage to stop and retreat?'

Gaunt shook his head. 'I think we've come in so deep, we can do some good. We'll wait for the scouts to return.'

The recon units returned to the shelter within half an hour. The scouts, some Vitrian, mostly Tanith, combined the data from their sweeps and built a picture of the area in a two kilometre radius for Gaunt and Zoren.

What interested Gaunt most was a structure to the west.

They moved through a wide section of drainage pipelines, through rain-washed concrete underpasses stained with oil and dust.

The cordite fog drifted back over their positions. To the west rose the great hill line, to the immediate north the shadowy bulk of habitat spires, immense conical towers for the workforce that rose out of the ground fog, their hundred thousand windows all blown out by shelling and air-shock. There were fewer drum-mills in this range of the enemy territory, but still no sign of a solitary living thing, not even vermin.

They began passing blast-proofed bunkers of great size, all empty except for scattered support cradles and stacking pallets of grey fibre-plast. A crowd of battered, yellow, heavy-lift trolleys were abandoned on the concourses before the bunkers.

'Munitions stores?' Zoren suggested to Gaunt as they advanced.

'They must have stockpiled a vast amount of shells for this bombardment and they've already emptied these sheds.'

Gaunt thought this a good guess. They edged on, cautious, marching half-time and with weapons ready. The structure the reconnaissance had reported was ahead now, a cargo loading bay of tubular steel and riveted blast-board. The bay was mounted with hydraulic cranes and derricks on the surface, poised to lower cargo into a cavity below ground.

The guardsmen descended on the metal grilled stairway onto a raised platform that lay alongside a wide, well-lit tunnel that ran off out of sight into the impacted earth. The tunnel was modular, circular in cross section, with a raised spine running along the lowest part. Feygor and Grell examined the tunnel and the armoured control post overlooking it.

'Maglev line,' said Feygor, who had done all he could to augment his basic engineering knowledge with off-world mechanisms. 'Still active. They cart the shells from the munitions dump and lower them into the bay, then load them onto bomb trains for fast delivery to the emplacements in the hills.'

He showed Gaunt an indicator board in the control position. The flat-plate glowed green, showing a flickering runic depiction of a track network. 'There's a whole transit system down here, purpose-built to link all the forge factories and allow for rapid transportation of material.'

'And this spur has been abandoned because they've exhausted the munitions stores in this area.' Gaunt was thoughtful. He took out his data-slate and made a working sketch of the network map.

The commissar ordered a ten-minute rest, then sat on the edge of the platform and compared his sketch with area maps of the old factory complexes from the slate's tactical archives. The Shriven had modified a lot of the details, but the basic elements were still the same.

Colonel Zoren joined him. 'Something's on your mind,' he began.

Gaunt gestured to the tunnel. 'It's a way in. A way right into the central emplacements of the Shriven. They won't have blocked it because they need these maglev lines active and clear to keep the bomb trains moving to feed their guns.'

'There's something odd, though, don't you think?' Zoren eased back the visor of his helmet.

'Odd?'

'Last night, I thought your assessment of their tactics was correct. They'd tried a frontal assault to pierce our lines, but when it failed they pulled back to an extreme extent to lure us in and then set the bombardment to flatten any Imperial forces they'd drawn out.'

'That makes sense of the available facts,' Gaunt said.

'Even now? They must know they could only have caught a few thousand of us with that trick, and logic says most of us would be dead by now. So why are they still shelling? Who are they firing at? It's exhausting their shell stocks, it must be. They've been at it for over a day. And they've abandoned such a huge area of their lines.'

Gaunt nodded. 'That was on my mind too when dawn broke. I think it began as an effort to wipe out any forces they had trapped. But now? You're right. They've sacrificed a lot of land and the continued bombardments make no sense.'

'Unless they're trying to keep us out,' a voice said from behind them. Rawne had joined them.

'Let's have your thoughts, major,' Gaunt said.

Rawne shrugged and spat heavily on to the floor. His black eyes narrowed to a frowning squint. 'We know the spawn of Chaos don't fight wars with any tactics we'd recognise. We've been held on this front for months. I think yesterday was a last attempt to break us with a conventional offensive. Now they've put up a wall of fire to keep us out while they switch to something else. Maybe something that's taken them months to prepare.'

'Something like what?' Zoren asked uncomfortably.

'Something. I don't know. Something using their Chaos power. Something ceremonial. Those drum-mills… maybe they aren't psychological warfare… maybe they're part of some vast… ritual.'

The three men were silent for a moment. Then Zoren laughed, a mocking snarl. 'Ritual magic?'

'Don't mock what you don't understand!' Gaunt warned. 'Rawne could be right. Emperor knows, we've seen enough of their madness.' Zoren didn't reply. He'd seen things too, per-haps things his mind wanted to deny or scrub out as impossible.

Gaunt got up and pointed down the tunnel. 'Then this is a way in. And we'd better take it – because if Rawne's right, we're the only units in a position to do a damn thing about it.'

* * *

Eight

It was possible to advance down the maglev tunnel four abreast, with two men on each side of the central rider spine. It was well lit by recessed blue-glow lighting in the tunnel walls, but Gaunt sent Domor and the other sweepers in the vanguard to check for booby traps.

An unopposed advance down the stuffy tunnels took them two kilometres east, passing another abandoned cargo bay and forks with two other maglev spurs. The air was dry and charged with static from the still-powered electromagnetic rail, and hot gusts of wind breathed on them periodically as if heralding a train that never came.

At the third spur, Gaunt turned the column into a new tunnel, following his map. They'd gone about twenty metres when Milo whispered to the commissar.

'I think we need to go back to the spur fork,' he said.

Gaunt didn't query. He trusted Brin's instincts like his own, and knew they stretched further. He retreated the whole company to the junction they had just passed. Within a minute, a hot breeze blew at them, the tunnel hummed and a maglev train whirred past along the spur they had been about to join. It was an automated train of sixty open carts, painted khaki with black and yellow flashing. Each cart was laden with shells and munitions, hundreds of tonnes of ordnance from distant bunkers destined for the main batteries. As the train rolled past on the magnetic-levitation rail, slick and inertia free, many of the men gawked openly at it. Some made signs of warding off and protection.

Gaunt consulted his sketch map. It was difficult to determine how far it was to the next station or junction, and without knowing the frequency of the bomb trains, he couldn't guarantee they'd be out of the tunnel before the next one rumbled through.

Gaunt cursed. He didn't want to turn back now. His mind raced as he reviewed his troop files, scrabbling to recall personal details.

'Domor!' he called, and the trooper hurried over.

'Back on Tanith, you and Grell were engineers, right?'

The young trooper nodded. 'I was apprenticed to a timber haulier in Tanith Attica. I worked with heavy machines.'

'Given the resources at hand, could you stop one of these trains?'

'Sir?'

'And then start it again?'

Domor scratched his neck as he thought. 'Short of blowing the mag-rail itself... You'd need to block or short out the power that drives the train. As I understand it, the trains move on the rails, sucking up a power source from them. It's a conductive electrical exchange, as I've seen on batteries and flux-units. We'd need some non-conductive material, fine enough to lay across the rider-spine without actually derailing the train. What do you have in mind, sir?'

'Stopping or slowing the next train that passes, jumping a ride and starting it again.'

Domor grinned. 'And riding it all the way to the enemy?' He chuckled and looked around. Then he set off towards Colonel

Zoren, who was conversing with some of his men as they rested. Gaunt followed.

'Excuse me, sir,' Domor began with a tight salute, 'may I examine your body armour?'

Zoren looked at the Tanith trooper with confusion and some contempt but Gaunt soothed him with a quiet nod. Zoren peeled off a gauntlet and handed it to Domor. The young Tanith examined it with keen eyes.

'It's beautiful work. Is this surface tooth made of glass bead?'

'Yes, mica. Glass, as you say. Scale segments woven onto a base fabric of thermal insulation.'

'Non-conductive,' Domor said, showing the glove to Gaunt. 'I'd need a decent-sized piece. Maybe a jacket – and it may not come back in one piece.'

Gaunt was about to explain, hoping Zoren would ask for a volunteer from among his men. But the colonel got to his feet, took off his helmet and handed it to his subaltern before stripping off his own jacket.

Standing in his sleeveless undervest, his squat, powerful frame, shaven black hair and black skin revealed for the first time, Zoren paused only to remove a slim, grey-sleeved book from a pouch in his jacket before handing it to Domor. Zoren carefully tucked the book into his belt.

'I take it this is part of a plan?' Zoren asked as Domor hurried away, calling to Grell and others to assist him.

'You'll love it,' Gaunt said.

* * *

FIRST AND ONLY

A warm gust of air announced the approach of the next train, some seventeen minutes or so after the first they had seen. Domor had wrapped the Vitrian major's jacket over the rider-rail just beyond the spur and tied a length of material cut from his own camo-cloak to it.

The train rolled into view. Every one of them watched with bated breath. The front cart passed over the jacket without any problem, suspended as it was just a few centimetres above the smooth rail by the electromagnetic repulsion so that the whole vehicle ran friction-free along the spine. Gaunt frowned. For a moment he was sure it hadn't worked.

But as soon as the front cart had passed beyond the non-conductive layer, the electromagnetic current was broken, and the train decelerated fast as the propelling force went dead. Forward momentum carried the train forward for a while – by the track-side, Domor prayed it would not carry the entire train beyond the circuit break, or it would simply start again – but it went dead at last and came to a halt, rocking gently on the suspension field.

There was a cheer.

'Mount up! Quick as you can!' Gaunt ordered, leading the company forward. Vitrians and Tanith alike clambered up onto the bomb-laden carriages, finding foot and handholds where they could, stowing weapons and holding out hands to pull comrades aboard. Gaunt, Zoren, Milo, Bragg and six Vitrians mounted the front cart alongside Mkoll, Curral and Domor, who still clutched the end of the cloth rope.

'Good work, trooper,' Gaunt said to the smiling Domor and

held a hand up as he watched down the train to make sure all had boarded and were secure. In short order, the entire company was in place, and relays of acknowledgements ran down the train to Gaunt.

Gaunt dropped his hand. Domor yanked hard on the cloth cord. It went taut, fought him and then flew free, pulling Zoren's jacket up and out from under the cart like a large flatfish on a line.

In a moment, as the circuit was restored, the train lurched and silently began to move again, quickly picking up speed. The tunnel lights began to strobe-flash as they flicked past them.

Clinging on carefully, Domor untied his makeshift cord and handed the jacket back to Zoren. Parts of the glass fabric had been dulled and fused by contact with the rail, but it was intact. The Vitrian pulled it back on with a solemn nod.

Gaunt turned to face the tunnel they were hurtling into. He opened his belt pouch and pulled out a fresh drum-pattern magazine for his bolt pistol. The sixty round capacity clip was marked with a blue cross to indicate the inferno rounds it held. He clicked it into place and then thumbed his wire headset.

'Ready, weapons ready. Word is given. We're riding into the mouth of hell and we could be among them any minute. Prepare for sudden engagement. Emperor be with you all.'

Along the train, lasguns whined as they powered up, launchers clicked to armed, plasma packs hummed into seething readiness and the ignitors on flamer units were lit.

* * *

Nine

'Come on,' Caffran said, wriggling up the side of the stinking shell-hole that had been home for the best part of a day. Zogat followed. They blinked up into the dawn light. The barrage was still thundering away, and smoke-wash fog licked down across no-man's-land.

'Which way?' Zogat asked, disorientated by the smoke and the light.

'Home.' Caffran said. 'Away from the face of hell while we have the chance.'

They trudged into the mud, struggling over wire and twisted shards of concrete.

'Do you think we may be the only two left?' the Vitrian asked, glancing back at the vast barrage.

'We may be, we may be indeed. And that makes me the last of the Tanith.'

The Jantine armoured unit stabbed into the Shriven positions behind the barrage, but in two kilometres or more of advancing they had met nothing. The old factory areas were lifeless and deserted.

Flense called a halt and rose out of the top hatch to scan the way ahead through his scope. The ruined and empty buildings stood around in the fog like phantoms. There was a relentless drumming sound that bit into his nerves.

'Head for the hill line,' he told his driver as he dropped back inside. 'If we do no more than silence their batteries, we will have entered the chapters of glory.'

* * *

Four kilometres, five, passing empty stations and unlit cargo bays. A spur to the left, then to the left again, and then an anxious pause of three minutes, waiting while another bomb train passed ahead of them from another siding. Then they were moving again.

The tension wrapped Gaunt like a straitjacket. All of the passing tunnel looked constant and familiar, there were no markers to forewarn or alert. Any moment.

The bomb train slid into a vast cargo bay on a spur siding, coming to rest alongside two other trains that were being offloaded by cranes and servitor lifters. An empty train was just leaving on a loop that would take it back to the munitions dumps.

The chamber was lofty and dark, lit by thousands of lanterns and the ruddy glare of work-lamps. It was hot and smelled bitter, like a furnace room. The walls, as they could see them, were inscribed with vast sigils of Chaos, and draped with filthy banners. The symbols made the guardsmen's eyes weep if they glanced at them and made their heads pound if they looked for longer. Unclean symbols, symbols of pestilence and decay.

There were upwards of two hundred Shriven in the dim, gantried chamber, working the lifters or sliding bomb trolleys. None of them seemed to notice the new train's extra cargo for a moment.

Gaunt's company dismounted from the train, opening fire as they went, laying down a hail of las-fire that cracked like electricity in the air. There was the whine of the Tanith guns on the lower setting and the stinging punch of the full-force Vitrian shots. Gaunt had forbidden the use of meltas, rockets and flamers until they were clear of the munitions bay. None of the shells were fused or set, but there was no sense cooking or exploding them.

Dozens of the Shriven fell where they stood. Two half-laden shell trolleys spilled over as nerveless hands released levers. Warheads rolled and chinked on the platform. A trolley of shells veered into a wall as its driver was shot, and overturned. A crane assembly exploded and collapsed.

The guardsmen surged onwards. The Vitrian Dragoons fanned out in a perfect formation, taking point of cover after point of cover and scything down the fleeing Shriven. A few had found weapons and were returning fire, but their efforts were dealt with mercilessly.

Gaunt advanced up the main loading causeway with the Tanith, blasting Shriven with his bolt pistol. Nearby, Mad Larkin and a trio of other Tanith snipers with the needle-pattern lasguns were ducked in cover and picking off Shriven on the overhead catwalks.

Trooper Bragg had an assault cannon which he had liberated from a pintle mount some weeks before. Gaunt had never seen a man fire one without the aid of a power armour's recoil compensators or lift capacity before. Bragg grimaced and strained with the effort of steadying the howling weapon with its six cycling barrels, and his aim was its usual miserable standard. He killed dozens of the enemy anyway. Not to mention a maglev train.

The Ghosts led the fight up out of the cargo bay and onto loading ramps which extended up through great caverns cut into the hillside. A layer of blue smoke rose up under the flickering pendulum lighting rigs.

Clear of the munitions deck, Gaunt ordered up his meltas, flamers and rocket launchers, and began to scour a path, blackening the concrete strips of the ramps and fusing Shriven bone into syrupy pools.

At the head of the ramps, at the great elevator assemblies which raised the bomb loads into the battery magazines high above them in the hillside, they met the first determined resistance. A massed force of Shriven troops rushed down at them, blasting with lasguns and autorifles. Rawne commanded a fireteam up the left flank and cut into them from the edge, matched by Corbec's platoons from the right, creating a crossfire that punished them terribly.

In the centre of the Shriven retaliation, Gaunt saw the first of the Chaos Space Marines, a huge horned beast, centuries old and bearing the twisted markings of the Iron Warriors Chapter. The monstrosity exhorted his mutated troops to victory with great howls from his augmented larynx. His ancient, ornate boltgun spat death into the Tanith ranks. Sergeant Grell was vaporised by one of the first hits, two of his fire-team a moment later.

'Target him!' Gaunt yelled at Bragg, and the giant turned his huge firepower in the general direction with no particular success. The Chaos Marine proceeded to punch butchering fire into the Vitrian front line. Then he exploded. Headless, armless, his legs and torso rocked for a moment and then fell.

Gaunt nodded his grim thanks to Trooper Melyr and his missile launcher. Las-fire and screaming autogun rounds wailed down from the Shriven units at the elevator assembly. Gaunt ducked behind some freight pallets and found himself sharing the cover with two Vitrians who were busy changing the power cells of their lasguns.

'How much ammo have you left?' Gaunt asked briskly as he swapped the empty drum of his bolt pistol with a fresh sickle-pattern clip of Kraken penetrators.

'Half gone already,' responded one, a Vitrian corporal.

Gaunt thumbed his micro-bead headset. 'Gaunt to Zoren!'

'I hear you, commissar-colonel.'

'Instruct your men to alter their settings to half-power.'

'Why, commissar?'

'Because they're exhausting their ammo! I admire your ethic, colonel, but it doesn't take a full power shot to kill one of the Shriven and your men are going to be out of clips twice as fast as mine!'

There was a crackling pause over the comm-line before Gaunt heard Zoren give the order.

Gaunt looked across at the two troopers who were adjusting their charge settings.

'It'll last longer, and you'll send more to glory. No point in overkill,' he said with a smile. 'What are you called?'

'Zapol,' said one.

'Zeezo,' said the other, the corporal.

'Are you with me, boys?' Gaunt asked with a wolfish grin as he hefted up his pistol and thumbed his chainsword to maximum revs. They nodded back, lasrifles held in strong, ready hands.

Gaunt and the two dragoons burst from cover firing. They

were more than halfway up the loading ramp to the elevators. Rawne's crossfire manoeuvre had fenced the Shriven in around the hazard-striped blast doors, which were now fretted and punctured with las-impacts and fusing burns.

As he charged, Gaunt felt the wash of fire behind him as his own units covered and supported.

He could hear the whine of the long-pattern sniper guns, the crack of the regular lasweapons, the rattle of Bragg's cannons.

'Keep your aim up, Try Again…' Gaunt hissed as he and the two dragoons reached the makeshift defences around the enemy.

Zeezo went down, clipped by a las-round. Gaunt and Zapol bounded up to the debris cover and cut into the now-panicked Shriven. Gaunt emptied his boltgun and ditched it, scything with his chainsword. Zapol laid in with his bayonet, stabbing into bodies and firing point blank to emphasise each kill.

It took two minutes. They seemed like a lifetime to Gaunt, each bloody, frenzied second playing out like a year. Then he and Zapol were through to the elevator itself and the Shriven were piled around them. Five or six more Vitrians were close behind.

Zapol turned to smile at the commissar.

The smile was premature.

The elevator doors ahead of them parted and a second Iron Warrior Chaos Marine lunged out at them. It was loftier than the tallest guardsman, and clad entirely in an almost insect-like carapace of ancient power armour dotted with insane runes in dedication to its deathless masters. It was preceded by a bow-wave of the most foetid stench, exhaled from its grilled mask, and accompanied by a howl that grazed Gaunt's hearing and sounded like consumptive lungs exploding under deep pressure.

The beast's chainfist, squealing like an enraged beast, pulped Zapol with a careless downwards flick. The Vitrian was crushed and liquefied. The creature began to blast wildly, killing at least four more of the supporting Vitrians.

Gaunt was right in the thing's face. He could do nothing but lunge with his chainsword, driving the shrieking blade deep into the Chaos Marine's armoured torso. The toothed blade screamed and protested, and then whined and smoked as the serrated, whirling cutting edge meshed and glued as it ate into the monster's viscous and toughened innards.

The Iron Warrior stumbled back, bellowing in pain and rage. The chainsword, smoking and shorting as it finally jammed, impaled its chest. Reeking ichor and tissue sprayed across the commissar and the elevator doorway.

Gaunt knew he could do no more. He dropped to the floor as the stricken creature rose again, hoping against hope.

His prayers were answered. The rearing thing was struck once, twice... four or five times by carefully placed las-shots which tore into it and spun it around. Gaunt somehow knew it was the sniper Larkin who had provided these marksman blasts.

On one knee, the creature rose and raged again, most of its upper armour punctured or shredded, smoke rising and black fluid spilling from the grisly wounds to its face, neck and chest.

A final, powerful las-blast, close range and full-power, took its head off.

Gaunt looked round to see the wounded Corporal Zeezo standing on the barricade.

The Vitrian grinned, despite the pain from his wound. 'I went against orders, I'm afraid,' he began. 'I reset my gun for full charge.'

'Noted… and excused. Good work!'

Gaunt got to his feet, wet and wretched with blood and fouler stuff. His Ghosts, and Zoren's Vitrians, were moving up the ramp to secure the position. Above them, at the top of the elevator shaft, were maybe a million Shriven, secure in their battery bunkers. Gaunt's expeditionary force was inside, right in the heart of the enemy stronghold.

Ibram Gaunt smiled.

Ten

It took another precious half hour to regroup and secure the bomb deck. Gaunt's scouts located all the entranceways and blocked them, checking even ventilation access and drainage gullies.

Gaunt paced, tense. The clock was ticking and it wouldn't take long for the massive forces above them to start wondering why the shell supply from below had dried up, and come looking for a reason.

There was the place itself too: the gloom, the taste of the air, the blasphemous iconography scrawled on the walls. It was as if they were inside some sacred place, sacred but unholy. Everyone was bathed in cold sweat and there was fear in everyone's eyes.

The comm-link chimed and Gaunt responded, hurrying

through to the control room of the bomb bays. Zoren, Rawne and others were waiting for him. Someone had managed to raise the shutters on the vast window ports.

'What in the name of the Emperor is that?' Colonel Zoren asked.

'I think that's what we've come to stop,' Gaunt said, turning away from the stained glass viewing ports.

Far below them, in the depths of the newly-revealed hollowed cavern, stood a vast megalith, a menhir stone maybe fifty metres tall that smoked with building Chaos energy. Its essence filled the bay and made all the humans present edgy and distracted. None could look at it comfortably. It seemed to be bedded in a pile of... blackened bodies. Or body parts.

Major Rawne scowled and flicked a thumb upwards.

'It won't take them long to notice the bomb levels aren't supplying them with shells any more. Then we can expect serious deployment against us.'

Gaunt nodded but said nothing. He crossed to the control suite where Feygor and a Vitrian sergeant named Zolex were attempting to access data. Gaunt didn't like Feygor. The tall, thin Tanith was Rawne's adjutant and shared the major's bitter outlook. But Gaunt knew how to use him and his skills, particularly in the area of cogitators and other thinking machines.

'Plot it for me,' he told the adjutant. 'I have a feeling there may be more of these stone things.'

Feygor touched several rune keys on the glass and brass machined device.

'We're there...' Feygor said, pointing at the glowing map

sigils. 'And here's a larger scale map. You were right. That menhir down there is part of a system buried in these hills. Seven all told, in a star pattern. Seven fething abominations! I don't know what they mean to do with them, but they're all charging with power right now.'

'How many?' Gaunt asked too quickly.

'Seven,' Feygor repeated. 'Why?'

Ibram Gaunt felt light-headed. 'Seven stones of power…' he murmured. A voice from years ago lilted in his mind. The girl. The girl back on Darendara. He could never remember her name, try as hard as he could. But he could see her face in the interrogation room, and hear her words.

When her words about the Ghosts had come true, two years earlier, he had been chilled and had spent several sleepless nights remembering her prophecies. He'd taken command of the worldless wretches of Tanith and then one of the troop, Mad Larkin, it was asserted, had dubbed them Gaunt's Ghosts. He'd tried to put that down to coincidence, but ever since, he'd watched for other fragments of the Night of Truths to emerge.

Cut them and you will be free, she had said. *Do not kill them.*

'What do we do?' asked Rawne.

'We have mines and grenades a plenty,' Zoren said. 'Let's blow it.'

Do not kill them.

Gaunt shook his head. 'No! This is what the Shriven have been preparing, some vast ritual using the stones, some industrial magic. That's what has preoccupied them, that's what they've tried to distract us from. Blowing part of their ceremonial ring would be a mistake. There's no telling what foul power we might unleash. No, we have to break the link…'

Cut them and you will be free.

Gaunt got to his feet and pulled on his cap again. 'Major Rawne, load as many hand carts as you can find with Shriven warheads, prime them for short fuse and prepare to send them up on the elevator on my cue. We'll choke the emplacements upstairs with their own weapons. Colonel Zoren, I want as many of your men as you can spare – or more specifically, their armour.'

The major and the colonel looked at him blankly.

'Now!' he added sharply. They leapt to their feet.

Gaunt led the way up the ramp towards the menhir. It smoked with energy and his skin prickled uncomfortably. Chaos energy smelt that way, like a tangy stench of cooked blood and electricity. None of them dared look down at the twisted, solidified mound below them.

'What are we doing?' Zoren asked by his side, clearly distressed about being this close to the unutterable.

'We're breaking the chain. We want to disrupt the circle without blowing it.'

'How do you know?'

'Inside information,' Gaunt said, trying hard to grin. 'Trust me. Let's short this out.'

The Vitrians by his side moved forward at a nod from their commander. Tentatively, they approached the huge stone and started to lash their jackets around the smooth surface. Zoren had collected the mica armoured jackets of more than fifty of his men. Now he fused them together as neat as a surgeon with a melta on the lowest setting. Gingerly the Vitrians wrapped the makeshift mica cloak around the stone, using meltas borrowed from the Tanith like industrial staplers to lock it into place over the stone.

'It's not working,' Zoren said.

It wasn't. After a few moments more, the glass beads of the Vitrian armour began to sweat and run, melting off the stone, leaving the fabric base layers until they too ignited and burned.

Gaunt turned away, his disheartened mind churning.

'What now?' Zoren asked, dispiritedly.

Cut them and you will be free.

Gaunt snapped his fingers. 'We don't blow them! We realign them. That's how we cut the circle.'

Gaunt called up Tolus, Lukas and Bragg. 'Get charges set in the supporting mound. Don't target the stone itself. Blow it so it falls away or drops.'

'The mound…' Lukas stammered.

'Yes, trooper, the mound,' Gaunt repeated. 'The dead can't hurt you. Do it!'

Reluctantly, the Ghosts went to work.

Gaunt tapped his micro-bead intercom. 'Rawne, send those warheads up.'

'Acknowledged.'

A 'sir' wouldn't kill him, Gaunt thought.

At the elevator head, the troops under Rawne's command thundered trolleys of warheads into the car.

'Shush!' a Vitrian said suddenly. They stopped. A pause – then they all heard the clanking, the distant tinny thumps. Rawne swung up his lasgun and moved into the elevator assembly. He pulled the lever that opened the upper inspection hatch.

Above him, the great lift shaft yawned like a beast's throat.

He stared up into the darkness, trying to resolve the detail.

The darkness was moving. Shriven were descending, clawing like bat-things down the sheer sides of the shaftway.

Terror punched Rawne's heart. He slammed the hatch and screamed out, 'They're coming!'

The intercom lines went wild with reports as sentries reported hammerings at the sealed hatches and entranceways all around. Hundreds of fists, thousands of fists.

Gaunt cursed, feeling the panic rising in his men. Trapped, entombed, the infernal enemy seeping in from all sides. Speakers mounted on walls and consoles all around squawked into life, and a rasping voice, echoing and overlaying itself from a hundred places, spat inhuman gibberish into the chambers.

'Shut that off!' Gaunt yelled at Feygor.

Feygor scrabbled desperately at the controls. 'I can't!' he cried.

A hatchway to the east exploded inwards with a shower of sparks. Men screamed. Las-fire began to chatter. A little to the north, another doorway blew inwards in a flaming gout and more Shriven began to battle their way inwards.

Gaunt turned to Corbec. The man was pale. Gaunt tried to think, but the rasping, reverberating snarls of the speakers clogged his mind. With a bark, he raised his pistol and blasted the nearest speaker set off the wall.

He turned to Corbec. 'Start the retreat. As many as we dare to keep the covering fire.'

Corbec nodded and hurried off. Gaunt opened his intercom to wide band. 'Gaunt to all units! Commence withdrawal, maximum retreating resistance!' He sprinted down through the mayhem into the megalith chamber, knocked back for a second by the noxious stench of the place. Lukas, Tolus and Bragg were just emerging, their arms, chests and knees caked with black, tarry goo. They were all ashen and hollow-eyed.

'It's done,' Tolus said.

'Then blow it! Move out!' Gaunt cried, pushing and shoving his stumbling men out of the cavern. 'Rawne!'

'Almost there!' Rawne replied from over at the elevator. He and the Ghost next to him looked up sharply as they heard a thump from the liftcar roof above them. Cursing, Rawne pushed the final trolley of shells into the elevator bay.

'Back! Back!' Rawne shouted to his men. He hit the riser stud of the elevator and it began to lift up the shaft towards the Shriven emplacements high above. They heard impacts and shrieks as it pulverised the Shriven coming down the shaft.

The Ghosts and Vitrians with Rawne were running for their lives. Somewhere far above, their payload arrived – and detonated hard enough to shake the ground and sprinkle earth and rock chips down from the cavern roof. Lamp arrays swung like pendulums.

Gaunt felt it all going off above them, and it strengthened his resolve. He was moving towards the maglev tunnel in the middle of a tumble of guardsmen, almost pushing the dazed Bragg by force of will. Shriven fire burned their way. A Ghost dropped, mid-flight. Others turned, knelt, returned fire. Las-fire glittered back and forth.

Behind them all, in the megalith chamber, the charges planted by Domor's team exploded. Its support blown away, the great crackling stone teetered and then slumped down into the pit. The speakers went silent.

Total silence. The Shriven firing had stopped. Those that had penetrated the chamber were prostrate, whimpering.

The only sound was the thumping footfalls and gasping breaths of the fleeing guardsmen.

Then a rumbling started. Incandescent green fire flashed and rippled out of the monolith chamber. Without warning the stained glass view ports of the control room exploded inwards. The ground rippled, ruptured; concrete churned like an angry sea.

'Get out! Get out now!' bellowed Ibram Gaunt.

Eleven

The shelling faltered, then stopped. Caffran and Zogat paused as they trudged back across the deadscape and looked back.

'Feth take me!' Caffran said. 'They've finally–'

The hills beyond the Shriven lines exploded. The vast shockwave threw them both to the ground. The hills splintered and puffed up dust and fire, swelling for a moment before collapsing into themselves.

'Emperor's throne!' Zogat said as he helped the young Tanith trooper up. They looked back at the mushroom cloud lifting from the sunken hills.

'Hah!' Caffran said. 'Someone just won something!'

In the villa, Lord High Militant General Dravere put down his cup and watched with faint curiosity as it rattled on the cart. He walked stiffly to the veranda rail and looked through the scope, though he hardly needed it. A bell-shaped cloud of ochre smoke boiled up over the horizon where the Shriven stronghold had once been. Lightning flared in the sky. The vox-caster speaker in the corner of the room wailed and then went dead. Secondary explosions, munitions probably, began to explode along the Shriven lines, blasting the heart out of everything they held.

Dravere coughed, straightened and turned to his adjutant. 'Prepare my transport for embarkation. It seems we're done here.'

A firestorm of shockwave and flame passed over the armoured vehicles of Colonel Flense's convoy. Once it had blown itself out, Flense scrambled out of the top hatch, looking towards the hills ahead of him, hills that were sliding down into themselves as secondary explosions went off.

'No…' he breathed, looking wide-eyed at the carnage.

'No!'

They had been knocked flat by the shockwave, losing many in the flare of green flame that followed them up the tunnel. Then they were blundering through darkness and dust. There were moans, prayers, coughs.

In the end it took almost five hours for them all to claw their way up and out of the darkness. Gaunt led the way up the tunnel himself. Finally the surviving Tanith and Vitrian units emerged, blinking, into the dying light of another day. Most flopped down, or staggered into the mud, sprawling, crying, laughing. Fatigue washed over them all.

Gaunt sat down on a curl of mud and took off his cap. He started to laugh, months of tension sloughing off him in one easy tide. It was over. Whatever else, whatever the mopping up, Fortis was won.

That girl, damn whatever her name was, had been right.

A MEMORY

Ignatius Cardinal,
Twenty-Nine Years Earlier

'What...' The voice paused for a moment, in deep confusion. 'What are you doing?'

Scholar Blenner looked up from the draughty tiles of the long cloister where he was kneeling. There was another boy standing nearby, looking down at him in quizzical fascination. Blenner didn't recognise him, though he was also wearing the sober black-twill uniform of the schola progenium.

A new boy, Blenner presumed.

'What do you think I'm doing?' he asked tersely. 'What does it look like I'm doing?'

The boy was silent for a moment. He was tall and lean, and Blenner guessed him to be about twelve years old, no more than a year or two less than his own age. But there was something terribly old and horribly piercing about the gaze of those dark eyes.

'It looks,' the new boy said, 'as if you're polishing the spaces between the floor tiles in this cloister using only a buckle brush.'

Blenner smirked humourlessly up at the boy and flourished the tiny brush in his grimy hand. It was a soft-bristle tool designed for buffing uniform buttons and fastenings. 'Then I think you'll find that you've answered your own question.' He dipped the tiny brush back into the bowl of chilly water at his side and began to scrub again. 'Now if you don't mind, I have three sides of the quadrangle still to do.'

The boy was silent for several minutes, but he didn't leave. Blenner scrubbed at the tiles and could feel the stare burning into his neck. He looked up again. 'Was there something else?'

The boy nodded. 'Why?'

Blenner dropped the brush into the bowl and sat back on his knees, rubbing his numb hands. 'I was reckless enough to use live rounds in the weapons training silos and somewhat – not to say completely – destroyed a target simulator. Deputy Master Flavius was not impressed.'

'So this is punishment?'

'This is punishment,' Blenner agreed.

'I'd better let you get on with it,' the boy said thoughtfully. 'I imagine I'm not even supposed to be talking to you.'

He crossed to the open side of the cloister and looked out. The inner quadrangle of the ancient missionary school was paved with a stone mosaic of the two-headed Imperial eagle. The air was full of thin rain, cast down by the cold wind which whined down the stone colonnades. Above the cloister roofs rose the ornate halls and towers of the ancient building, its carved guttering and gargoyles worn almost featureless by a thousand years of erosion. Beyond the precinct of the Schola stood the skyline of the city itself, the capital of the mighty Cardinal World, Ignatius. Dominating the western horizon was the black bulk of the Ecclesiarch Palace, its slab-like towers over two kilometres tall, their up-link masts stabbing high into the cold, cyan sky.

It seemed a damp, dark, cold place to live. Ibram Gaunt had been stung by its bone-deep chill from the moment he had stepped out of the shuttle which had conveyed him down to the landing fields from the frigate ship that had brought him here. From this cold world, the Ministorum ruled a segment of the galaxy with the iron hand of the Imperial faith. He had been told that it was a great honour for him to be enrolled in a schola progenium on Ignatius. Ibram had been taught to love the Emperor by his father, but somehow this honour didn't feel like much compensation.

Even with his back turned, Ibram knew that the older, thicker-set boy scrubbing the tiles was now staring at him.

'Do you now have a question?' he asked without turning.

'The usual,' the punished boy said. 'How did they die?'

'Who?'

'Your mother, your father. They must be dead. You wouldn't be here in the orphanage if they weren't gone to glory.'

'It's the schola progenium, not an orphanage.'

'Whatever. This hallowed establishment is a missionary school. Those who are sent here for education are the offspring of Imperial servants who have given their lives for the Golden Throne.

'So how did they die?'

Ibram Gaunt turned. 'My mother died when I was born. My father was a colonel in the Imperial Guard. He was lost last autumn in an action against the orks on Kentaur.'

Blenner stopped scrubbing and got up to join the other boy. 'Sounds juicy!' he began.

'Juicy?'

'Guard heroics and all that. So what happened?'

Ibram Gaunt turned to regard him and Blenner flinched at the depth of the gaze. 'Why are you so interested? How did your parents die to bring you here?'

Blenner backed off a step. 'My father was a Space Marine. He died killing a thousand daemons on Futhark. You'll have heard of that noble victory, no doubt. My mother, when she knew he was dead, took her own life out of love.'

'I see,' Gaunt said slowly.

'So?' Blenner urged.

'So what?'

'How did he die? Your father?'

'I don't know. They won't tell me.'

Blenner paused. 'Won't tell you?'

'Apparently it's… classified.'

The two boys said nothing for a moment, staring out at the rain which jagged down across the stone eagle.

'Oh. My name's Blenner, Vaynom Blenner,' the older boy said, turning and sticking out a hand.

Gaunt shook it. 'Ibram Gaunt,' he replied. 'Maybe you should get back to your–'

'Scholar Blenner! Are you shirking?' a voice boomed down the cloister. Blenner dived back to his knees, scooping the buckle brush out of the bowl and scrubbing feverishly.

A tall figure in flowing robes strode down the tiles towards them. He came to a halt over Blenner and stood looking down at him. 'Every centimetre, scholar, every tile, every line of junction.'

'Yes, deputy master.'

Deputy Master Flavius turned to face Gaunt. 'You are scholar-elect Gaunt.' It wasn't a question. 'Come with me, boy.'

Ibram Gaunt followed the tall master as he paced away over the tiles. He turned back for a moment. Blenner was looking up, miming a throat-cut with his finger and sticking his tongue out in a choking gag.

Young Ibram Gaunt laughed for the first time in a year.

The high master's chamber was a cylinder of books, a veritable hive-city of racks lined with shelf after shelf of ancient tomes and data-slates. There was a curious cog trackway that spiralled up the inner walls of the chamber from the floor, a toothed brass mechanism whose purpose utterly baffled Ibram Gaunt.

He stood in the centre of the room for four long minutes until High Master Boniface arrived.

The high master was a powerfully-set man in his fifties – or at least he had been until the loss of his legs, left arm and half of his face. He sailed into the room on a wheeled brass chair that supported a suspension field generated by the three field-buoys built into the chair's framework. His mutilated body moved, inertia-less, in the shimmering globe of power.

'You are Ibram Gaunt?' The voice was harsh, electronic.

'I am, master,' Gaunt said, snapping to attention as his uncle had trained him.

'You are also lucky, boy,' Boniface rasped, his voice curling out of a larynx enhancer. 'The Schola Progenium Prime of Ignatius doesn't take just anyone.'

'I am aware of the honour, high master. General Dercius made it known to me when he proposed my admission.'

The high master referred to a data-slate held upright in his suspension field, keying the device with his whirring, skeletal, artificial arm. 'Dercius. Commander of the Jantine regiments. Your father's immediate superior. I see. His recommendations for your placement here are on record.'

'Uncle… I mean, General Dercius said you would look after me, now my father has gone.'

Boniface froze, before swinging around to face Gaunt. His harshness had gone suddenly, and there was a look of – was it affection? – in his single eye.

'Of course we will, Ibram,' he said.

Boniface rolled his wheelchair into the side of the room and engaged the lateral cogs with the toothed trackway which spiralled up around the shelves. He turned a small handle and his chair started to lift up along the track, raising him up in widening curves over the boy.

Boniface stopped at the third shelf up and took out a book. 'The strength of the Emperor…? Finish it.'

'Is Humanity, and the strength of Humanity is the Emperor.

The sermons of Sebastian Thor, volume twenty-three, chapter sixty-two.'

Boniface wound his chair up higher on the spiral and selected another book.

'The meaning of war?'

'Is victory!' Gaunt replied eagerly. 'Lord Militant Gresh, *Memoirs*, chapter nine.'

'How may I ask the Emperor what he owes of me?'

'When all I owe is to the Golden Throne and by duty I will repay,' Gaunt returned. '*The Spheres of Longing* by Inquisitor Ravenor, volume… three?'

Boniface wound his chair down to the carpet again and swung round to face Gaunt. 'Volume two, actually.'

He stared at the boy. Gaunt tried not to shrink from the exposed gristle and tissue of the half-made face.

'Do you have any questions?'

'How did my father die? No one's told me, not even Un– I mean, General Dercius.'

'Why would you want to know, lad?'

'I met a boy in the cloisters. Blenner. He knew the passing of his parents. His father died fighting the Enemy at Futhark, and his mother killed herself for the love of him.'

'Is that what he said?'

'Yes, master.'

'Scholar Blenner's family were killed when their world was virus bombed during a genestealer insurrection. Blenner was off-planet, visiting a relative. An aunt, I believe. His father was an Administratum clerk. Scholar Blenner always has had a fertile imagination.'

'His use of live rounds? In training? The cause of his punishment?'

'Scholar Blenner was discovered painting rude remarks about the deputy high master on the walls of the latrine. That is the cause of his punishment duty. You're smiling, Gaunt. Why?'

'No real reason, high master.'

There was a long silence, broken only by the crackle and fizz of the high master's suspension field.

'How did my father die, high master?' Ibram Gaunt asked.

Boniface clenched the data-slate shut with an audible snap. 'That's classified.'

PART FOUR

Cracia City, Pyrites

One

The Imperial Needle was quite a piece of work, Colonel Colm Corbec decided. It towered over Cracia, the largest and oldest city on Pyrites, a three thousand metre ironwork tower, raised four hundred years before, partly to honour the Emperor but mostly to celebrate the engineering skill of the Pyriteans. It was taller than the jagged turrets of the Arbites Precinct, and it dwarfed even the great twin towers of the Ecclesiarch Palace. On cloudless days, the city became a giant sundial, with the spire as the gnomon. City dwellers could tell precisely the time of day by which streets of the city were in shadow.

Today was not a cloudless day. It was winter season in Cracia and the sky was a dull, unreflective white like an untuned vista-caster screen. Snow fluttered down out of the leaden sky to ice the gothic rooftops and towers of the old, grey city, edging the ornate decorations, the wrought-iron guttering and brass eaves, the skeletal fire-escapes and the sills of lancet windows.

But it was warm down here on the streets. Under the stained glass-beaded ironwork awnings which edged every thoroughfare, the walkways and concourses were heated. Kilometres below the city, ancient turbines pumped warm air up to the hypocaust beneath the pavements, which circulated under the awning levels. A low-power energy sheath broadcast at first floor height stopped rain or snow from ever reaching the pedestrian levels, for the most part.

At a terrace cafe, Corbec, the jacket of his Tanith colonel's uniform open and unbuckled, sipped his beer and rocked back on his black, ironwork chair. They liked black ironwork here on Pyrites. They made everything out of it. Even the beer, judging by the taste.

Corbec felt relaxation flood into his limbs for the first time in months. The hellhole of Fortis Binary was behind him at last: the mud, the vermin, the barrage.

It still flickered across his dreams at night and he often woke to the thump of imagined artillery. But this – a beer, a chair, a warm and friendly street – this was living again.

A shadow apparently bigger than the Imperial Needle blotted out the daylight. 'Are we set?' Trooper Bragg asked.

Corbec squinted up at the huge, placid-faced trooper, by some way the biggest man under his command. 'It's still early. They say this town has quite a nightlife, but it won't get going until after dark.'

'Seems dead. No fun,' Bragg said drearily.

'Hey, lucky we got Pyrites rather than Guspedin. By all accounts that's just dust and slag and endless hives.'

The lighting standards down each thoroughfare and under the awnings were beginning to glow into life as the automated cycle took over, though it was still daylight.

'We've been talking–' Bragg began.

'Who's we?' Corbec said.

'Uh, Larks and me... and Varl. And Blane.' Bragg shuffled a little. 'We heard about this little wagering joint. It might be fun.'

'Fine.'

''Cept it's, uh–'

'What?' Corbec said, knowing full well what the 'uh' would be.

'It's in a cold zone,' Bragg said.

Corbec got up and dropped a few coins of the local currency on the glass-topped table next to his empty beer glass. 'Trooper, you know the cold zones are off limits,' he said smoothly. 'The regiments have been given four days' recreation in this city, but that recreation is contingent on several things. Reasonable levels of behaviour, so as not to offend or disrupt the citizens of this most ancient and civilised burg. Restrictions as to the use of prescribed bars, clubs, wager-halls and brothels. And a total ban on Imperial Guard personnel leaving the heated areas of the city. The cold zones are lawless.'

Bragg nodded. 'Yeah... but there are five hundred thousand guardsmen on leave in Cracia, clogging up the star ports and the tram depots. Each one has been to fething hell and back in the last few months. Do you honestly think they're going to behave themselves?'

Corbec pursed his lips and sighed. 'No, Bragg. I suppose I do not. Tell me where this place is. The one you're talking about. I've an errand or two to run. I'll meet you there later. Just stay out of trouble.'

Two

In the mirror-walled, smoke-wreathed bar of the Polar Imperial, one of the better hotels in uptown Cracia, right by the Administratum complex, Commissar Vaynom Blenner was describing the destruction of the enemy battleship, *Eradicus*. It was a complex, colourful evocation, involving the skilled use of a lit cigar, smoke rings, expressive gestures and throaty sound effects. Around the table, there were appreciative hoots and laughs.

Ibram Gaunt, however, watched and said nothing. He was often silent. It disarmed people.

Blenner had always been a tale-spinner, even back in their days at the schola progenium. Gaunt always looked forward to their reunions. Blenner was about as close as he came to having an old friend, and it strangely reassured him to see Blenner's face, constant through the years when so many faces perished and disappeared.

But Blenner was also a terrible boast, and he had become weak and complacent, enjoying a little too much of the good life. For the last decade, he'd served with the Greygorian Third. The Greys were efficient, hard working and few regiments were as unswervingly loyal to the Emperor. They had spoiled Blenner.

Blenner hailed the waiter and ordered another tray of drinks for the officers at his table. Gaunt's eyes wandered across the crowded salon, where the officer classes of the Imperial Guard relaxed and mixed.

On the far side of the room, under a vast, glorious gilt-framed oil painting of Imperial Titans striding to war, he caught sight of officers in the chrome and purple dress uniform of the Jantine Patricians, the so-called 'Emperor's Chosen'. Amidst them was a tall, thickset figure with an acid-scarred face that Gaunt knew all too well – Colonel Draker Flense.

Their gaze met for a few seconds. The exchange was as warm and friendly as a pair of automated range finders getting a mutual target lock. Gaunt cursed silently to himself. If he'd known the Jantine officer cadre was using this hotel, he would have avoided it. The last thing he wanted was a confrontation.

'Commissar Gaunt?'

Gaunt looked up. A uniformed hotel porter stood by his armchair, his head tilted to a position that was both obsequious and superior. Snooty ass, thought Gaunt; loves the Guard all the while we're saving the universe for him, but let us in his precious hotel bar to relax and he's afraid we'll scuff the furniture.

'There is a boy, sir,' the porter said disdainfully. 'A boy in reception who wishes to speak with you.'

'Boy?' Gaunt asked.

'He said to give you this,' the porter continued. He held out a silver Tanith ear hoop suspiciously between velveted finger and thumb.

Gaunt nodded, got to his feet and followed him out.

Across the room, Flense watched him go. He beckoned over his aide, Ebzan, with a surly curl of his finger. 'Go and find Major Brochuss and some of his clique. I have a matter I wish to settle.'

Gaunt followed the strutting porter out into the marble foyer. His distaste for the place grew with each second. Pyrites was soft, pampered, so far away from the harsh warfronts. They paid their tithes to the Emperor and in return ignored completely the darker truths of life beyond their civilised domain. Even the Imperium troops stationed here as a permanent garrison seemed to have gone soft.

Gaunt broke from his reverie and saw Brin Milo hunched under a potted ouroboros tree. The boy was wearing his Ghost uniform and looked most unhappy.

'Milo? I thought you were going with the others. Corbec said he'd take you with the Tanith. What are you doing in a stuffy place like this?'

Milo fetched a small data-slate out of his thigh pocket and presented it. 'This came through the vox-cast after you'd gone, sir. Executive Officer Kreff thought it best it was brought straight to you. And as I'm supposed to be your adjutant... well, they gave the job to me.'

Gaunt almost grinned at the boy's weary tone. He took the slate and keyed it open. 'What is it?' he asked.

'All I know, sir, is that it's a personal communiqué delivered on an encrypted channel for your attention forty–' He paused to consult his timepiece. 'Forty-seven minutes ago.'

Gaunt studied the gibberish on the slate. Then the identifying touch of his thumbprint on the decoding icon unscrambled it. For his eyes only indeed.

'Ibram. You only friend in area close enough to assist. Go to 1034 Needleshadow Boulevard. Use our old identifier. Treasure to be had. Vermilion treasure. Fereyd.'

Gaunt looked up suddenly and snapped the slate shut as if caught red-handed. His heart pounded for a second. Throne of Earth, how many years had it been since his heart had pounded with that feeling – was it really fear? Fereyd? His old, old friend, bound together in blood since–

Milo was looking at him curiously. 'Trouble?' the boy asked innocuously.

'A task to perform…' Gaunt murmured. He opened the data-slate again and pressed the 'Wipe' rune to expunge the message.

'Can you drive?' he asked Milo.

'Can I?' the boy said excitedly.

Gaunt calmed his bright-eyed enthusiasm with a flat patting motion with his hands. 'Go down to the motor-pool and scare us up some transport. A staff car. Tell them I sent you.'

Milo hurried off. Gaunt stood for a moment in silence. He took two deep breaths – then a hearty slap on the back almost felled him.

'Bram! You dog! You're missing the party!' Blenner growled.

'Vay, I've got a bit of business to take care–'

'No no no!' the tipsy, red-faced commissar said, smoothing the creases in his leather greatcoat. 'How many times do we get together to talk of old times, eh? How many? Once every damn decade it seems like! I'm not letting you out of my sight! You'll never come back, I know you!'

'Vay… really, it's just tedious regimental stuff…'

'I'll come with you then! Get it done in half the time! Two commissars, eh? Put the fear of the Throne itself into them, I tell you!'

'Really, you'd be bored… it's a very boring task…'

'All the more reason I come! To make it less boring! Eh? Eh?' Blenner exclaimed. He edged the vintage brandy bottle that he had commandeered out of his coat pocket so that Gaunt could see it. So could everyone else in the foyer.

Any more of this, thought Gaunt, and I might as well announce my activities over the tannoy. He grabbed Blenner by the arm and led him out of the bar.

'You can come,' he hissed, 'just… behave! And be quiet!'

Three

The girl gyrating on the apron stage to the sounds of the tambour band was quite lovely and almost completely undressed, but Major Rawne was not looking at her.

He stared across the table in the low, smoky light as Vulnor Habshept kal Geel filled two shot glasses with oily, clear liquor.

Even as a skeleton, Geel would have been a huge man. But upholstered as he was in more than three hundred kilos of chunky flesh he made even Bragg look undernourished.

Major Rawne knew full well it would take over three times his own body-mass to match the opulently dressed racketeer. Rawne was also totally unafraid.

'We drink, soldier boy,' Geel said in his thick Pyritean accent, lifting one shot glass with a gargantuan hand.

'We drink,' Rawne agreed, picking up his own glass. 'Though I would prefer you address me as "Major Rawne"… racketeer boy.'

There was a dead pause. The crowded cold zone bar was silent in an instant. The girl stopped gyrating.

Geel laughed.

'Good! Good! Very amusing, such pluck! Ha ha ha!' He chuckled and knocked his drink back in one. The bar resumed talk and motion, relieved.

Rawne slowly and extravagantly gulped his drink. Then he lifted the decanter and drained the other litre of liquor without even blinking. He knew that it was a rye-based alcohol with a chemical structure similar to that used in Chimera and Rhino anti-freeze. He also knew that he had taken four anti-intoxicant tablets before coming in. Four tabs that had cost a fortune from a black market trader, but it was worth it. It was like drinking spring water.

Geel forgot to close his mouth for a moment and then recovered his composure.

'Major Rawne can drink like Pyritean!' he said with a complimentary tone.

'So the Pyriteans would like to think…' Rawne said. 'Now let's to business.'

'Come this way,' Geel said and lumbered to his feet. Rawne fell into step behind him and Geel's four huge bodyguards moved in behind.

Everyone in the bar watched them leave by the back door.

On stage, the girl had just shed her final, tiny garment and was in the process of twirling it around one finger prior to hurling it into the crowd. When she realised no one was watching, she stomped off in a huff.

In a snowy alley behind the club, a grey, beetle-nosed six-wheeled truck was waiting.

'Hocwheat liquor. Smokes. Text-slates with dirty pictures. Everything you asked for,' Geel said expansively.

'You're a man of your word,' Rawne said.

'Now, to the money. Two thousand Imperial credits. Don't waste my time with local rubbish. Two thousand Imperial.'

Rawne nodded and clicked his fingers. Trooper Feygor stepped out of the shadows carrying a bulging rucksack.

'My associate, Mr Feygor,' Rawne said. 'Show him the stuff, Feygor.'

Feygor stood the rucksack down in the snow and opened it. He reached in and pulled out a laspistol.

The first two shots hit Geel in the face and chest, smashing him back down the alley.

With practiced ease, Feygor grinned as he put an explosive blast through the skulls of each outraged bodyguard.

Rawne dashed over to the truck and climbed up into the cab.

'Let's go!' he roared to Feygor who scrambled up onto the side even as Rawne threw it into gear and roared it out of the alley.

As they screamed away under the archway at the head of the alley, a big dark shape dropped down into the truck, landing on the tarpaulin-wrapped contraband in the flatbed. Feygor, hanging on tight and monkeying up the restraints onto the cargo bed, saw the stowaway and lashed out at him. A powerful jab laid him out cold in the canvas folds of the tarpaulin.

At the wheel, Rawne saw Feygor fall in the rear-view scope and panicked as the attacker swung into the cab beside him.

'Major,' Corbec said.

'Corbec!' Rawne exploded. 'You! Here?'

'I'd keep your eyes on the road if I were you,' Corbec said glancing back, 'I think Geel's men are after a word with you.'

The truck raced on down the snowy street. Behind it came four angry limousines.

'Feth!' Major Rawne said.

Four

The big, black staff-track roared down the boulevard under the glowing lamps in their ironwork frames. Smoothly and deftly it slipped around the light evening traffic, changing lanes.

Drivers seemed more than willing to give way to the big, sinister machine with its throaty engine note and its gleaming double-headed eagle crest.

Behind armoured glass in the tracked passenger section, Gaunt leaned forward in the studded leather seats and pressed the speaker switch. Beside him, Blenner poured two large snifters of brandy and chuckled.

'Milo,' Gaunt said into the speaker, 'not so fast. I'd like to draw as little attention to ourselves as possible, and it doesn't help with you going for some new speed record.'

'Understood, sir,' Milo said over the speaker.

Sitting forward astride the powerful nose section, Milo flexed his hands on the handlebar grips and grinned. The speed dropped. A little.

Gaunt ignored the glass Blenner was offering him and flipped open a data-slate map of the city's street-plan.

Then he thumbed the speaker again. 'Next left, Milo, then follow the underpass to Zorn Square.'

'That… that takes us into the cold zones, commissar,' Milo replied over the link.

'You have your orders, adjutant,' Gaunt said simply and snapped off the intercom.

'This isn't Guard business at all, is it, old man?' Blenner said wryly.

'Don't ask questions and you won't have to lie later, Vay. In fact, keep out of sight and pretend you're not here. I'll get you back to the bar in an hour or so.'

I hope, Gaunt added under his breath.

Rawne threw the truck around a steep bend. The six chunky wheels slid alarmingly on the wet snow. Behind it, the heavy pursuit vehicles thrashed and slipped.

'This is the wrong way!' Rawne said. 'We're going deeper into the damn cold zone!'

'We didn't have much choice,' Corbec replied. 'They're boxing us in. Didn't you plan your escape route?'

Rawne said nothing and concentrated on his driving. They were flung around another treacherous turn.

'What are you doing here?' he asked Corbec at last.

'Just asking myself the same thing,' Corbec reflected lightly. 'Well, truth is, I thought I'd do what any good regimental colonel does for his men on a shore leave rotation after a nightmare tour of duty in a hell-pit like Fortis, and take a trip into the downtown districts to rustle up a little black market drink and the like. The men always appreciate a colonel who looks after them.'

Rawne scowled, fighting the wheel.

'Then I happened to see you and your sidekick, and I realised that you were doing what any good sneaking low-life weasel would do on shore leave rotation. To wit, scamming some local out of contraband so he can sell it to his comrades. So I thought to myself – I'll join forces. Rawne's got exactly what I'm after and without my help, he'll be dead and floating down the River Cracia by dawn.'

'Your help?' Rawne spat. The glass at the rear of the cab shattered suddenly as bullets smacked into it. Both men ducked.

'Yeah,' Corbec said, pulling an autopistol out of his coat. 'I'm a better shot than that feth-wipe Feygor.'

Corbec wound his door window down and leaned out, firing back a quick burst of heavy fire from the speeding truck.

The front screen of one of the black vehicles exploded and it skidded sharply, clipping one of its companions before slamming into a wall and spinning nose to tail three times before coming to rest in a spray of glass and debris.

'I rest my case,' Corbec said.

'There are still three of them out there!' Rawne said.

'True,' Corbec said, loading a fresh clip, 'but, canny chap that I am, I thought of bringing spare ammo.'

Gaunt made Milo park the staff-track around the corner from Needleshadow Boulevard. He climbed out into the cold night. 'Stay here,' he told Blenner, who waved back jovially from the cabin. 'And you,' Gaunt told Milo, who was moving as if to follow him.

'Are you armed, sir?' the boy asked.

Gaunt realised he wasn't. He shook his head.

Milo drew his silver Tanith dagger and passed it to the commissar. 'You can never be sure,' he said simply.

Gaunt nodded his thanks and moved off.

The cold zones like this were a grim reminder that society in a vast city like Cracia was deeply stratified. At the heart were the great palace of the Ecclesiarch and the Needle itself. Around that, the city centre and the opulent, wealthy residential areas were patrolled, guarded, heated and screened, safe little microcosms of security and comfort. There, every benefit of Imperial citizenship was enjoyed.

But beyond, the bulk of the city was devoid of such luxuries. League after league of crumbling, decaying city blocks, buildings and tenements a thousand years old, rotted on unlit, unheated, uncared for streets. Crime was rife here, and there were no Arbites. Their control ran out at the inner city limits.

It was a human zoo, an urban wilderness that surrounded civilisation. In some ways it almost reminded Gaunt of the Imperium itself – the opulent, luxurious heart surrounded by a terrible reality it knew precious little about. Or cared to know.

Light snow, too wet to settle, drifted down. The air was cold and moist.

Gaunt strode down the littered pavement. 1034 Needleshadow Boulevard was a dark, haunted relic. A single, dim light glowed on the sixth floor.

Gaunt crept in. The foyer smelled of damp carpet and mildew. There were no lights, but he found the stairwell lit by hundreds of candles stuck in assorted bottles. The light was yellow and smoky.

By the time he reached the third floor, he could hear the music. Some kind of old dancehall ballad by the sound of it. The old recording crackled. It sounded like a ghost.

Sixth floor, the top flat. Shattered plaster littered the worn hall carpet. Somewhere in the shadows, vermin squeaked. The music was louder, murmuring from the room he was approaching on an old audio-caster. The apartment door was ajar, and light, brighter than the hall candles, shone out, the violet glow of a self-powered portable field lamp.

His fingers around the hilt of the knife in his greatcoat pocket, Gaunt entered.

Five

The room was bare to the floorboards and the peeling paper. The audio-caster was perched on top of a stack of old books, warbling softly. The lamp was in the corner, casting its spectral violet glow all around the room.

'Is there anyone here?' Gaunt asked, surprised at the sound of his own voice.

A shadow moved in an adjoining bathroom.

'What's the word?' it said.

'What?'

'I haven't got time to humour you. The word.'

'Eagleshard,' Gaunt said, using the code word he and Fereyd had shared years before on Pashen Nine-Sixty.

The figure seemed to relax. A shabby, elderly man in a dirty civilian suit entered the room so that Gaunt could see him. He was lowering a small, snub-nosed pistol of a type Gaunt wasn't familiar with.

Gaunt's heart sank. It wasn't Fereyd.

'Who are you?' Gaunt asked.

The man arched his eyebrows in reply. 'Names are really quite inappropriate under these circumstances.'

'If you say so,' Gaunt said.

The man crossed to the audio-caster and keyed in a new track. Another old-fashioned tune, a jaunty love song full of promises and regrets, started up with a flurry of strings and pipes.

'I am a facilitator, a courier and also very probably a dead man,' the stranger told Gaunt. 'Have you any idea of the scale and depth of this business?'

Gaunt shrugged. 'No. I'm not even sure what business you refer to. But I trust my old friend, Fereyd. That is enough for me. By his word, I have no illusions as to the seriousness of this matter, but as to the depth, the complexity...'

The man studied him. 'The Navy's intelligence network has

established a web of spy systems throughout the Sabbat Worlds to watch over the Crusade.'

'Indeed.'

'I'm a part of that cobweb. So are you, if you but knew it. The truth we are uncovering is frightening. There is a grievous power struggle under way in the command echelon of this mighty Crusade, my friend.'

Gaunt felt impatience rising in him. He hadn't come all this way to listen to arch speculation. 'Why should I care? I'm not part of High Command. Let them squabble and backstab and—'

'Would you throw it all away? A decade of liberation warfare? All of Warmaster Slaydo's victories?'

'No,' Gaunt admitted darkly.

'The intrigue threatens everything. How can a Crusade force this vast continue when its commanders are at each other's throats? And if we're fighting each other, how can we fight the foe?'

'Why am I here?' Gaunt cut in flatly.

'He said you would be cautious.'

'Who said? Fereyd?'

The man paused, but didn't reply directly. 'Two nights ago, associates of mine here in Cracia intercepted a signal sent via an astropath from a scout ship in the Nubila Reach. It was destined for Lord High Militant General Dravere's fleet headquarters. Its clearance level was Vermilion.'

Gaunt blinked. *Vermilion level.*

The man took a small crystal from his coat pocket and held it up so that it winked in the violet light.

'The data is stored on this crystal. It took the lives of two psykers to capture the signal and transfer it to this. Dravere must not get his hands on it.'

He held it out to Gaunt.

Gaunt shrugged. 'You're giving it to me?'

The man pursed his lips. 'Since my network here on Cracia intercepted this, we've been taken apart. Dravere's own counter-spy network is after us, desperate to retrieve the data. I have no one left to safeguard this. I contacted my off-world superior, and he told me to await a trusted ally. Whoever you are, friend, you are held in high regard. You are trusted. In this secret war, that means a lot.'

Gaunt took the crystal from the man's trembling fingers. He didn't quite know what to say. He didn't want this vile, vital thing anywhere near himself, but he was beginning to realise what might be at stake.

The older man smiled at Gaunt. He began to say something.

The wall behind him exploded in a firestorm of light and vaporising bricks. Two fierce blue beams of las-fire punched into the room and sliced the man into three distinct sections before he could move.

Six

Gaunt dived for cover in the apartment doorway. He drew Milo's blade, for all the good that would do.

Feet were thundering up the stairs.

From his vantage point at the door he watched as two armoured troopers swung in through the exploded wall. They were big, clad in black, insignia-less combat armour, carrying compact, cut-down lasrifles. Adhesion clamps on their knees and forearms showed how they had scaled the outside walls to blow their way in with a directional limpet mine. They surveyed the room, sweeping their green laser tagger beams. One spotted Gaunt prone in the doorway and opened fire. The blast punched through the doorframe, kicking up splinters and began stitching along the plasterboard wall.

Gaunt dived headlong. He was dead! Dead, unless–

The old man's pistol lay on the worn carpet under his nose. It must have skittered there when he was cut down. Gaunt grabbed it, thumbed off the safety and rolled over to fire.

The gun was small, but the odd design clearly marked it as an ancient and priceless specialised weapon. It had a kick like a mule and a roar like a Basilisk.

The first shot surprised Gaunt as much as the two stealth troops and it blew a hatch-sized hole in the wall. The second shot exploded one of the attackers.

A little rune on the grip of the pistol had changed from 'V' to 'III'. Gaunt sighed. This thing clearly wasn't over-blessed with a capacious magazine.

The footfalls on the stairway got louder and three more stealth troopers stumbled up, wafting the candle flames as they ran.

Gaunt dropped to a kneeling pose and blew the head off the first. But the other two opened fire up the well with their lasguns and then the remaining trooper in the apartment behind him began firing too. The cross-blast of three lasguns on rapid-burst tore the top hallway to pieces. Gaunt dropped flat so hard he smashed his hand on the boards and the gun pattered away down the top steps.

After a moment or two, the firing stopped and the attackers began to edge forward to inspect their kill. Dust and smoke drifted in the half-light. Some of the shots had punched up through the floor and carpet a whisker from Gaunt's nose, leaving smoky, dimpled holes. But Gaunt was intact.

When the trooper from the apartment poked his head round the door, a cubit of hard-flung Tanith silver impaled his skull and dropped him to the floor, jerking and spasming. Gaunt leapt up. A second, two seconds, and he would have the fallen man's lasgun in his hands, ready to blast down the stairs.

But the other two from below were in line of sight. There was a flash and he realised their green laser taggers had swept over his face and dotted on his heart. There was a quick and frantic burst of lasgun fire and a billow of noxious burning fumes washed up the stairs over Gaunt.

Blenner climbed the stairs into view, carefully stepping over the smouldering bodies, a smoking laspistol in his hand.

'Got tired of waiting,' the commissar sighed. 'Looks like you needed a hand anyway, eh, Bram?'

Seven

The grey truck, with its single remaining pursuer, slammed into high gear as it went over the rise in the snowy road, leaving the ground for a stomach-shaking moment.

'What's that?' Rawne said wildly, a moment after they landed again and the thrashing wheels re-engaged the slippery roadway.

'It's called a roadblock, I believe,' Corbec said.

Ahead, the cold zone street was closed by a row of oilcan fires, concrete poles and wire. Several armed shapes were waiting for them.

'Off the road! Get off the road!' Corbec bawled. He leaned over and wrenched at the crescent steering wheel.

The truck slewed sideways in the slush and barrelled beetle-nose-first through the sheet-wood doors of an old, apparently abandoned warehouse. There, in the dripping darkness, it grumbled to a halt, its firing note choking away to a dull cough.

'Now what?' Rawne hissed.

'Well, there's you, me and Feygor…' Corbec began. Already the trooper was beginning to pull himself groggily up in the back. 'Three of Gaunt's Ghosts, the best damn fighting regiment in the Guard. We excel at stealth work and look, we're here in a dark warehouse!'

Corbec readied his automatic. Rawne pulled his laspistol and did the same. He grinned.

'Let's do it,' he said.

Years later, in the speakeasies and clubs of the Cracian cold zones, the story of the shoot-out at the old Vinchy Warehouse would do the rounds. Thousands of shots were heard, they say, mostly the bass chatter of the autogun sidearms carried by twenty armed men, mob overbaron Vulnor Habshept kal Geel's feared enforcers, who went in to smoke out the off-world gangsters.

All twenty died. Twenty further shots, some from laspistols, some from a big-bore autogun, were heard. No more, no less.

No one ever saw the off-world gangsters again, or found the truck laden with stolen contraband that had sparked off the whole affair.

The staff-track whipped along down the cold zone street, heading back to the safety of the city core. In the back, Blenner poured another two measures of his expensive brandy. This time, Gaunt took the one offered and knocked it back.

'You don't have to tell me what's going on, Bram. Not if you don't want to.'

Gaunt sighed. 'If I had to, would you listen?'

Blenner chuckled. 'I'm loyal to the Emperor, Gaunt, and doubly loyal to my old friends. What else do you need to know?'

Gaunt smiled and held his glass out as Blenner refilled it.

'Nothing, I suppose.'

Blenner leaned forward, earnest for the first time in years. 'Look, Bram... I may seem like an old fogey to you, grown fat on the luxuries of having a damn near perfect regiment... but I haven't forgotten what the fire feels like. I haven't forgotten the reason I'm here. You can trust me to hell and back, and I'll be there for you.'

'And the Emperor,' Gaunt reminded him with a grin.

'And the bloody Emperor,' Blenner said and they clinked glasses.

'I say,' Blenner said a moment later, 'why is your boy slowing down?'

Milo pulled up, wary. The two tracked vehicles blocking the road ahead had their headlamps on full beam, but Milo could see they were painted in the colours of the Jantine Patricians. Large, shaven-headed figures armed with batons and entrenching tools were climbing out to meet them.

Gaunt climbed out of the cabin as Milo brought them to a halt. Snow drifted down. He squinted at the men beyond the lights.

'Brochuss,' he hissed.

'Colonel-Commissar Gaunt,' replied Major Brochuss of the Jantine Patricians, stepping forward. He was stripped to his vest and oiled like a prize fighter. The wooden spoke in his hands slapped into a meaty palm.

'A reckoning, I think,' he said. 'You and your scum-boys cheated us of a victory on Fortis. You bastards. Playing at soldiers when the real thing was ready to take the day. You and your pathetic Ghosts should have died on the wire where you belong.'

Gaunt sighed. 'That's not the real reason, is it, Brochuss? Oh, you're still smarting over the stolen glory of Fortis, but that's not it. After all, why were you so unhappy we won the day back there? It's the old honour thing, isn't it? The old debt you and Flense still think has to be paid. You're fools. There's no honour in this, in back-street murder out here, in the cold zones, where our bodies won't be reported for months.'

'I don't believe you're in a position to argue,' said Brochuss. 'We of Jant will take our repayment in blood where it presents itself. Here is as good a place as any other.'

'So you'd act with dishonour, to avenge a slight to honour? Brochuss, you ass – if you could only see the irony! There was no dishonour to begin with. I only corrected what was already at fault. You know where the real fault lies. All I did was expose the cowardice in the Jantine action.'

'Bram!' Blenner hissed in Gaunt's ear. 'You never were a diplomat! These men want blood! Insulting them isn't going to help their mood.'

'I'm dealing with this, Vay,' Gaunt said archly.

'No you're not, I am...' Blenner pushed Gaunt back and faced the Jantine mob. 'Major... if it's a fight you want I won't disappoint you. A moment? Please?' Blenner said holding up a finger. He turned to Milo and whispered, 'Boy, just how fast can you drive this buggy?'

'Fast enough,' Milo whispered, 'and I know exactly where to go...'

Blenner turned back to the Patrician heavies in the lamplight and smiled. 'After due consultation with my colleagues, Major Brochuss, I can now safely say... burn in hell, you shit-eating dog!'

He leapt back aboard, pushing Gaunt into the cabin ahead of him. Milo had the staff-track gunned and slewed around in a moment, even as the enraged troopers rushed them.

Another three seconds and Gaunt's ride was roaring off down the snowy street at a dangerous velocity, the engines raging. Squabbling and cursing, Brochuss and his men leapt into their own machines and gave chase.

'So glad I left that to you, Vay,' Gaunt grinned. 'I don't think I would've have been that diplomatic.'

* * *

FIRST AND ONLY

Eight

Trooper Bragg kissed his lucky dice and let all three of them fly. A cheer went up across the wagering room and piles of chips were pushed his way.

'Go on, Bragg!' Mad Larkin chuckled at his side. 'Do it again, you fething old drunk!'

Bragg chuckled and scooped up the dice.

This was the life, he thought. Far away from the warzone of Fortis, the mayhem and the death, here in a smoke-filled dome in the cold zone back-end of an ancient city, him and his few true friends, a good number of pretty girls and wager tables open all night.

Varl was suddenly at his side. His intended friendly slap was hard and stinging – Varl had still to get used to the cybernetic implant shoulder joint the medics had fitted him with on Fortis.

'The game can wait, Bragg. We've got business.'

Bragg and Larkin kissed their painted lady-friends goodbye and followed Varl out through the rear exit of the gaming club onto the boarding ramp. Suth was there: Melyr, Meryn, Caffran, Curral, Coll, Baru, Mkoll, Raglon… almost twenty of the Ghosts.

'What's going on?' Bragg asked.

Melyr jerked his thumb down to where Corbec, Rawne and Feygor were unloading booze and smokes from a battered six wheeler.

'Colonel's got us some tasty stuff to share, bless his Tanith heart.'

'Very nice,' Bragg said, licking his lips, not entirely sure why Rawne and Feygor looked so annoyed. Corbec smiled up at them all.

'Get everyone out here! We're having a party, boys! For Tanith! For us!'

There was cheering and clapping. Varl leapt down into the bay and opened a box with his Tanith knife. He threw bottles up to those clustered around.

'Hey!' Raglon said suddenly, pointing out into the snowy darkness beyond the club's bay. 'Incoming!'

The staff track slid into the bay behind Corbec's truck and Gaunt leapt out. A cheer went up and somebody tossed him a bottle. Gaunt tore off the stopper and took a deep swig, before pointing back out into the darkness.

'Lads! I could do with a hand...' he began.

Major Brochuss leaned forward in the cab of his speeding staff-track and looked through the screen where the wiper was slapping snow away.

'Now we have him! He's stopped at that place ahead!'

Brochuss flexed his hand and struck it with his baton.

Then he saw the crowds of jeering Ghosts around the drive-in bay. A hundred... two hundred.

'Oh balls,' he managed.

The bar was almost empty and it was nearly dawn. Ibram Gaunt sipped the last of his drink and eyed Vaynom Blenner who was asleep face-down on the bar beside him.

Gaunt took out the crystal from the inside pocket where he had secreted it and tossed it up in his hand once, twice.

Corbec was suddenly beside him.

'A long night, eh, commissar?'

Gaunt looked at him, catching the crystal in a tight fist.

'Maybe the longest so far, Colm. I hear you had some fun.'

'Aye, and at Rawne's expense, you'll no doubt be pleased to hear. Do you want to tell me about what's going on?'

Gaunt smiled. 'I'd rather buy you a drink,' he said, motioning to the weary barkeep. 'And yes, I'd love to tell you. And I will, when the time comes. Are you loyal, Colm Corbec?'

Corbec looked faintly hurt. 'To the Emperor, I'd give my life,' he said, without hesitating.

Gaunt nodded. 'Me too. The path ahead may be truly hard. As long as I can count on you.'

Corbec said nothing but held out his glass. Gaunt touched it with his own. There was a tiny chime.

'First and Last,' Corbec said.

Gaunt smiled softly. 'First and Only,' he replied.

A MEMORY

Manzipor, Thirty Years Earlier

They had a house on the summit of Mount Resyde, with long colonnades that overlooked the cataracts. The sky was golden, until sunset, when it caught fire. Light-bugs, heavy with pollenfibres, ambled through the warm air in the atrium each evening. Ibram imagined they were navigators, charting secret paths through the empyrean, between the hidden torments of the warp.

He played on the sundecks overlooking the mists of the deep cataract falls that thundered down into the eight kilometre chasms of the Northern Rift. Sometimes from there, you could see fighting ships and Imperium cutters lifting or making planetfall at the great landing silos at Lanatre Fields. From this distance they looked just like light-bugs in the dark evening sky.

Ibram would always point, and declare his father was on one.

His nurse, and the old tutor Benthlay, always corrected him. They had no imagination. Benthlay didn't even have any arms. He would point to the lights with his buzzing prosthetic limbs and patiently explain that if Ibram's father had been coming home, they would have had word in advance.

But Oric, the cook from the kitchen block, had a broader mind. He would lift the boy in his meaty arms and point his nose to the sky to catch a glimpse of every ship and every shuttle. Ibram had a toy Dreadnought that his Uncle Dercius had carved for him from a hunk of plastene. Ibram would swoop it around in his hands as he hung from Oric's arms, dog-fighting the lights in the sky.

Oric had a huge lightning flash tattoo on his left forearm that fascinated Ibram. 'Imperial Guard,' he would say, in answer to the child's questions. 'Jantine Third for eight years. Mark of honour.'

He never said much else. Every time he put the boy down and returned to the kitchens, Ibram wondered about the buzzing noise that came from under his long chef's overalls. It sounded just like the noise his tutor's arms made when they gestured.

The night Uncle Dercius visited, it was without advance word of his coming.

Oric had been playing with him on the sundecks, and had carved him a new frigate out of wood. When they heard Uncle Dercius's voice, Ibram had leapt down and run into the parlour.

He hit against Dercius's uniformed legs like a meteor and hugged tight.

'Ibram, Ibram! Such a strong grip! Are you pleased to see your uncle, eh?'

Dercius looked a thousand metres tall in his mauve Jantine uniform. He smiled down at the boy, but there was something sad in his eyes.

Oric entered the room behind them, making apologies. 'I must get back to the kitchen,' he averred.

Uncle Dercius did a strange thing; he crossed directly to Oric and embraced him. 'Good to see you, old friend.'

'And you, sir. Been a long time.'

'Have you brought me a toy, uncle?' Ibram interrupted, shaking off the hand of his concerned-looking nurse.

Dercius crossed back to him.

'Would I let you down?' he chuckled. He pulled a signet ring off his left little finger and hugged Ibram to his side. 'Know what this is?'

'A ring!'

'Smart boy! But it's more.' Dercius carefully turned the milled edge of the ring setting and it popped open. A thin, truncated beam of laser light stabbed out. 'Do you know what this is?'

Ibram shook his head.

'It's a key. Officers like me need a way to open certain secret dispatches. Secret orders. You know what they are?'

'My father told me! There are different codes... it's called "security clearance".'

Dercius and the others laughed at the precocity of the little boy. But there was a false note in it.

'You're right! Codes like Panther, Esculis, Cryptox, or the old colour-code levels: cyan, scarlet, it goes up, magenta, obsidian and vermilion,' Dercius said, taking the ring off. 'Generals like me are given these signet rings to open and decode them.

'Does my father have one, uncle?'

A pause. 'Of course.'

'Is my father coming home? Is he with you?'

'Listen to me, Ibram, there's–'

Ibram took the ring and studied it. 'Can I really have this, Uncle Dercius? Is it for me?'

Ibram looked up suddenly from the ring in his hands and found that everyone was staring at him intently.

'I didn't steal it!' he announced.

'Of course you can have it. It's yours...' Dercius said, hunkering down by his side, looking as if he was preoccupied by something.

'Listen, Ibram, there's something I have to tell you... About your father.'

PART FIVE

The empyrean

One

Gaunt had been talking to Fereyd. They had sat by a fuel-drum fire in the splintered shadows of a residence in the demilitarised zone of Pashen Nine-Sixty's largest city. Fereyd was disguised as a farm boss, in the thick, red-wool robes common to many on Pashen, and he was talking obliquely about spy work, just the sort of half-complete, enticing remarks he liked to tease his commissar friend with. An unlikely pair, the commissar and the Imperial spy: one tall, lean and blond, the other compact and dark. Thrown together by the circumstances of combat, they were bonded and loyal despite the differences of their backgrounds and duties.

Fereyd's intelligence unit, working the city-farms of Pashen in deep cover, had revealed the foul Chaos cult – and the heretic Navy officers in their thrall. A disastrous fleet action, brought in too hastily in response to Fereyd's discovery, had led to open war on the planet itself and the deployment of the Guard. Chance had led Gaunt's Hyrkans to the raid which had rescued Fereyd from the hands of the Pashen traitors. Together, Gaunt and Fereyd had unveiled and executed the traitor Baron Sylag.

They were talking about loyalty and treachery, and Fereyd was saying how the vigilance of the Emperor's spy networks was the only thing that kept the private ambitions of various senior officers in check. But it was difficult for Gaunt to follow Fereyd's words because his face kept changing. Sometimes he was Oktar, and then, in the flame-light, his face would become that of Dercius or Gaunt's father.

With a grunt, Gaunt realised he was dreaming, bade his friend goodbye and, dissatisfied, he awoke.

The air was unpleasantly stuffy and stale. His room was small, with a low, curved ceiling and inset lighting plates that he had turned down to their lowest setting before retiring. He got up and pulled on his clothes, scattered where he had left them: breeches, dress shirt, boots, a short leather field-jacket with a high collar embossed with interlocked Imperial eagles. Firearm-screening fields meant there was no bolt pistol in his holster on the door hook, but he took his Tanith knife.

He opened the door-hatch and stepped out into the long, dark space of the companionway. The air here was hot and stifling too, but it moved, wafted by the circulation systems under the black metal grille of the floor.

A walk would do him good.

It was night cycle, and the deck lamps were low. There was the ever-present murmur of the vast power plants and the resulting micro-vibration in every metal surface, even the air itself.

Gaunt walked for fifteen minutes or more in the silent passageways of the great structure, meeting no one. At a confluence of passageways, he entered the main spinal lift and keyed his pass-code into the rune-pad on the wall. There was an electronic moan as cycles set, and a three-second chant sung by non-human throats to signal the start of the lift. The indicator light flicked slowly up twenty bas-relief glass runes on the polished brass board.

Another burst of that soft artificial choir. The doors opened.

Gaunt stepped out into the Glass Bay. A dome of transparent, hyper-dense silica a hundred metres in radius, it was the most serene place the structure offered. Beyond the glass, a magnificent, troubling vista swirled, filtered by special dampening fields. Darkness, striated light, blistering strands and filaments of colours he wasn't sure he could put a name to, bands of light and dark shifting past at an inhuman rate.

The empyrean. Warp space. The dimension beyond reality through which this structure, the Mass Cargo Conveyance *Absalom*, now moved.

He had first seen the *Absalom* through the thick, tinted ports of the shuttle that had brought him up to meet it in orbit. He was in awe of it. One of the ancient transport-ships of the Adeptus Mechanicus, a veteran vessel. The Tech-Lords of Mars had sent a massive retinue to aid the disaster at Fortis, and now in gratitude for the liberation they subordinated their vessels to the Imperial Guard. It was an honour to travel on the *Absalom*,

Gaunt well knew. To be conveyed by the mysterious, secret carriers of the God-Machine cult.

From the shuttle, he'd seen sixteen solid kilometres of grey architecture, like a raked, streamlined cathedral, with the tiny lights of the troop transports flickering in and out of its open belly-mouth. The crenellated surfaces and towers of the mighty Mechanicus ship were rich with bas-relief gargoyles, out of whose wide, fanged mouths the turrets of the sentry guns traversed and swung. Green interior light shone from the thousands of slit windows. The pilot tug, obese and blackened with the scorch marks of its multiple attitude thrusters, bellied in the slow solar tides ahead of the transport vessel.

Gaunt's flagship, the great frigate *Navarre*, had been seconded for picket duties to the Nubila Reach so Gaunt had chosen to travel with his men on the *Absalom*. He missed the long, sleek, waspish lines of the *Navarre*, and he missed the crew, especially Executive Officer Kreff, who had tried so hard to accommodate the commissar and his unruly men.

The *Absalom* was a different breed of beast, a behemoth. Its echoing bulk capacity allowed it to carry nine full regiments, including the Tanith, four divisions of the Jantine Patricians, and at least three mechanised battalions, including their many tanks and armoured transport vehicles.

Fat lift-ships had hefted the numerous war machines up into the hold from the depots on Pyrites.

Now they were en route – a six-day jump to a cluster of warworlds called the Menazoid Clasp, the next defined line of battle in the Sabbat Worlds campaign. Gaunt hoped for deployment with the Ghosts into the main assault on Menazoid Sigma, the capital planet, where a large force of Chaos was holding the line against a heavy Imperial advance.

But there was also Menazoid Epsilon, the remote, dark death world at the edge of the Clasp. Gaunt knew that Warmaster Macaroth's planning staff were assessing the impact of that world. He knew some regimental units would be deployed to take it.

No one wanted Epsilon. No one wanted to die.

He looked up into the festering, fluctuating light of the empyrean beyond the glass and uttered a silent prayer to the Most Blessed Emperor: spare us from Epsilon.

Other, even gloomier thoughts clouded his mind. Like the infernal, invaluable crystal that had come into his hands on Pyrites. Its very presence, its unlockable secret, burned in the back of his mind like a meltagun wound. No further word had come from Fereyd, no signal, not even a hint of what was expected of him. Was he to be a courier – if so, for how long? How would he know who to trust the precious jewel to when the time came? Was something else wanted from him? Had some further, vital instruction failed to reach him? Their long friendship aside, Gaunt cursed the memory of Fereyd. This kind of complication was unwelcome on top of the demands of his commissarial duties.

He resolved to guard the crystal. Carry it, until Fereyd told him otherwise. But still, he fretted that the matter was of the highest importance, and time was somehow slipping away.

He crossed to the knurled rail at the edge of the bay and leaned heavily on it. The enormity of the warp shuffled and spasmed in front of him, milky tendrils of proto-matter licking like ribbons of fluid mist against the outside of the glass. The Glass Bay was one of three immaterium observatories on the *Absalom*, allowing the navigators and the clerics of the Astrographicus Division visual access to the void. In the centre of the bay's deck, on a vast platform mechanism of oiled cogs and toothed gears, giant sensorium scopes, aura-imagifiers and luminosity evaluators cycled and turned, regarding the maelstrom: charting, cogitating, assessing and transmitting the assembled data via chattering relays and humming crystal stacks to the main bridge eight kilometres away at the top of the *Absalom's* tallest command spire.

The observatories were not forbidden areas, but their spaces were not recommended for those new to space crossings. It was said that if the glass wasn't shielded, the view could derange and twist the minds of even hardened astrographers. The elevator's choral chime had been intended to warn Gaunt of this. But he had seen the empyrean before, countless times on his voyages. It no longer scared him. Filtered in this way, he found the fluctuations of the warp somehow easeful, as if its cataclysmic turmoil allowed his own mind to rest. He could think here.

Around the edge of the dome, the names of militant commanders, lord-generals and master admirals were etched into the polished ironwork of the sill in a roll of honour. Under each name was a short legend indicating the theatres of their victories. Some names he knew, from the history texts and the required reading at the schola back on Ignatius. Some, their inscriptions old and faded, were unknown, ten centuries dead. He worked his way around the edge of the dome, reading the plaques. It took him almost half a circuit before he found the name of the one he had actually known personally: Warmaster Slaydo, Macaroth's predecessor, dead at the infamous triumph of Balhaut in the tenth year of this crusade through the Sabbat Worlds.

Gaunt glanced around from his study. The elevator doors at the top of the transit shaft hissed open and he caught once more a snatch of the chanted warning chime. A figure stepped onto the deck; a Navy rating, carrying a small instrument kit. The rating looked across at the lone figure by the rail for a moment and then turned away and disappeared from view behind the lift assembly. An inspection patrol, Gaunt decided absently.

He turned back to the inscriptions and read Slaydo's plaque again. He remembered Balhaut, the firestorms that swept the night away and took the forces of Chaos with it. He and his beloved Hyrkans had been at the centre of it, in the mudlakes, struggling through the brimstone atmosphere under the weight of their heavy rebreathers. Slaydo had taken credit for that famous win, rightly enough as warmaster, but in sweat and blood it had been Gaunt's. His finest hour, and he had Slaydo's deathbed decoration to prove it.

He could hear the grind of the enemy assault carriers even now, striding on their long, hydraulic legs through the mud, peppering the air with sharp needle blasts of blood-red light, washing death and fire towards his men. A physical memory of the tension and fatigue ran down his spine, the superhuman effort with which he and his best fire-teams had stormed the Oligarchy Gate ahead of even the glorious forces of the Adeptus

Astartes, driving a wedge of las-fire and grenade bursts through the overlapping plates of the enemy's buttress screens.

He saw Tanhause making his lucky shot, still talked about in the barracks of the Hyrkan: a single las-bolt that penetrated a foul, demented Chaos Dreadnought through the visor-slit, detonating the power systems within. He saw Veitch taking six of the foe with his bayonet when his last powercell ran dry.

He saw the Tower of the Plutocrat combust and fall under the sustained Hyrkan fire.

He saw the faces of the unnumbered dead, rising from the mud, from the flames.

He opened his eyes and the visions fled. The empyrean lashed and blossomed in front of him, unknowable. He was about to turn and return to his quarters.

But there was a blade at his throat.

Two

There was no sense of anyone behind him – no shadow, no heat, no sound or smell of breath. It was as if the cold sharpness under his chin had arrived there unaccompanied. He knew at once he was at the mercy of a formidable opponent.

But that alone gave him a flicker of confidence. If the blade's owner had simply wanted him dead, then he would already be dead and none the wiser. There was something that made him more useful alive. He was fairly certain what that was.

'What do you want?' he asked calmly.

'No games,' a voice said from behind him. The tone was low and even, not a whisper but of a level that was somehow softer and lower still. The pressure of the cold blade increased against the skin of his neck fractionally. 'You are reckoned to be an intelligent man. Dispense with the delaying tactics.'

Gaunt nodded carefully. If he was going to live even a minute more, he had to play this precisely right.

'This isn't the way to solve this, Brochuss,' he said carefully.

There was a pause. 'What?'

'Now who's playing games? I know what this is about. I'm sorry you and your Patrician comrades lost face on Pyrites. Lost a few teeth too, I'll bet. But this won't help.'

'Don't be a fool! You've got this wrong! This isn't about some stupid regimental rivalry!'

'It isn't?'

'Think hard, fool! Think why this might really be happening! I want you to understand why you are about to die!' The weight of the blade against his throat shifted slightly. It didn't lessen its pressure, but there was a momentary alteration in the angle. Gaunt knew his comments had misdirected his adversary for a heartbeat.

His only chance. He struck backwards hard with his right elbow, simultaneously pulling back from the blade and raising his left hand to fend it off. The knife cut through his cuff, but he pulled clear as his assailant reeled from the elbow jab.

Gaunt had barely turned when the other countered, striking high. They fell together, limbs twisting to gain a positive hold. The wayward blade ripped Gaunt's jacket open down the seam of the left sleeve.

Gaunt forced the centre of balance over and threw a sideways punch with his right fist that knocked his assailant off him. A moment later the commissar was on his feet, drawing the silver Tanith blade from his belt.

He saw his opponent for the first time. The Navy rating, a short, lean man of indeterminate age. There was something strange about him. The way his mouth was set in a determined grimace while his wide eyes seemed to be... pleading? The rating flipped up onto his feet with a scissor of his back and legs, and coiled around in a hunched, offensive posture, the knife held blade-uppermost in his right hand.

How could a deck rating know moves like that? Gaunt worried. The practised movements, the perfect balance, the silent resolve – all betrayed a specialist killer, an adept in the arts of stealth and assassination. But close up, Gaunt saw the man was just an engineer, his naval uniform a little tight around a belly going to fat. Was it just a disguise? The rank pins, insignia and the coded identity seal mandatory for all crew personnel all seemed real.

The blade was short and leaf-shaped, shorter than the rubberised grip it protruded from. There was a series of geometric holes in the body of the blade itself, reducing the overall weight whilst retaining the structural strength. It plainly wasn't metal; it was matte blue, ceramic, invisible to the ship's weapon-scan fields.

Gaunt stared into the other's unblinking eyes, searching for recognition or contact. The gaze which met him was a desperate, piteous look, as if from something trapped inside the menacing body.

They circled, slowly. Gaunt kept his body angled and low as he had learned in bayonet drill with the Hyrkans. But he held the Tanith blade loosely in his right hand with the blade descending from the fist and tilted in towards his body. He'd watched the odd style the Ghosts had used in knife drill with interest, and one long week in transit aboard the *Navarre*, he had got Corbec to train him in the nuances. The method made good use of the weight and length of the Tanith war-knife. He kept his left hand up to block, not with a warding open palm as the Hyrkans had practised – and as his opponent now adopted – but in a fist, knuckles outward. 'Better to stop a blade with your hand than your throat,' Tanhause had told him, years before. 'Better the blade cracks off your knuckles than opens a smile in your palm,' Corbec had finessed more recently.

'You want me dead?' Gaunt hissed.

'That was not my primary objective. Where is the crystal?' Gaunt started as the man replied. Though the mouth moved, the voice was not coming from it. The lip movements barely synched with the words. He'd seen that before somewhere, years ago. It looked like… possession. Gaunt bristled as fear ran down his back. More than the fear of mortal combat. The fear of witchcraft. Of psykers.

'A commissar-colonel won't be easily missed,' Gaunt managed.

The rating shrugged stiffly as if to indicate the infinite raging vastness beyond the glass dome. 'No one is so important he won't be missed out here. Not even the warmaster himself.'

They had circled three times now. 'Where is the crystal?' the rating asked again.

'What crystal?'

'The one you acquired in Cracia City,' returned the killer in that floating, unmatched voice. 'Give it up now, and we can forget this meeting ever took place.'

'Who sent you?'

'Nothing in the known systems would make me answer that question.'

'I have no crystal. I don't know what you're talking about.'

'A lie.'

'Even if it was, would I be so foolish to carry anything with me?'

'I've searched your quarters twice. It's not there. You must have it. Did you swallow it? Dissection is not beyond me.'

Gaunt was about to reply when the rating suddenly stamped forward, circling his blade in a sweep that missed the commissar's shoulder by a hair's breadth. Gaunt was about to feint and counter when the blade swept back in a reverse of the slice. The touch of a stud on the grip had caused the ceramic blade to retract with a pneumatic hiss and re-extend through the flat pommel of the grip, reversing the angle. The tip sheared through his blocking left forearm and sprayed blood across the deck.

Gaunt leapt backwards with an angry curse, but the rating followed through relentlessly, reversing his blade again so it poked up forward of his punching fist. Gaunt blocked it with an improvised turn of his knife and kicked out at the attacker, catching his left knee with his boot tip.

The man backed off but the circling did not recommence. This was unlike the sparring in bayonet training, the endless measuring and dancing, the occasional clash and jab. The man rallied immediately after each feint, each deflection, and struck in once more, clicking his blade up and down out of the grip to wrong-foot Gaunt, sometimes striking with an upwards blow on the first stroke and thumbing the blade downwards to rake on the return.

Gaunt survived eight, nine, ten potentially lethal passes, thanks only to his speed and the attacker's unfamiliarity with the curious Tanith blade technique.

They clashed again, and this time Gaunt jabbed not with his knife but with his warding left hand, directly at the man's weapon. The blade cut a stinging gash in his knuckles, but he slipped in under the knife and grabbed the man by the right wrist. They clenched, Gaunt driving forwards with his superior size and height. The man's left hand found his throat and clamped it in an iron grip. Gaunt gagged, choking, his vision swimming as his neck muscles fought against the tightening grip.

Desperately, he slammed the man backwards into the guard rail. The rating thumbed his blade catch again and the reversing tongue of ceramic stabbed down into Gaunt's wrist. In return he plunged his own knife hard through the tricep of the arm holding his throat.

They broke, reeling away from each other, blood spurting from the stab wounds in their arms and hands. Gaunt was panting and short of breath from the pain, but the man made no sound. As if he felt no pain, or as if pain was no hindrance to him.

The rating came at him again, and Gaunt swung low to block,

but at the last moment, the man tossed the ceramic blade from his right hand to his left, the blade reversing itself through the grip in mid air so that what had started as an upwards strike from the right turned into a downward stab from the left. The blade dug into the meat of Gaunt's right shoulder, deadened only by the padding and leather of his jacket. White-hot pain lanced down his right side, crushing his ribs and the breath inside them.

The blade slid free cleanly and blood drizzled after it. The hot warmth was coursing down the inside of his sleeve and slickening his grip on the knife handle. It dripped off his knuckles and the silver blade. If he kept bleeding at that rate, even if he could hold off his assailant, he knew he would not survive much longer.

The rating crossed his guard again, switching hands like a juggler, to the right and then back to the left, reversing the blade direction with each return. He feinted, sliced in low at Gaunt's belly with a left-hand pass and then pushed himself at the commissar.

Gaunt stabbed in to meet the low cut, and caught the point of his silver blade through one of the perforations in the ceramic blade.

Instinctively, he wrenched his blade back and levered at the point of contact. A second later, the ceramic tech-knife whirled away across the Glass Bay and skittered out of sight over the cold floor. Suddenly disarmed, the rating hesitated for a heartbeat and Gaunt rammed his Tanith knife up and in, puncturing the man's torso and cracking his sternum.

The rating reeled away sharply, sucking for air as his lungs failed. The silver knife was stuck fast in his chest. Thin blood jetted from the wound and gurgled from his slack mouth. He hit the deck, knees first, then fell flat in his face, his torso propped up like a tent on the hard metal prong of the knife.

Gaunt stumbled back against the rail, gasping hoarsely, his body shaking and burning pain jeering at him. He wiped a bloody hand across his clammy, ashen face and gazed down at the rating's body as it lay on the floor in a pool of scarlet fluid.

He sank to the deck, trembling and weak. A laugh, half chuckle, half sob broke from him. When next he saw Colm Corbec, he would buy him the biggest–

The rating got up again.

The man wriggled back on his knees, rippling the pool of blood around him, and then swung his body up straight, arms swaying limp at his sides. Kneeling, he slowly turned his head to face the prone, dismayed Gaunt. His face was blank, and his eyes were no longer pleading and trapped. They were gone, in fact. A fierce green light raged inside his skull, making his eyes pupilless slits of lime fire. His mouth lolled open and a similar glow shone out, back-lighting his teeth. With one simple, direct motion, he pulled the Tanith knife out of his chest. There was no more blood, just a shaft of bright green light poking from the wound.

With a sigh of finality, Gaunt knew that the psychic puppetry was continuing. The man, who had been a helpless thrall of the psyker magic when he first attacked, was now reanimated by abominable sorcery.

It would function long enough to win the fight.

It would kill him.

Gaunt battled with his senses to keep awake, to get up, to run. He was blacking out.

The rating swayed towards him, like a *zumbay* from the old myths of the non-dead, eyes shining, expression blank, the Tanith blade that had killed him clutched in his claw of a hand.

The dead thing raised the knife to strike.

Three

Two las-shots slammed it sideways. Another tight pair broke it open along the rib cage, venting an incandescent halo of bright psychic energy. A fifth shot to the head dropped the thing like it had been struck in the ear with a sledgehammer.

Colm Corbec, the laspistol in his hand, stalked across the deck of the Glass Bay and stood looking down at the charred and smouldering shape on the floor, a shape that had self-ignited and was spilling vaporous green energies as it ate itself up.

Somewhere, the weapons interdiction alarm started wailing.

Using the rail for support, Gaunt was almost on his feet again by the time Corbec reached him.

'Easy there, commissar…'

Gaunt waved him off, aware of the way his blood was still freely dribbling onto the deck.

'Your timing…' he grunted, 'is perfect… colonel.'

Corbec grimly gestured over his shoulder. Gaunt turned to look where he pointed. Brin Milo stood by the elevator assembly, looking flushed and fierce.

'The lad had a dream,' Corbec said, refusing to be ignored and looping his arm under his commander's shoulder. 'Came to me at once when he couldn't find you in your quarters.'

Milo crossed to them. 'The wounds need attention,' he said.

'We'll get him to the apothecarion,' Corbec began.

'No,' Milo said firmly and, despite the pain, Gaunt almost laughed at the sudden authority his junior aide directed at the shaggy brute who was the company commander. 'Back to our barrack decks. Use our own medics. I don't think the commissar wants this incident to become a matter for official inquiry.'

Corbec looked at the boy curiously but Gaunt nodded. In his experience, there was no point fighting the boy's gift for judgement.

Milo never intruded into the commissar's privacy, but he seemed to understand instinctively Gaunt's intentions and wishes. Gaunt could not keep secrets from the boy, but he trusted him – and valued his insight beyond measure.

Gaunt looked at Corbec. 'Brin's right. There's more to this… I'll explain later, but I want the ship hierarchy kept out of it until we know who to trust.'

The weapons alarm continued to sound.

'In that case, we better get out of here–' Corbec began.

He was cut off by the elevator shutters gliding open with a breathy hiss and a choral exhalation. Six Imperial Navy troopers in fibre-weave shipboard armour and low-brimmed helmets exited in a pack and dropped to their knees, covering the trio with compact stub-guns. One barked curt orders into his helmet vox-link. An officer emerged from the elevator in their wake.

Like them, his uniform was emerald with silver piping, the colours of the Segmentum Pacificus Fleet, but he was not armoured like his detail. He was tall, a little overweight and his puffy flesh was unhealthily pale.

A career spacer, thought Corbec. Probably hasn't stood on real soil in decades.

The officer stared at them: the shaggy Guard miscreant with his unauthorised laspistol; the injured, bloody man leaning against him and bleeding on the deck; the rangy, strange-eyed boy.

He pursed his lips, spoke quietly into his own vox-link and then touched a stud on the facilitator wand he carried, waving it absently into the air around him. The alarm shut off mid-whine.

'I am Warrant Officer Lekulanzi. It is my responsibility to oversee the security of this vessel on behalf of Lord Captain Grasticus. I take a dim view of illicit weapons on this holy craft, though I always expect Imperial Guard scum to try something. I look with even greater displeasure on the use of said weapons.'

'Now, this is not how it loo–' Corbec began, moving forward with a reassuring smile. Six stub-gun muzzles swung their attention directly at him. The detail's weapons were short-line, pump-action models designed for shipboard use.

The glass shards and wire twists wadded into each shell would roar out in a tightly packed cone of micro-shrapnel, entirely capable of shredding a man at close range. But unlike a lasgun or a bolter, there was no danger of them puncturing the outer hull.

'No hasty movements. No eager explanations.' Lekulanzi

stared at them. 'Questions will be answered in due time, under the formal process of your interrogation. You are aware that the firing of a prohibited weapon on a transport vessel of the Adeptus Mechanicus is an offence punishable by court martial. Surrender your weapon.'

Corbec handed his laspistol to the trooper who rose smartly to take it from him.

'This is stupid,' Gaunt said abruptly. The guns turned their attention to him. 'Do you know who I am, Lekulanzi?'

The warrant officer tensed as his name was used without formal title. He narrowed his flesh-hooded eyes.

Gaunt hauled himself forward and stood free of Corbec's support. 'I am Commissar-Colonel Ibram Gaunt.'

Warrant Officer Lekulanzi froze. Without the coat, the cap, the badges of authority, Gaunt looked like any low-born Guard officer.

'Come here,' Gaunt told him. The man hesitated, then crossed to Gaunt, whispering a low order into his vox-link. The guard detail immediately rose from their knees, snapped to attention and slung their weapons.

'That's better…' Corbec smiled.

Gaunt placed a hand on Lekulanzi's shoulder, and the officer stiffened with outrage. Gaunt was pointing to something on the deck, a charred, greenish slick or stain, oily and lumpy. 'Do you know what that is?'

Lekulanzi shook his head.

'It's the remains of an assassin who set upon me here. The weapon's discharge was my First Officer saving my life. I will formally caution him for concealing a firearm aboard, strictly against standing orders.'

Gaunt smiled to see a tiny bead of nervous perspiration begin to streak Lekulanzi's pallid brow.

'He was one of yours, Lekulanzi. A rating. But he was in the sway of others, dark forces that beguiled and drove him like a toy. You don't like illicit weapons on your ship, eh? How about illicit psykers?'

Some of the security troopers muttered and made warding gestures. Lekulanzi stammered. 'But who... who would want to kill you, sir?'

'I am a soldier. A successful soldier,' Gaunt smiled coldly. 'I make enemies all the time.'

He gestured down at the remains. 'Have this analysed. Then have it purged. Make sure no foul, unholy taint has touched this precious ship. Report any findings directly to me, no matter how insignificant. Once my wounds have been treated, I will report to Lord Captain Grasticus personally and submit a full account.'

Lekulanzi was lost for words.

With Corbec supporting him, Gaunt left the Glass Bay. At the elevator doors, Lekulanzi caught the hard look in the boy's eyes. He shuddered.

In the elevator, Milo turned to Gaunt. 'His eyes were like a snake's. He is not trustworthy.'

Gaunt nodded. He had changed his mind. Just minutes before, he had reconciled himself to acting as Fereyd's courier, guardian to the crystal. But now things had changed. He wouldn't sit by idly waiting. He would act with purpose. He would enter the game, and find out the rules and learn how to win.

That would mean learning the contents of the crystal.

Four

'Best I can do,' murmured Dorden, the Ghosts' chief medic, making a half-hearted gesture around him that implicated the whole of the regimental infirmary. The Ghosts' infirmary was a suite of three low, corbel-vaulted rooms set as an annex to the barrack deck where the Tanith First were berthed. Its walls and roof were washed with a greenish off-white paint and the hard floors had been lined with scrubbed red stone tiles. On dull steel shelves in bays around the rooms were ranked fat, glass-stoppered bottles with yellowing paper labels, mostly full of treacly fluids, surgical pastes, dried powders and preparations, or organic field-swabs in clear, gluey suspensions. Racks of polished instruments sat in pull-out drawers and plastic waste bags, stale bedding and bandage rolls were packed into low, lidded boxes around the walls that doubled as seats. There was a murky autoclave on a brass trolley, two resuscitrex units with shiny iron paddles, and a side table with an apothecary's scales, a diagnostic probe and a blood cleanser set on it. The air was musty and rank, and there were dark stains on the flooring.

'We're not over-equipped, as you can see,' Dorden added breezily. He'd patched the commissar's wounds with supplies from his own field kit, which sat open on one of the bench lockers. He hadn't trusted the freshness or sterility of any of the materials provided by the infirmary.

Gaunt sat, stripped to the waist, on one of the low brass gurneys which lined the centre of the main chamber, its wheels locked into restraining lugs in the tiled floor. The gurney's springs squeaked and moaned as Gaunt shifted his weight on the stained, stinking mattress.

Dorden had patched the wound in the commissar's shoulder with sterile dressings, washed the whole limb in pungent blue sterilising gel and then pinched the mouth of the wound shut with bakelite suture clamps that looked like the heads of biting insects. Gaunt tried to flex his arm.

'Don't do that,' Dorden said quickly. 'I'd wrap it in false-flesh if I could find any, but besides, the wound should breathe. Honestly, you'd be better off in the main hospital ward.'

Gaunt shook his head. 'You've done a fine job,' he said. Dorden smiled. He didn't want to press the commissar on the issue. Corbec had muttered something about keeping this private.

Dorden was a small man, older than most of the Ghosts, with a grey beard and warm eyes. He'd been a doctor on Tanith, running an extended practice through the farms and settlements of Beldane and the forest wilds of County Pryze.

He'd been drafted at the Founding to fulfil the Administratum's requirements for regimental medical personnel. His wife had died a year before the Founding and his only son was a trooper in the ninth platoon. His one daughter, her husband and their first born had perished in the flames of Tanith. He had left nothing behind in the embers of his home world except the memory of years of community service, a duty he now carried on for the good of the last men of Tanith.

He refused to carry a weapon, and thus was the only Ghost that Gaunt couldn't rely on to fight... but Gaunt hardly cared. He had sixty or seventy men in his command who wouldn't still be there but for Dorden.

'I've checked for venom taint or fibre toxin. You're lucky. The blade was clean. Cleaner than mine!' Dorden chuckled and it made Gaunt smile. 'Unusual...' Dorden added and fell silent.

Gaunt raised an eyebrow. 'How so?'

'I understood assassins liked to toxify their blades as insurance.' Dorden said simply.

'I never said it was an assassin.'

'You didn't have to. I may be a non-combatant. Feth, I may be an old fool, but I didn't come down in the last barrage.'

'Don't trouble yourself with it, Dorden,' Gaunt said, flexing his arm again against the medic's advice. It stung, ached, throbbed. 'You've worked your usual magic. Stay impartial. Don't get drawn in.'

Dorden was scrubbing his suture clamp and wound probes in a bowl of filmy antiseptic oil. 'Impartial? Do you know something, Ibram Gaunt?'

Gaunt blinked as if slapped. No one had spoken to him with such paternal authority since the last time he had been in the company of his Uncle Dercius. No... not the last time...

Dorden turned back, wiping the tools on sheets of white lint. 'Forgive me, commissar. I– I'm speaking out of turn.'

'Speak anyway, friend.'

Dorden jerked a lean thumb to indicate out beyond the archway into the barrack deck. 'These are all I've got. The last pitiful scraps of Tanith genestock, my only link to the past and to the green, green world I loved. I'll keep patching and mending and binding and sewing them back together until they're all gone, or I'm gone, or the horizons of all known space have withered and died. And while you may not be Tanith, I know many of the men now treat you as such. Me, I'm not sure. Too much of the chulan about you, I'd say.'

'Koolun?'

'Chulan. Forgive me, slipping in to the old tongue. Outsider. Unknown. It doesn't translate directly.'

'I'm sure it doesn't.'

'It wasn't an insult. You may not be Tanith-breed, but you're for us every way. I think you care, Gaunt. Care about your Ghosts. I think you'll do all in your power to see us right, to take us to glory, to take us to peace. That's what I believe, every night when I lay down to rest, and every time a bombardment starts, or the drop-ships fall, or the boys go over the wire. That matters.'

Gaunt shrugged – and wished he hadn't. 'Does it?'

'I've spoken to medics with other regiments. At the field hospital on Fortis, for instance. So many of them say their commissars don't care a jot about their men. They see them as fodder for the guns. Is that how you see us?'

'No.'

'No, I thought not. So, that makes you rare indeed. Something worth hanging on to, for the good of these poor Ghosts. Feth, you may not be Tanith, but if assassins are starting to hunger for your blood, I start to care. For the Ghosts, I care.'

He fell silent.

'Then I'll remember not to leave you uninformed,' Gaunt said, reaching for his undershirt.

'I thank you for that. For a *chulan*, you're a good man, Ibram Gaunt. Like the *anroth* back home.'

Gaunt froze. 'What did you say?'

Dorden looked round at him sharply. 'Anroth. I said anroth. It wasn't an insult either.'

'What does it mean?'

Dorden hesitated uneasily, unsettled by Gaunt's hard gaze. 'The anroth... well, household spirits. It's a cradle-tale from Tanith. They used to say that the anroth were spirits from other worlds, beautiful worlds of order, who came to Tanith to watch over our families. It's nothing. Just an old memory. A forest saying.'

'Why does it matter, commissar?' said a new voice.

Gaunt and Dorden looked around to see Milo sat on a bench seat near the door, watching them intently.

'How long have you been there?' Gaunt asked sharply, surprising himself with his anger.

'A few minutes only. The anroth are part of Tanith lore. Like the *drudfellad* who ward the trees, and the *nyrsis* who watch over the streams and waters. Why would it alarm you so?'

'I've heard the word before. Somewhere,' Gaunt said, getting to his feet. 'Who knows, a word like it? It doesn't matter.'

He went to pull on his undershirt but realised it was ripped and bloody, and cast it aside. 'Milo. Get me another from my quarters,' he snapped.

Milo rose and handed Gaunt a fresh undershirt from his canvas pack. Dorden covered a grin. Gaunt faltered, nodded his thanks, and took the shirt.

Both Milo and the medical officer had noticed the multitude of scars which laced Gaunt's broad, muscled torso, and had made no comment. How many theatres, how many fronts, how many life-or-death combats had it taken to accumulate so many marks of pain?

But as Gaunt stood, Dorden noticed the scar across Gaunt's belly for the first time and gasped. The wound line was long and ancient, a grotesque braid of buckled scar-tissue.

'Sacred Feth!' Dorden said too loudly. 'Where–'

Gaunt shook him off. 'It's old. Very old.'

Gaunt slipped on his undershirt and the wound was hidden. He pulled up his braces and reached for his tunic.

'But how did you get such a–'

Gaunt looked at him sharply. 'Enough.'

Gaunt buttoned his tunic and then put on the long leather coat which Milo was already holding for him. He set his cap on his head.

'Are the officers ready?' he asked.

Milo nodded. 'As you ordered.'

With a nod to Dorden, Gaunt marched out of the infirmary.

Five

It had crossed his mind to wonder who to trust. A few minutes' thought had brought him to the realisation that he could trust them all, every one of the Ghosts from Colonel Corbec down to the lowliest of the troopers. His only qualm lay with the malcontent Rawne and his immediate group of cronies in the third platoon, men like Feygor.

Gaunt left the infirmary and walked down the short companionway into the barrack deck proper. Corbec was waiting.

Colm Corbec had been waiting for almost an hour. Alone in the antechamber of the infirmary, he had enjoyed plenty of time to fret about the things he hated most in the universe. First and last of them was space travel.

Corbec was the son of a machinesmith who had worked his living at a forge beneath a gable-barn on the first wide bend of the River Pryze. Most of his father's work had come from log-handling machines: rasp-saws, timber-derricks, trak-sleds. Many times, as a boy, he'd shimmied down into the oily service trenches to hold the inspection lamp so his father could examine the knotted, dripping axles and stricken synchromesh of a twenty-wheeled flatbed, ailing under its cargo of young, wet wood from the mills up at Beldane or Sottress.

Growing up, he'd worked the reaper mills in Sottress and seen men lose fingers, hands and knees to the screaming bandsaws and circular razors. His lungs had clogged with saw mist and he had developed a hacking cough that lingered even now. Then he'd joined the militia of Tanith Magna on a dare and on top of a broken heart, and patrolled the sacred stretches of the Pryze County nalwood groves for poachers and smugglers.

It had been a right enough life. The loamy earth below, the trees above and the far starlight beyond the leaves. He'd come to understand the ways of the twisting forests, and the shifting nal-groves and clearings. He'd learned the knife, the stealth patterns and the joy of the hunt. He'd been happy. So long as the stars had been up there and the ground underfoot.

Now the ground was gone. Gone forever. The damp, piney scents of the forest soil, the rich sweetness of the leaf-mould, the soft depth of the nalspores as they drifted and accumulated. He'd sung songs up to the stars, taken their silent blessing, even cursed them. All so long as they were far away. He never thought he would travel in their midst.

Corbec was afraid of the crossings, as he knew many of his company were afraid, even now after so many of them. To leave soil, to leave land, sea and sky behind, to part the stars and crusade through the immaterium. That was truly terrifying.

He knew the *Absalom* was a sturdy ship. He'd seen its vast bulk from the viewspaces of the dock-ship that had brought him aboard. But he had also seen the great timber barges of the mills founder, shudder and splinter in the hard water courses of the Beldane rapids. Ships sailed their ways, he knew, until the ways got too strong for them and gave them up.

He hated it all. The smell of the air, the coldness of the walls, the inconstancy of the artificial gravity, the perpetual constancy of the vibrating empyrean drives. All of it. Only his concern for the commissar's welfare had got him past his phobias onto the nightmare of the Glass Bay Observatory. Even then, he'd focussed his attention on Gaunt, the troopers, that idiot warrant officer – anything at all but the cavorting insanity beyond the glass.

He longed for soil underfoot. For real air. For breeze and rain and the hush of nodding branches.

'Corbec?'

He snapped to attention as Gaunt approached. Milo was a little way behind the commissar.

'Sir?'

'Remember what I was telling you in the bar on Pyrites?'

'Not precisely, sir... I... I was pretty far gone.'

Gaunt grinned. 'Good. Then it will all come as a surprise to you too. Are the officers ready?'

Corbec nodded perfunctorily. 'Except Major Rawne, as you ordered.'

Gaunt lifted his cap, smoothed his cropped hair back with his hands and replaced it squarely again.

'A moment, and I'll join you in the staff room.'

Gaunt marched away down the deck and entered the main billet of the barracks.

The Ghosts had been given barrack deck three, a vast honeycomb of long, dark vaults in which bunks were strung from chains in a herringbone pattern. Adjoining these sleeping vaults was a desolate recreation hall and a trio of padded exercise chambers. All forty surviving platoons, a little over two thousand Ghosts, were billeted here.

The smell of sweat, smoke and body heat rose from the bunk vaults. Rawne, Feygor and the rest of the third platoon were waiting for him on the slip-ramp. They had been training in the exercise chambers, and each one carried one of the shock-poles provided for combat practice. These neural stunners were the only weapons allowed to them during a crossing. They could fence with them, spar with them and even set them to long range discharge and target-shoot against the squeaking, moving, metal decoys in the badly-oiled automatic range.

Gaunt saluted Rawne. The men snapped to attention.

'How do you read the barrack deck, major?'

Rawne faltered. 'Commissar?'

'Is it secure?'

'There are eight deployment shafts and two to the drop-ship hangar, plus a number of serviceways.'

'Take your men, spread out and guard them all. No one must get in or out of this barrack deck without my knowledge.'

Rawne looked faintly perplexed. 'How do we hold any intruders off, commissar, given our lack of weapons?'

Gaunt took a shock-pole from Trooper Neff and then laid him out on the deck with a jolt to the belly.

'Use these,' Gaunt suggested. 'Report to me every half hour. Report to me directly with the name of anyone who attempts access.' Pausing for a moment to study Rawne's face and make sure his instructions were clearly understood, Gaunt turned and walked back up the ramp.

'What's he up to?' Feygor asked the major when Gaunt was out of earshot. Rawne shook his head. He would find out. Until he did, he had a sentry duty to organise.

Six

The staff room was an old briefing theatre next to the infirmary annex. Steps led down into a circular room, with three tiers of varnished wooden seats around the circumference and a lacquered black console in the centre on a dais. The console, squat and rounded like a polished mushroom, was an old tactical display unit, with a mirrored screen in its top which had once broadcast luminous three-dimensional hololithic forms into the air above it during strategy counsels. But it was old and broken; Gaunt used it as a seat.

The officers filed in: Corbec, Dorden, and then the platoon leaders, Meryn, Mkoll, Curral, Lerod, Hasker, Blane, Folore... thirty-nine men, all told. Last in was Varl, recently promoted. Milo closed the shutter hatch and perched at the back. The men sat in a semi-circle, facing their commander.

'What's going on, sir?' Varl asked. Gaunt smiled slightly. As a newcomer to officer-level briefings, Varl was eager and forth-right, and oblivious to the usually reserved protocols of staff discussions. I should have promoted him earlier, Gaunt thought wryly.

'This is totally unofficial. Ghost business, but unofficial. I want to advise you of a situation so that you can be aware of it and act accordingly if the need arises. But it does not go beyond this chamber. Tell your men as much as they need to know to facilitate matters, but spare them the details.'

He had their attention now.

'I won't dress this up. As far as I know – and believe me, that's no further than I could throw Bragg – there's a power strug-gle going on. One that threatens to tear this whole Crusade to tatters.

'You've all heard how much infighting went on after War-master Slaydo's death. How many of the Lord High Militants wanted to take his place.'

'And that weasel Macaroth got it,' Corbec said with a rueful grin.

'That's Warmaster Weasel Macaroth, colonel,' Gaunt corrected. He let the men chuckle. Good humour would make this easier. 'Like him or not, he's in charge now. And that makes it simple for us. Like me, you are all loyal to the Emperor, and therefore to Warmaster Macaroth. Slaydo chose him to be successor. Macaroth's word is the word of the Golden Throne itself. He speaks with Imperium authority.'

Gaunt paused. The men watched him quizzically, as if they had missed the point of some joke.

'But someone's not happy about that, are they?' Milo said dourly, from the back. The officers snapped around to stare at him and then turned back equally sharply as they heard the commissar laugh.

'Indeed. There are probably many who resent his promotion over them. And one in particular we all know, if only by name. Lord Militant General Dravere. The very man who commands our section of the Crusade force.'

'What are you saying, sir?' Lerod asked with aghast disbelief. Lerod was a large, shaven-headed sergeant with an Imperial eagle tattoo on his temple. He had commanded the militia unit in Tanith Ultima, the Imperial shrine-city on the Ghost's lost home world, and as a result he, along with the other troopers from Ultima, were the most devoted and resolute Imperial servants in the Tanith First. Gaunt knew that Lerod would be perhaps the most difficult to convince. 'Are you suggesting that Lord General Dravere has renegade tendencies? That he is... disloyal? But he's your direct superior, sir!'

'Which is why this discussion is being held in private. If I'm right, who can we turn to?'

The men greeted this with uncomfortable silence.

Gaunt went on. 'Dravere has never hidden the fact that he felt Slaydo snubbed him by appointing the younger Macaroth. It must rankle deeply to serve under an upstart who has been promoted past you. I am pretty certain that Dravere plans to usurp the warmaster.'

'Let them fight for it!' Varl spat, and others concurred. 'What's another dead officer – begging your pardon, sir.'

Gaunt smiled. 'You echo my initial thoughts on the matter, sergeant. But think it through. If Dravere moves his own forces against Macaroth, it will weaken this entire endeavour. Weaken it at the very moment we should be consolidating for the push into new, more hostile territories. What good are we against the forces of the enemy if we're battling with ourselves? If it came to it, we'd be wide open, weak... and ripe for slaughter. Dravere's plans threaten the entire future of us all.'

Another heavy silence. Gaunt rubbed his lean chin. 'If Dravere goes through with this, we could throw everything away. Everything we've won in the Sabbat Worlds these last ten years.'

Gaunt leaned forward. 'There's more. If I was going to usurp the warmaster, I'd want a whole lot more than a few loyal regiments with me. I'd want an edge.'

'Is that what this is about?' Lerod asked, now hanging on Gaunt's words.

'Of course it is. Dravere is after something. Something big. Something so big it will actually place him on an equal footing with the warmaster. Or even make him stronger. And that is where we pitiful few come into the picture.'

He paused for a moment. 'When I was on Pyrites, I came into possession of this...'

Gaunt held up the crystal.

'The information encrypted onto this crystal holds the key to it all. Dravere's spy network was transmitting it back to him and it was intercepted.'

'By who?' Lerod asked.

'By Macaroth's loyal spy network, Imperial intelligence, working to undermine Dravere's conspiracy. They are covert, vulnerable, few, but they are the only things working against the mechanism of Dravere's ascendancy.'

'Why you?' Dorden asked quietly.

Gaunt paused. Even now, he could not tell them the real reason. That it was foretold. 'I was there, and I was trusted. I don't understand it all. An old friend of mine is part of the intelligence hub, and he contacted me to caretake this precious cargo. It seemed there was no one else on Pyrites close enough or trusted enough to do it.'

Varl shifted in his seat, scratching his shoulder implant. 'So? What's on it?'

'I have no idea,' Gaunt said. 'It's encoded.'

Lerod started to say something else, but Gaunt added, 'It's Vermilion level.'

There was a long pause, accompanied only by Blane's long, impressed whistle.

'Now do you see?' Gaunt asked.

'What do we do?' Varl said dully.

'We find out what's on it. Then we decide.'

'But how–' Meryn began, but Gaunt held up a calming hand.

'That's my job, and I think I can do it. Easily, in fact. After that… well, that's why I wanted you all in on this. Already, Dravere's covert network has attempted to kill me and retrieve the crystal. Twice. Once on Pyrites and now here again on the ship. I need you with me, to guard this priceless thing, to keep the Lord Militant General's spies from it. To cover me until I can see the way clear to the action we should take.'

Silence reigned in the staff room.

'Are you with me?' Gaunt asked.

The silence beat on, almost stifling. The officers exchanged furtive glances.

In the end, it was Lerod who spoke for them. Gaunt was particularly glad it was Lerod.

'Do you have to ask, commissar?' he said simply.

Gaunt smiled his thanks. He got up from the display unit and stepped off the dais as the men rose. 'Let's get to it. Rawne's already setting patrols to keep this barrack deck secure. Support and bolster that effort. I want to feel confident that the area of this ship given over to us is safe ground. Keep intruders out, or escort them directly to me. If the men question the precautions, tell them we think that those damn Patricians might try something to ease their grudge against us. Terra knows, that's true enough, and there are over four times our number of Patricians aboard this vessel on the other barrack decks. And the Patricians are undoubtedly in Dravere's pocket.

'I also want the entire deck searched for hidden vox-relays and vista-lines. Hasker, Varl… use any men you know with technical aptitude to perform the sweep. They may be trying all manner of ways of spying on us. From this moment on, trust no one outside our regiment. No one. There is no way of telling who might be part of the conspiracy around us.'

The officers seemed eager but unsettled. Gaunt knew that this was strange work for regular soldiers. They filed out, faces grave.

Gaunt looked at the crystal in his hand. What are you hiding? he wondered.

Seven

Gaunt returned to his quarters with the silent Milo in tow. Corbec had set two Ghosts to guard the commissar's private room. Gaunt sat at the cogitator set into a wall alcove, and began to explore the shipboard information he could access through the terminal. Lines of gently flickering amber text scrolled across the dark vista-plate. He was hoping for a personnel manifest, searching for names that might hint at the identity of those that opposed him. But the details were jumbled and incomplete. It wasn't even clear which other regiments were actually aboard. The Patricians were listed, and a complement of mechanised units from the Bovanian Ninth. But Gaunt knew there must be at least two other regimental strengths aboard, and the listing was blank. He also tried to view the particulars of the *Absalom's* officer cadre, and any other senior Imperial servants making the crossing with them, but those levels of data were locked by naval cipher veils, and Gaunt did not have the authority to penetrate them.

Technology, such as it was, was a sandbagged barricade keeping him out. He sat back in his chair and sighed. His shoulder was sore. The crystal lay on the console near his hand. It was time to try it. Time to try his guess. He'd been putting it off, in case it didn't work really. He got up.

Milo had begun to snooze on a seat by the door and the sudden movement startled him.

'Sir?'

Gaunt was on his feet, carelessly pulling his kitbag and luggage trunks from the wall locker.

'Let's hope the old man wasn't lying!' was all Gaunt said.

Which old man, Milo had no idea.

Gaunt rifled through his baggage. A silk-swathed dress uniform ended up on the floor. Books and data-slates spewed from pulled-open pouches.

Milo was fascinated for a moment. The commissar always packed his own effects, and Milo had never seen the few possessions Gaunt valued enough to carry with him. The boy glimpsed a bar of medals wound in tunic cloth; a larger, grand silver starburst rosette that fell from its velvet-lined case; a faded forage cap with Hyrkan insignia; a glass box of painkiller tablets; a dozen large, yellow slab-like teeth – ork teeth – drilled and threaded onto a cord; an antique scope in a wooden case; a worn buckle brush and a tin of silver polish; a tarot gaming deck which spilled out of its ivory box. The cards were stiff pasteboard, decorated with commemorative images of a liberation festival on somewhere called Gylatus Decimus. Milo bent to collect them up before Gaunt trampled them. They were clean and new, never used; the lid of the box was inscribed with the letters D. O.

Unheeding, Gaunt pulled handfuls of clothes out of his kitbag and flung them aside.

Milo grinned. He felt somehow privileged to see this stuff, as if the commissar had let him into his mind for a while.

Then something else bounced off the accumulating clutter on the deck and Milo paused. It was a toy battleship, rudely carved from a hunk of plastene. Enamel paint was flaking away, and some of the towers and gun turrets had broken off. Milo turned away. There was something painful about the toy, something that let him glimpse further into Ibram Gaunt's private realm of loss than he wanted to go.

The feeling surprised him. He retreated a little, dropping some of the cards he had been shuffling back into their ivory box, and was glad of the excuse to busy himself picking them up.

Gaunt suddenly turned from the mess, a look of triumph in his eyes. He held up an old, tarnished signet ring between his fingers.

'What you were looking for, commissar?' Milo asked brightly, feeling a comment was expected.

'Oh yes. Dear old Uncle Dercius, that bastard. Gave it me as a distraction that night—' Gaunt stopped suddenly, thoughts clouding his face.

He sat down on the bunk next to Milo, glancing over and chuckling sadly as he saw the deck the boy was sorting. 'Souvenirs. Hnh. Emperor knows why I keep them. Never glance at them for years and then they only dredge up black memories.'

He took the cards and rifled through them, holding up some to show Milo, laughing sourly as he did so, as if the Tanith youth could understand the reason for humour. One card showed a Hyrkan flag flying from some tower or other, another showed a heraldic design with an ork's skull, another a moon struck by lightning from the beak of an Imperial eagle.

'Seventy-two reasons to forget our noble victory in the Gylatus World Flock,' he said mockingly.

'And the ring?' Milo asked.

Gaunt put the cards aside. He turned the milling on the signet mount and a short beam of light stabbed out of the ring. 'Feth! Still power in the cell, after all this time!'

Milo smiled, uncertain.

'It's a decryption ring. Officer level. A key to let senior staff access private or veiled data. A general's plaything. They used to be quite popular. This was issued to the commander-in-chief of the noble Jantine regiments, a lord of the very highest standing. And that old bastard gave it to a little boy on Manzipor.'

Gaunt dug the crystal out of his tunic pocket and held it over the ring's beam. He glanced at Milo for a second. There was a surprisingly impish, youthful glee in Gaunt's eyes that made Milo snort with laughter.

'Here goes,' Gaunt said. He slipped the base of the crystal onto the ring mount. It fitted perfectly and engaged with a tiny whirr. Locked in place, as if the stone was now set on the ring band like an outrageously showy gem, it was illuminated by the beam of light. The crystal glowed.

'Come on, come on…' Gaunt said.

Something started to form in the air a few centimetres above the ring, a pict-form, neon bright and lambent in the dimness of the cabin.

The tight, small holographic runes hanging in the air read: 'Authority denied. This document may only be opened by Vermilion level decryption as set by order of Senthis, Administratum Elector, Pacificus calendar 403457.M41. Any attempts to tamper with this data-receptacle will result in memory wipe.'

Gaunt cursed and slipped the crystal off the mount, cancelling the ring's beam. 'Too old, too damn old! Feth, I thought I had it!'

'I don't understand, sir.'

'The clearance levels remain the same, but they revise the codes required to read them at regular intervals. Dercius's ring would certainly have opened a Vermilion text thirty years ago, but the sequences have been overwritten since then. I should have expected Dravere to have set his own confidence codes. Damn!'

Gaunt looked like he was going to continue cursing, but there was a sharp knock at the door of his quarters. Gaunt pocketed the crystal smartly and opened the door. Trooper Uan, one of the corridor sentries, looked in at him.

'Sergeant Blane has brought visitors to you, sir. We've checked them for weapons, and they're clean. Will you see them?'

Gaunt nodded, pulling on his cap and longcoat. He stepped out into the corridor. When he saw the identity of the visitors, Gaunt waved his men back and walked down to greet them.

It was Colonel Zoren, the Vitrian commander, and three of his officers.

'Well met, commissar,' Zoren said curtly. He and his men were dressed in ochre fatigues and soft caps.

'I didn't realise you Vitrians were aboard,' Gaunt said.

'Last minute change. We were bound for the *Japhet* but there was a problem with the boarding tubes. They re-routed us here. The regiments scheduled for the *Absalom* took our places on the *Japhet* once the technical problems were solved. My platoons have been given the barrack decks aft of here.'

'It's good to see you, colonel.'

Zoren nodded, but there was something he was holding back, Gaunt sensed. 'When I learned we were sharing the same transport as the Tanith, I thought perhaps an interaction would be appropriate. We have a mutual victory to celebrate. But–'

'But?'

Zoren dropped his voice. 'I was attacked in my quarters this morning. A man dressed in unmarked Navy overalls was searching my belongings. He rounded on me when I came in. There was a struggle. He escaped.'

Gaunt felt his anger return. 'Go on.'

'He was looking for something. Something he thought I might have, something he had failed to find elsewhere. I thought I should tell you directly.'

Milo, Uan and everyone in the corridor, including Zoren himself, was surprised when Gaunt grabbed the Vitrian colonel by the front of his tunic and dragged him into his quarters.

Gaunt slammed the door shut after them.

Alone in the room, Gaunt turned on Zoren, who looked hurt but somehow not surprised.

'That was a terribly well-informed statement, colonel.'

'Naturally.'

'Start making sense, Zoren, or I'll forget our friendship.'

'No need for unpleasantness, Gaunt. I know more than you imagine and, I assure you, I am a friend.'

'Of whom?'

'Of you, of the Throne of Terra, and of a mutual acquaintance. I know him as Bel Torthute. You know him as Fereyd.'

Eight

'It's...' Colonel Draker Flense began. 'It's a lot to think about.'

He was answered by a snigger that did nothing to calm his nerves. The snigger came from a tall, hooded shape at the rear of the room, a figure silhouetted against a window of stained glass imagery which was lit by the flashes and glints of the immaterium.

'You're a soldier, Flense. I don't believe thinking is part of the job description.'

Flense bit back on a sharp answer. He was afraid, terribly afraid of the man in the multi-coloured shadows of the window. He shifted uneasily, dying for a breath of fresh air, his throat parched. The chamber was thick with the smoke from the obscura water-pipe on its slate plinth by the steps to the window. The nectar-sweet opiate smoke swirled around him and stole all humidity from the air. His mind was slack and torpid from breathing it in.

Warrant Officer Lekulanzi stood by the door, and the three shrouded astropaths grouped in a huddle in the shadows to his left didn't seem to mind. The astropaths were a law unto themselves, and Flense had recognised the pallor of an obscura addict in Lekulanzi's face the moment the warrant officer had arrived at his quarters to summon him. Flense had led an assault into an addict-hive on Poscol years before. He had never forgotten the sweet stench, nor the pallor of the half-hearted resistance.

The figure at the window stepped slowly down to face him. Flense, two metres tall without his jackboots, found himself looking up into the darkness of the cowl.

'Well, colonel?' whispered the voice inside the hood.

'I– I don't really understand what is expected of me, my lord.'

Inquisitor Golesh Constantine Pheppos Heldane sniggered again. He reached up with his ring-heavy fingers and turned back his cowl. Flense blinked. Heldane's face was high and long, like some equine beast. His wet, sneering mouth was full of blunt teeth and his eyes were round and dark. Fluid tubes and fibre-wires laced his long, sloped skull like hair braids. His huge skull was hairless, but Flense could see the matted fur that coated his neck and throat. He was human, but his features had been surgically altered to inspire terror and obedience in those he... studied. At least, Flense hoped it was a surgical alteration.

'You seem uneasy, colonel. Is it the circumstance, or my words?'

Flense found himself floundering for speech again. 'I've never been admitted to a sacrosanctorium before, my lord,' he began.

Heldane extended his arms wide – too wide for anything but a skeletal giant like Heldane, Flense shuddered – to encompass the chamber. Those present were standing in one of the *Absalom's* astropath sanctums, a chamber screened from all intrusion. The walls were null field dead spaces designed to shut out both the material world and the screaming void of the immaterium. Sound-proofed, psyker-proofed, wire-proofed, these inviolable cocoons were dedicated and reserved for the astropathic retinue alone. They were prohibited by Imperial law. Only a direct invitation could admit a blunt human such as Flense.

Blunt. Flense didn't like the word, and hadn't been aware of it until Lekulanzi had used it.

Blunt. A psyker's word for the non-psychic. Blunt. Flense wished by the Ray of Hope he could be elsewhere. Any elsewhere.

'You are discomforting my cousins,' Heldane said to Flense, indicating the three astropaths, who were fidgeting and murmuring. 'They sense your reluctance to be here. They sense their stigma.'

'I have no prejudices, inquisitor.'

'Yes, you have. I can taste them. You detest mind-seers. You despise the gift of the astropath. You are a blunt, Flense. A sense-dead moron. Shall I show you what you are missing?'

Flense shook. 'No need, inquisitor!'

'Just a touch? Be a sport.' Heldane sniggered, droplets of spittle flecking off his thick teeth.

Flense shuddered. Heldane turned his gaze away slowly and then snapped back suddenly. Impossible light flooded into Flense's skull. For one second, he saw eternity. He saw the angles of space, the way they intersected with time. He saw the tides of the empyrean, and the wasted fringes of the immaterium, the fluid spasms of the warp. He saw his mother, his sister, both long dead. He saw light and darkness and nothingness. He saw colours without name. He saw the birth torments of the gene-stealer whose blood would scar his face. He saw himself on the drill-field of the Schola on Primagenitor. He saw an explosion of blood. Familiar blood. He started to cry. He saw bones buried in rich, black mud. He realised they, too, were his own. He looked into the sockets. He saw maggots. He screamed. He vomited. He saw a red-dark sky and an impossible number of suns. He saw a star overload and collapse. He saw–

Too much.

Draker Flense fell to the floor of the sacrosanctorium, soiled himself and started to whimper.

'I'm glad we've got that straight,' Inquisitor Heldane said. He raised his cowl again. 'Let me start over. I serve Dravere, as you do. For him, I will bend the stars. For him, I will torch planets. For him, I will master the unmasterable.'

Flense moaned.

'Get up. And listen to me. The most priceless artefact in space awaits our lord in the Menazoid Clasp. Its description and circumstance lies with Commissar Gaunt. We will obtain that secret. I have already expended precious energies trying to reach it. This Gaunt is... resourceful. You will allow yourself to be used in this matter. You and the Patricians. You already have a feud with them.'

'Not this... not this...' Flense rasped from the floor.

'Dravere spoke highly of you. Do you remember what he said?'

'N– no…'

Heldane's voice changed and became a perfect copy of Dravere's. 'If you win this for me, Flense, I'll not forget it. There are great possibilities in my future, if I am not tied here. I would share them with you.'

'Now is the time, Flense,' Heldane said in his own voice once more. 'Share in the possibilities. Help me to acquire what my Lord Dravere demands. There will be a place for you, a place in glory. A place at the side of the new warmaster.'

'Please!' Flense cried. He could hear the astropaths laughing at him.

'Are you still undecided?' Heldane asked. He stepped towards the curled, foetal colonel. 'Another look?' he suggested.

Flense began to shriek.

Nine

'They're excluding us,' Feygor said out of the silence.

Rawne snapped an angry glance round at his adjutant, but he knew what the lean man meant. It had been four hours since the rest of the officers had been called into their meeting with Gaunt. How convenient that he and his platoon had been excluded. Of course, if what Corbec said was true and there was trouble aboard, a good picket was essential. But in the natural order of things, it should have been Folore's platoon, the sixteenth, who took first shift.

Rawne grunted a response and led his team of five men down to the junction with the next corridor. They'd swept this area six times since they had begun. Just draughty hull-spaces, dark corners, empty stores, dusty floors and locked hatches. He checked the time. A radio message from Lerod twenty minutes earlier had informed him that the shift change would take place on the next hour. He ached. He knew the men with him were tired and cold and in need of stove-warmth, caffeine and relaxation. By extension, all of his platoon, all fifty of them spread out patrolling the perimeter of the Ghosts' barrack deck in squads of five, would be demoralised and hungry too.

Rawne thought, as he often did, of Gaunt. Of Gaunt's motives. From the start, back at the bloody hour of the Founding itself, he had shown no loyalty to the commissar. It had astonished him when Gaunt had raised him to major and given him the tertiary command of the regiment. He'd laughed at it at first, then qualified that laughter by imagining Gaunt had recognised his leadership qualities. Sometime later, Feygor, the only man in the regiment he thought of as a friend, and then only barely, had reminded him of the old saying: 'Keep your friends close and your enemies closer.'

There was no escape from the Guard, so Rawne had got on with making the best of his job. But he always wondered at Gaunt. If he'd been the colonel-commissar, with a danger like himself at his heels, he'd have called up a firing squad long since.

Ahead, Trooper Lonegin was checking the locks on a storage bin. Rawne scanned the length of the corridor they had just advanced through.

Feygor watched his commander slyly. Rawne had been good to him – and they had worked together in the militia of Tanith Attica before the Founding. Quite a tasty racket they had running there until the fething Imperium rolled up and ruined it. Feygor was the bastard son of a black marketeer, and only his sharp mind and formidable physical ability had got him a place in the militia, and then the Imperial Guard. Rawne's background had been select. He didn't talk about it much, but Feygor knew enough to know that Rawne's family had been rich merchants, local politicians, local lords. Rawne had always had money, stipends from his father's empire of timber mills. But as the third son, he was never going to be the one to inherit the fortune. The militia service – and the opportunities for self advancement – had been the best option.

Feygor didn't trust Rawne. Feygor didn't trust anyone. But he never thought of the major as evil. Just... bitter. Bitterness was what had ruined him, bitterness was what had scalded his nature early on.

Like Feygor, the men of Rawne's platoon were the misfits and troublemakers of the surviving Tanith. They gravitated towards Rawne, seeing him as a natural leader, the man who would make the best chances for them. During the draft process, Rawne had selected most of them for his own squads.

One day, Feygor thought, one day Rawne will kill Gaunt and take his place. Gaunt, Corbec, any who opposed. Rawne will kill Gaunt. Or Gaunt will kill Rawne. Whatever, there will be a reckoning. Some said Rawne had already tried.

Feygor was about to suggest they double back into the storerooms to the left when Trooper Lonegin cried out and spun across the deck, hit by something from behind. He curled, convulsing, on the grill-walkway and Feygor could clearly see the short boot-knife jutting from the man's ribs where it had impacted.

Rawne was already yelling when the attackers emerged around them from all sides. Ten men, dressed in the work uniforms of the Purpure Patricians. They had knives, stakes, clubs made from bunk-legs. A frenzy of close-quarter brutality exploded in the narrow confines of the hallway.

Trooper Colhn was smashed into a wall by a blow to the head and sank without a murmur before he could even turn. Trooper Freul struck one attacker hard with his shock-pole and knocked him over in a cascade of sparks before three knife jabs from as many assailants ripped into him and dropped him in a bloody mass. Feygor could see two of the Patricians clubbing the wounded, helpless Lonegin repeatedly.

Feygor hurled his shock-pole at the nearest Patrician, blasting him backwards and burning through the belly of his uniform with the discharge, and then pulled out his silver Tanith blade. He screamed an obscenity and hurled forward, ripping open a throat with his first attack. With a savage turn, using the moves that had won him respect in the backstreets of Tanith Attica, he wheeled, kicked the legs out from under another and took a knife-wielding hand off at the wrist.

'Rawne! Rawne!' he bellowed, fumbling for his radio bead. He was hit from behind. Stunned, he took two more strikes and dropped, rolling. Feet kicked into him. Something that felt white hot dug into his chest. He bellowed with pain and rage. The sound was diffused by the gout of blood in his mouth.

Rawne struck down one with his pole, wheeling and blocking.

He cursed them with every oath in his vocabulary. A blade ripped open his tunic and spilled blood from a long, raw scratch. A heavy blow struck his temple and he went over, vision fogging.

The major tried to move but his body wouldn't respond. The cold grille of the deck pushed into his cheek and his slack mouth. Wet warmth ran down his neck. His unfocussed eyes looked up at the bulky Patrician who stood over him, a long-armed wrench raised ready to pulp his skull.

'Stay your hand, Brochuss!' a voice said. The wrench lowered, reluctantly.

Immobile, Rawne wished he could see more. Another figure replaced the shape of his wrench-swinging attacker. Rawne's eyes were dim and filmy. He wished he could see clearly. The man who stooped by him looked like an officer.

Colonel Flense hunkered down beside Rawne, looking sadly at the blood matting the hair and the twisted spread of the limbs.

'See the badge, Brochuss?' Flense said. 'He's the major, Rawne. Don't kill him. Not yet, at least.'

Ten

'How do you know him?' Gaunt demanded.

Colonel Zoren made a slight, shrugging gesture, the typically unemphatic body language of the Vitrians. 'Likely the same way you do. A chance encounter, a carefully established measure of trust, an informal working relationship during a crisis.'

Gaunt rubbed his angular chin and shook his head. 'If this conversation is going to get us anywhere, you'll have to be more specific. If you honestly do appreciate the critical nature of this situation, you'll understand why I need to be sure and certain of those around me.'

Zoren nodded. He turned, as if to survey the room, but the close confines of Gaunt's quarters allowed for little contemplation. 'It was during the Famine Wars on Idolwilde, perhaps three standard years ago. My Dragoons were sent in as a peacekeeping presence in the main city-state, Kenadie. That was just before the food riots began in earnest and before the fall of the local government. The man you know as Fereyd was masquerading as a local grain broker called Bel Torthute, a trade-banker with a place on the Idolwilde Senate. His cover was perfect. I had no idea he was an off-world operative. No idea he wasn't a native. He had the language, the customs, the gestures–'

'I know how Fereyd works. Observational perfection is his speciality, and that mimicry thing.'

'Then you'll know his modus operandi too. To work with what he calls the "trustworthy salt" of the Imperium.'

Gaunt nodded, a half-smile curving his mouth.

'To work in such environments, so alone, so vulnerable, our mutual friend needs to nurture the support of those elements of the Imperium he deems uncorrupted. Rooting out corruption and taint in Imperium-sponsored bureaucracies, he can't trust the Administratum, the Ministorum, or any ranking officials who might be part of the conspiratorial infrastructure. He told me that he always found his best allies in the Guard in those circumstances, in men drafted into crisis flash-points, plain soldiery who like as not were newcomers to any such event, and thus not part of the problem. That is what he found in me and some of my officer cadre. It took him a long time and much careful investigation to trust me, and just as long to win my trust back. Eventually, in the midst of the food riots, we Vitrians were the only elements he could count on. The Famine Wars had been orchestrated by a government faction with ties into the Departmento Munitorium. They were able to field two regiments of Imperial Guard turned to their purpose. We defeated them.'

'The Battle of Altatha. I have read some of the details. I had no idea Imperial corruption was behind the Famine Wars.'

Zoren smiled sadly. 'Such information is often suppressed. For the good of morale. We parted company as allies. I never thought to meet him again.'

Gaunt sat down on his cot. He leaned his elbows onto his knees, deep in thought. 'And now you have?'

'I received a message, encrypted, during my disembarkation from shore leave on Pyrites. Shortly after that, a meeting.'

'In person?'

Zoren shook his head. 'An intermediary.'

'And how did you know to trust this intermediary?'

'He used certain identifiers. Code words Bel Torthute and I had developed and used on Idolwilde. Cipher syllables from Vitrian combat-cant that only he would have known the significance of. Torthute made a point of studying the cultural heritage of the Vitrian Byhata, our Art of War. Only he could have sent the message and couched it so.'

'That's Fereyd. So you are my ally? I have a feeling you know more about this situation than me, Zoren.'

Zoren watched the tall, powerful man as he sat on the cot, his chin resting on his hands. He'd come to admire him during the Fortis action, and Fereyd's message had contained details specific to Gaunt. It was clear the Imperial covert agent trusted Commissar-Colonel Ibram Gaunt more than almost anyone in the sector. More than myself, Zoren thought.

'I know this much, Gaunt. A group of high-ranking conspirators in the Sabbat Worlds Crusade High Command is hunting for something precious. Something so vital they may be prepared to twist the overall purpose of the crusade to achieve it. The key that unlocks that something has been deflected out of their waiting hands and diverted to you for safekeeping, as you were the only one of Fereyd's operatives in range to deal with it.'

Gaunt rose angrily. 'I'm no one's operative!' he snarled.

Zoren waved him back with a deft apologetic gesture to the mouth that indicated a misprision with language. Gaunt reminded himself that Low Gothic was not the colonel's first tongue. 'A trusted partner,' he corrected. 'Fereyd has been careful to establish a wide, remote circle of friends on whom he can call at times like this. You were the only one able to intercept and safeguard the key on Pyrites. After some further manipulation, he made sure I was on the same transport as you to assist. How else do you think we Vitrians ended up on the *Absalom* so conveniently? I imagine Fereyd and his agents in the warmaster's command staff risked great exposure arranging for us to be diverted to this ship. It would be about as overt an action as a covert dared.'

'Did he tell you anything else, this intermediary?' Gaunt said.

'That I was to offer you all assistance, up to and beyond coun-termanding the direct orders of my superiors.'

There was a long quiet space as the enormity of this sunk in. 'And then?' Gaunt asked.

'The instructions said that you would make the right choice. That Fereyd, unable to directly intercede here, would trust you to carry this forward until his network was able to involve itself again. That you would assess the situation and act accordingly.'

Gaunt laughed humourlessly. 'But I know nothing! I don't know what this is about, or where it's going! This shadowplay isn't what I'm good at!'

'Because you're a soldier?'

'What?'

Zoren repeated it. 'Because you're a soldier? Like me, you deal in orders and commands and direct action. This doesn't sit easy with any of us that Fereyd employs. Us "Imperial salt" may be trustworthy and able to be recruited to his cause, but we lack the sophistication to understand the war. This isn't something we solve with flamers and fire-teams.'

Gaunt cursed Fereyd's name. Zoren echoed him, and they both began to laugh.

'Unless you can,' Zoren said, suddenly serious.

'Why?'

'Why? Because he trusts you. Because you're a colonel second and a commissar first, a political officer. And this war is all politics. Intrigue. We were both on Pyrites, Gaunt. Why did he divert the key to you and not me? Why am I here to help you, and not the other way around?'

Gaunt cursed Fereyd's name again, but this time it was low and bitter.

He was about to speak again when there was a fierce hammering at the door to the quarters. Gaunt swept to his feet and pulled the door open. Corbec stood outside, his face flushed and fierce.

'What?' managed Gaunt.

'You'd better come, sir. We've got three dead and another critical. The Jantine are playing for keeps.'

Eleven

Corbec led Gaunt, Zoren and a gaggle of others into the Infirmary annex where Dorden awaited them.

'Colhn, Freul, Lonegin...' Dorden said, gesturing to three shapes under sheets on the floor. 'Feygor's over there.'

Gaunt looked across at Rawne's adjutant, who lay, sucking breath through a transparent pipe, on a gurney in the corner.

'Puncture wound. Knife. Lungs are failing. Another hour unless I can get fresh equipment.'

'Rawne?' Gaunt asked.

Corbec edged forward. 'Like I said, sir, no sign. It was hit and run. They must have taken him with them. But they left this to let us know.'

Corbec showed the commissar the Jantine cap badge. 'Pinned it to Colhn's forehead,' he said with loathing.

Zoren was puzzled. 'Why such an outward show of force?'

'The Jantine are a part of all of this. But they also have a declared rivalry with the Ghosts. This comes to light, it'll look like inter-regiment feuding. There'll be reprimands, but it will cloud the true matter. They want to take credit… under cover of an open feud they can do anything they like.'

Gaunt realised they were all looking at him. His mind was racing. 'So we do the same. Colm, maintain the perimeter patrols on this deck, double strength. But also organise a raid on the Jantine. Lead it yourself. Kill some for me.'

A great smile crossed Corbec's face.

'Let's play along with their game and use it to our own ends. Doctor,' he gestured to Dorden, 'you're going to get medical supplies with my authority now you have a critical case.'

'What are you going to do?' Dorden asked, wiping his hands on a gauze towel.

Gaunt was thinking hard. He needed a plan now, a second option now that Dercius's ring had failed. He cursed his overconfidence in it. Now they had to start from scratch, both to safeguard themselves and to learn the crystal's secrets. But Gaunt was determined now. He would see this through. He would take the fight to the enemy.

'I need access to the bridge. To the captain himself. Colonel Zoren?'

'Yes?' Colonel Zoren moved up close to join Gaunt. He was entirely unprepared for the punch that laid him out, lip split and already bloody.

'Report that,' Gaunt said. His plan began to fall into place.

Twelve

Chief Medical Officer Galen Gartell of the Jantine Patricians turned slowly from his patient in the bright, clean medical bay of the Jantine barrack deck. He had been tending the man since he had been brought in: a lout, a barbarian. One of the Tanith, the stretcher bearers had told him.

The patient was a slim, powerful man with hard, angular good looks and a blue starburst tattoo over one eye. Currently the lean, handsome temple was disfigured by a bloody impact wound. 'Keep him alive!' Major Brochuss had hissed as he had helped to carry the man in.

Such damage… such a barbarian… Gartell had mused as he had begun work, cleaning and healing. He disliked using his skill on animals like this, but clearly his noble regiment had shown mercy to some raiding rival scum and were going to heal his wounds and send him off as a gesture of their benign superiority to the deck rats they were bunked with. The voice that made him turn was that of Colonel Flense. 'Is he alive, doctor?'

'Just. I don't know why I should be saving a wretch like this, wasting valuable medical commodities.'

Flense hushed him and moved into the infirmary. A tall hooded figure followed him.

Gartell took a step back. The figure was well over two metres tall and there was a suggestion of smoke around him that fluctuated and masked his presence.

Who is this? Gartell wondered. The shadow-cloak – only a formidable scion of the Imperium would have such a device.

'What do you need?' Flense asked, addressing the figure. It hovered forward, past Gartell and looked down at the patient.

'Cranial clamps, a neural probe, perhaps some long, single-edged scalpels,' it said in a hollow voice.

'What?' Gartell stammered. 'What in the name of the Emperor are you about to do?'

'Teach this thing. Teach it well,' the figure replied, reaching out a huge, twisted hand to stroke the Ghost's brow. The finger-nails were hooked and brown, like claws.

Gartell felt anger rise. 'I am chief medical officer here! No one performs any procedure in this infirmary without my–'

The hooded figure flicked its arm.

Galen Gartell suddenly found himself staring at his booted toes. It took the rest of his life for him to realise that something was wrong. Only when his headless body fell onto the deck next to him did he realise that... his head... cut... bastard... no.

'Flense? Clear that up, would you?' Inquisitor Heldane asked, gesturing to the corpse at his feet with a swish of the blood-wet, long-bladed scalpel in his hands. He turned back to the patient.

'Hello, Major Rawne,' he crooned softly. 'Let me show you your heart's desire.'

Thirteen

Reclining in his leather upholstered command throne, Lord Captain Itumade Grasticus, commander of the Adeptus Mechanicus Mass Conveyance *Absalom*, raised his facilitator wand in a huge, baby-fat hand and gestured gently at one of the many hololithic plates which hovered around him on suspensor fields, bobbing gently like a cluster of buoys in an ebb-tide.

The matt, dark surface of the chosen plate blinked, and a slow swirl of amber runes played across it. Grasticus carefully noted the current warp displacement of his vast ship, and then selected another plate to appraise himself of the engine tolerances.

Through reinforced metal cables that grew from the deck plates under his throne and clung like thick growths of creeper to the back of his chair, Grasticus felt his ship. The data-cables, many of them tagged with paper labels bearing codes or prayers, spilled over the headrest of his throne and entered his cranium, neck, spine and puffy cheeks through sutured bio-sockets. They fed him the sum total of the ship's being, the structural integrity, the atmospheric levels, the very mood of the great spacecraft. Through them, he experienced the actions of every linked crewman and servitor aboard, and the distant rhythm of the engines set the pace of his own pulse.

Grasticus was immense. Three hundred kilos of loose meat hung from his great frame. He seldom left his throne, seldom ventured outside the quiet peace of his private strategium, an armoured dome at the heart of the busy bridge vault, set high on the command spire at the rear of the *Absalom*.

One hundred and thirty standard years before, when he had inherited this vessel from the late Lord Captain Ulbenid, he had been a tall, lean man. Indolence, and the addictive sympathy with the ship, had made him throne-bound. His body, as if sensing he was now one with such a vast machine, had slowed his metabolism and increased his mass, as if it wanted him to echo the swollen bulk of the *Absalom*. The conveyance vessels of the Adeptus Mechanicus were not like ships of the Imperial Navy. Immeasurably older and often much larger, they had been made to carry the engines of war from Mars to wherever they were needed. Their captains were more like the Princeps of great walking Titans, hard-wired into the living machines through mind-impulse links. They were living ships.

Grasticus wanded another screen which allowed him direct observation of his beloved navigators, husks of men wired into their shrine, set in an alcove a few marble steps down from the main bridge. Their chanting voices sang him the immaterium coordinates and their progress, forming them into a data-plainsong which resonated a pale harmony through his mind. He listened, understood, was reassured.

There was a slight course adjustment which he relayed to the senior helm officers. The Menazoid Clasp was now just two day-cycles away. The ether showed no signs of storm fronts or warp pools, and the signal from the Astronomican beacon, whose psychic light guided all ships through the empyrean, was clear and clean. Blessed are the songs of the Navis Nobilite, murmured Grasticus in his thick voice, pronouncing part of the Navis Blessing Creed, for from them shines the Ray of Hope that lights our Golden Path.

Grasticus frowned suddenly. There was an uproar outside his hard-wired womb. Human voices raised in urgent conference. His flesh-heavy brow furrowed like sand-dunes slipping, and he wanded his throne to revolve to face the arched opening to the strategium.

'Warrant Officer Lekulanzi,' he said into his intercom horn, hanging on taut brass wires from the vaulted roof, 'enter and explain this disturbance.'

He dropped the storm shield guarding the entry arch with a

flick of his wand and Lekulanzi hurried in, looking alarmed. The warrant officer gazed up at the obese bulk in the hammock-like throne above him and toyed with compulsive agitation at the hem of his uniform and his own facilitator wand. He seldom saw the captain face to face.

'Lord captain, a senior officer of the Imperial Guard petitions for audience with you. He wishes to make a formal complaint.'

'An item of cargo wishes to complain?' Grasticus said with slow wonder.

'A passenger,' Lekulanzi said, shuddering at the direct sound of the captain's seldom-heard voice.

Grasticus brushed the correction aside as he always did. He wasn't used to carrying humans. Compared to the beloved God-Machines it was his given task to convey, they seemed insignificant. But the humans had liberated Fortis Binary, and the tech-priests had sent him and his ship to assist them. It was a kind of gratitude, he supposed.

Grasticus disliked Lekulanzi. The whelp had been transferred to his command three months earlier on the orders of the Adeptus after Grasticus's acting warrant officer was killed during a warp storm. He doubted the man's ability. He loathed his spare, fragile build.

'Admit him,' Grasticus said, diverted by the unusual event. It would make a change to speak to people. To use his mouth. To see a body and smell its warm, fleshy breath.

Colonel Zoren entered the strategium flanked by two Navy troopers with shotguns. The man's face was marked by a bruise and a dressed cut.

'Speak,' said Grasticus.

'Lord captain,' the soldier began, uttering in the delicious accent-tones of a far-worlder. Grasticus hooded his eyes and smiled. The noise delighted him.

'Colonel Zoren, Vitrian Dragoons. We have the privilege of transport on your great vessel. However, I wish to complain strongly about the lack of inter-barrack security. Feuding has begun with those uncouth barbarians, the Tanith. Their commanding officer struck me when I approached him to complain about several brawling incidents.'

Through his data-conduits, Grasticus felt the waft of the psychic truth-fields that layered and screened his strategium. The man was speaking honestly; the Tanith commander – a... Gaunt? – had indeed struck him. There were lower levels of inconsistency and falsehood registered by the fields, but Grasticus put that down to the man's nervousness about approaching him directly.

'This is a matter for my security aide, the warrant officer here. Shipboard manners and protocol are his domain. Do not trouble me with such irrelevancies.'

Zoren cast a look at the agitated Lekulanzi, who dearly wished to be elsewhere.

Before either could speak, a new figure marched directly into the strategium, a tall man in the long coat and cap of an Imperial commissar. The troopers turned their weapons on him reflexively but he did not even blink.

'Lekulanzi is a fop. He is unable to perform his duties, let alone command peace on this ship. You must deal with it.'

The newcomer was astonishingly bold and direct. No formal address, no humble approach. Grasticus was impressed – and wrong-footed.

'I am Gaunt,' the newcomer said. 'My Tanith barracks have been raided and attempts have been made on my own life. Three of my men are dead, another critical and another missing. I mistook Zoren and his men as the culprits, hence my assault on him. The guilty party is in fact the Jantine Regiment. I ask you now, directly, to confine them and put their commanding officers on report.'

Again, Grasticus felt a hint of deceit in the flow of the astro-pathic truth-fields, but once more he put this down to the disarming awe of being in his presence. Essentially, this Gaunt was reading as utterly truthful and shamelessly direct.

'You have men dead?' Grasticus asked, almost alarmed.

'Three. More urgently, I require your authorisation to admit my medical officer to the stores of the Munitorium to obtain medical commodities to save my injured soldier.'

This insect is shaming me! In my own strategium! Grasticus thought with sudden revulsion.

His mind whirled and he shut out sixty percent of the data-flow entering his skull so he could concentrate. This was the first time in a dozen years he had to deal with a problem involving his cargo. Passengers! Passengers, that was what Lekulanzi had called them. Grasticus writhed gently in his throne. This was unseemly. This was insulting. This matter should have been contained long before now, before cargo was damaged, died, before complaints were brought to his feet.

He raised his facilitator wand and flicked it at a hovering plate. He would not lose face before these walking flesh-worms. He would show he was the captain, the lord captain, and that they all owed their safety and lives to him.

'I have given your medical officer authority. He has my formal mark to expedite his access to the stores.'

Gaunt smiled 'That's a start. Now confine the Jantine and punish their officers.'

Grasticus was amazed. He raised himself up on his ham-like elbows to study Gaunt, hefting his upper body free of the leather for the first time in fifteen months. There was a squeak of sweat-wet leather and a scent of stale filth wafted into the air of the strategium.

'I will not brook such insubordination,' Grasticus hissed, his cotton-soft words spitting from the loose folds of spare flesh that surrounded his small, glistening mouth like curtains on a proscenium arch. 'No one demands of me.'

'That's not good enough. Don't belabour us with threats. We require action!' This from Zoren now, stood side by side with the hawk-faced Gaunt. Grasticus reacted in surprise. He had thought the Vitrian more subdued, more deferential, but now he too challenged directly. 'Contain the Jantine and curtail their feuding or you'll have an uprising on your hands! Thousands of trained troopers, hungry for blood! More than your trooper details can handle!' Zoren cast a contemptuous glance at the Navy escort.

'Do you threaten me?' Grasticus almost gasped. The very thought of it. 'I will see you in chains for such a remark!'

'Is that how you deal with things you don't want to hear?' Gaunt snapped, pushing aside a trooper to approach Grasticus's throne. The trooper grappled with the larger commissar but Gaunt sent him sprawling with a deft swing of his arm.

'Are you the commander of this vessel, or a weak, fat nothing who hides at its heart?'

Lekulanzi fell back against the wall of the strategium, aghast and hyperventilating. No one spoke to the lord captain like that! No one–

Grasticus writhed ever-upwards from his bed-throne, sweeping the hovering plates aside with his hands so that they parted and cowered at the edges of the chamber behind him. He glared down at the Guard officers, rage rippling through his vast mass.

'Well?' Gaunt said.

Grasticus began to bellow, raising his thick, swollen voice for the first time in years.

Zoren cast a nervous glance at Gaunt. Weren't they pushing the lord captain too hard? Something in Gaunt's calm reassured him. He remembered the elements of their plan and started to send his own jibes at the captain in tune with Gaunt's.

Gaunt grinned inwardly. Now they had Grasticus's entire attention.

Outside the strategium, on the lower levels of the high-roofed, cool-aired bridge vault, the senior helm officers looked up from their dark, oiled gears and levers, and exchanged wondering glances. The basso after-echo of their captain rolled out of the armoured dome. The lord captain was clearly so angry he had diverted his attention from most of the systems temporarily. This was unheard of, unprecedented.

A detachment of ship troopers milled cautiously outside the door-arch of the strategium. 'Do we enter?' rasped one through his helmet intercom. None of them felt like confronting the lord captain's wrath.

They pitied the idiot Guard officers who had created this commotion.

Gaunt did not care. This was exactly what he had been after.

Fourteen

Chief Medic Dorden led his party in through the armoured hatchway of the Munitorium depot deck. Flanking him, Caffran, Brin Milo and Bragg formed a motley honour guard of uneven height for the elderly medico.

They entered a wide bay that smelled of antiseptic and ionisation filters. The grey deck was dusted with clean sand. Dorden consulted his chronometer.

'Cometh the hour...' he said.

'Come who?' Bragg asked.

'What I mean is, it's now or never. We've given the commissar long enough. He should be with the captain now,' Dorden said.

'I still don't get any of this,' Bragg said, scratching his lantern jaw. 'How's this meant to work? What's the old Ghostmaker trying to do?'

'It's called a diversion,' Milo said quietly. 'Don't worry about the details, just play along and act dumb.'

'Not a problem!' Bragg announced, baffled by Caffran's subsequent smirk.

Beyond metal cage doors at the end of the bay, three robed officials of the Munitorium were at work at low-set consoles. There were at least seven Navy troopers on watch around the place.

Dorden marched forward and rapped on the metal grille. 'I need supplies!' he called. 'Hurry now; a man is dying!'

One of the Munitorium men got up from his console, leaving his cloak draped over the seat back. He was a short, bulky man with physical power under his khaki Munitorium tunic. Glossy, chrome servitor implants were stapled into his cheek, temple and throat. He disconnected a cable from his neck socket as he approached them.

Dorden thrust his data-slate under the man's nose. 'Requisition of medical supplies,' he snapped.

The man viewed the slate. As he scrolled down the slate file, the troopers suddenly came to attention and grouped in the centre of the bay. Milo could hear the muffled back and forth of their helmet vox-casters. One of them turned to the Munitorium staff.

'Trouble on the bridge!' he said through his speaker, his voice tinny. 'Bloody Guard are feuding again. We've been detailed down to the barrack decks to act as patrol.'

The Munitorium officer waved them off with his hand. 'Whatever.' The troopers exited, leaving just one watching the grille entry.

The Munitorium officer slid back the cage grille and let the four Ghosts inside. He eyed the slate before directing them down an aisle to the left. 'Lord Captain Grasticus has issued you with clearance. Down there, chamber eleven. Get what you need. Just what you need. I'll be checking the inventory on the way out. No analgesics without a signed chit from the warrant officer, no purloining.'

'Feth you,' Dorden said, snatching back the slate and beckoning the others after him. 'We've got a life to save! Do you think we'd waste time trying to rustle some booty?'

The official turned away, disinterested. Dorden led the trio down the dark aisle, between racks of air-tanks, amphorae of wine and food crates stacked up to the high roof. They entered a junction bay in the dark depths of the storage holds, and through several hatches ahead saw the vast commodity stockpiles of the huge ship.

'Medical supplies down there,' Caffran said, noting the white marker tags on one of the hatch frames.

'There's a console,' Milo said, pointing down another of the aisles into a dark hold. They could see the dull, distant green glow of a Munitorium artificer. Dorden glanced at his chronometer again. 'Right, as we planned. Five minutes! Go!'

With Bragg at his heels, Dorden strode into the medical supply vault and started pulling bundles of sterile gauze, jars of counter-septic wash and packs of clean surgical tools off the black metal shelves. Bragg requisitioned a wheeled cargo trolley from an alcove near the door and followed him.

Milo and Caffran slunk down into the darker chamber, and the boy swung onto the low bench-seat in front of the console. He fumbled in his pocket and produced the memory tile that Gaunt had give him, gingerly fitting it into the slot on the desk-edge of the machine. Two teal-coloured lights winked and flashed as the artificer recognised the blank tile. His hands trembled. He tried to remember what the commissar had told him.

'Will this work?' Caffran asked, pulling out his blade and watching the door anxiously.

The Munitorium data banks were slaved directly to the ship's main cogitator. Remembering Gaunt's instructions piece by piece, Milo entered key search words via the ivory-toothed keyboard. The banks had full access to the ship's information stockpile, including the security clearance Gaunt's artificer lacked.

'Hurry up, boy!' Caffran snapped, edgy.

Milo ignored him, but that 'boy' nagged him and made him unhappy. His trembling fingers conducted his way across the worn keys into new levels of instruction that glowed in runic cursors on the flat plate of the console, just as the commissar had laid it out.

'Here!' Milo said suddenly, 'I think...' He awkwardly touched a rune-inscribed command key and the console hummed. Data began to download onto the blank tile. Gaunt would be proud. Milo had listened to his arcane ramblings about the use of machines well.

In the medical store, Dorden looked up from the cargo trolley he was filling and glanced once more at his chronometer. Bragg watched him, cautiously.

'This is taking too fething long!' Dorden said irritably.

'I can go back–' Bragg suggested.

'No, we've not got everything yet,' Dorden said, searching the racks for jars of pneumeno-thorax resin.

Milo's fingers hovered over the keys. 'We've got it!' he exclaimed.

Caffran didn't answer. Milo turned and saw Caffran frozen, the blunt nose of a deck-shotgun pressed to his temple. The Imperial Navy trooper said nothing, but nodded his helmet-clad head at Milo, indicating he should get up from the bench rapidly.

Milo rose, his hands where the trooper could see them.

'That's good,' the trooper said through the dull resonator of his headset. He pointed the muzzle of his gun at where he wanted Milo to stand.

Caffran slammed back, jabbing his elbow at the trooper's sternum, aiming for the solar plexus in one desperate move. The fibre-weave armour of the trooper's uniform stopped the blow and he swung around, smashing Caffran into the wall-racks with an open hand.

Milo tried to move.

The shotgun fired, a wide burst of incandescent fury in the darkness.

Fifteen

As they waited in the shadows, they noted that the Jantine had been issued with the finest barrack decks on the ship. The approach colonnade was a spacious embarkation hall, wide enough for the bulkiest of equipment. The glittering wall burners cast long purple shadows across the tiles.

Two Jantine Patricians in full dress armour, training shock-poles held ready, patrolled the far end. They were exchanging inconsequential remarks when Larkin appeared down the colonnade, bumbling along as if he'd missed his way. They snapped round in disbelief and Larkin froze, a look of horror on his leathery, narrow face. With an oath, he turned and began to run back the way he had come.

The two guards thundered after him with baying blood-cries. They'd gone ten metres before the shadows behind them unfolded and Ghosts emerged, dropping stealth cloaks and seizing them from behind. Mkoll, Baru, Varl and Corbec fell on the two Jantine, struck with shock-poles and Tanith blades, and dragged the fallen men into the darkness off the main hall.

'Why am I always the fething bait?' the returning Larkin asked, stopping by Corbec, who was wiping a trace of blood from the floor with the hem of his cape.

'You've got that kind of face,' Varl said, and Corbec smiled.

'Look here!' Baru called in a hiss from the end of the hall. They moved to join him and he grinned as he pulled his find from the corner of the archway the Jantine sentries had been watching. Guns! A battered old exotic bolt-action rifle with a long muzzle and ornately decorated stock, and a worn but serviceable pump stub-gun with a bandolier strap of shells. Neither were regular issue Guard pieces, and both were much lower tech than Guard standard-pattern gear. Corbec knew what they were.

'Souvenirs, spoils of war,' he murmured, his hands running a check on the stub-gun. All soldiers collected trophies like these, stuck them away in their kits to sell on, keep as mementoes, or simply use in a clinch. Corbec knew many of the Ghosts had their own... but they had dutifully handed them in with their issued weapons when they'd come aboard. He was not the least surprised that the Jantine had kept hold of their unrecorded weapons. The sentries had left them here as back up in case of an assault their shock-poles couldn't handle.

Varl handed the rifle to Larkin. There was no question who should carry it.

The weight of a gun in his hands again seemed to calm the old sniper. He licked his almost lip-less mouth, which cut the leather of his face like a knife-slash. He'd been complaining incessantly since they had set out, unwilling to be part of a vendetta strike.

'If they catch us, we'll be for the firing squad! This ain't right!'

Corbec had been firm, fully aware of how daring the mission was. 'We're in a regimental feud, Larks,' he had said simply, 'an honour thing. They killed Lonegin, Freul and Colhn. You think what they did to Feygor, and what they might be doing to the major. The commissar's asked us to avenge the blood-wrong, and I for one am happy to oblige.'

Corbec hadn't mentioned that he'd only selected Larkin because of his fine stealth abilities, nor had he made clear Gaunt's real reason for the raid: distraction, misdirection – and, like the Jantine, to promote the notion that what was really happening aboard the *Absalom* was a mindless soldier's feud.

Now, checking the long gun, Larkin seemed to relax. His only eloquence was with a firearm. If he was going to break ship-law, then best do it full-measure, with a gun in his hands; and they all knew he was the best shot in the regiment.

They edged on into the Jantine barrack area. From down one long cross-hallway came the sounds of singing and carousing, from another, the clash of shock-poles in a training vault.

'How far do we go with this?' Mkoll whispered.

Corbec shrugged. 'They killed three, wounded two. We should match that at least.'

He also had an urge to discover Rawne's fate, and rescue him if they could. But he suspected the major was already long dead.

Mkoll, the commander of the scout platoon, was the best stealther they had.

With Baru at his side, the pair melted into the hall shadows and swept ahead.

The other three waited. There seemed to be something sporadic and ill-at-ease in the distant rhythm of the ship's engines as they vibrated the deck. I hope we're not running into some fething warp-madness, Corbec mused, then lightened up as he realised that it may be Gaunt's work. He'd said he was going to distract and upset the captain.

Baru came back to them. 'We've hit lucky, really lucky,' he hissed. 'You'd better see.'

Mkoll was waiting in cover in an archway around the next bend. Ahead was a lighted hatchway.

'Infirmary,' he whispered. 'I went up close to the door. They've got Rawne in there.'

'How many Jantine?'

'Two troopers, an officer – a colonel – and someone else. Robed. I don't like the look of him at all…'

A scream suddenly cut the air, sobbing down into a whimper. The five Ghosts stiffened. It had been Rawne's voice.

Sixteen

The Navy trooper kicked Caffran's fallen body hard and then swung his shotgun round to finish him. Weapon violation sirens were sounding shrilly in the close air of the Munitorium store. The trooper pumped the loader-grip and then was smashed sideways into the packing cartons to his left by a massive fist.

Bragg lifted the crumpled form of the dazed trooper and threw him ten metres down the vault-way. He landed hard, broken.

'Brinny! Brinny boy!' Bragg called anxiously over the siren. Milo raised himself up from under the artificer. The shot had exploded the vista-plate, just missing him. 'I'm okay,' he said.

Bragg got the dazed Caffran to his feet as Brin slid the tile from the artificer slot.

'Go!' he said, 'Go!'

In under a minute, they had rejoined Dorden, helping him to push his laden trolley back out of the vault. By then, Munitorium officials and Navy troopers were rushing in through the cage.

Dorden was a master of nerve. 'Thank feth you're here!' he bellowed, his voice cracking. 'There are Jantine in there, madmen! They attacked us! Your man engaged them, but I think they got him. Quickly! Quickly now!'

Most of the detail moved past at a run, racking weapons. One stayed, eyeing the Ghost party cautiously.

'You'll have to wait. We're going to check this.'

Dorden strode forward, steely-calm now and held up his data-slate to show the man.

'Does this mean anything to you? A direct authorisation from your captain? I've got a man dying back in my infirmary! I need these supplies! Do you want a death on your hands, because by feth you're–'

The trooper waved them on, and hurried after his comrades.

'I thought this place was meant to be secure,' Dorden spat at the Munitorium official as they pushed past him towards the exit.

They slammed the cart into a lift and slumped back against the walls as it began to rise.

'Did you get it?' Dorden asked, after a few deep breaths.

Milo nodded. 'Think so.'

Caffran looked at the elderly doctor with a wide-eyed grin. '"There are Jantine in there, madmen! They attacked us! Your man engaged them, but I think they got him. Quickly!" What the feth was that all about?'

'Inspired, I'd say,' Bragg said.

'Back home, I was a doctor… and also secretary of the County Pryze Citizens' Players. My Prince Teygoth was highly regarded.'

Their relieved laughter began to fill the lift.

Seventeen

Corbec's revenge squad was about to move when the deck vox-casters started to relay the scream of a weapons violation alert. The dull choral wails echoed down the hallway and 'Alert' runes began to blink above all of the archways.

The colonel pulled his men into cover as figures strode out of the infirmary, looking around. Squads of Jantine guards came up from both sides, milling around as vox-checks tried to ascertain the nature of the incident.

Corbec saw Flense and Brochuss, the Jantine senior officers, and another man, a hugely tall and grotesque figure in shimmering, smoke-like robes who filled him with dread.

'Weapons discharge on the Munitorium deck!' a Jantine trooper with a vox-caster on his back reported. 'The Navy details are closing to contain it… Sir, the channels are alive with cross-reports. They're blaming it on the Jantine! They say we conducted a feud strike on Tanith-scum in the supply vaults!'

Flense cursed. 'Gaunt! The devil's trying to match our game!' He turned to his men. 'Brochuss! Secure the deck! Security detail with me!'

'I'll stay and finish my work,' the robed figure said in a deep, liquid tone that quite chilled Corbec. As the various men moved off to comply with orders, the robed figure stopped Flense with a hand to his shoulder. Or rather, what seemed more like a long-fingered claw than a hand, Corbec noticed with a shudder.

'This isn't good, Flense,' the figure breathed at the suddenly trembling colonel. 'Use violence against a soldier like Gaunt and you can be assured he will use it back. And you seem to have underestimated his political abilities. I fear he has outplayed you. And if he has, you should fear for yourself.'

Flense shook himself free and hurried away. 'I'll deal with it!' he snarled defensively over his shoulder. The robed figure watched him leave and then withdrew into the infirmary.

'What do we do?' Varl hissed.

'Tell me we go back now,' Larkin whispered urgently.

Another scream issued from the chamber beyond.

'What do you think?' Corbec asked.

Eighteen

Sirens wailed in the normally tranquil strategium. Grasticus shifted in his cot-throne, wanding screens to him and cursing at the information he was reading.

Gaunt and Zoren exchanged glances.

I hope this confusion is the confusion we planned, Gaunt thought.

Grasticus rose up on his elbows and bawled at the quaking Lekulanzi. 'Weapons fire on the Munitorium deck! My data says it's Jantine feuders!'

'Are any of mine hurt?' Gaunt asked, pushing forward, urgent. 'I told you the Jantine were out for blood–'

'Shut up, commissar,' the captain said with a suddenly sour look. His day had been disrupted enough. 'The reports are unconfirmed. Get down there and see to it, warrant officer!'

Lekulanzi scurried out of the chamber. Grasticus turned back to the two Imperial Guard colonels.

'This matter needs my undivided attention. I will summon you when we can speak further.'

Zoren and Gaunt nodded and backed out of the strategium smartly. Side by side they crossed the nave of the bridge, through the hubbub of bridge crew, and entered the lifts.

'Is it working?' Zoren asked as the doors closed and the choral chime sang out.

'Pray by the Throne that it is,' Gaunt said.

Nineteen

They took the infirmary in a textbook move.

The room was wide, long and low. The robed figure was bent over Rawne, who was strapped, screaming, to a gurney. A pair of Jantine troopers stood guard at the door. Corbec came in between them, ignoring them both as he dived into a roll, his shotgun raised up to fire. The robed figure turned, as if sensing the sudden intrusion. The shotgun blast blew him backwards into a stack of wheezing resuscitrex units.

The guards began to turn when Mkoll and Baru launched in on Corbec's heels and knifed them both. Corbec rolled up onto his feet, slung his shotgun by the strap and grabbed Rawne.

'Sacred Feth…' he murmured, as he saw the head wound, and the insidious pattern of scalpel cuts across the major's face, neck and stripped body. Rawne was slipping in and out of consciousness.

'Come on, Rawne, come on!' Corbec snapped, hauling the major up over his shoulder.

'We have to move now!' Mkoll bellowed, as secondary weapons violation sirens began to shrill. Corbec threw the shotgun over to him.

'Take point! We shoot our way out if we have to!'

'Colonel!' Baru yelled. Weighed down by Rawne, Corbec couldn't turn in time. The robed figure was clawing its way back onto its feet behind him. Its hood was thrown back, and they gasped to see the equine extension and bared teeth of the head. Fury boiled in the eyes of the man-monster, and violet-dark energy crackled around him.

Corbec felt the room temperature drop. Fething magic, was all he had time to think – before a shot took the man-monster's throat clean away.

Larkin stood in the doorway, the old rifle raised in his hands. 'Now we're leaving, right?' he said.

Twenty

Gaunt took the tile Milo held out for him. Then he shut the door of his quarters on the faces of the men crowded outside. Inside, Corbec, Zoren and Milo watched him carefully.

'This had better be worth all that damn effort,' Corbec said eventually, voicing what they all thought.

Gaunt nodded. The gamble had been immense. But for the Jantine's bloodthirsty and brutal methods of pursuing their intrigue, they would never have got this far. The ship was still full of commotion. Adeptus Mechanicus security details clogged every corridor, conducting barrack searches. Rumour, accusation and threat rebounded from counter-rumour, counter-accusation and promise.

Gaunt knew his hands weren't spotless in this, and he would make no attempt to hide that his men fought back against the Jantine in a feud. There would be reprimands, punishment details, rounds of questioning that would lead to nothing conclusive. But, like him, the Jantine would not take the matter beyond a simple regimental feud. Only he and those secret elements pitched against him would know precisely what had been at stake.

He slotted the tile into his artificer, and then set the crystal in the read-slot. He touched a few keys.

There was a pause.

'It isn't working,' Zoren began.

It wasn't. As far as Gaunt could tell, Milo had indeed downloaded the latest clearance ciphers via the Munitorium artificer, but still they would not open the crystal. In fact, he couldn't even open the ciphers and set them to work.

Gaunt cursed.

'What about the ring?' Milo asked.

Gaunt paused, then fished Dercius's ring from his pocket. He fitted that into the read-slot beside the one that held the crystal and activated it.

Old and too out of date to open the dedicated ciphers of the crystal, the ring was nevertheless standardised in its cryptography enough to authorise use of the downloaded codes. The vista-plate scrolled nonsense for a moment, as runic engram languages translated each other and overlaid data, transcribing and interpreting, rereading and re-setting. The crystal opened, spilling its contents up in a hololithic display which projected up off the vista-plate.

'Oh feth... what's this mean?' Corbec murmured, instantly overwhelmed by the magnitude of what he saw.

Milo and Gaunt were silent, as they read on for detail.

'Schematics,' Zoren said simply, an awed note in his voice.

Gaunt nodded. 'By the Golden Throne, I don't pretend to understand much of this, but from what I do… now I see why they were so keen to get it.'

Milo pointed to a side bar of the display. 'A chart. A location. Where is that?'

Gaunt looked and nodded again, slowly. Things now made sense. Like why Fereyd had chosen him to be the bearer of the crystal. Things had just become a great deal harder than even he had feared.

'Menazoid Epsilon,' he breathed.

A MEMORY

Khedd 1173, Sixteen Years Earlier

The Kheddite had not expected them to move in winter, but the High Lords of Terra's Imperial Guard, whose forces dwelt in seasonless ship holds plying the ever-cold of space, made no such distinction between campaigning months and resting months. They burned two clan-towns at the mouth of the River Heort, where the deep fjord inlets opened to the icy sea and the archipelago, and then moved into the glacial uplands to prosecute the nomads who had spent the summer harrying the main Imperial outposts with guerrilla strikes.

Up here, the air was clear like glass, and the sky was a deep, burnished turquoise. Their column of Chimera troop transports, ski-nosed half-traks commandeered locally, Hellhounds and Leman Russ tanks with big bulldozer blades, made fast going over the sculptural ice desert, snorting exhaust smoke and ice-spumes in their wake. The khaki body-camouflage from their last campaign in the dust-thick heatlands of Providence Lenticula had been painted over with leopard-pelt speckles of grey and blue on white. Only the silver Imperial eagles and the purple insignia of the Jantine Patricians remained on the flanks of the rushing, bouncing, roaring vehicles.

The Sentinel scouts, stalking as swift outriders to the main advance, had located a nomad heluka three kilometres away over a startlingly vivid glacier of green ice. General Aldo Dercius swung the column to a stop and sat on the turret top of his command tank, pulling off his fur mittens so he could sort through the sheaf of flimsy vista-prints the sentinels had brought back.

The heluka seemed of normal pattern – a stockade of stripped fir-stems surrounding eighteen bulbous habitat tents of tanned mahish hide supported on umbrella domes of the animals' treated rib-bones. There was a corral adjacent to the stockade, holding at least sixty anahig, the noxious, hunch-backed, flightless bird-mounts that the Kheddite favoured. Damn things – ungainly and comical in appearance, but the biped steeds could run faster than an unladen Chimera across loose snow, turn much faster, and the scales under their oily, matted down-fur could shrug off las-fire while their toothed beaks sliced a man in two like toffee.

Dercius slid his flare goggles up for a better look at the vista-prints, and winced at the glare of the open snow. Down on the prow of the Leman Russ, his crew were taking time to stretch their limbs and relax. A stove boiled water for treacly caffeine and Dercius's two adjutants/bodyguards were applying mahish fat to their snow-burned cheeks and noses out of small, round tins they had bartered from the local population. Dercius smiled to himself at this little thing. His Patricians had a reputation for aristo snobbery, but they were resourceful men – and certainly not too proud to follow the local wisdom and smear their faces with cetacean blubber to block the unforgiving winter suns.

His face caked in the pungent white grease, Adjutant Brochuss slid his tin away in the pocket of his fur-trimmed, purple-and-chrome Patrician battledress and took a wire-handled can of caffeine up to the turret.

Dercius accepted it gratefully. Brochuss, a young and power-fully built trooper, nodded down at the prints spread out on the turret canopy.

'A target? Or just another collection of *thlak* hunters?'

'I'm trying to decide,' Dercius said.

Since they had left the mouth of the Heort eight days before, they had made one early, lucky strike at a camp of nomad guerrilla Kheddite, and then wasted four afternoons assaulting helukas that had sheltered nothing more than herders and hunters in ragged family groups. Dercius was eager for another success. The Imperial Guard had strength, technology and firepower in their corner, but the nomad rebels had patriotic determination, a fanatical mindset and the harsh environment in theirs.

Dercius knew that many campaigns had faltered when the initially victorious forces had driven the natives back onto the advantage of inhospitable home turf. The last thing he wanted was a war of attrition that locked him here in a police action against elusive guerrillas for years. The Kheddite knew and used this beautiful, cruel environment well, and Dercius knew they could be hunting them for months, all the while suffering a slow erosion of strength to lightning strikes by the fast-moving foe. If they only had a base, a static HQ, a city that could be assaulted. But the Kheddite culture out here was fierce and nomadic. This was their realm, and they would be masters of it until he could catch them.

Still, he reassured himself that Warmaster Slaydo had promised him three more Guard units to help his Jantine Fourth and Eleventh in their hunt. Just a day or two more…

He looked back at the prints, and saw something. 'This is promising,' he told Brochuss, sipping his caffeine. 'It's a large settlement. Large by comparison with the herder/hunter helukas we've seen. Sixty plus animals. Those anahig are big; they look like war-mounts to me.'

'Veritable destrier!' Brochuss laughed, referring to the beautiful, sixteen-hand beasts traditionally bred in the stud-farms of the baronies on Jant Normanidus Prime.

Dercius enjoyed the joke. It was the sort of quip his old major, Gaunt, would have made; a pressure-release for the slow-building tension bubble of a difficult campaign. He rubbed the memory away. That was done, left behind on Kentaur.

'Look here,' he said, tapping a particular print. Brochuss leaned closer.

'What does that look like to you?' Dercius asked.

'The main habitat tent? Where your finger is? I don't know – a smoke flue? An airspace?'

'Maybe,' Dercius said and lifted the print so that his adjutant could get a closer look. 'There's certainly smoke issuing from it, but we all know how easy smoke is to make. That wink of light… there.'

Brochuss chuckled, nodding. 'Throne! An up-link spine. No doubt. They've got a vox-vista set in that place, with the mast extending up out of the opening. You've got sharp eyes, general.'

'That's why I'm the general, Trooper Brochuss!' Dercius snorted with ample good humour. 'So what does that give us? A larger than normal heluka, sixty head of war-mount in the pen…'

'And since when did thlak herders need an intercontinental up-link unit?' finished the adjutant.

'I think the Emperor has smiled on our fortune. Have Major Saulus circle the tanks into a crescent formation around the edge of the glacier. Bring the Hellhounds forward, and hold the troops back for final clearing. We will engulf them.'

Brochuss nodded and jumped back off the track bed of the Leman Russ, running to shout his orders.

Dercius poured the last dregs of his caffeine away over the side of the turret. It melted and stained the snow beside the tank's treads.

Just before sunset, with the first sun a frosty pink semi-circle dipping below the horizon and the second a hot apricot glow in the wispy clouds of the blackening sky, the heluka was a dark stain too.

The Kheddite had fought ferociously… as ferociously as

any fur-clad ice-soldier whose tented encampment had been pounded by tank shells and hosed by infernos unleashed from the trundling Hellhounds. Most of the dead and the debris were fused into thick curls of the rapidly refreezing ice-cover: twisted, broken, blackened shapes around which the suddenly liquid ice had abruptly solidified and set.

Some twenty or so had made it to their anahig mount and staged a countercharge along the north flank. A few of his infantry had been torn apart by the clacking beaks or churned under the heavy, three-toed feet. Dercius had pulled the troops back and sent in the tanks with their relentless dozer blades.

The sunset was lovely on Khedd. Dercius pulled his vehicle up from the glacier slope until he overlooked the ocean. It was vibrant red in the failing light, alive with the flashing bioluminescence of the micro-growth and krill which prospered in the winter seas. Every now and then, the dying light caught the slow glitter of a mahish as it surfaced its great bulk to harvest the surface. Dercius watched the flopping thick-red water for the sudden breaks of twenty-metre flukes and dorsal spines and the sonorous sub-bass creaks of deep-water voices.

The vox-caster set in the lit turret below him was alive with back-chat, but he started as he heard a signal cut through: a low, even message couched in simple Jantine combat-cant.

'Who knows that... who's broadcasting?' he murmured, dropping into the turret and adjusting the dial of the set.

He smiled at first. Slaydo's promised reinforcements were coming in. The Hyrkan Fifth and Sixth. The message was from the Hyrkan commissar, little Ibram Gaunt.

Fog lights lit the glacier crest as the armoured column of the Hyrkan hove in to view, kicking up snow-dust from their tracks as they bounced down towards the Jantine column.

It will be good to see Ibram, Dercius thought. What's it been… thirteen, fourteen years? He's grown up since I last saw him, grown up like his father. Served with the Hyrkan, made commissar.

Dercius had kept up with the long-range reports of Ibram's career. Not just an officer, as his father intended, a commissar no less. Commissar Gaunt. Well, well, well. It would be good to see the boy again.

Despite everything.

Gaunt's half-trak slewed up in the snow next to the general's Leman Russ. Dercius was descending to meet it, putting his cap on, adjusting his regimental chainsword in its decorative sheath.

He hardly recognised the man who stepped out to meet him.

Gaunt was grown. Tall, powerful, thin of face, his eyes as steady and penetrating as targeting lasers. The black uniform storm-coat and cap of an Imperial commissar suited him.

'Ibram…' Dercius said with a slow smile. 'How long has it been?'

'Years,' the commissar said flatly, face expressionless. 'Space is wide and too broad to be spanned. I have looked forward to this. For too long. I always hoped circumstance would draw us together again, face to face.'

'Ah… so did I, Ibram! It's a joy to see you.' Dercius held his arms out wide.

'Because I am, as my father raised me, a fair man, I will tell you this, Uncle Dercius,' Gaunt said, his voice curiously low. 'Four years ago on Darendara, I experienced a revelation. A series of revelations. I was given information. Some of it was nonsense, or was not then applicable. Some of it was salutary. It told me a truth. I have been waiting to encounter you ever since.'

Dercius stiffened. 'Ibram... my boy... what are you saying?'

Gaunt unsheathed his chainsword. It murmured waspishly in the cold air. 'I know what happened on Kentaur. I know that, for fear of your own career, my father died.'

Dercius's adjutant was suddenly between them. 'That's enough!' Brochuss spat. 'Back off!'

Major Tanhause and Sergeant Kleff of the Hyrkan stood ready to second Gaunt.

'You're speaking to an Imperial commissar, friend,' Gaunt said. 'Think hard about your objections.' Brochuss took a pace back, uncertainty warring with duty.

'Now I am a commissar,' Gaunt continued, addressing Dercius, 'I am empowered to deliver justice wherever I see it lacking. I am empowered to punish cowardice. I am granted the gift of total authority to judge, in the name of the Emperor, on the field of combat.'

Suddenly realising the implications behind Gaunt's words, Dercius pulled his own chainsword and flew at the commissar. Gaunt swung his own blade up to block, his grip firm.

Madness and fear filled the Jantine commander... how had the little bastard found out? Who could have known to tell him? The calm confidence, which had filled his mind since the

Khedd campaign began, washed away as fast as the dying light was dulling the ice-glare around them. Little Ibram knew. He knew! After all this time, all his care, the boy had found out! It was the one thing he always dreaded, always promised himself would never happen.

The scything chainswords struck and shrieked, throwing sparks into the cold night, grinding as the tooth belts churned and repelled each other. Broken sawteeth spun away like shrapnel. Dercius had been tutored in the duelling schools of the Jant Normanidus Military Academy. He had the ceremonial honour scars on his cheek and forearms to bear it out. A chain-blade was a different thing, of course; ten times as heavy and slow as a coup-epee, and the clash-torsion of the chewing teeth was an often random factor. But Dercius had retrained his swordsmanship in the nuances of the chainsword on admission to the Patricians. A duel, chainsword to chainsword, was rare these days, but not unheard of. The secrets were wrist strength, momentum and the calculated use of reversal in chain direction to deflect the opponent and open a space.

There was no feinting with a weapon as heavy as a chainsword. Only swing and re-address. They turned, clashed, broke, circled, clashed again. The men were calling out, others running to see. No one dared step in. From the frank determination of the officers, it was clear this was an honour bout.

Dercius hooked in low, cycling the action of his blade to a fast reversal and threw Gaunt's weapon aside with a shriek of tortured metal.

An opening. He sliced, and the sweep took Gaunt across the gut. His commissar's coat and tunic split open, and blood exploded from a massive cut across his lower belly.

Gaunt almost fell. The pain was immense, and he knew the ripped, torn wound was terrible. He had failed. Failed his honour and his father. Dercius was too big, too formidable a presence in his mind to be defeated. Uncle Dercius, the huge man, the laughing, scolding, charismatic giant who had strode into his life from time to time on Manzipor, full of tales and jokes and wonderful gifts. Dercius, who had carved toy frigates for him, told him the names of the stars, sat him on his knee and presented him with ork tooth souvenirs.

Dercius, who, with the aid of awning rods, had taught him to fence on the sundecks over the cataracts. Gaunt remembered the little twist-thrust that always left him sitting on his backside, rubbing a bruised shoulder. Deft with an épée, impossible with a chainsword.

Or perhaps not. Trailing blood and tattered clothes and flesh, Gaunt twisted, light as a child, and thrust with a weapon not designed to be thrust.

There was a look of almost unbearable surprise on Dercius's face as Gaunt's chainsword stabbed into his sternum and dug with a convulsive scream through bone, flesh, tissue and organs until it protruded from between the man's shoulder blades, meat flicking from the whirring teeth. Dercius dropped in a bloody quaking mess, his corpse vibrating with the rhythm of the still-active weapon impaling it.

Gaunt fell to his knees, clutching his belly together as warm blood spurted through the messy gut-wound. He was blacking out as Tanhause got to him.

'You are avenged, father,' Ibram Gaunt tried to say to the evening sky, before unconsciousness took him.

PART SIX

Menazoid Epsilon

One

No one wanted Epsilon. No one wanted to die.

Colonel-Commissar Gaunt recalled his own deliberations in the Glass Bay of the *Absalom* with a rueful grin. He remembered how he had prayed his Ghosts would be selected for the main offensive on the main planet, Menazoid Sigma. How things change, he laughed to himself. How he would have scoffed back then in the Glass Bay if he had been told he would deliberately choose this action.

Well, choose was perhaps too strong a word. Luck, and invisible hands, had been at work. When the *Absalom* had put in at one of the huge beachhead hexathedrals strung out like beads across the Menazoid Clasp, there had been a bewildering mass of regiments and armoured units assembling to deploy at the Menazoid target zones. Most of the regimental officers had been petitioning for the glory of advancing on Sigma, and Warmaster Macaroth's tactical counsel had been inundated with proposals and counter-proposals as to the disposition of the Imperial armies. Gaunt had thought of the way that Fereyd, the unseen Fereyd and his network of operatives, had arranged for the Vitrians to support him on the *Absalom*. With no direct means of communication, he trusted that they would observe him again and where possible facilitate his needs, tacitly understanding them to be part of the mutual scheme.

So he had sent signals to the tactical division announcing that he believed his Ghosts, with their well-recognised stealth and scout attributes, would be appropriate for the Epsilon assault.

Perhaps it was chance. Perhaps it was because no other regiment had volunteered. Perhaps it was that Fereyd and his network had noted the request and manipulated silently behind the scenes to ensure that it happened. Perhaps it was that the conspiring enemy faction, rebuffed in their attempts to extract the secrets of the crystal from him, had decided the only way to reveal the truth was to let him have his way and follow him. Perhaps he was leading them to the trophy they so desired.

It mattered little. After a week and a half of levy organisation, resupply and tactical processing at the hexathedrals, the Ghosts had been selected to participate in the assault on Menazoid Epsilon, advancing before an armoured host of forty thousand vehicles from the Lattarii Gundogs, Ketzok 17th, Samothrace 4th, 5th and 15th, Borkellid Hellhounds, Cadian Armoured 3rd and Sarpoy Mechanised Cavalry. With the Tanith First in the field would be eight Mordian and four Pragar regiments, the

Afghali Ravagers 1st and 3rd, six battalions of Oudinot Irregulars – and the Vitrian Dragoons.

The inclusion of the Vitrians gave Gaunt confidence that deployment decisions had been influenced by friendly minds.

The fact that the Jantine Patricians were also part of the first wave, and that Lord General Dravere was in overall charge of the Epsilon theatre, made him think otherwise.

How much of it was engineered by Fereyd's hand; how much by the opposing cartel? How much was sheer happenstance? Only time would tell. Time... and slaughter.

The lord general's strategists had planned out six dispersal sites for the main landing along a hundred and twenty kilometre belt of lowlands adjacent to a hill range designated Shrine Target Primaris on all field charts and signals. Four more dispersal sites were spread across a massive salt basin below Shrine Target Secundus, a line of steeple-cliffs fifteen hundred kilometres to the west, and three more were placed to assault Shrine Target Tertius on a wide oceanic peninsula two thousand kilometres to the south.

The waves of landing ships came in under cover of pre-dawn light, tinting the dark undersides of the clouds red with their burners and attitude thrusters. As the sun came up, pale and weak, the lightening sky was thick with ships... the heavy-weight troop carriers, glossy like beetles, the smaller munitions and supply lifters moving in pairs and trios, the quick, cross-cutting threads of fighter escort and ground cover. Some orbital bombardment – jagging fire-ripples of orbit-to-surface missiles and the occasional careful stamp of a massive beam weapon

– softened the empty highlands above the seething dispersal fields.

Down in the turmoil, men and machines marshalled out of black ships into the dawn light. Troops components formed columns or waiting groups, and armour units ground forward, making their own roads along the lowlands, assembling into packs and advance lines on the churned, rolling grasses. The air was thick with exhaust fumes, the growl of tank engines, the roar of ship-thrusters and the crackle of vox-chatter. Platoon strength retinues set dispersal camps, lit fires, or were seconded to help erect the blast-tents of the field hospitals and communication centres. Engineer units dug fortifications and defence baffles. Munitorium supply details broke out the crates from the material ships, and distributed assault equipment to collection parties from each assembling platoon. Amid the hue and cry, the Ministorum priesthood moved solemnly through their flock, chanting, blessing, swinging incense burners and singing unceasing hymns of valour and protection.

Gaunt came down the bow-ramp of his drop-ship into the early morning air and onto a wide mud-plain of track-chewed earth. The noise, the vibration, the petrochemical smell, was intense and fierce. Lights flashed all around, from campfires and hooded lanterns, from vehicle headlights, from the winking hazard lamps of landing ships or the flicking torch-poles of dispersal officers directing disembarking troop columns or packs of off-loading vehicles.

He looked up at the highland slopes beyond: wide, rising hills thick with dry, ochre bracken. Beyond them was the suggestion of crags and steeper summits: the Target Primaris. There, if the Vermilion-level data was honest, lay the hopes and dreams of Lord High Militant General Dravere and his lackeys – the destiny of Ibram Gaunt and his Ghosts too.

Further down the field, Devourer drop-ships slackened their metal jaws and disgorged the infantry. The Ghosts came out blinking, in platoon formation, gazing out at the rolling ochre-clad hills and the low, puffy cloud cover. Gaunt moved them up and out, under direction of the marshals, onto the rise that was their first staging post. Clearing the exhaust smog which choked the dispersal site, they got their first taste of Menazoid Epsilon. It was dry and cool, with a cutting wind and a permeating scent of honeysuckle. At first, the sweet, cold smell was pleasing and strange, but after a few breaths it became cloying and nauseating.

Gaunt signalled his disposition and quickly received the command to advance as per the sealed battle orders. The Ghosts moved forward, rising up through the bracken, leaving countless trodden trails in their wake. The growth was hip-high and fragile as ash, and the troopers were encumbered by tripping roots and wiry sedge weeds.

Gaunt led them to the crest of the hill and then turned the regiment west, as he had been ordered. Two kilometres back below them, on the busy dispersal field, burners flared and several of the massive drop-ships rose, swinging low above the hillside, shuddering the air and billowing up a storm of bracken fibres as they lifted almost impossibly into the cloudy sky.

Three kilometres distant, Gaunt could see through his scope two regiments of Mordian Iron Guard forming up as they advanced from their landing points. Another two kilometres beyond them, the Vitrian Dragoons were advancing from their first staging. The rolling hilly landscape was alive with troops, clusters of black dots marching up from the blasted acres of the dispersal site, forward through the scrub.

By mid-morning, the parallel-advancing regiments of Imperial Guard armour and infantry were pushing like fingers through the bracken and scree-marked slopes of the highlands. At the dispersal sites now left far behind, ships were still ferrying components of the vast assault down from orbit. Thruster-roar rolled like faraway thunder around the sleeve of hills.

They began to see the towers: forty-metre tall, irregular piles of jagged rock rising out of the bracken every five hundred metres or so. Gaunt quickly passed the news on to command, and heard similar reports on the vox-caster's cross-channel traffic. There were lines of these towers all across the highland landscape. They looked like they had been piled from flat slabs, wide at the base, narrowing as they rose and then wider and flat again at the top. They were all crumbling, mossy, haphazard, and in places time had tumbled some of their number over in wide spreads of broken stone, half-hidden amidst the bracken.

Gaunt wasn't sure if they were natural outcrops, their spacing and linear form seemed to suggest otherwise. He was disheartened as he remembered the singular lack of data on Epsilon that had been available at the orbital preparatory briefings.

'Possibly a shrineworld' had been the best the Intelligence cadre had had to offer. 'The surface of the planet is covered in inexplicable stone structures, arranged in lines that converge on the main areas of ruins – the targets Primaris, Secundus and Tertius.'

Gaunt sent Mkoll's scouting platoon ahead, around the breast of the hill through a line of mouldering towers and into the valley beyond. He flipped out the data-slate which he had secreted in his storm-coat pocket for two days and consulted the crystal's data.

Calling up Trooper Rafflan, he took the speaker-horn from the field-caster on his back and relayed further orders. His units would scout ahead and the Mordians, advancing in their wake, would lay behind until he signalled. It was now local noon.

Turning back to his men, Gaunt saw Major Rawne nearby, standing in a grim hunch, his lasgun hanging limply in his hands.

Gaunt had all but refused to allow Rawne to join them, but the hexathedral medics had pronounced him fit. He was a shadow of his former self since the torture by the Jantine and that mysterious robed monster which Larkin had shot. Gaunt missed the waspish, barbed attitude that had made Rawne a dangerous ally – and a good squad leader.

Feygor, his adjutant, was here too, his life owed to Dorden. Feygor was a loose cannon now, an angry man with an axe to grind. He'd railed against the Jantine in the barracks and cursed that they were sharing this expedition. Gaunt feared what might happen if the Ghosts and the Jantine crossed on Epsilon, particularly without Rawne sharp enough to keep his adjutant in line.

What will happen will happen, Gaunt decided, hearing Fereyd's counsel in his head. He checked his boltgun for luck and was about to turn and tell Milo to play up when the shivering notes of a march spilled from the chanters of the Tanith pipes and echoed across the curl of the valley.

They were here. Now they would do this.

Two

Lord General Dravere's Command Leviathan, a vast armoured, trundling fortress the size of a small city, crawled forward across the loamy soil of the lowland slope overlooking one of the main dispersal sites for the Primaris target.

At its heart, Dravere swung around in his leather command g-hammock. He was in a good mood. Thanks to his urgent requests, Warmaster Macaroth had personally instructed him to the command of the Epsilon offensive. The fool! Here lay the secret that the freak-beast Heldane had told him of on Fortis Binary. The reward. The prize that would win him everything.

Dravere had spent two days reviewing the available data on Menazoid Epsilon before the drop. Little more than a moon compared to its vast partner Sigma, it was reckoned to be a shrine world to the Dark Powers. Vast, mouldering structures of inexplicable ancient design dominated the northern uplands, arranged in patterns that could only be appreciated from high orbit. The vast bulk of the Chaos legions arrayed against them had dug in to defend their cities on the primary world, but intelligence reports had picked up hints of an unknown mass of defence established here. It was clear that, though there was no obvious wealth or value to the moon-world, the foe regarded it as significant. Why else would they have risked splitting their forces?

Dravere had heard talk of simply obliterating Epsilon from orbit, but had fiercely vetoed the Navy plan. He wanted Epsilon taken on the ground, so that they might capture and examine whatever it was the enemy held in such regard. That was the authorised explanation for this assault.

Dravere knew more. He knew that the fact the rebellious Gaunt had requested this theatre alone made it significant. Dravere readied himself. He knew how to use manpower. He had based his career upon it. He would use Gaunt now. The commissar had not given up the priceless data, so they would instead use Gaunt to lead them to it.

Dravere pulled on a lever to rotate his command hammock, speed-reading the deposition reports from the repeater plates that hung around his station. He linked in with the command globes of Marshal Sendak and Marshal Tarantine, who were overseeing the assaults on target locations Secundus and Tertius respectively. They reported their dispersal complete and their forces in advance. No contact with any enemy thus far.

The afternoon was half gone, and the first day with it. Dravere was unhappy that fighting had not yet begun at any of the three battlefronts, but he was gratified in the knowledge that he had supervised the landing of an expeditionary force of this size, divided between three targets, in less than a single day. He knew of few Imperial Guard commanders who could have done the same in treble that time.

He selected other plates and surveyed the disposition of the army under his direct command, the Primaris invasion. The infantry regiments were down and advancing strongly from the dispersal sites, and the motorised armour were disembarking from their landing craft into the lower valleys. He was pushing on three prongs to encircle the ancient mountainside structures of Shrine Target Primaris, fanning his armour out to support three infantry advances, led by the Mordian to the west, the Lattarii to the east and the Tanith to the south. So far there had been no sign of an enemy to engage. No sign at all, in fact, that there were anything other than Imperium forces alive on Epsilon.

Dravere took up a stylus and inscribed a short message on a data-slate to Colonel Flense of the Jantine. Flense would be his eyes and ears on the ground, tailing the Tanith Ghosts and standing ready to intercede. Gaunt's advance was the only one he was interested in.

Dravere coded the message in Jantine combat-cant and broadcast it to the Patricians on a stammered vox-burst. Flense would not fail him.

He sat back in his harness and allowed a smile to cross his thin lips. He knew this gambit would cost him, but he had lives enough to pay. The lives of the fifty thousand infantry under his command here on Epsilon. He considered them a down-payment on his apotheosis.

He decided to take the opportunity to rest and meditate.

The second day was dawning when he returned to his command-hammock, and overviewed the intelligence from the night. All of his units had advanced as expected until dark and then established watch-camps and stagings. At first light, they were moving again. The night had brought no sign of the foe, nor had Dravere expected such news. His staff would have roused him immediately at the first shot fired.

Chatter and industry filled the command globe beyond the circular guard rail surrounding his hammock-pit. Navy officers and Munitorium aides mixed with Guard tactical officials and members of his own staff, manning the artificers and codifiers, processing, analysing and charting movement on the huge hololithic deployment map, a three-dimensional light-shape projecting down from the domed roof.

A sudden call rang through the deck: 'Marshal Tarantine reports his Cadian and Afghali units have engaged. Heavy fighting now at Shrine Target Tertius!'

First blood, Dravere thought, at last. Red indicator runes flashed on the continental deployment map. Stains of tell tale brown and crimson shone out to delineate firefight spread and range at the Tertius location. Enemy positions flashed into life as they were assessed, appearing as aggressive little yellow stars.

He issued more orders, bringing the heavy artillery and tanks around to begin bombardment to cover Tarantine's line. Two more heavy fighting zones erupted on the map, as the Secundus push suddenly ground hard into hidden enemy emplacements. A counter-bombardment opened up from the enemy forces. More stains, more yellow stars. Dravere kept one eye fixed on the jinking signals that flagged the swift Tanith advance, with Mordian, Jantine and Vitrian columns at its heels. The Primaris assault was unopposed so far.

'It begins, lord,' a voice said to his left. Dravere looked up into the face of Imperial Tactician Wheyland. Wheyland was a grizzled, bald man with a commanding frame and piercing eyes. He wore the black and red-braid uniform of Macaroth's tactical advisors, but Dravere had known who the man really was when he first met him. A spy, a watcher, an observer, sent by Macaroth to supervise Dravere's efforts.

'Your assessment, Wheyland?' Dravere said smoothly.

The tactician scrutinised the deployment map. 'We expected fierce resistance. I anticipate they have more than this up their sleeves.'

'Nothing yet here at Primaris. We expected this to be the worst, didn't we?'

'Indeed.' Wheyland seemed oblivious to Dravere's sarcasm. 'Not yet, but it will come. If this is the shrineworld we fear it to be, their defence will be more indomitable and fanatical than we can imagine. Do not advance your forces too swiftly, lord general, or you will render them vulnerable and over-extended.'

Dravere wished he could tell the tactician exactly what he thought of his advice, but Wheyland was part of Macaroth's military aristocracy and an insult would be counter-productive. He wanted to shout: I've dispersed this invasion faster and more efficiently than any commander in the fleet and you dare advise me to slow? But he simply nodded, biting his tongue for now.

Wheyland sat on the guard rail and sighed reflectively. 'It's been a long time for us, eh, Hechtor?'

Dravere looked at him crossly. 'Long time? What do you mean?'

Wheyland smiled at him. 'The heat of combat? We were both

footsloggers once. Last action I saw was against the accursed eldar on Ondermanx, twenty years past. Now we're data-slate watchers, plate-pushers. Command is an honourable venture, but sometimes I miss the sweat and toil of combat.'

Dravere licked his lips at the delicious thought which had just come to him. 'I can use any able-bodied, willing fighting man, Wheyland. Do you want to get out there?'

Wheyland looked startled for a moment, then grinned suddenly, getting up. 'I never refuse such an opportunity. The combat technique of this much-celebrated Tanith regiment fascinates me. I'm sure the tactical counsel could incorporate many new ideas from close observation of their stealth methods. With your permission, I'd gladly join them.'

You're so damn transparent, Dravere thought sullenly. You want to see for yourself, don't you? But he also knew he couldn't argue. To deny an Imperial tactician now might risk compromising his plan. I can deal with you later, he decided.

'Would you care to deploy in the field as an observer? I could always use an eye on the ground.'

'With your permission,' Wheyland said, making to leave. 'I'll take a Chimera from the reserve and move up the line. I have a detail of bodyguards who can act as a fire-team squad. Naturally, I'll report all findings to you.'

'Naturally,' Dravere agreed humourlessly. 'I'll enter your identifier on the chart. Your battle code will be what?'

Wheyland seemed to think for a moment. 'How about my old unit call sign? Eagleshard.'

Dravere noted it and passed the details to his aide.

'Good hunting… tactician,' he said as the man left the command dome.

Three

Gaunt looked up from the inscription that Communications Officer Rafflan had made of the intercepted vox-burst.

'Mean anything to you, sir?' he asked. 'I logged it yesterday afternoon.'

Gaunt nodded. It was a message in Jantine combat-cant. Watchful of Macaroth's agencies, he had instructed Rafflan to keep his vox-cast unit open to listen for all battlefield traffic. The message was from Dravere to Flense – a direct order to shadow the Ghosts. Gaunt rubbed his chin. Slowly, the enemies were showing their hand.

He looked ahead, up the high mountain pass, choked with bracken, and its lines of slumping towers. He was tempted to send Rawne back down the slope to mine the way in advance of the Jantine at their heels, but when all was said and done, they were on the same side. Word had come that the fighting had opened at the other two target sites, heavy and bloody.

There was no telling what they would encounter up ahead in the thin altitude. He dared not drive back the units which might be the only forces to support the Tanith in a direct action.

Gaunt pulled a notepad from the pocket of his storm-coat and consulted several pages that Colonel Zoren had written. Carefully, with uncertainty, he composed a message in the Vitrian battlefield language, using the code-words Zoren had told him. Then he had Rafflan send it.

'Speaking in tongues, sir?' the vox-officer laughed, ironically using the Tanith's own war-dialect that Gaunt had made sure he had learned early on. Many of the regiments used their own languages or codes for internal messages. On the battlefield, secrecy was imperative in vox-commands, and Dravere couldn't know Gaunt had a working knowledge of Jantine combat-cant.

Gaunt called up Sergeant Blane. 'Take the seventh platoon and function as a rearguard,' he told Blane directly.

'You're expecting a hindquarters strike, then?' asked Blane, puzzled. 'Mkoll's scouts have covered the hill line. The enemy won't be sneaking round on us.'

'Not the given enemy,' Gaunt said. 'I want you watching for the Jantine who are following us up. Our code word will be "Ghostmaker". Given from me to you, or you back to me, it will indicate the Jantine have made a move. I don't want to be fighting our own… but it may come to that. When you hear the word, do not shrink from the deed. If you signal me, I will send everything back to support you. As far as I am concerned, the Jantine are as much our foe as the things that dwell up here.'

'Understood,' Blane said, looking darkly at his commander. Corbec had briefed the senior men well after Gaunt's unlocking of the crystal. They knew what was at stake, and were keeping the thought both paramount and away from their men, who had enough to concern them. Gaunt had a particular respect for the gruff, workmanlike Blane. He was as gifted and loyal an officer as Corbec, Mkoll or Lerod, but he was also dependable and solid. Almost despite himself, Gaunt found himself offering Blane his hand.

They shook. Blane realised the weight of the duty, the potentially terrible demands.

'Emperor go with you, sir,' he said, as he broke the grip and turned to retreat down the bracken slope.

'And may He watch over you,' Gaunt returned.

Nearby, Milo saw the quiet exchange. He shook spit from the chanters of his Tanith pipes and prepared to play again. This is it, he thought. The commissar expects the worst.

Sergeant Mkoll's scouts were returning from the higher ground. Gaunt joined them to hear their report.

'I think it's best if you see it yourself,' Mkoll said simply and gestured back at the heights.

Gaunt spread the fire-teams of three platoons along the width of the valley slope and then moved forward with Mkoll's scout unit. By now, all of the Ghosts had rubbed the absorbent fabric of their stealth cloaks with handfuls of ochre bracken and dusted them so that they blended into the ground cover. Gaunt smiled as Mkoll scolded the commissar's less than Tanith-like abilities, and scrupulously damped down the colour of Gaunt's cloak with a scrub of ashy bracken. Gaunt removed his cap and edged forward, trying to hang the cloak around him as deftly as the Tanith scout. Behind them, there were two thousand Ghosts on the bracken-thick mountainside, but their commanding officer could see none of them.

He reached the rise, and borrowed Mkoll's scope as they bellied down in the fern and the dust.

He hardly needed the scope. The rise they were ascending dropped away and a cliff face rose vertically ahead of them, looking like it was ten thousand metres tall. The milky-blue granite face was carved into steps like a ziggurat, a vast steepled formation of weather-worn storeys, rows of archways and slumped blocks. Gaunt knew that this was his first look at Shrine Target Primaris. Other than that, he had no idea what it was. A burial place, a temple, a dead hive? It simply smacked of evil, of the darkness. A vile corruption seeped up from every pore of the rock face, every dark alcove and pillared recess.

'I don't like the look of it,' Mkoll said flatly.

Gaunt smiled grimly and consulted his own data-slate. 'Neither do I. We don't want to approach it directly. We need to sweep around to the left and follow the valley line.' Gaunt scoped down to the left. The carved granite structure extended away beyond the curve of the vale and several of the stalking lines of towers marched up the bracken slopes to meet it, as if they were feelers spread out from the immense shrine itself. Beyond and higher, he could now see towers of blue granite in the clouds: spires, steeples and buttresses. This was just the outskirts of an ancient necropolis, a city long dead that had been raised by inhuman hands before the start of recorded time.

The honeysuckle scent in the air was becoming a stench. Vox-level chatter over the micro-bead in his ear told him that his men were starting to succumb to a vague, indefinable nausea.

'You want to go left?' Mkoll asked. 'But that's not in accord with the order of battle.'

'I know.'

'The lord general will be furious if we divert from the given advance.'

'I have my own orders,' Gaunt said, tapping his data-slate.

'And the Emperor love you for your loyalty!' Mkoll shook his head. 'Sir, we were told to assault this... this place directly.'

'And we will, Mkoll – just not here.'

Mkoll nodded. 'How far down?'

'A kilometre or two. The crystal spoke of a dome. Find it for me.'

'Gladly,' Mkoll said. 'You know that if we alter our advance it will give the Jantine dogs more reason to come for us.'

'I know,' Gaunt said. More than ever he appreciated the way his senior officers had accommodated the truth of their endeavour. They knew what was at stake and what the real dangers were.

Mkoll and Corporal Baru led the advancing Ghosts along the top of the valley, just under the crest, and past the threatening, tower-haunted steppes of the graven hillside.

Scout Trooper Thark was the first to spot it. He voxed back to the command group: a dome, a massive, bulbous dome swelling from the living rock of the cliff face, impossibly carved from granite.

Gaunt moved up to see it for himself. It was like some vast stone onion, a thousand metres in diameter, sunk into the stepped rock wall around it, the surface inscribed with billions of obscure sigils and marks.

Thark was also the first to die. A storm of autocannon rounds whipped up the slope, exploding bracken into dust, spitting up soil and punching him into four or five bloody parts. At the cue, other weapon placements in the steppe alcoves of the facing cliff opened fire, raining las-fire, bullets and curls of plasma down at the Ghosts.

The answering fire laced a spider's web of las-light, tracer lines and fire wash between the sides of the valley.

The dying began.

Four

Marshal Gohl Sendak, the so-called Ravager of Genestock Gamma, had abandoned his Command Leviathan to lead his forces from the front. He rode a Leman Russ battle tank of the Borkellid regiments, heading a fast-moving armoured phalanx that was smashing its way across the rocky escarpments below the weathered stone structures of Shrine Target Secundus.

Laying down a ceaseless barrage, they broke through two lines of crumbling curtain walls and into the lower perimeters of the shrine structure itself. Wide, rubble-strewn slopes faced them, dotted with the lines of those infernal towers. Sendak voxed to the Oudinot infantry at his tail and urged them to follow him in. Fire as heavy as he had ever known blazed down from the archways and alcoves facing them

Sendak felt a dry stinging in his nose, and snorted it away. That damn honeysuckle odour, it was beginning to get to him like it was getting to his men.

He felt a wetness heavy his moustache and wiped it. Fresh blood smeared his grey-cloth sleeve. There was more in his mouth and he spat, his ears throbbing. Looking around in the green-lit interior of the tank, he saw all the crew were suffering spontaneous nose-bleeds, or were retching and hacking blood.

There was a vibration singing in the air: low, lazy, ugly.

Sendak swung the tank's periscope around to scan the scene outside. Something was happening to the lines of towers which flanked them on either side. They were glowing, fulminating with rich curls of vivid damask energy. Mist was columnating around the old stones.

'Blood of the Emperor!' Sendak growled, his teeth and lips stained red with his own dark blood.

Outside, in the space of a human heartbeat, two things happened. The lines of towers, just ragged rows of stone spines a moment before, exploded into life and became a fence, a raging energy field forty metres tall. Lashing and fizzling lines of force whipped and crackled from tower to tower like giant, supernatural barbed wire. Each tower connected blue and white brambles of curling energy with its neighbour. Any man or machine caught in the line between towers was, in two heartbeats, burned or exploded or ripped into pieces. The rest were penned between the sudden barriers, hemmed in and unable to turn or flank.

As the energy wires ignited between the previously dormant stone stacks, something else happened on the flat tops of each tower. In puffs of pinkish, coloured gas, figures appeared on each tower platform.

Teleported into place by sciences too dark and heretical for a sane mind to understand, these squads of soldiers instantly deployed heavy weapons on tripods and laid down fire on the penned aggressors beneath them. The Chaos forces were thin, wasted beings in translucent shrouds and scowling masks made of bone. They manned tripod-mounted lascannons, meltaguns and other more arcane field weapons with hands bandaged in soiled strips of plastic. Amongst them were their corrupt commanders, quasi-mechanical Chaos Marines, Obliterators.

Sendak screamed orders, trying to turn his advance in the chaos. Two tanks to his right swung blindly round into the nearest energy fence and were obliterated, exploding in huge clouds of flame as their munitions went off. Another tank was riddled with fire from the tops of the two nearest towers.

Sendak suddenly found the enemy had heavy weapon emplacements stretching back along the tower-lines around, between and behind his entire column.

He almost admired the tactic, but the technology was beyond him, and his eyes were so clouded and swimming with the blood-pain in his sinuses he could barely think.

He grabbed the vox-caster horn and fumbled for the command channel. 'It's worse than we feared! They are luring us in and using unholy science to bracket us and cut us to pieces! Inform all assault forces! The towers are death! The towers are death!'

A cannon round punched through the turret and exploded Sendak and his gunner. The severed vox-horn clattered across the deck, still clutched by the marshal's severed hand. A second later, the tank flipped over as a frag-rocket blew out its starboard track, skirt and wheelbase. As it landed, turret-down, in the mud, it detonated from within, blowing apart the Leman Russ next to it.

Behind the decimated tanks, the Oudinot were fleeing.

But there was nowhere to flee to.

* * *

Five

Every opening in the stepped structure which rose above the Tanith Ghosts along the far side of the cliff around that gross, inscribed dome seemed to be spitting fire. Las-fire, bolter rounds, the heavier sparks of cannon fire, and other exotic bursts, odd bullets that buzzed like insects and flew slowly and lazily.

Corbec ran the line of the platoons which had reached the crest, his great rich voice bawling them into cover and return-fire stances.

There was little natural cover up here except the natural curl of the hill brow, and odd arrangements of ancient stones which poked like rotten, discoloured teeth from the bracken.

'Dash! Down! Crawl! Look!' Corbec bellowed, repeating the training chant they had first heard on the Founding Fields of lost Tanith. 'Take your sight and aim! Spraying and praying is not good enough!'

Down the crest, near Lerod's command position, Bragg opened up with the rocket launcher, swiftly followed by Melyr and several other heavy weapons troopers. Tank-busting missiles whooped across the gully into the crumbling stone facade of the tumbled structure, blowing gouts of stone and masonry out in belches of flame.

On hands and knees, Gaunt regrouped with Corbec under the lip of the hill. The barrage of shots whistled over their heads and the honeysuckle stench was augmented by the choking scent of ignited bracken.

'We have to get across!' Gaunt yelled to Corbec over the firing of ten thousand sidearms and the scream of rockets.

'Love to oblige!' returned Corbec ruefully, gesturing at the scene. Gaunt showed him the data-slate and they compared it to the edifice beyond, gingerly keeping low for fear of the whinnying shot.

'It isn't going to happen,' Corbec said. 'We'll never get inside against a frontal opposition like this!'

Gaunt knew he was right. He turned back to the slate. The data they had downloaded from the crystal was complex and in many places completely impenetrable. It had been written, or at least translated, from old code notations, and there was as much obscure about it as there was comprehensible. Some more of it made sense now – now Gaunt had the chance to compare the information with the actual location. One whole part seemed particularly clear.

'Hold things here,' he ordered Corbec curtly and rolled back from the lip, gaining his feet in the steep bracken and hurrying down the slope they had advanced up.

He found the tower quickly enough, one of the jagged, mouldering stone formations, a little way down the slope. He pulled bracken away from the base and uncovered the top of an old, decaying shaft he hoped – knew – would be there. He crouched at the mouth and gazed down into the inky depths of the drop beneath.

Gaunt tapped his micro-bead to open the line, and then ordered up personnel to withdraw to his position: Mkoll, Baru, Larkin, Bragg, Rawne, Dorden, Domor, Caffran.

They assembled quickly, eyeing the black shaft suspiciously.

'Our back door,' Gaunt told them. 'According to the old

data, this sink leads down some way and then into the cata-combs beneath the shrine structure. We'll need ropes, pins, a hammer.'

'Who'll be going in there?' Rawne asked curtly.

'All of us... me first,' Gaunt told him.

Gaunt beaded to Corbec and instructed him to marshal the main Tanith levies and sustain fire against the facade of the structure.

He stripped off his storm-coat and cloak, and slung his chains-word over his back. Mkoll had tapped plasteel rooter pins into the stonework at the top of the shaft and played a length of cable around them and down into the darkness.

Gaunt racked the slide of his bolt pistol and holstered it again. 'Let's go,' he said, wrapping the cord around his waist and slid-ing into the hole.

Mkoll grabbed his arm to stop him as Trooper Vench hurried down the slope from the combat-ridge, calling out. Gaunt slid back out of the cavity and took the data-slate from Vench as he stumbled up to them.

'Message from Sergeant Blane,' Vench gasped. 'There's a Chi-mera coming up the low pass, sending signals that it desires to join with us.'

Gaunt frowned. It made no sense. He studied the slate's transcript. 'Sergeant Blane wants to know if he should let them through,' Vench added. 'They're identifying themselves as a detail of tactical observers from the warmaster's counsel. They use the code-name "Eagleshard".'

Gaunt froze as if he had been shot. 'Sacred Feth!' he spat.

The men murmured and eyed each other. It was a pretty pass when the commissar used a Tanith oath.

'Stay here,' Gaunt told the insurgence party and unlashed the rope, heading downhill at the double. 'Tell Rafflan to signal Blane!' he yelled back at Vench. 'Let them through!'

Six

The Chimera, its hull armour matt-green and showing no other markings than the Imperial crest, rumbled up the slope from Blane's picket and slewed sidelong on a shelf of hillside, chewing bracken under its treads. Gaunt scrambled down to meet it, warier than he had ever been in his life.

The side hatch opened with a metallic clunk and three troopers leapt out, lasguns held ready. They wore combat armour in the red and black liveries of the Imperial Crusade staff, elite bodyguard troops for the officer cadre. Reflective visor masks hid their faces. A taller, heftier figure in identical battledress joined them and stood, hands on hips, surveying the scene as Gaunt approached.

The figure slid back his visor and then pulled the helmet off. Gaunt didn't recognise him… until he factored in a few years, some added muscle and the shaven head.

'Eagleshard,' Gaunt said.

'Eagleshard,' responded the figure. 'Ibram!'

Gaunt shook his old friend's hand. 'What do I call you?'

'I'm Imperial Tactician Wheyland here, but my boys are trustworthy,' the big man said, gesturing to the troopers, who now relaxed their spread. 'You can call me by the name you know.'

'Fereyd…'

'So, Ibram… bring me up to speed.'

'I can do better. I can take you to the prize.'

The stone chimney was deep and narrow. Gaunt half-climbed, half-rappelled down the flue, his toes and hands seeking purchase in the mouldering stonework. He tried to imagine what this place had been at the time of its construction; perhaps a city, a living place built into and around the cliff. This flue was probably the remains of an air-duct or ventilator, dropping down to Emperor-knew-what beneath.

Gaunt's feet found the rock floor at the base, and he straightened up, loosening the ropes so that the others could join him. It smelled of sweaty damp down here, and the tunnel he was in was low and jagged.

'Lasgun!' came a call from above. The weapon dropped down the flue and Gaunt caught it neatly, immediately igniting the lamp pack which Dorden had webbed to the top of the barrel with surgical tape. He played the light over the dirty, low walls, his finger on the trigger. Above him came the sounds of others scrambling down the ragged chimney.

It took thirty minutes for the rest to join him. They all held lasguns with webbed-on lamps, except Dorden, who was unarmed but carried a torch, and Bragg, who hefted a massive autocannon. Bragg had enjoyed the hardest descent; bulky and uncoordinated, he had struggled in the flue and begun to panic.

Larkin was moaning about death and claustrophobia, young Caffran was clearly alarmed, Dorden was sour and defeatist,

Baru was scornful of them all and Rawne was silent and surly. Gaunt smiled to himself. He had selected them well. They were all exhibiting their angst and worries up front. Nothing would linger to come out later. But between them, they encompassed the best stealth, marksmanship, firepower, medical ability and bravery the Tanith First and Only had to offer.

All of them seemed wary of the Imperial tactician and his trooper bodyguard which the commissar had suddenly decided to invite along. The troopers were tough, silent types who had scaled the chimney with professional ease. They stuck close to their leader, limpet-like, guns ready.

The party moved down the passage, stooping under outcrops and sags of rock and twisted stone. Their lamps cut obscure shadows and light from the uneven surfaces.

After two hundred careful steps and another twenty minutes, they emerged into a dripping, glistening cavern where the ancient rock walls were calcified and sheened with mineral moisture. Ahead of them, their lamps picked out an archway of perfectly fitted, dressed stone.

Gaunt raised his weapon and flicked the lamp as an indicator. 'After me,' he said.

Seven

'He wants to see you, sir,' the aide said.

Lord General Dravere didn't want to hear. He was still staring at the repeater plates which hung in front of him, showing the total, desperate carnage that had befallen Marshal Sendak's advance on Target Secundus. Even now, plates were fizzing out to blankness or growing dim and fading. He had never expected this. It was… It was not possible.

'Sir?' the aide said again.

'Can you not see this is a crisis moment, you idiot?' Dravere raged, swinging around and buffeting some of the floating plates out of his way. 'We're being murdered on the second front! I need time to counter-plan! I need the tactical staff here now!'

'I will assemble them at once,' the aide said, speaking slowly, as if he was scared of a thing far greater than the raging commander. 'However, the inquisitor insists.'

Dravere hesitated, and then released the toggle of his harness and slid out of the hammock. He didn't like fear, but fear was what now burned in his chest. He crossed the command globe to the exit shutter and turned briefly to order his second-in-command to take over and assemble the advice of the tactical staff as it came in.

'Signal whatever remains of Sendak's force to withdraw to staging ground A11-23. Alert the other forces to the danger of the towers. I want assessments and counter-strategies by the time I return.'

A brass ladder led down into the isolation sphere buried in the belly of the command globe.

Dravere entered the dimly-lit chamber. It smelled of incense and disinfectant. There was a pulse tone from the medical diagnosticators, and pale steam rose from the plastic sheeting tented over the cot in the centre of the room. Medical staff in cowled red scrubs left silently as soon as he appeared.

'You wanted to see me, Inquisitor Heldane?' Dravere began.

Heldane moved under the loose semi-transparent flaps of the tent. Dravere got a glimpse of tubes and pipes, draining fluid from the ghastly rent in the man's neck, and of the ragged wound in the side of his head, which was encased in a swaddling package of bandage, plastic wrap and metal braces.

'It is before us, my Lord Hechtor,' Heldane said, his voice a rasping whisper from vox-relays at his bedside. 'The prize is close. I sense it through my pawn.'

'What do we do?'

'We move with all stamina. Advance the Jantine. I will guide them in after Gaunt. This is no time for weakness or subtlety. We must strike.'

Eight

Death flurried down over the Tanith ranks from the stepped arches of the necropolis. A blizzard of las-shot showered down, along with the arcing stings of arcane electrical weapons. The air hummed, too, with the whine of the slower metal projectile-casters the enemy were using. Barb-like bullets, slow-moving enough to be seen, buzzed down at them like glittering hornets. Where they hit flesh, they did untold explosive damage. Corbec saw men rupture and come apart as the barbed rounds hit. Others were maimed by shrapnel as the vile shells hit stone or metal beside them and shattered.

A barbed round dug into the turf near Corbec's foxhole cover and became inert.

The colonel flicked it out with his knife-point and studied it – a bulb of dull metal with forward-pointing, overlaid leaves of razor-sharp alloy. The blackened, fused remains of a glass cartridge at the base showed its method of propulsion. Shot from simple tube-launchers, Corbec decided, the propellant igniting as the firing pin shattered the glass capsule. He turned it over in one hand, protected by the edge of his stealth cape. Evil and ingenious, the barb's leaves were scored to ease impact-shatter – either against a hard surface to produce a cloud of shrapnel, or against bone as it chewed through tissue to effect the worst wounds possible. The leaves were slightly spiralled too, suggesting that the launcher's rifling set them spinning as they fired. Corbec decided he had never seen a more savage, calculated, more grotesque instrument of death and pain.

He sighed as the firestorm raged above him. Still no word had come from the commissar's infiltration team, and only Corbec's knowledge of Gaunt's secret agenda allayed his fears at the high-risk tactic.

Corbec contacted his platoon leaders and had them edge the men forward along the facing lip, winning any inch they could. He had close on two thousand lasguns and heavier weapons raking the front of the pile, and the alcove-lined facade was shattering, slumping and collapsing under the fusillade. But the return fire was as intense as ever.

Trooper Mahan, communications officer for Corbec's own platoon command, crouched in the foxhole beside him, talking constantly into the voice-horn of his heavy vox-set, relaying and processing battle-reports from all the units. Mahan suddenly leaned back, grabbed the colonel by a cuff and dragged him close, pushing the headset against his ear.

'…are death! The towers are death!' Corbec heard.

He shot a stare at Mahan, who was encoding the information on his data-slate.

'Target Secundus is routed,' Mahan said grimly, scribing as he spoke and relaying the data in stuttered code-bursts through the handset of the vox-caster. 'Sendak is dead… Feth, it sounds like they're all dead. Dravere is signalling a total withdrawal. The towers–'

Corbec grabbed the slate and studied the scrolling text Mahan was direct-receiving from High Command. There were flickering, indistinct images captured from Sendak's last transmission. He saw the towers erupt into life, laying down their destructive fences, saw the forces of the enemy manifest on the tower tops.

Instinctively, he looked up at the towers nearest them. If it happened here, they would suffer a similar fate.

Even as he formed the thought, a ragged flurry of frenzied reports flooded the comm-lines. The towers had ignited at Target Tertius too. Marshal Tarantine had received enough warning from the Secundus advance to protect the advance of his forces, but still he was suffering heavy losses. They were generally intact, but their assault was stymied.

'Sacred Feth!' Corbec hissed, heating the air with his curse. He keyed his micro-bead to open traffic and bellowed an order.

'Any Ghosts within twenty metres of a tower! Use any and all available munitions to destroy those towers! Do it, for the love of us all!'

Answering links jabbered back at him and he had to shout to be heard. 'Now, you fething idiots!' he bawled.

Two hundred metres away, a little way down a slope in the hill, Sergeant Varl's platoon reacted fastest, turning their rocket launchers on the nearest two towers and toppling them in earthy *crumps* of dirt and flame. Folore and Lerod's platoons quickly followed suit to the left of Corbec's position. Seven or more of the towers were demolished in the near vicinity. Sergeant Curral's platoon, guarding the rear of the main defence, set to blasting towers further down the slope with their missile launchers. Stone dust and burnt bracken fibres drifted in the scorched air.

There was a report from Sergeant Hasker, whose platoon had lost all of its heavy weapon troops in the first exchange. Hasker was sending men up close to the towers in his sector to mine them with grenade strings and tube bombs.

By Corbec's side, Mahan was about to say something, but stopped short in surprise, suddenly wiping fresh blood from his upper lip. Corbec felt the hot dribble in his own nose too, and sensed the sickly tingle in the air.

'Oh—' he began.

Mahan shook his head, trying to clear it, blood streaming from his nose. Suddenly he convulsed as catastrophic static noise blasted through his headset to burst his eardrums. He winced up in pain, crying out and tearing at his ear pieces.

He rose too far. A barbed round found him as he exposed his head and shoulders over the cover, and tore everything above his waist into bloody spatters. The comms unit on his back exploded. Corbec was drenched in bloody matter and took a sidelong deflection of shrapnel in the ribs, a piece of the barbed round that had fractured on impact with Mahan's sternum.

Corbec slumped, gasping. The pain was hideous. The broken leaf of metal had gone deep between his ribs and he knew it had ruptured something inside him. Blood pooled in the bracken roots beneath him.

Fighting the agony, he looked up. The air-sting and the nosebleeds could only mean one thing – and Corbec had fought through enough theatres against Chaos to know the cursed signs.

The Primaris target had activated its towers.

Almost doubled up, clutching his side with bloodstained fingers, Corbec looked down the length of the assault line. His warning had come just in time. The Ghosts had demolished enough of the towers to break the chains. Foetid white energy billowed out of the necropolis, swirling in grasping tendrils that whipped forward to find the relay towers that were no longer there. Corbec's orders had cut the insidious counter-defences of the enemy.

Unable to link with the tower relays, the abysmal energy launched from the necropolis wavered and then boiled backwards into the city. In an instant, the enemy's own thwarted weapons did more damage to the city façade than Corbec's regiment could have managed in a month of sustained fire. Entire plateaux of stone work exploded and collapsed as the untrained energy snapped back into the dead city. Granite shards blasted outwards in choking fireballs, and sections of the edifice slipped away like collapsing ice-shelves, baring tunnelled rock faces beneath.

Down the Tanith line, Hasker's platoon had not been so lucky. Their mining efforts were only partially complete when the defence grid activated. The better part of fifty men, Dorain Hasker with them, were caught in the searing energy-fence and burned.

But Hasker had his revenge at the last, as the tower's energy set off his munitions. The whole slope shuddered at the simultaneous report. Crackling towers dissolved in sheets of flame and great explosions of earth and stone. The feedback there was far greater. The flickering, blazing fence wound back on itself as the towers collapsed, lashing back into the necropolis and scourging a new ravine out of the mountainside.

As if stunned, or mortally crippled, the enemy gunfire trailed away and died.

Corbec rolled in the belly of the foxhole, awash with his own blood, and Mahan's. He pulled a compress from his field kit and slapped it over the wound in his side, and then gulped down a handful of fat counter-pain tablets from his medical pouch with three swigs from his water flask while reciting a portion of the Litany for Merciful Healing.

More than the recommended dose, he knew. His vision swam, and then he felt a strength return as the pain dulled. His ribs and his chest throbbed, but he felt almost alive again. Alive enough to function, though at the back of his mind he knew it was no more than a bravura curtain call.

There were eight tablets left in his kit. He put them in his pocket for easy access. A week's worth of dose, and he'd use it in an hour if he had to. He would fight until pain and death clawed through the analgesic barriers and stopped him.

He hefted himself up, recovered his lasgun and keyed his micro-bead.

'Corbec to all the Ghosts of Tanith… now we advance!'

Nine

Over the vale beyond them, Colonel Draker Flense and his Patrician units saw the flicker of explosions that backlit the hills and underlit the clouds. Night was falling. The concussion of distant explosions, too loud and large for any Guard ground-based weaponry, stung the air around them.

Trooper Defraytes, Flense's vox-officer, stood to attention by him and held out the handset plate on which the assimilated data of Command flickered like an endless litany.

Flense read it, standing quite still in the dusk, amid the bracken and the soft flutter of evening moths.

The Tanith had met fierce opposition, but thanks to the warnings from the other target sites, they had broken the Chaos defence grid and blasted the opposition. Those thunderclaps still rolling off the far hills were the sounds of their victory.

'Sir?' Defraytes said, holding out his data-slate. A battle-coded relay from Dravere was forming itself across the matt screen in dull runes.

Flense took it, pressing his signet ring against the reader plate so that it would decode. The knurled face of the ring turned and stabbed a stream of light into the slate's code-socket. Magenta clearance, for his eyes only.

The message was remarkably direct and certain.

Flense allowed himself a moment to smile. He turned to his

men, all six thousand of them spread in double file swirls down the scarp.

Nearby, Major Brochuss stared at his commander under hooded lids.

Flense keyed his micro-bead.

'Warriors of Jant Normanidus Prime, the order has come. Evidence has now proved to our esteemed commander Lord General Dravere that the Colonel-Commissar Gaunt is infected with the taint of Chaos, as are his so-called Ghosts. They, and they alone, have passed through the defences of Chaos which have halted Marshal Sendak and Marshal Tarantine. They are marked with the badge of evil. Lord General Dravere has granted us the privilege of punishing them.'

There was a murmur in the ranks, and an edgy eagerness.

Flense cleared his throat. 'We will take the scarp and fall upon the Tanith from behind. No longer think of them as allies, or even human. They are stained with the foul blackness of our eternal foe. We will engage them – and we will exterminate them.'

Flense cut his link and turned to face the top of the scarp. He flicked his hand to order the advance and knew without question that they would follow.

Ten

The light died.

Gaunt tore the lamp pack off the muzzle of his lasgun and tossed it away. Dorden was at his side, handing him another.

'Eight left,' the elderly medic said, holding out a roll of

surgical tape to help Gaunt wrap the lamp in place.

Neither of them wanted to talk about the darkness down here. A Guard issue lamp-pack was meant to last six hundred hours. In less than two, they had exhausted the best part of twenty between them. It was as if the dark down in the underworld of the necropolis ate up the light. Gaunt shuddered. If this place could leach power from energetic sources like lamp packs, he dared not think what it might be doing to their human frames.

They still edged forward: first the scouts, Mkoll and Baru, silent and almost invisible in the directionless dark, then Larkin and Gaunt. Gaunt noticed that Larkin was sporting some ancient firing piece instead of his lasgun, a long-limber rifle of exotic design. He had been told this was the weapon Larkin had used to take down the Inquisitor Heldane, and so it was now his lucky weapon. There was no time to chastise the man for superstitious foolishness. Gaunt knew Larkin's mental balance hung by a thread as it was. He simply hoped that, come a firefight, the strange weapon would have a cycle rate commensurate to the lasgun.

Behind them came Rawne, Domor and Caffran, all with lamp pack equipped lasguns at the ready. Domor had his sweeper set slung on his shoulder too, if the need came to scan for mines. Dorden followed, unarmed, and then Bragg with his massive autocannon. Behind them came Fereyd, with his anonymous, still visored troops as their rearguard.

Gaunt called a halt while the scouts took fresh bearings and inspected the tunnels ahead. Fereyd moved over to him.

'Been a long time, Bram,' he said in a smooth voice that was almost a whisper.

He doesn't want the men to hear, thought Gaunt. He doesn't know how much I've told them. He doesn't even know what I know.

'Aye, a long time,' Gaunt replied, tugging the straps of his rifle sling tighter and casting a glance in the low lamplight at Fereyd's unreadable face. 'And now barely time for a greeting and we're in it again.'

'Like Pashen.'

'Like Pashen,' Gaunt nodded with a phantom smile. 'We do always seem to make things up as we go along.'

Fereyd shook his head. 'Not this time. This is too big. It makes Pashen Nine-Sixty look like a blank-round exercise. Truth is, Bram, we've been working together on this for months, had you but realised it.'

'Without direct word from you, it was hard to know anything. First I knew was Pyrites, when you volunteered me as custodian for the damn crystal.'

'You objected?'

'No,' Gaunt said, tight and mean. 'I'd never shirk from service to the Throne, not even dirty clandestine shadowplay like this. But that was quite a task you dropped in my lap.'

Fereyd smiled. 'I knew you were up to it. I needed someone I could trust. Someone there…'

'Someone who was part of the intricate web of friends and confidantes you have nurtured wherever you go?'

'Hard words, Ibram. I thought we were friends.'

'We are. You know your friends, Fereyd. You made them yourself.'

There was a silence.

'So tell me… from the beginning.' Gaunt raised a questioning eyebrow.

Fereyd shrugged. 'You know it all, don't you?'

'I've had gobbets of it, piecemeal… bits and scraps, educated guesses, intuitions. I'd like to hear it clean.'

Fereyd put down his lasgun, drew off his gloves and flexed his knuckles. The gesture made Gaunt smile. There was nothing about this man, this Tactician Wheyland, that remotely resembled the Fereyd he'd known on the city farms of Pashen Nine-Sixty, such was the spy's mastery of disguise. But now that little gesture, an idiosyncrasy even careful disguise couldn't mask. It reassured the commissar.

'It is standard Imperial practice for a warmaster to establish a covert network to observe all of his command. Macaroth is cautious, a son of the Emperor in instinct. And glory knows, he's got a lot of shadows to fear. Slaydo's choice wasn't popular. Many resent him, Dravere most of all. Power corrupts, and the temptation of power corrupts even more. Men are just men, and they are fallible. I've been part of the network assigned by Macaroth to keep watch and check on his Crusade's officers. Dravere is a proud man, Bram, he will not suffer this slight.'

'You've said as much before. Hell, I've even paraphrased you to my men.'

'You've told your men?' Fereyd asked quickly, with a sharp look.

'My officers. Just enough to make sure they are with me, just enough to give them an edge if it matters. Fact is, I've probably told them all I know, which is precious little. The prize, the Vermilion trophy… that's what has changed everything, isn't it?'

'Of course. Even with regiments loyal to him, Dravere could never hope to turn on our beloved warmaster. But if he had something else, some great advantage, something Macaroth didn't have…'

'Like a weapon.'

'Like a great, great weapon. Eight months ago, part of my network on Talsicant first got a hint that Dravere's own covert agencies had stumbled upon a rumour of some great prize. We don't know how, or where… we can only imagine the efforts and sacrifices made by his operatives to locate and recover the data. But they did. A priceless nugget of ancient, Vermilion level secrets snatched from some distant, abominable reach of space and conveyed from psyker to psyker, agent to agent, back to the Lord High Militant General. It couldn't be sent openly, of course, or Macaroth would have intercepted it. Nor was it possible to send it directly, as it was being carried out of hostile space, far from Imperial control. On the last leg of its journey, transmitted from the Nubila Reach to Pyrites, we managed to track it and intercept it, diverting it from Dravere's agents. That was when it fell into your hands.'

'And the general's minions have been desperate to retrieve it ever since.'

Fereyd nodded. 'In anticipation of its acquisition, Dravere has set great wheels in motion. He knew its import, and the location it referred to. With it now in our hands – just – we couldn't allow it to fall back into Dravere's grasp. But we were not positioned strongly or closely enough to recover it. It was decided – I decided, in fact – that our best choice was to let you run with it, in the hope that you would get to it for us before the Lord General and his coterie of allies.'

'You have terrifying faith in my abilities, Fereyd. I'm just a footslogger, a commander of infantry.'

'You know you're more than that. A loyal hero of unimpeachable character, resourceful, ruthless… one of Warmaster Slaydo's chosen few, a man on whom the limelight of fame fell full enough to make it difficult for Dravere to move against you directly.'

Gaunt laughed. 'If the attempts to kill me and my men recently weren't direct, I hate to think what direct means!'

Fereyd caught his old friend with a piercing look. 'But you did it! You made it this far! You're on top of the situation, close to the prize, just as I knew you would be! We did everything we could behind the scenes, to facilitate your positioning and give you assistance. The deployment of the Tanith in the frontline here was no accident. And I'm just thankful I was able to manipulate my own cover as part of the Tactical Counsel to get close enough to join you now.'

'Well, we're here now, right enough, and the prize is in our grasp…' Gaunt began, hefting up his rifle again and preparing to move.

'May I see the crystal, Bram? Maybe it's time I read its contents too… if we're to work together on this.'

Gaunt swung round and gazed at Fereyd in slow realisation. 'You don't know, do you?'

'Know?'

'You don't know what it is we're here risking our lives for?'

'You thought I did? Even Macaroth and his allies don't know for sure. All any of us are certain of is that it is something that could make Dravere the man to overthrow the Crusade's High Command. As far as I know, you're the only person who's decoded it. Only you know – you and the men you've chosen to share it with.'

Gaunt began to laugh. The laughter rolled along the low stone tunnel and made all the men look round in surprise.

'I'll tell you then, Fereyd, and it's as bad as you fear–'

Mkoll's hard whistle rang down the space and cut them all silent.

Gaunt spun around, raising his rifle and looked ahead into the blackness, his fresh lamp pack already dimmer. Something moved ahead of him in the darkness. A scrabbling sound.

A barbed round hummed lazily out of nowhere, missing the flinching Larkin by a whisker and exploding against the stone wall of the corridor. Domor started screaming as Caffran held him. Shrapnel had taken his eyes and his face was a mask of flowing blood.

Gaunt seared five shots off into the darkness, and heard the chatter of Bragg's autocannon starting up behind him. The party took up firing positions along the rough-hewn walls of the tunnel.

Now the endgame, Gaunt thought.

* * *

Eleven

The medics, trailing their long red scrubs like priests' robes, their faces masked by gauze, moved silently around the isolation sphere in the belly of the Leviathan. They reset diagnosticators and other gently pulsing machines, muttering low intonations of healing invocations.

Heldane knew they were the best medics in the Segmentum Pacificus fleet. Dravere had transferred a dozen of his private medical staff to Heldane when he learned of the inquisitor's injury. It mattered little, Heldane knew as a certainty. He was dying. The rifle round, fired at such close range, had destroyed his neck, left shoulder and collarbone, left cheek and throat. Without the supporting web of the medical bay and the Emperor's grace, he would already be cold.

He eased back in his long-frame cot, as far as the tubes and regulator pipes piercing his neck and chest would allow. Beyond the plastic sheeting of his sterile tent, he could see the winking, pumping mechanisms on their brass trolleys and racks that were keeping him alive. He could see the dark fluids of his own body cycling in and out of centrifuge scrubs, squirting down ridged plastic tubes supported by aluminium frames.

Every twenty seconds, a delicate silvered scorpion-form device screwed into the bones of his face bathed his open wound with a mist of disinfectant spray from its hooked tail. Soothing smoke rose from incense burners around the bed.

He looked up through the plastic veil at the ceiling of the sphere, lucidly examining the zigzag, black and white inlay of the roof-pattern. With his mind, the wonderful mind that could pace out the measures of unreal space and stay sane in the full light of the immaterium, he considered the overlaid pattern, the interlocking chevrons of ivory and obsidian. The nature of eternity lay in their pattern. He unlocked it, psychically striding beyond his ruined physicality, penetrating the abstract realms of light and dark, the governing switches on which all reality was triggered.

Light interlocked with dark. It pleased him. He knew, as he had always known, that his place lay somehow in the slivered cracks of shadow between the contrasting white and black. He entered this space between, and it embraced him. He understood, as he was sure the Emperor himself did not understand, the miraculous division between the Light of mankind and the Darkness of the foe. It was a distinction so obvious and yet so overlooked. Like any true son of the Imperium of Man, he would fight with all his soul and vigour against the blackness, but he would not do so standing in the harshness of the pure white. There was a shadow between them, a greyness, that was his to inhabit. The Emperor, and his heir Macaroth, were oblivious to the distinction and that was what made them weak. Dravere saw it, and that is why Heldane bent his entire force of will to support the lord general. What did he care if the weapon they hunted for was made by, or polluted by, Chaos? It would still work against the Darkness.

If man was to survive, he must adjust his aspect and enter the shadow. Ninety years as an inquisitor had shown Heldane that much at least. The political and governing instincts of mankind had to shift away from the stale Throne of Earth. The blackness without was too deep, too negative for such complacency.

Despite his weakness, Heldane lazily read the blunt minds of the medics around him, as a man might flick through the pages of open books. He knew they feared him, knew that some found his inhuman form repulsive. One, a medic called Guylat, dared to regard him as an animal, a beast to be treated with caution. Heldane had been happy to work on Guylat's prejudices, and from time to time he would slide into the man's mind anonymously, fire a few of the synapses he found, and send the medic racing to the latrine rooms beyond the sphere with a loose bowel or a choking desire to vomit.

Usable minds. They were Heldane's favourite tools.

He scanned out again, thumbing through blunt intelligences that frankly alarmed him with their simple limits. Two medics were talking softly by the door – out of earshot, they thought, from the patient in the bed. One supposed Heldane to be insane, such was the damage to his brain. The other concurred.

They were afraid of him. How delightful, Heldane chuckled.

He had exercised his mind enough. It was free and working. He could perform his task. He knitted his raking brow and summoned one of the medics. The medic came at once, unsure as to why he was lifting the edge of the plastic tent and approaching Heldane.

'A mirror. I require a mirror,' Heldane said through the larynx augmenters. The man nodded, swept back out of the tent, and returned in a moment with a round surgical mirror.

Heldane took hold of it with his right hand, the only limb that would still function. He dismissed the blunt with a curt thought and the medic went back to his work.

Heldane raised the mirror and looked into it, glimpsing the steepled line of his own skull, the grinning mouth, the bloody wound edges and medical instrumentation. He looked into the mirror.

Creating a pawn was not easy. It involved a complex focusing of pain and a training of response, so that the pawn-mind became as a lock shaped to fit Heldane's psychic key. The process could be done rudely with the mind, but was better effected through surgery and the exquisite use of blades.

Heldane enjoyed his work. Through the correct application of pain and the subtle adjustment of mind response, he could fashion any man into a slave, a psychic puppet through whose ears and eyes he could sense – and through whose limbs he could act.

Heldane used the mirror to summon his pawn. He focused until the face appeared in the mirror, filmy and hazed. The pawn would do his bidding. The pawn would perform. Through the pawn, he would see everything. It was as good as being there himself. As he had promised Dravere, his pawn was with Gaunt now. He sensed everything the pawn could: the wet rock, the swallowing darkness, the exchange of fire.

He could see Gaunt, without his cap and storm-coat, dressed in a short leather jacket, blasting at the foe with his lasgun.

Gaunt.

Heldane reached out and took control of his pawn, enjoyed the rich seam of hatred for Ibram Gaunt that layered through his chosen pawn's mind. That made things so much easier. Before he submitted to death, Heldane told himself, he would use his pawn to win the day. To win everything.

Twelve

Rawne threw himself flat as laser fire and barb-shells winnowed down the corridor. He raised his lasgun, hunting for a target. A flat pain, like a migraine headache, darted through his head, disturbing memories of sharp physical pain. In his mind, Rawne saw the beast, the arch-manipulator, the inquisitor, with his hooked blades and micro-surgery drills, leaning over him.

Heldane. The bastard's name had been Heldane. His blades had opened Rawne's body and unshackled his mind. Heldane's venomous, obscene mind had swept into the breach...

He shook his head and felt droplets of sweat flick away. Heldane be damned. He fired off a trio of shots into the darkness of the vault and silently thanked the mad sniper, Larkin, and his shot that had blasted Heldane apart. He had never thanked Larkin personally, of course. A man like him verbally acknowledge a peasant like Mad Larkin?

The infiltration team had all made cover, except for Baru who had lost a knee to a las-round and was fallen in the open, crawling and gasping.

Gaunt bellowed a command down the narrow tunnel and Bragg swept out of cover, thumping sizzling shots from his auto-cannon in a wide covering spread, which gave Gaunt and Mkoll time to drag Baru into shelter. Domor was still screaming, even as Caffran tried to bind his face wounds from the field kit.

Las-fire whickered along the passage around them, but Rawne

feared the barbs more. Even missing or deflecting or ricocheting, they could do more damage. He squeezed off two hopeful shots, breathless for a target. Unease coiled in his mind, a faint, stained darkness that had been there since his torture at the hands of the lean giant, Heldane. He fought it off, but it refused to go away.

Gaunt slid across to Domor, taking the shuddering man's bloody hands in his own.

'Easy, trooper! Easy, friend! It's me, the commissar... I've come all the way from Tanith with you, and I won't leave you to die!'

Domor stopped whimpering, biting on his lip. Gaunt saw that his face was an utter mess. His eyes were ruined and the flesh of his right check hung shredded and loose. Gaunt took the ribbons of bandage from Caffran and strapped the trooper's head back together, winding the tape around his eyes in a tight blindfold. He hissed to Dorden, who was just finishing field-dressing Baru's knee. The medical officer wriggled over under the sporadic fire. Gaunt had stripped Domor's sleeve away from his forearm with a jerking cut of his blade and Dorden quickly sunk a dose of painkiller into the man's bulging wrist veins.

Gaunt had seen death wounds before, and knew that Domor would not live long outside of a properly-equipped infirmary. The eye wounds were too deep, and already rusty smears of blood were seeping through the pale white bindings. Dorden shook his head sadly at Gaunt, and the commissar was glad Domor couldn't see the unspoken verdict.

'You'll make it,' Gaunt told him, 'if I have to carry you myself!'

'Leave me…' Domor moaned.

'Leave the trooper who hijacked the maglev train and led us to our victory battle on Fortis? We won a world with your help, Domor. I'd rather hack off an arm and leave that behind!'

'You're a good man,' Domor said huskily, his breathing shallow, 'for an anroth.'

Gaunt allowed himself a thin smile.

Behind him, Larkin sighted the ancient weapon he had adopted and dropped a faint figure in the darkness with a clean shot.

Fereyd's troopers, supported by Rawne and Mkoll, fired lasrounds in a pulsing rhythm that battered into the unseen foe.

Then it fell suddenly quiet.

Together with one of Fereyd's men, Mkoll, a shadow under his stealth cloak, edged forward. After a moment, he shouted back: 'Clear!'

The party moved on, Caffran supporting the weakening Domor and Dorden helping the limping Baru. At a turn in the corridor, they picked their way between the fallen foe: eight dead humans, emaciated and covered in sores, dressed in transparent plastic body gloves, their faces hidden by snarling bone masks. They were inscribed with symbols: symbols that made their minds hurt; symbols of plague and invention. Gaunt made sure that the dead were stripped of all plasma ammo packs. Rawne slung his lasgun over his shoulder and lifted one of the barb-guns – a long, lance-tube weapon with a skate-like bayonet fixed underneath. He pulled a satchel of barb-rounds off the slack arm of one of the corpses.

Gaunt didn't comment. Right now, anything they could muster to their side was an advantage.

Thirteen

The citadel had fallen silent. Smoke, some thin and pale, some boiling and black, vented from the jagged stone facade.

Breathlessly light-headed on painkillers, Colonel Colm Corbec led the first advance down into the steep, rubble-strewn ditch and up into the cliff face of buildings. Silent, almost invisible waves of Tanith warriors crept down after him, picking their way into the ruins, lasguns ready.

Corbec had not sent any signals back to Command. This advance would be as unknown as he could manage. This would be the Ghosts alone, taking what ground they could before crying for help.

They edged through stone, shattered and fused into black bubbles, crushing the ashen remains of the foe underfoot. The feedback of the fence weapons had done greater damage than Corbec could have imagined. He called up Varl's platoon and sent them forward as scouts, using double the number of sweepers.

Corbec turned suddenly, to find Milo standing next to him.

'No tunes now, I'd guess, sir,' the boy said, his Tanith pipes slung safely under his arm.

'Not yet,' Corbec smiled thinly.

'Are you all right, colonel?'

Corbec nodded, noticing for the first time there was the iron tang of blood in his mouth. He swallowed.

'I'm fine...' he said.

* * *

Fourteen

'What do you make of that, sir?' Trooper Laynem asked, passing the scope to his platoon sergeant, Blane. The seventh platoon of the Ghosts were, as per Gaunt's instructions, hanging back to guard the back slopes of the rise over which the main force were advancing. Blane knew why; the commissar had made it plain. But he hadn't found the right way to tell his men.

He squinted through the scope. Down the valley, massed formations of the Jantine Patricians were advancing up towards them, in fire-teams formed up in box-drill units. It was an attack dispersal. There could be no mistake.

Blane swung back into his bracken-edged foxhole and beckoned his comms officer, Symber. Blane's face was drawn.

'They... they look like they mean to attack us, sergeant,' Laynem said in disbelief. 'Have they got their orders scrambled?'

Blane shook his head. Gaunt had been over this and had seemed quite certain, but still Blane had fought to believe it. Guard assaulting Guard? It was... not something to even think about. He had obeyed the commissar's directive, of course – it had been so quietly passionate and direct – but he still had not understood the enormity of the command. The Jantine were going to attack them. He took the speakerhorn Symber offered.

'Ghosts of the Seventh,' he said simply, 'form into defensive file along the slope and regard the Jantine advance. If they fire upon us, it is not a mistake. It is real. Know that the commissar himself warned me of this. Do not hesitate. I count on you all.'

As if on cue, the first blistering ripple of las-fire raked up over their heads from the Jantine lines.

Blane ordered his men to hold fire. They would wait for range. He swallowed. It was hard to believe. An entire regiment of elite Jantine heavy infantry against his fifty men?

Las-fire cracked close to him. He took the speakerhorn and made Symber select the commissar's own channel.

He paused. The word hung like a cold, heavy marble in his dry mouth until he made himself say it.

'Ghostmaker,' he breathed.

Fifteen

Dank, clammy darkness dripped down around them. Gaunt moved his team along through the echoing chambers and caves of wet stone. Caffran led Domor by the hand and one of Fereyd's elite and anonymous troopers assisted the limping Baru.

The place was lifeless except for the cockroaches which swarmed all around them. At first, there had been just one or two of the black-bodied vermin bugs, then hundreds, then thousands. Larkin had taken to stamping on them but gave up when they became too numerous. Now they were everywhere. The darkness all around the infiltration team murmured and shifted with beetles, coating the walls, the floor, the roof. The insistent chattering of the insects susurrated in the gloom, a low, crackling slithering from the shifting blanket of bodies instead of distinct, individual sounds.

Shuddering, the Tanith moved on, finally leaving the mass of beetles behind and heading into galleries that were octagonal in cross section, the walls made of glass blocks fused together. The glass, its surface a dark, crazed patina where the slow passage of time had abraded it, cast back strange translucent phantoms from their failing lights; sometimes sharp reflections, sometimes wispy glows and embers.

Mkoll's sharp eyes saw shapes in the glass, indistinct relics of semi-molten bone set in the vitreous wall like flecks of grit in pearls... or the tan-flies he used to find set in hard, amber nodes of sap while scouting the nalwood forests back home.

Mkoll, a youthful-looking fifty year-old with a wiry frame and a salting of grey in his hair and beard, remembered the forests keenly for a moment. He remembered his wife, dead of canth-fever for twelve years now, and his sons who had timbered on the rivers rather than follow his profession and become woodsmen.

There was something about this place, this place he could never in all his life have imagined himself in all those years ago when his Eiloni still lived, that reminded him of the nal-forests.

Sometime after the First Founding, when the commissar had noted his background from the files and appointed him sergeant of the scouting platoon with Corbec's blessing, he had sat and talked of the nalwood to Gaunt. Commissar Gaunt had remarked to him that the unique shifting forests of Tanith had taught the Ghosts a valuable lesson in navigation. He conjectured that was what made them so sure and able when it came to reconnaissance and covert insertion.

Mkoll had never thought about it much before then, but the suggestion rang true. It had been second nature to him, an instinct thing, to find his way through the shifting trees, locating paths and tracks which came and went as the fibrous evergreens stalked the sun. It had been his life to track the cuchlain herds for pelts and horn, no matter how they used the nal to obscure themselves.

Mkoll was a hunter, utterly attuned to the facts of his environs, utterly aware of how to read solid truth from ephemerally-shifting inconsequence. Since Gaunt had first remarked upon this natural skill, a skill shared by all Tanith but distilled in him and the men of his platoon, he'd prided himself in never failing the task.

Yes, now he considered, there was something down here that reminded him very strongly of lost Tanith.

He signalled a halt. The crusade staff trooper whom Tactician Wheyland – or Fereyd, as the commissar called him – had sent forward to accompany him glanced around. Probably asking an unvoiced question, but any expression was hidden by the reflective visor of his red and black armour. Mkoll inherently mistrusted the tactician and his men. There was just something about them. He disliked any man who hid his face and even when Wheyland had revealed himself, Mkoll had found little to trust there. In his imagination he heard Eiloni tut-tutting, scolding him for being a loner, slow to trust.

He blinked the memory of his wife away. He knew he was right. These elite bodyguard troops were certainly skilled; the trooper had moved along with him as silently and assuredly as the best in his platoon. But there was just something, like there was something about this place.

Gaunt moved up to join the head of the advance.

'Mkoll?' he asked, ignoring Wheyland's trooper, who was standing stiffly to attention nearby.

'Something's wrong here,' Mkoll said. He pointed left and right with a gesture. 'The topography is, well, unreliable.'

Gaunt frowned. 'Explain?'

Mkoll shrugged. Gaunt had made him privy to the unlocked data back on the *Absalom*, and Mkoll had studied and restudied the schematics carefully. He had felt privileged to be taken that close to the commissar's private burden.

'It's all wrong, sir. We're still on the right tack, and I'll be fethed if I don't get you there – but this is different.'

'To the map I showed you?'

'Yes… And worse, to the way it was five minutes ago. The structure is static enough,' Mkoll slapped the glass-brick wall as emphasis, 'but it's like direction is altering indistinctly. Something is affecting the left and right, the up and down…'

'I've noticed nothing,' Wheyland's trooper interrupted bluntly. 'We should proceed. There is nothing wrong.'

Gaunt and Mkoll both shot him a flat look.

'Perhaps it's time I saw your map,' a voice said from behind. Tactician Wheyland had approached, smiling gently. 'And your data. We were… interrupted before.'

Gaunt felt a sudden hesitation. It was peculiar. He would trust Fereyd to the Eye of Terror and back, and he had shown the data to chosen men like Mkoll. But something was making him hold back.

'Ibram? We're in this together, aren't we?' Fereyd asked.

'Of course,' Gaunt said, pulling out the slate and drawing Fereyd aside. What in the Emperor's name was he thinking? This was Fereyd. Fereyd! Mkoll was right; there was something down here, something that was even affecting his judgement.

Mkoll stood back, waiting. He eyed the Crusade trooper at his side. 'I don't even know your name,' he said at last. 'I'm called Mkoll.'

'Cluthe, sergeant, Tactical Counsel war staff.'

They nodded to each other. Can't show me your fething face even now, Mkoll thought.

Back down the gallery, Domor was whimpering gently and Dorden was inspecting his eyes again. Larkin hunted the shadows with his gun-muzzle.

Rawne was staring into the glass blocks of the wall with a hard-set face. 'Those are bones in there,' he said. 'Feth, what manner of carnage melted bones into glass so it could be made into slabs for this place?'

'What manner and how long ago?' Dorden returned, rewinding Domor's gauze.

'Bones?' Bragg asked, looking closer at what Rawne had indicated. He shuddered. 'Feth this place for a bundle of nal-sticks!'

Behind them, Caffran hissed for quiet. He had been carrying the team's compact vox-set ever since Domor had been injured, and had plugged the wire of his micro-bead earpiece into it to monitor the traffic. The set was nothing like as powerful as the heavy vox-casters carried by platoon comm-officers like Raglon and Mkann, and its limited range was stunted further by the depth of the rock they were under. But there was a signal: inter-mittent and on a repeating automatic vox-burst. The identifier was Tanith, and the platoon series code that of the Seventh. Blane's men.

'What is it, Caff?' Larkin asked, his eyes sharp.

'Trooper Caffran?' Major Rawne questioned.

Caffran pushed past them both and hurried up the tunnel to where Gaunt stood with the Imperial tactician.

As he approached, he saw Wheyland gazing at the lit displays of Gaunt's data-slate, his eyes wide.

'This is… unbelievable!' Fereyd breathed. 'Everything we hoped for!'

Gaunt shot a sharp glance at him. 'Hoped for?'

'You know what I mean, Bram. Throne! That something like this could still exist… that it could be so close. We were right to chase this without hesitation. Dravere cannot be allowed to gain control of… of this.'

Fereyd paused, reviewing the data again, and looked back at the commissar. 'This makes all the work, all the loss, all the effort… worthwhile. To know there really was a prize here worth fighting for. This proves we're not wasting our time or jumping at ghosts – no offence to the present company.' He said this with a diplomatic smile at Caffran as the trooper edged up closer.

Watching the tactical officer, Mkoll stiffened. Was it the fething place again, screwing with his mind? Or was there something about this grand Imperial tactician that even Gaunt hadn't noticed?

'Caffran?' Gaunt said, turning to his make-do vox-officer.

Caffran handed him the foil from the field-caster that he had just printed out. 'A signal from Sergeant Blane, sir. Very indistinct, very chopped. Took me a while to get it.'

'It says "Ghostmaker", sir.'

Gaunt screwed his eyes shut for a moment.

'Bram?'

'It's nothing, Fereyd,' Gaunt said to his old friend. 'Just what I was expecting and hoped wouldn't come to pass. Dravere is making his counter-move.'

Gaunt turned to Caffran. 'Can we get a signal out?' he asked, nodding to the voxer on its canvas sling over Caffran's shoulder.

'We can try fething hard and repeatedly,' responded Caffran, and Gaunt and Mkoll both grinned. Caffran had borrowed the line from comms-officer Raglon, who had always used that retort when the channels were particularly bad.

Gaunt handed Caffran a pre-prepared message foil. A glance showed Caffran it wasn't in Tanith battle-tongue, or Imperial Guard Central Cipher either.

He couldn't read it, but he knew it was coded in Vitrian combat-cant.

Caffran fed the foil into the vox-set, let the machine read it and assemble it and then flicked the 'send' switch, marked by a glowing rune at the edge of the set's compact fascia.

'It's gone.'

'Repeat every three minutes, Caffran. And watch for an acknowledgement.'

Gaunt turned back to Fereyd. He took the data-slate map back from him smartly.

'We advance,' he told the Imperial tactician. 'Tell your men,' he nodded at the Crusade troopers, 'to follow every instruction my scout gives, without question.'

With Mkoll in the front, the raiding party moved on.

A long way behind, back down the team, Major Rawne shuddered. The image of the monster Heldane had just flickered across his mind again. He felt the seeping blackness of Heldane's touch and felt his surly consciousness wince.

Get out! His thoughts shrilled in his head. Get out!

Sixteen

It was, Sergeant Blane decided, ironic.

The defence was as epic as any hallowed story of the Guard. Fifty men gainsaying the massed assault of almost a thousand. But no one would ever know. This story, of Guard against Guard, was too unpalatable for stories. The greatest act of the Tanith First and Only would be a record hushed up and unspoken of, even by High Command.

The Jantine units, supported by light artillery and heavy weapons in the valley depths, swung up around the rise Blane's men commanded in a double curl, like the arms of a throat-torc, extending overlapping fans of las-fire in disciplined, double-burst shots. The rain of shots, nearly fifteen hundred every twenty seconds, spat over the Ghosts' heads or thumped into the sloping soil, puffing up clods of smoky dust and igniting numerous brush fires through the cloaking bracken.

Sergeant Blane watched them from cover through his scope, his flesh prickling as he saw the horribly assured way they covered the ground and made advance. The warrior-caste of Jant were heavy troops, their silver and purple combat armour made for assault, rather than speed or stealth. They were storm troopers, not skirmishers; the Tanith were the light, agile, stealthy ones. But for all that, the drilled brilliance of the Jantine was frightening. They used every ounce of skill and every stitch of cover to bring the long claw of their attack up and around to throttle the Ghosts' seventh platoon.

Blane had fought the temptation to return fire when the Jantine first addressed them. They had nothing to match the range of the Jantine heavy weapons and Blane told himself that the las-fire fusillade was as much a psychological threat as anything.

His fifty men were deployed along the ridge line in a straggled stitch of natural foxholes that the Ghosts had augmented with entrenching tools and sacking made of stealth cloaks and sleeping rolls, lashed into bags and filled with dust and soil. Blane made his command instructions clear: fix blades, set weapons to single shot, hold fire and wait for his signal.

For the first ten minutes, their line was silent as las-fire crackled up at them and the air sifted with white smoke plumes and drifting dust. Light calibre field shells fluttered down, along with a few rocket-propelled grenades, most falling way short and creating new foxholes on the slope. Blane first thought they were aiming astray until he saw the pattern. The field guns were digging cover-holes and craters in the flank of the hillside for the Jantine infantry to advance into. Already, to his west, Jantine squads had crossed from their advance and dug in to a line of fresh shell-holes a hundred metres short of the Ghosts' line. Immediately, the field guns adjusted their range and began digging the next line for advance.

Blane cursed the Jantine perfection. Commissar Gaunt had

always said there were two foes most to be feared, the utterly feral and the utterly intelligent, and of the pair, the second were the worst. The Jantine were schooled and educated men who excelled at the intricacies of war. They were justly feared. Blane had, in fact, heard stories of the Jantine Patricians even before he had entered the Guard. He could hear them singing now, the long, languid, low hymn of victory, harmonised by nearly a thousand rich male voices, beautiful, oppressive... demoralising. He shuddered.

'That damn singing,' Trooper Coline hissed beside him.

Blane agreed but said nothing. The first las-rounds were now crossing overhead and if the Jantine guns were reaching them it meant one reassuring fact: the Jantine were in range.

Blane tapped his microbead link, selecting the open command channel. He spoke in Tanith battle-cant: 'Select targets carefully. Not a wasted shot now. Fire at will.'

The Ghosts opened fire. Streams of single-shot cover fire whipped down from their hidden positions into the advancing fans of the Jantine. In the first salvo alone, Blane saw ten or more of the Jantine jerk and fall. Their rate of fire increased. The wave punctured the Jantine ranks in three dozen places and made the incoming rain of fire hesitate and stutter.

The infantry duel began: two lines of dug-in troopers answering each other volley for volley up and down a steeply angled and thickly covered slope. The very air became warm and electric-dry with the ozone stench of las-fire. It was evenly pitched, with the Tanith enjoying the greater angle of coverage and the greater protection the hill afforded. But, unlike the Jantine, they were not resupplied every minute by lines of reinforcement.

Even firing off a well-placed round every six seconds, and scoring a kill one out of four shots, Blane felt they were helpless. They could not retreat, neither could they advance in a charge to use the ground to their advantage. Defeat one way, overwhelming death the other; the Ghosts could do nothing but hold their line and fight to the last.

The Jantine had more options, but the one they decided to use amazed Blane. After a full thirty minutes of fire exchange, the Patricians charged. En masse. Close on a thousand heavy troopers, bayonets fixed to muzzle-clips, rose as one from the bracken-choked foxholes and stormed up the slope towards his platoon.

It was an astonishing decision. Blane gasped and his first thought was that madness had gripped the Jantine command. A sort of madness had, but one that would surely win the day. The fifty guns of the Ghosts had more targets then they could pick. Dozens, hundreds of Jantine never made it up the slope, their twitching thrashing or limp bodies collapsing brokenly into the ochre undergrowth. But there was no way Blane's men could cut them all down before they reached the hill line.

'Blood of the Emperor!' spat Blane as he understood the tactic: superior numbers, total loyalty and an unquenchable thirst for victory. The Jantine commander had deployed his troops as expendable, using their sheer weight to soak up the Ghosts' fire and overwhelm them.

Three hundred Jantine Patricians were dead before the charge made it into Tanith lines. Dead to the Tanith guns, the slope of the hill, the angles of death. But that still left close on seven hundred of them to meet head on in screaming waves at the ditch line of the slit-trenches.

Singing the ancient war-hymn of Jant Normanidus, the Alto Credo, Major Brochuss led the assault over the Tanith Ghosts' paltry defence line. A las-round punched through his cloth-armoured sleeve and scorched the flesh of one arm. He swung around, double-blasting the Ghost before him as teams of his soldiery came in behind him.

The Ghosts were nothing... and to tear into them like this was a joy that exorcised Brochuss's own ghosts, ghosts which had been with him one way or another since the humiliation on Khedd, and which had been further reinforced on Fortis Binary and Pyrites. Anger, battle-joy, lust, rage – they thrilled through the powerful body of the Jantine Patrician.

The tempered steel of his bayonet slashed left and right, impaling and killing. Twice he had to fire his rifle point-blank to loosen a corpse stuck on his blade.

The nobility of his upbringing made him recognise the courage and fighting skill of the spidery black-clad men they crushed in this trench. They fought to the last, and with great skill. But they were light troops, dressed in thin fabrics, utterly unmatching the physical strength and resilience of his hard-armoured Jantine. His men had the discipline of the military academies of Jant in their blood, the fierce will to win. That was what made them Patricians, what made them as feared by others of the Imperial Guard as the Guards feared the Adeptus Astartes.

If Brochuss thought of the cost, which had earned them the route to the top of the hill, it was only in terms of the victory hymns they would sing at the mass funerals. If it cost one or a thousand, victory was still victory – and a punishment victory over traitor scum like this was the most cherished of all. The Ghosts were vermin to be exterminated. Colonel Flense had been right to give the order to charge, even though he had seemed strangely pale and horrified when he had given it.

Victory was theirs.

Sergeant Blane caught the first Jantine over the lip of the ditch in the belly with his bayonet and threw him over his head as he rolled. The man screamed as he died. A second bayoneted Blane's left thigh as he followed in and the sergeant bellowed in pain, swinging his lasgun so that the blade cut open the man's throat under the armour of the helmet. Then Blane fired a single shot point-blank into the writhing man's face.

Coline shot two Jantine on the lip of the line and then fell under a hammer-blow of fixed blades. Fighting was now thick, face to face, close-quarter. Symber shot three of Coline's killers before a loose las-shot took the top of his head off and dropped his twitching body into a narrow ditch already blocked by a dozen dead.

Killing another Jantine with a combination of bayonet thrust and rifle butt swipe, Blane saw the vox-caster spin from Symber's dying grasp, and wished he had the time to grab it and send a signal to Gaunt or Corbec. But the top of the ridge was a seething mass of men, stabbing, striking, firing, dying, and there was no pace to give and no moment to spare. This was the heat of battle, white heat, hate heat, as it is often spoken of by soldiers but seldom seen.

Blane shot another Patrician dead through the chest at a range of two metres and then swung his blade around into the chin of another that lunged at him. Something hot and hard nudged him from behind. He looked down and saw the point of a Jantine bayonet pushing out through his chest, blood gouting around its steel sheen.

Snarling with glee, Major Brochuss fired his lasgun and let the shot blow the stumbling Ghost off his blade. Sergeant Blane fell on his face without a murmur.

Seventeen

It was as hot as Milo had ever known it.

The main column of the Ghosts was slowly advancing through the tumbled stones of the necropolis, and had emerged into a long valley of ancient colonnades which rose on either hand in sun-blocking shadows. The valley, a natural rift in the mountain on either side of which the primitive architects had built towering formations of alcoves, was nearly eight kilometres long, and its floor, half a kilometre wide, was treacherous with the slumped stonework and rockfalls cast down from the high structures by slow time.

The energetic feedback of the defence grid had exploded ruinously in here as well and the fallen rocks, tarry-black and primeval, had soaked it up and were now radiating it out again. It was past sixty degrees down here, and dry-hot. Sweat streaked every Tanith man as he crept forward. Their black fatigues were heavy with damp and none except the scouts still wore cloaks.

Trooper Desta, advancing alongside Milo, hawked and spat at the gritty black flank of a nearby slab and tutted as his spittle fizzled and fried into evaporated nothingness.

Milo looked up. The gash of sky above the rift sides was pale and blue, and bespoke a fair summer's day. Down here, the long shadows and rocky depth suggested a cool shelter. But the heat was overwhelming, worse than the jungle miasma of the tropical calderas on Caligula, worse than the humid reaches of Voltis, worse than anything he had ever known, even the parching hot-season of high summer at Tanith Magna.

The radiating rocks glowed in his mind, aching their way into his drying bones and sinuses. He longed for moisture. He teased himself with memories of Pyrites, where the stabbing wet-cold of the outer city reaches had seemed so painful. Would he was there now. He took out his water flask and sucked down a long slug of stale, blood-warm water.

A half-shadow fell across him. Colonel Corbec stayed his hand.

'Not so fast. We need to ration in this heat and if you take it down too fast you'll cramp and vomit. And sweat it out all the faster.'

Milo nodded, clasping his bottle. He could see how pale and drawn Corbec had become, his flesh pallid and wet in the deep shadows of the rift's belly.

But there was more. More than the others were suffering. Pain.

'You're wounded, aren't you, sir?'

Corbec glanced at Milo and shook his head.

'I'm fine and bluff, lad. Yes, fine and bluff.' Corbec laughed, but there was no strength in his voice. Milo clearly saw the puncture rip in the side of Corbec's tunic which the colonel tried to hide.

Black fabric showed little, but Milo was sure that the wet patches on Corbec's fatigues were not sweat, unlike the patches on the other men.

A cry came back down the rift from the scout units and a moment later something creaked on the wind.

Corbec howled an order and the Ghosts fanned out between the sweltering rock, rock that afforded them cover but which they dare not touch. The enemy was counter-attacking.

They came at them down the valley, some on foot, most in the air. Dozens of small, missile-shaped airships, garish and fiercely-bright in colour and adorned with the grotesque symbols of Chaos, powered down the rift towards them, propellers thumping in their diesel-smoking nacelles, their belly-slung baskets, gondolas and platforms filled with armed warriors of Chaos. The swarm of airships drifted down across the Ghosts, raking the ground with fire.

Now it was all or nothing.

Eighteen

Dravere, his face angry and hollow-eyed, pushed aside the medics in the isolation sphere and yanked apart the plastic drapes veiling Inquisitor Heldane's cot. The inquisitor gazed up at him with fathomlessly calm eyes from beneath the clamped medical support devices covering him.

'Hechtor?'

Dravere flung a data-slate on the cot. The inquisitor's one good hand carefully put down the small mirror he had been holding and took up the slate, keying the data-flow with his long-nailed thumb.

'Madness!' Dravere spat. 'The Jantine have taken the rise and exterminated Gaunt's rearguard, but Flense reports that the main Tanith unit has actually advanced into Target Primaris. What by the Throne do we do now? We're losing more men to our own than to the foe, and I still require victory here! I'll not face Macaroth for this!'

Heldane studied the slate's information. 'Other regiments are moving in. The Mordian here, the Vitrians… they're close too. Let Gaunt's Ghosts lead the assault on the Target as they have begun. Sacrifice them to open a wedge. Move the Patricians in behind to consolidate this and finish off the Ghosts. Your main forces should be ready to advance after them by then.'

Dravere took a deep breath. Tactically, the advice was sound. There was still a good opportunity to silence the Ghosts without witnesses and still effect a victory. 'What of Gaunt?'

Heldane took up his mirror again and gazed into it. 'He progresses well. My pawn is still at his side, primed to strike when I command it. Patience, Hechtor. We play games within games, and all are subservient to the intricate processes of war.'

He fell silent, resolving images in the distances of the mirror invisible to the lord general.

Dravere turned away. The inquisitor was still useful to him, but as soon as that usefulness ended he would not hesitate to remove him.

Gazing into the mirror, Heldane absently recognised the malicious thought in Dravere's blunt intellect. Dravere utterly misunderstood his place in the drama. He thought himself a leader, a manipulator, a commander. But in truth, he was nothing more than another pawn – and just as expendable.

Nineteen

Colonel Flense led the Jantine Patricians down the great outer ditch and into the outskirts of the necropolis ruins, passing through the exploded steatite fragments and blackened corpses left by Corbec's assault. Distantly, through the archways and stone channels they could hear gunfire. The Ghosts had plainly met more opposition inside.

The afternoon was lengthening, the paling sky striated with lingering bands of smoke from the fighting. Flense had six hundred and twelve men left, forty of that number so seriously injured they had been retreated to the field hospitals far back at the deployment fields. Fifty Tanith, fighting to the last, had taken over a third of his regiment. He felt bitterness so great that it all but consumed him. His hatred of Ibram Gaunt, and the rivalry with the Tanith First that it had bred, had been a burning frustration. Now when they actually had the chance to face them on the field, the Tanith skirmishers had fought above their weight and scored a huge victory, even in defeat.

He cared little now what happened. The other Ghosts could live or die. All he wanted was one thing: Gaunt. He sent a Magenta level communiqué to Dravere, expressing his simple wish.

The reply surprised and delighted him. Dravere instructed Flense to place his main force under Brochuss's direct command to continue the advance into the Target Primaris. The battle orders were to neutralise the Ghosts and then prosecute a direct assault on the enemy itself. With luck, the Tanith would be crushed between the Jantine and the forces of Chaos.

But for Flense there was a separate order. Dravere had learned from the Inquisitor Heldane that Gaunt was personally leading an insertion team into the city from below. The entry point, a shaft beneath an outcrop of stones on the hillside, was identified and a route outlined. On Dravere's personal orders, Flense was to lead a fire-team in after the commissar and destroy him.

Flense quietly conveyed the directive to Brochuss as they stood watching the men advance in three file-lines up into the vast ancient necropolis. Brochuss was swollen with pride at this command opportunity. The big man turned to face his colonel with a battle-light firing his eyes. He drew off his glove and held out his hand to Flense. The colonel removed his own gauntlet and they shook, the thumb-clasping grip of brotherhood learned in the honour schools of Jant Normanidus.

'Advance with hope, fight with luck, win with honour, Brochuss,' Flense said.

'Sheath your blade well, colonel,' his second replied.

Flense turned, pulling his glove back on and tapping his micro-bead. 'Troopers Herek, Stigand, Unjou, Avranche and Ebzan report to the colonel. Bring climbing rope.'

Flense took a lasrifle from one of the dead, blessed it silently to assuage the soul of its previous owner, and checked the ammo clips. Brochuss had two of his platoon gather spare lamp packs from the passing men. The rearguard platoon watched over Flense and his team as they made ready and descended into the shaft under the stones.

In the isolation sphere of the command globe, Heldane sensed this manoeuvre. He hadn't been inside the fool Flense's mind for long enough to turn him, but he had left his mark there, and through that psychic window he could sense and feel so much already. Above all, he could feel Flense's bitter hatred.

So, Dravere was trying a ploy of his own, playing his own man Flense into the intrigue, anxious to secure his own leverage. Aching with dull pain, Heldane knew he should be angry with the lord general. But there was no time, and he hadn't the willpower to spare for such luxuries. He would accommodate Dravere's counter-ploy, and appropriate what elements of it he could use for his own devices. For mankind, for the grand scheme at hand, he would serve and manipulate and win the Vermilion treasure hidden beneath Target Primaris. Then, and only then, he would allow himself to die.

He swallowed his pain, blanked out the soft embrace of death. The pain was useful in one sense; just as it allowed him to co-opt the minds of blunt tools, so it gave his own mind focus. He could dwell upon his own deep agony and drive it on like a psychic scalpel to slit open the reserve of his pawn and make him function more ably.

He looked at the mirror again, the life-support machines around him thumping and wheezing. He saw how his hand trembled, and killed the shake with a stab of concentration.

He saw into the small mind of his pawn again, sensed the close, cold, airless space of the tunnels he moved through, far beneath the tumbling steatite of the necropolis. He branched out with his thoughts, seeing and feeling his way into the spaces ahead of his pawn. There was warmth there, intellect, pulsing blood.

Heldane tensed, and sent a jolt of warning to his pawn: ambush ahead!

Twenty

They had reached a long, low cistern of rock, pale-blue and glassy, which branched off ahead in four directions. Oily black water trickled and pooled down the centre of the sloping floor-space.

Rawne felt himself tense and falter. He reached out a hand to support himself against the gritty wall as a stabbing pain entered his head and clung like a great arachnid, biting into the bones of his face. His vision doubled, then swirled.

It was like a warning... warning him that something ahead was...

The major screeched an inarticulate sound that made the others turn or drop in surprise. The noise had barely begun to echo back down the cistern when Wheyland was firing, raking the darkness ahead with his lasgun, bellowing deployment orders.

A volley of barbs and las-blasts spat back at them.

Gaunt dropped against a slumped rock as gunfire cracked and fizzed against the glassy walls over him. They almost walked into that! If it hadn't been for Rawne's warning and Fereyd's rapid reaction… But how had Rawne known? He was well back in the file. How could he have seen anything that Mkoll's sharp eyes, right at the front, had missed?

Fereyd was calling the shots at the moment but Gaunt didn't resent the abuse of command. He trusted his friend's tactical instinct and Fereyd was in a better position and line of sight to direct the tunnel fight. Gaunt clicked off his lamp pack to stop himself becoming a target and then swung his lasrifle up to sight and fire. Mkoll, Caffran, Baru and the tactician's troopers were sustaining fire from their own weapons, and Larkin was using his exotic rifle to cover Bragg while he moved the hefty auto-cannon up into a position to fire. Dorden cowered with Domor.

Rawne bellied forward and fitted a barbed round to his stolen weapon. He rose, fingers feeling their way around the unfamiliar trigger grip, and blasted a buzzing barb up the throat of the passage. There was a *crump* and a scream. Rawne quickly reloaded and fired again, his shot snaking like a slow, heavy bee between the darting light-jags of the other men's lasguns.

Larkin's rifle fired repeatedly with its curious clap-blast double sound. Then Bragg opened up, shuddering the entire chamber with his heavy, rapid blasts. The close air was suddenly thick with cordite smoke and spent fycelene.

'Cease fire! Cease!' Gaunt yelled with a downward snap of his hand. Silence fell.

Heartbeats pounded for ten seconds, twenty, almost a minute, and then the charge came. The enemy swarmed down into the chamber, flooding out of two of the tunnel forks ahead.

Gaunt's men waited, disciplined to know without order how long to pause. Then they opened up again: Rawne's barb-gun, Bragg's autocannon, Larkin's carbine, the lasguns of Gaunt, Fereyd, Mkoll, Baru, Caffran, and the three Crusade bodyguards. The cistern boxed the target for them. In ten seconds there were almost thirty dead foe bunched and crumpled in the narrow chamber, their bodies impeding the advance of those behind, making them easier targets.

Gaunt knelt in concealment, firing his lasgun over a steatite block with the drilled track-sight fire readdress pattern which he had trained into his men. He expected it of them and knew they expected no less in return. They were slaughtering the enemy, every carefully placed shot exploding through plastic body suits and masked visors. But there was no slowing of the tide. Gaunt began to wonder what would run out first: the flow of enemy, his team's ammo or airspace in the cistern not filled with dead flesh.

Twenty-One

They emerged from the stifling shadows of the necropolis arches and into a vast interior valley of baking heat and warmth-radiating rock. Brochuss and his men blinked in the light, eyes watering at the intense heat. The major snapped orders left and right, bringing his men up and thinning the file, extending in a wide front between the jumbled monoliths and splintered boulders. He kept as many of his soldiers in the sweeping overhanging shadows of the valley sides as he could.

Ahead, no more than two kilometres away, a great combat was taking place. Brochuss could see the las-fire flashing over and between the rocky outcrops of the valley basin, and the boiling smoke plumes of a pitched infantry battle were rising up into the pale light above the valley. He could hear laser blasts, the rasp of meltas, the occasional fizz of rockets, and knew that Colonel Corbec's despicable Ghosts had engaged ahead. There were other sounds too: the whirr of motors, the buzz of barbs, the chatter of exotic repeater cannons, and bellows and screams of men, a long, backwash of noise that ululated up and down the sound-box of the valley.

Brochuss tapped his micro-bead link. 'A tricky play, my brave boys. We come upon the Tanith from the rear to crush them. But defend against the vermin they are engaging. Kill the Ghosts so we get to face the enemy ourselves. Face them and carry back the glory of victory to the ancestral towers of Jant Prime! Normanidus excelsius!'

Six hundred voices answered in a ripple of approval, uttering the syllables of the devotional creed, and the war hymn began spontaneously, echoing like the sonorous swell of an Ecclesiarchy litany from the rock faces around and above them, as if from the polished basalt of a great cathedral.

Most of the Patricians had raised their blast-cowls because of the heat, but now they snapped the visors back down in place, covering their faces with the diamond eye-slit visages of war. Their battle hymn moved to the channels of their micro-beads, resounding in the ears of every man present.

Brochuss slid down his own blast-cowl so that the hymn swam in his earpiece and around the close, hot-metal confines of his battledress helmet. He turned to Trooper Pharant at his side and unslung his lasgun. Wordlessly, Pharant exchanged his heavy stubber and ammunition webbing for his commander's rifle. He nodded solemnly at the honour; the commander would carry his heavy weapon into combat at the head of the Patricians, the Emperor's Chosen.

Brochuss arranged the heavy webbing around his waist and shoulders with deft assistance from Pharant, settling the weighty pouches with their drum-ammo feeders against his back and thighs. Then he braced the huge stubber in his gloved fists, right hand around the trigger grip, the skeleton stock under his right armpit, his left hand holding the lateral brace so that he could sweep the barrel freely. His right thumb hit the switch that cycled the ammo-advance. The belt feed chattered fat, ugly cartridges into place and the water-cooled barrel began to steam and hiss gently.

Brochuss had advanced to the head of his phalanx when one of his rearguard voxed directly to him. 'Troop units! Inbound to our rear!'

Brochuss turned. At first he saw nothing, then he detected faint movement against the milky-blue and charred blocks of the archway curtain behind them. Soldiers were coming through in their wake. Hundreds of them, almost invisible in the treacherous side-light of the valley. The body-armour they wore was reflective and shimmering. The Vitrians.

Brochuss smiled under his blast-cowl and prepared to signal the

Vitrian commander. With the support of the Vitrian Dragoons, they could–

Las-fire erupted along the rear line of his regiment.

Colonel Zoren led his men directly down onto the exposed and straggling line of the Jantine Patricians. They were upwards of six hundred in number and the Vitrians only four hundred, but he had them on the turn.

Gaunt's message had been as per their agreement, though it was still the worst, most devastating message he had received in sixteen years as a fighting man. Their mutual enemies had shown their hands and now the success of the venture depended upon his loyalty. To Colonel-Commissar Gaunt. To the man called Fereyd, among other things. To the Emperor.

It went against all his schooling as an Imperial Guardsman, all his nature. It went against the intricate teachings of the Byhata. But still, the Byhata said there was honour in friendship, and friendship in valour. Loyalty and honour, the twinned fundamental aspects of the *Vitrian Art of War*.

Let Dravere have him shot, him and all four hundred of his men. This was not insubordination, nor was it insurrection. Gaunt had shown the colonel what was at stake. He had shown him the greater levels of loyalty and honour at stake on Menazoid Epsilon. He had been truer to the Emperor and truer to the teachings of the Byhata than Dravere could ever have been.

In a triple arrowhead formation, almost invisible in their glass armour, the Vitrian Dragoons punched into the hindquarters of Brochuss's extended advance line; a tight, dense triple wedge where the Patricians were loose and extended. The Jantine had formed a lateral file to embrace the enemy, utterly useless for countering a rearguard sweep. So it said in the Byhata: book six, segment thirty-one, page four hundred and six.

The Patricians had greater strength, but their line was convex where it should have been concave. Zoren's men tore them apart. Zoren had ordered his men to set lasweapons for maximum discharge. He hoped Colonel-Commissar Gaunt would forgive the extravagance, but the Jantine heavy troops wore notoriously thick armour.

The First Regiment of the Jantine Patricians, the so-called Emperor's Chosen, the Imperial Guard elite, was destroyed that late afternoon in the valley inside the necropolis of the Target Primaris. The noble forces of the Vitrian Dragoon's Third, years later to be decorated and celebrated as one of the foremost Guard armies, took on their superior numbers and vanquished them in a pitched battle that lasted twenty-eight minutes and relied for the most part on tactical discretion.

Major Brochuss denied the Vitrians for as long as he was able. Screaming in outrage and despair, he smashed back through his own ranks to confront the Vitrians with Pharant's massive autocannon. It was in no way the death he had foreseen for himself, nor the death of his celebrated company.

He bellowed at his men, admonishing them for dying, kicking at corpses as they fell around him in a raging despair to get them to stand up again. In the end, Brochuss was overwhelmed by a stinging wash of anger that having come so far, fought so hard, he and his Patricians would be cheated.

Cheated of everything they deserved. Cheated of glory by this inglorious end. Cheated of life by lesser, weaker men who nevertheless had the resolve to fight courageously for what they believed in.

He was amongst the last to die, as the last few shells clattered out of his ammo drums, raining into the Vitrian advance as he squeezed the trigger of the smoking, hissing stubber on full rapid. Brochuss personally killed forty-four Vitrian Dragoons in the course of the Jantine First's last stand. His autocannon was close to overheating when he was killed by a Vitrian sergeant called Zogat.

His armoured torso pulverised by Zogat's marksmanship, Brochuss toppled into the flecked mica sand of the valley floor, and his name, bearing, manner and being was utterly extinguished from the Imperial Record.

Twenty-Two

Then Baru died. The filthy barbed round smelted into the rockface behind him and ribboned him with its lethal backwash of shrapnel. He didn't even have time to scream.

From his cover, seeing the death and regretting it desperately, Gaunt slid around and set his lasgun to full auto, bombarding the torrent of foe with a vivid cascade of phosphorescent bolts. He heard Rawne scream something unintelligible.

Baru, one of his finest, as good a scout and stealther as Mkoll, pride of the Tanith. Pulling back into cover to exchange ammo clips, Gaunt glanced back at the wet ruin that had been his favoured scout. Claws of misery dug into him. For the first time since Khedd, the commissar tasted the acrid futility of war. A soldier dies, and it is the responsibility of his commander to rise above the loss and focus. But Baru: sharp, witty Baru, a favourite of the men, the clown and joker, the invisible stealther, the truest of true. Gaunt found he could not look at the corpse, at the torn mess that had once been a man he called friend and whom he trusted beyond simple trust.

Around him, and he was oblivious to it, the other Guard soldiers blasted into the ranks of the enemy. Abruptly, as if turned off like a tap, the flow of charging cultists faltered and stopped. Larkin continued to pop away with his long-snouted carbine, and Rawne sent round after round of barb-heads into the dark. Then silence, darkness, except for the fizzle of ignited clothing and the seep of blood.

Fereyd's voice lifted over them, urgent and strong, 'They're done! Advance!'

He's too eager, thought Gaunt, too eager… and I'm the commander here. He rose from cover, seeing the other troopers scrambling up to follow Fereyd. 'Hold!' he barked.

They all turned to face him, Fereyd blinking in confusion.

'We do this my way or not at all,' Gaunt said sternly, crossing to Baru's remains. He knelt over them, plucking the Tanith silver icon up and over his shirt collar, dangling it on the neck chain. In low words, echoed by Dorden, Larkin and Mkoll, he pronounced the funeral rites of the Tanith, one of the first things Milo had taught him. Rawne, Bragg and Caffran lowered their heads. Domor slumped in uneasy silence.

Gaunt stood from the corpse and tucked the chain-hooked

charm away. He looked at Fereyd. The Imperial tactician had marshalled his men in a solemn honour guard, heads steepled low, behind the Tanith.

'A good man, Bram; a true loss,' Fereyd said with import.

'You'll never know,' Gaunt said, snatching up his lasgun in a sudden turn and advancing into the thicket of enemy dead.

He turned. 'Mkoll! With me! We'll advance together!'

Mkoll hustled up to join him.

'Fereyd, have your men watch our backs,' Gaunt said.

Fereyd nodded his agreement and pulled his troopers back into the van of the advance. Now it went Gaunt and Mkoll, Bragg, Rawne and Larkin, Dorden with Domor, Caffran, Fereyd and his bodyguard.

They trod carefully over and between the fallen bodies of the foe and found the tunnel dipped steeply into a wider place. Light, like it was being emitted from the belly of a glowing insect, shone from the gloom ahead, outlining an arched doorway. They advanced, weapons ready, until they stood in its shadows.

'We're there,' Mkoll said with finality.

Gaunt slipped his data-slate out of his pocket and thought to consult his portable geo-compass, but Mkoll's instinct was far more reliable than the little purring dial. The commissar looked at the slate, winding the decoded information across the little plate with a touch of the thumb wheel.

'The map calls this the Edicule – a shrine, a resting place. It's the focus of the entire necropolis.'

'And it's where we'll find this... thing?' Mkoll asked darkly.

Gaunt nodded, and took a step into the lit archway. Beyond the crumbling black granite of the arch, a great vault stretched away, floor, walls and roof all fashioned from opalescent stone lit up by some unearthly green glow. Gaunt blinked, accustoming his eyes to the lambent sheen. Mkoll edged in behind him, then Rawne. Gaunt noticed how their breaths were steaming in the air. It was many degrees colder in the vault, the atmosphere damp and heavy. Gaunt clicked off his now redundant lamp pack.

'It looks empty,' Major Rawne said, looking about them. They all heard how small and muffled his voice sounded, distorted by the strange atmospherics of the room. Gaunt gestured at the far end wall, sixty metres away, where the thin scribing of a doorway was marked on the stone wall. A great rectangular door or doors, maybe fifteen metres high, set flush into the wall itself.

'This is the outer approach chamber. The Edicule itself is beyond those doors.'

Rawne took a pace forward, but pulled up in surprise as Sergeant Mkoll placed an arresting hand on his arm.

'Not so fast, eh?' Mkoll nodded at the floor ahead of them. 'These vaults have been teeming with the enemy, but the dust on that floor hasn't been disturbed for decades, at least. And you see the patterning in the dust?'

Both Rawne and Gaunt stooped their heads to get an angle to see what Mkoll described. Catching the light right they could see almost invisible spirals and circles in the thick dust, like droplet ripples frozen in ash.

'Your data said something about wards and prohibitions on

the entrance to the Edicule. This area hasn't been traversed in a long while, and I'd guess those patterns are imprints in the dust made by energies or force screens. Like a storm shield, maybe. We know the enemy here has some serious crap at their disposal.'

Gaunt scratched his cheek, thinking. Mkoll was right, and had been sharp-witted to remember the data notes at a moment where Gaunt was all for rushing ahead, so close was the prize. Somehow, Gaunt had expected gun emplacements, chain-fences, wire-strands – conventional wards and prohibitions. He caught Rawne's eye, and saw the resentment burning there. Gaunt had still managed to exclude the major from the details he had shared with the other officers, and Rawne remained in the dark as to the nature of this insertion, if not its importance. Gaunt had only brought him along because of his ruthless expertise in tunnel fighting.

Because, after the business on the *Absalom*, he wanted to keep Rawne where he could see him. And, of course, there was…

Gaunt blinked off the thoughts. 'Get me Domor's sweeper set. I'll sweep the room myself.'

'I'll do it, sir,' a voice said from behind them. The others had edged into the chamber behind them, with Fereyd's men watching the arch, though even they were clearly more interested in what lay ahead. Domor himself had spoken. He was standing by himself now, a little shaky but upright. Dorden's high-dose painkillers had given him a brief respite from pain and a temporary renewal of strength.

'It should be me,' Gaunt said softly, and Domor angled his

blind face slightly to direct himself at the sound of the voice.

'Oh no, sir, begging your pardon.' Domor smiled below the swathe of eye-bandage. He tapped the sweeper set slung from his shoulder. 'You know I'm the best sweeper in the unit... and it's all a matter of listening to the pulse in the headset. I don't need to see. This is my job.'

There was a long silence in which the dense air of the ancient vault seemed to buzz in their ears. Gaunt knew Domor was right about his skills, and moreover, he knew what Domor was really saying: I'm a ghost, sir, expendable.

Gaunt made his decision, not based on any notion of expendability. Here was a task Domor could do better than any of them, and if Gaunt could still make the man feel a useful part of the team, he would not crush the pride of a soldier already dying.

'Do it. Maximum coverage, maximum caution. I'll guide you by voice and we'll string a line to you so we can pull you back.'

The look on what was left of Domor's face was worth more than anything they could find beyond those doors, Gaunt thought.

Caffran stepped forward to attach a rope to Domor as Mkoll checked the test-settings on the sweeper set, and adjusted the headphones around Domor's ears.

'Gaunt, you're joking!' Fereyd snapped, pushing forward. His voice dropped to a hiss. 'Are you seriously going to waste time with this charade? This is the most important thing any of us are ever going to do! Let one of my men do the sweep! Hell, I'll do the sweep–'

'Domor is sweeper officer. He'll do it.'

'But—'

'He'll do it, Fereyd.'

Domor began his crossing, moving in a straight line across the ancient floor, one step at a time. He stopped after each footfall to retune the clicking, pulsing sweeper, listening with experience-attuned ears to every hiss and murmur of the set. Caffran played out the line behind him. After a few yards, he edged to the right, then a little further on, jinked left again. His erratic path was perfectly recorded in the dust.

'There are… cones of energy radiating from the floor at irregular intervals,' Domor whispered over the micro-bead intercom. 'Who knows what and for why, but I'm betting it wouldn't be a good idea to interrupt one.'

Time wound on, achingly slow. Domor slowly, indirectly, approached the far side of the chamber.

'Gaunt! The line! The fething line!' Dorden said abruptly, pointing.

Gaunt immediately saw what the doctor was referring to. Domor was safely negotiating the invisible obstacles, but his safety line was trailing behind him in a far more economical course between the sweeper and his team. Any moment, and its dragging weight might intersect with an unseen energy cone.

'Domor! Freeze!' Gaunt snarled into the intercom. On the far side of the vault, Domor stopped dead. 'Untie your safety line and let it drop,' the commissar instructed him. Wordless, Domor complied, fumbling blindly to undo the slip-knot Caffran had tied. It would not come free. Domor tried to gather some slack from the line to ease the knot, and in jiggling it, shook the strap of the sweeper set off his shoulder. The rope came free and dropped, but the heavy sweeper slipped down his arm and his arm spasmed to hook it on his elbow. Domor caught the set, but the motion had pulled on the cord of his headset and plucked it off. The headset clattered onto the dusty floor about a metre from his feet.

Everyone on Gaunt's side of the chamber flinched but nothing happened. Domor struggled with the set for a moment and returned it to his shoulder. 'The headset? Where did it go?' he asked over the micro-bead.

'Don't move. Stay still.' Gaunt threw his lasgun to Rawne and as quickly as he dared followed Domor's route in the dust across the chamber. He came up behind the frozen blind man, spoke low and reassuringly so as not to make Domor turn suddenly, then reached past him, crouching low, to scoop up the headset. He plugged the jack back into its socket and placed the ear-pieces back around Domor's head.

'Let's finish this,' Gaunt said.

They moved on, close together, Gaunt letting Domor set the pace and direction. It took another four minutes to reach the doorway.

Gaunt signalled back at his team and instructed them to follow the pair of them over on the path Domor had made. He noticed that Fereyd was first in line, his face set with an urgent, impatient scowl.

As they came, Gaunt turned his attention back to the door. It was visible only by its seams in the rock, a marvellously smooth piece of precision engineering. Gaunt did what the data crystal had told him he should; he placed an open palm against the right hand edge of the door and exerted gentle pressure.

Silently, the twin, fifteen metre tall blocks of stone rolled back and opened. Beyond lay a huge chamber so brightly lit and gleaming it made Gaunt close his eyes and wince.

'What? What do you see?' Domor asked by his side.

'I don't know,' Gaunt said, blinking, 'but it's the most incredible thing I've ever seen.'

The others closed in behind them, looking up in astonishment, crossing the threshold of the Edicule behind Gaunt and the eager Fereyd. Rawne was the last inside.

Twenty-Three

Inquisitor Heldane allowed himself a gentle shudder of relief. His pawn was now inside the sacred Edicule of the Menazoid necropolis, and with him went Heldane's senses and intellect. After all this time, all this effort, he was right there, channelled through blunt mortal instruments until his mind was engaging first hand with the most precious artefact in space.

The most precious, the most dangerous, the most limitless of possibilities. A means at last, with all confidence, to overthrow Macaroth and the stagnating Imperial rule he espoused. It would make Dravere warmaster, and Dravere would in turn be his instrument. All the while mankind fought the dark with light, he was doomed to eventual defeat. The grey, thought Heldane, the secret weapons of the grey, those things that the hard-liners of the Imperium were too afraid to use, the devices and possibilities that lay in the blurred moral fogs beyond the simple and the just. That is how he would lead mankind out of the dark and into true ascendancy, crushing the perverse alien menaces of the galaxy and all those loyal to the old ways alike.

Of course, if Dravere used this weapon and seized control of the Crusade, used it to push the campaign on to undreamed-of victory, then the High Lords of Terra would be bound to castigate him and declare him treasonous. But they wouldn't know until it was done; and then, in the light of those victories, how could they gainsay his decision?

Some of the orderlies in the isolation bay began to notice the irregularities registering in the inquisitor's bio-monitors and started forward to investigate. He sent them scurrying out of sight with a lash of his psyche.

Heldane took up the hand mirror again and gazed into it until his mind loosed once more and he was able to psychically dive into its reflective skin like a swimmer into a still pool.

Invisible, he surfaced amongst Gaunt's wondering team in the Edicule. He turned the eyes of his pawn to take it all in: a cylindrical chamber a thousand metres high and five hundred in diameter, the walls fibrous and knotted with pipes and flutes and tubes of silver and chromium. Brilliant white light shafted down from far above. The floor underfoot was chased with silver, richly inscribed with impossibly complex algorithmic paradoxes, a thousand to a square metre. Heldane expanded his mind in a heartbeat and read them all... solved them all.

Bounding eagerly beyond this trifle, he looked around and focused on the great structure which dominated the centre of the chamber. A machine, a vast device made of brilliant white ceramics, silver piping, chromium chambers.

A Standard Template Constructor. Intact.

The secrets of originating technology had been lost to mankind for so long. Since the Dark Ages, the Imperium, even the Adeptus Mechanicus could only manufacture things they had learned by recovering the processes of the ancient STC systems. From scraps and remnants of shattered STC systems on a thousand dead worlds, the Imperium had slowly relearned the secrets of construction, of tanks and machines and laser weapons. Every last fragment was priceless.

To find a dedicated Constructor intact was a find made once a generation, a find from which the entire Imperium benefited.

But to find one like this intact was surely without precedent. All of the speculation had been correct. Long ago, thousands of years before Chaos had overwhelmed it, Menazoid Epsilon had been an arsenal world, manufacturing the ultimate weapon known to those lost ages. The secrets of its process and purpose were contained within those million and a half algorithms etched into the wide floor.

The Men of Iron. A rumour so old it was a myth, a myth from the oldest times, before the Age of Strife, from the Dark Age of Technology, when mankind had reached a state of glory as the masters of a techno-automatic Empire, the race that had perfected the standard template construct. They created the Men of Iron, mechanical beings of power and sentience but no human soul. Heretical devices in the eyes of the Imperium. War with the self-aware Men of Iron had led to the fall of that distant Empire and, if the old, deeply arcane records Heldane had been privy to were correct, that was why the Imperium had outlawed any soulless mechanical intelligence. But as servants, implacable warriors – what could not be achieved with Men of Iron at your side?

Here, at the untouched heart of the ancient arsenal world, was the STC system to make such Men of Iron.

There was more! Heldane broadened his focus and took in the walls of the chamber for the first time. At floor level, all around, were alcoves screened by metal grilles. Behind them, as still and silent as terracotta statues guarding a royal tomb, stood phalanxes Men of Iron. Hundreds, hundreds of hundreds, ranked back in symmetrical rows into the shadows of the alcove. Each stood far taller than a man, with faces like sightless skulls of burnished steel, the sinews and arteries of their bodies formed from cable and wire encased in anatomical plate-sections of lustreless alloy. They slept, waiting the command to awaken, waiting to receive orders, waiting to ignite the great device once more and multiply their forces again.

Heldane breathed hard to quell his excitement. He wound his senses back into his pawn and surveyed the gathered men.

Gaunt gazed in solemn wonder; the Ghosts were transfixed with awe and bafflement, the Crusade staff alert and eager to investigate. Gaunt turned to Dorden and ordered him to take Domor aside and let him rest. He told the other Ghosts to stand down and relax. Then he crossed to Fereyd, who was standing before the vast STC device, his helmet dangling by its chin-strap from his hand.

'The prize, old friend,' Fereyd said, without turning.

'The prize. I hope it was worth it.'

Now Fereyd turned to look. 'Do you have any idea what this is?'

'Ever since I unlocked that crystal, you know that I have. I don't pretend to understand the technology, but I know that's an intact standard template weapons maker. And I know that's as unheard of as a well-manicured ork.'

Fereyd laughed. 'Sixty years ago on Geyluss Auspix, a rat-water world a long way from nothing in Pleigo Sutarnus, a team of Imperial scouts found an intact STC in the ruins of a pyramid city in a jungle basin. Intact. You know what it made? It was the standard template constructor for a type of steel blade, an alloy of folded steel composite that was sharper and lighter and tougher than anything we've had before. Thirty whole Chapters of the great Astartes are now using blades of the new pattern. The scouts became heroes. I believe each was given a world of his own. It was regarded as the greatest technological advance of the century, the greatest discovery, the most perfect and valuable STC recovery in living memory.'

'That made knives, Bram... knives, daggers, bayonets, swords. It made blades and it was the greatest discovery in memory. Compared to this... it's less than nothing. Take one of those wonderful new blades and face me with the weapon this thing can make.'

'I read the crystal before you did, Fereyd. I know what it can do. Men of Iron: the old myth, one of the tales of the Great Old Wars.'

Fereyd grinned. 'Then breathe in this moment, my friend. We've found the impossible here. A device to guarantee the ascendancy of man. What's a stronger, lighter, sharper, better blade when you can overrun the home world of the man wielding it with a legion of deathless warriors? This is history, you know, alive in the air around us. This makes us the greatest of men. Don't you feel it?'

Gaunt and Fereyd both turned slowly, surveying the silent ranks of metal beings waiting behind the grilles.

Gaunt hesitated. 'I feel... only horror. To have fought and killed and sacrificed just to win a device that will do more of the same a thousandfold. This isn't a prize, Fereyd. It is a curse.'

'But you came looking for it? You knew what it was.'

'I know my responsibilities, Fereyd. I dedicate my life to the service of the Imperium, and if a device like this exists then it's my duty to secure it in the name of our beloved Emperor. And you gave me the job of finding it, after all.'

Fereyd set his helmet on the silver floor and began to unlace his gloves, shaking his head. 'I love you like a brother, old friend, but sometimes you worry me. We share a discovery like this and you trot out some feeble moral line about lives? That's called hypocrisy, you know. You're a killer, slaved to the greatest killing engine in the known galaxy. That's your work, your life, to end others. To destroy. And you do it with relish. Now we find something that will do it a billion times better than you, and you start to have qualms? What is it? Professional jealousy?'

Gaunt scratched his cheek, thoughtful. 'You know me better. Don't mock me. I'm surprised at your glee. I've known the

Princeps of Imperial Titans who delight in their bloodshed, and who nevertheless regard the vast power at their disposal with caution. Give any man the power of a god, and you better hope he's got the wisdom and morals of a god to match. There's nothing feeble about my moral line. I value life. That is why I fight to protect it. I mourn every man I lose and every sacrifice I make. One life or a billion, they're all lives.'

'One life or a billion?' Fereyd echoed. 'It's just a matter of proportion, of scale. Why slog in the mud with your men for months to win a world I can take with Men of Iron… and not spill a drop of blood?'

'Not a drop? Not ours, maybe. There is no greater heresy than the thinking machines of the Iron Age. Would you unleash such a heresy again? Would you trust these… things not to turn on us as they did before? It is the oldest of laws. Mankind must never again place his fate in the hands of his creations, no matter how clever. I trust flesh and blood, not iron.'

Gaunt found himself almost hypnotised by the row of dark eye-sockets behind the grille. These things were the future? He didn't think so. The past, perhaps, a past better forgotten and denied.

How could any one wake them? How could anyone even think of making more and unleashing them against…

Against who? The enemy? Warmaster Macaroth and his retinue? This was how Dravere planned to usurp control of the Crusade? This was what it had all been about?

'You've really taken your poor orphan Ghosts into your heart, haven't you, Bram? The concern doesn't suit you.'

'Maybe I sympathise. Orphans stick with orphans.'

Fereyd walked away a few paces. 'You're not the man I knew, Ibram Gaunt. The Ghosts have softened you with their wailing and melancholy. You're blind to the truly momentous possibilities here.'

'You're not, obviously. You said "I".'

Fereyd stopped in his tracks and turned around. 'What?'

'"A world I can take without spilling a drop of blood." Your words. You would use this, wouldn't you? You'd use them.' He gestured to the sleeping iron figures.

'Better I than no one.'

'Better no one. That's why I came here. It's why I thought you had come here too, or why you'd sent me.'

Fereyd's face turned dark and ugly. 'What are you blathering about?'

'I'm here to destroy this thing so that no one can use it,' said Colonel-Commissar Ibram Gaunt.

He turned away from Fereyd's frozen face and called to Caffran and Mkoll. 'Unpack the tube charges,' he instructed. 'Put them where they count. Rawne knows demolition better than any. That's why I brought him along. Get him to supervise. And signal Corbec, or whoever's left up top. Tell them to pull out of the necropolis right now. I dare not imagine what will happen when we do this.'

In the isolation sphere, Heldane froze and clenched the mirror so tightly that it cracked. Thin blood oozed out from under his hooked thumb. He had entirely underestimated this Gaunt, this blunt fool. Such power, such scope; if only he had been given the chance to work on Gaunt and make him the pawn.

Heldane swallowed. There was no time to waste now. The prize was in his grasp. No Imperial Guard nobody would thwart him now. Discretion and subterfuge went to the winds. He lanced his mind down into the blunt skull of his pawn, urging him to act and throw off the deceit. To kill them all, before this madman Gaunt could damage the holy relic and kill the Men of Iron.

Sitting at the edge of the Edicule chamber, checking his barb-lance with his back resting against the silver wall, Rawne shuddered and blood seeped down out of his nose, thick in his mouth. He felt the touch of the bastard monster Heldane more strongly than ever now, clawing at his skull, digging in his eyes like scorpion claws. His guts churned and trembling filled his limbs.

Major Rawne stumbled to his feet, sliding a barb-round into the lance-launcher and swinging it to bear.

Twenty-Four

With the sudden reinforcement of Zoren's Vitrians, Corbec's platoons pushed the Chaos elements back into the ruins of the necropolis, slaughtering as they went. The misshapen forces of madness were in rout.

Leaning on a boulder and wheezing at the pain flooding through his ribs, Corbec thought to order up a vox-caster and signal command that the victory was theirs, but Milo was suddenly at his side, holding a foil-print out from a vox-caster.

'It's the commissar,' he said, 'We have to get clear of the Target Primaris. Well clear.'

Corbec studied the film slip. 'Feth! We spend all day getting in here…'

He waved Raglon over and pulled the speakerhorn from the caster set on the man's back.

'This is Corbec of the Tanith First and Only to all Tanith and Vitrian officers. Word from Gaunt: pull back and out! I repeat, clear the necropolis area!'

Colonel Zoren's voice floated across the speaker channel. 'Has he done it, Corbec? Has he achieved the goal?'

'He didn't say, colonel,' Corbec snapped in reply. 'We've done this much on his word, let's do the rest. Withdrawal plan five-ninety! We'll cover and support your Dragoons in a layered fall back.'

'Acknowledged.'

Replacing the horn, Corbec shuddered. The pain was almost more than he could bear and he had taken his last painkiller tab an hour before.

He returned to his men.

Twenty-Five

Bragg cried out in sudden shock, his voice dwarfed by the vastness of the Edicule. Gaunt, walking towards Dorden and Domor by the doorway, spun around in surprise, to find Fereyd and his bodyguard raising their lasrifles to bear on the Ghosts.

For a split second, as Fereyd swung his gun to aim, Gaunt locked eyes with him. He saw nothing in those deep, black irises he recognised of old. Only hate and murder.

In a heartbeat...

Gaunt flung himself down as Fereyd's first las-bolt cut through the air where his head had been.

Fereyd's elite troopers began firing, winging Bragg and scattering the other Ghosts. Dorden threw himself flat over Domor's yelling body.

Rawne sighted and fired the barb-lance.

The buzzing, horribly slow round crossed the bright space of the Edicule and hit Fereyd's face on the bridge of the nose. Everything of Imperial Tactician Wheyland above the sternum explosively evaporated in a mist of blood and bone chips.

Larkin howled as he fell, shot through the forearm by a las-round from one of the elite troopers flanking the tactician.

Caffran and Mkoll, both sprawling, whipped around to return fire with their lasguns, toppling one of the bodyguards with a double hit neither could truly claim.

Gaunt rolled as he dived, pulling out his laspistol and bellowing curses as he swung and fired. Another of Fereyd's troopers fell, blasted backwards by a trio of shots to his chest. He jerked back, arms and legs extended, and died.

Gaunt squeezed the trigger again, but his lasgun just retched and fizzed. The energy draining effect of the catacombs, which had sapped their lamp packs, had wasted ammo charges too. His weapon was spent.

The remaining bodyguard lurched forward to blast Gaunt,

helpless on the floor – and dropped with a laser-blasted hole burned clean through his skull. His body smashed back hard against the side of the STC machine and slid down, leaving a streak of blood down the chased silver facing. Gaunt scrambled around to look.

Clutching the bawling Domor to him, Dorden sat half-raised with Domor's laspistol in his hand.

'Needs must,' the doctor said quietly, suddenly tossing the weapon aside like it was an insect which had stung him.

'Great shot, doc,' Larkin said, getting up, clutching his seared arm.

'Only said I wouldn't shoot, not that I couldn't,' Dorden said.

The Ghosts got back to their feet. Dorden hurried to treat the wounds Bragg and Larkin had received.

'What's that sound?' Domor asked sharply. They all froze.

Gaunt looked at the great machine. Amber lights were flicking to life on a panel on its flank. In death, the last Crusader had been blown back against the main activation grid. Old technologies were grinding into life. Smoke, steam perhaps, vented from cowlings near the floor. Processes moved and turned and murmured in the device.

There was another noise too. A shuffling.

Gaunt turned slowly. Behind the dark grilles in the alcoves, metal limbs were beginning to flex and uncurl. As he watched, eyes lit up in dead sockets. Blue. Their light was blue, cold, eternal. Somehow, it was the most appalling colour Gaunt had ever seen. They were waking. As their creator awoke, they awoke too.

Gaunt stared at them for a long, breathless moment, his heart pounding. He looked at them until he had lost count of the igniting blue eyes. Some began to jerk forward and slam against the grilles, rattling and shaking them. Metal hands clawed at metal bars. There were voices now too. Chattering, just at the edge of hearing. Codes and protocols and streams of binary numbers. The Men of Iron hummed as they woke.

Gaunt looked back at the STC. 'Rawne!'

'Sir?'

'Destroy it! Now!'

Rawne looked at him, wiping the blood from his lip.

'With respect, colonel-commissar… is this right? I mean – this thing could change the course of everything.'

Gaunt turned to look at Major Rawne, his eyes fiercely dark, his brow furrowed. 'Do you want to see another world die, Rawne?'

The major shook his head.

'Neither do I. This is the right thing to do. I… I have my reasons. And are you blind? Do you want to greet these sleepers as they awake?'

Rawne looked round. The cold blue stares seemed to stab into him too. He shuddered.

'I'm on it!' he said with sudden decisiveness and moved off, calling to Mkoll and Caffran to bring up the explosives.

Gaunt yelled after him. 'These things are heresies, Rawne! Foul heresies! And if that wasn't enough, they've been sleeping here on a Chaos-polluted world for thousands of years! Do any of us really want to find out how that's altered their thinking?'

'Feth!' Dorden said, from nearby. 'You mean this whole thing could be corrupted?'

'You'd have to be the blindest fool in creation to want to find out, wouldn't you?' Gaunt replied.

He stared down at the remains of his friend Fereyd. 'It wasn't me who changed, was it?' he murmured.

Twenty-Six

Heldane was totally unprepared for the death of his pawn. It had been such a victory to identify and capture Macaroth's little spy, and then such a privilege to work on him. It had taken a long time to turn Fereyd, a long time and a lot of painful cutting. But the conceit had been so delicious: to take the greatest of the warmaster's agents and turn him into a tool. Heldane had learned so much more through Fereyd than he would have through a lesser being. Duplicity, deceit, motive. To use one of the men the warmaster had been channelling to undermine him? It had been beautiful, perfect, daring.

In his final moments, Heldane wished he could have had time to finish with Rawne. *There* had been a likely mind, however blunt. But the Ghosts Corbec and Larkin had cheated him of that, and left Rawne merely aware of his influence rather than controlled by it.

It mattered little. Heldane had miscalculated. Impending death had slackened his judgement. He had put too much of himself into his pawn. The backlash when the pawn died was too much. He should have shielded his mind to the possible onrush of death-trauma. He had not.

Fereyd had suffered the most painful, hideous death imaginable. All of it crackled down the psychic link to Heldane. He felt every moment of Fereyd's death. In it, he felt his own.

Heldane spasmed, burst asunder. Untameable psychic energies erupted out of his dead form, lashing outwards indiscriminately. Impact resounded on impact. Above in his command seat, Hechtor Dravere noticed the shuddering of the deck, and began to look around for the cause.

In a mushroom of light, the unleashed psychic energies of the dying inquisitor blew the entire Leviathan apart, atom from atom.

Twenty-Seven

'We're clear!' Rawne yelled as he sprinted across the chamber with Caffran next to him. Gaunt had marshalled the others at the doorway. By now, the huge machine was rumbling and the gas-venting was continuous.

'Mkoll! Come on!' Gaunt shouted.

On the far side of the chamber, a section of the ancient grille finally gave way. Men of Iron stumbled forward out of their alcove, their metal feet crunching over the fallen grille sheet. All around, their companions rattled and shook at their pens, eyes burning like the blue-hot backwash of missile tubes, murmuring their sonorous hum.

The metal skeletons spilling out of the cage began to advance across the chamber, bleary and undirected. Mkoll, fixing the last set of charges to the side of the vibrating STC, looked round in horror at their jerking advance.

There was a sudden rush of noise beside him and a hatch aperture slid open in the side of the STC, voiding a great gout of steam. Caught in it, Mkoll fell to his knees, choking and gagging.

'Mkoll!'

Kneeling with his back turned to the hot steam, the coughing Mkoll couldn't see what was looming out of the swirling gas behind him.

A newborn Man of Iron. The first to be produced by the STC after its long slumber. As soon as it appeared, the others, those loosed and those still caged, began keening, in a long, continuous, piteous wail that was at once a human shriek and a rapid broadcast of machine code sequences.

There was something wrong with the newborn. It was malformed, grotesque compared to the perfect anatomical symmetry of the other Men of Iron. A good head taller, it was hunched, blackened, one arm far longer than the other, draped and massive, the other hideously vestigial and twisted. Corrupt horns sprouted from its over-long skull and its eyes shone a deadened yellow. Oil like stringy pus wept from the eye sockets. It shambled, unsteady. Its exposed teeth and jaws clacked and mashed idiotically.

Dorden howled out something about Gaunt being right, but Gaunt was already moving and not listening. He dived across the chamber at full stretch and tackled the coughing Mkoll onto the floor a second before the newborn's larger arm sliced through the space the stealther had previously occupied.

The respite was brief. Rolling off Mkoll and trying to pull him up, Gaunt saw the newborn turn to address them again, its jaw champing mindlessly. Behind it, in the reeking smoke of the hatchway, a second newborn was already emerging.

Two las-rounds punched into the newborn and made it stagger backwards. Caffran was trying his best, but the dully reflective carapace of the newborn shrugged off all but the kinetic force of the shots.

It struck at Gaunt and Mkoll again, but the commissar managed to roll himself and the scout out of the way. Its great metal claw sparked against the algorithm-inscribed floor, incising an alteration to the calculations that was permanent and insane.

Gaunt struggled to drag Mkoll away from the shambling metal thing, cursing out loud. In a second, Dorden and Bragg were with him, easing his efforts, pulling Mkoll upright.

The unexpected blow smashed Gaunt off his feet. The newborn had reached out a glancing blow and taken a chunk of cloth and flesh out of his back. How could it–

Gaunt rolled and looked up. The newborn's massive forelimb had grown, articulating out on extending metallic callipers, forming new pistons and extruded pulleys as it morphed its mechanical structure.

The monstrous thing struck at him again. The commissar flopped left to dodge and then right to dodge again. The metal claw cracked into the floor on either side of him.

Rawne, Larkin and Caffran sprang in. Caffran tried to shoot at close range but Larkin got in his way, capering and shouting to distract the machine. A second later, Larkin was also sent flying by a backhanded swipe.

Rawne hadn't had time to load another barbed round into his lance, so he used it like an axe, swinging the bayonet blade so that it reverberated against the creature's iron skull. Cable-sinews sheared and the newborn's head was knocked crooked.

The machine-being swung round with its massive fighting limb and smacked Rawne away, extending its reach to at least five metres. Gaunt dived across the floor and came up holding Rawne's barb-lance. He scythed down with it and smashed the Man of Iron's limb off at the second elbow, cutting through the increasingly diminished girth of the extending limb. Then Gaunt plunged the weapon, point first, into the newborn's face. The blade came free in an explosion of oil and ichor-like milky fluid.

The monstrosity fell back, cold and stiff, the light dying in its eyes.

By then, six new demented newborns had spilled from the STC's hatch. Behind them, forty or more of the Men of Iron had burst from their cages and were thumping forward. The others rattled their pens and began to howl.

'Now! Now we're fething leaving!' Gaunt yelled.

Twenty-Eight

It had taken them close on four hours to find and fight their way in; four hours from the bottom of the chimney shaft on the hillside to the doors of the Edicule. Now they had closed the doors on the shuffling blue-eyed metal nightmares and were ready to run. But even with the simple confidence of retracing their steps, Gaunt knew he had to factor in more time, so in the end he had Rawne set the tube-charge relays for four and three-quarter standard hours.

Already their progress back to the surface was flagging. Domor was getting weaker with each step, and though able-bodied, both Bragg and Larkin were slowing with the dull pain of their wounds from the firefight. Most of their weapons had been dumped, as the powercells were now dead. There was no point carrying the excess weight. Rawne's barb-lance was still functioning and he led the way with Mkoll, whose lasrifle had about a dozen gradually dissipating shots left in its dying clip.

Dorden, Domor, and Larkin were unarmed except for blades. Larkin's carbine, still functioning thanks to its mechanical function, was of no use to him with his wounded arm, so Gaunt had turned it over to Caffran to guard the rear. Bragg insisted on keeping his autocannon, but there was barely a drum left to it, and Gaunt wasn't sure how well the injured trooper would manage it if it came to a fight.

Then there was the darkness of the tunnels, which Gaunt cursed himself for forgetting. All of their lamp packs were now dead, and as they moved away from the Edicule chambers into the darker sections of the labyrinth, they had to halt while Mkoll and Caffran scouted ahead to salvage cloth and wood from the bodies of the dead foe in the cistern approach. They fashioned two dozen makeshift torches, with cloth wadded around wooden staves and lance-poles, moistened with the pungent contents of Bragg's last precious bottle of sacra liquor. Lit by the flickering flames, they moved on, passing gingerly through the cistern and beyond.

As they lumbered through the stinking mass of enemy corpses choking the cistern, Gaunt thought to search them for other weapons, mechanical weapons that were unaffected by the energy-drain. But the scent of meat had brought the insect swarms down the passage, and the twisted bodies were now a writhing, revolting mass of carrion.

There was no time. They pressed on. Gaunt tried not to think what wretchedness Mkoll and Caffran had suffered to scavenge the material for the torches.

The torches themselves burned quickly, and illuminated little but the immediate environs of the bearer. Gaunt felt fatigue growing in his limbs, realising now more than ever that the energy-leaching affected more than lamp packs and lasgun charges. If he was weary, he dreaded to think what Domor was like. Twice the commissar had to call a halt and regroup as Mkoll and Rawne got too far ahead of the struggling party.

How long had it been? His timepiece was dead. Gaunt began to wonder if the charges would even fire. Would their detonator circuits fizzle and die before they clicked over?

They reached a jagged turn in the ancient, sagging tunnels. They must have been moving now for close on three hours, he guessed. There was no sign of Mkoll and Rawne ahead. He lit another torch and looked back as Larkin and Bragg moved up together past him, sharing a torch.

'Go on,' he urged them, hoping this way was the right way. Without Mkoll's sharp senses, he felt lost. Which turn was it? Larkin and Bragg, gifted with that uncanny Tanith sixth sense of direction themselves, seemed in no doubt. 'Just move on and out. If you find Sergeant Mkoll or Major Rawne, tell them to keep moving too.'

The huge shadow of Bragg and his wiry companion nodded silently to him and soon their guttering light was lost in the tunnel ahead.

Gaunt waited. Where the feth were the others?

Minutes passed, lingering, creeping.

A light appeared. Caffran moved into sight, squinting out into the dark with Larkin's carbine held ready.

'Sir?'

'Where are Domor and the doctor?' Gaunt asked.

Caffran looked puzzled. 'I haven't passed—'

'You were the rearguard, trooper!'

'I haven't passed them, sir!' Caffran barked.

Gaunt bunched a fist and rapped his own forehead with it. 'Keep going. I'll go back.'

'I'll go back with you, sir—' Caffran began.

'Go on!' Gaunt snapped. 'That's an order, trooper! I'll go back and look.'

Caffran hesitated. In the dim fire-flicker, Gaunt saw distress in the young man's eyes.

'You've done all I could have asked of you, Caffran. You and the others. First and Only, best of warriors. If I die in this pit, I'll die happy knowing I got as many of you out as possible.'

He made to shake the man's hand. But Caffran seemed over-whelmed by the gesture and moved away.

'I'll see you on the surface, commissar,' Caffran said firmly.

Gaunt headed back down the funnel of rock. Caffran's light remained stationary behind him, watching him until he was out of sight.

The rocky tunnel was damp and stifling. There was no sign of Dorden or the wounded Domor. Gaunt opened his mouth to call out and then silenced himself. The blackness around him was too deep and dark for a voice. By now, the awakened Men of Iron could be lumbering down the tunnels, alert to any sound.

The passage veered to the left. Gaunt fought a feeling of panic. He didn't seem to be retracing his steps at all. He must have lost a turn somewhere. Lost, a voice hissed in his mind. Fereyd's voice? Dercius's? Macaroth's? You're lost, you witless, compassionate fool!

His last torch sputtered and died. Darkness engulfed him. His eyes adjusted and he saw a pale glow far ahead. Gaunt moved towards it.

The tunnel, now crumbling underfoot even as it sloped away, led into a deep cavern, natural and rocky, lit by a greenish bioluminescent growth throbbing from fungus and lichens caking the ceiling and walls. It was a vast cavern full of shattered rock and dark pools. His foot slipped on loose pebbles and he struggled to catch himself. Almost invisible in the darkness, a bottomless abyss yawned to his right. A few steps on and he fumbled his way around the lip of another chasm. Black, oily fluid bubbled and popped in crater holes. Grotesque blind insects with dangling legs and huge fibrous wings whirred around in the semi-dark.

Domor lay on his side on a shelf of cool rock, still and silent. Gaunt crawled over to him. The trooper had been hit on the back of the head with a blunt instrument. He was alive, just, the blow adding immeasurably to the damage he had already suffered. A burned-out torch lay nearby, and there was a spilled medical kit, lying half-open, with rolls of bandages and flasks of disinfectant scattered around it.

'Doctor?' Gaunt called.

Dark shapes leapt down on him from either side. Fierce hands grappled him. He caught a glimpse of Jantine uniform as he fought back. The ambush was so sudden, it almost overwhelmed him, but he was tensed and ready for anything thanks to the warning signs of Domor and the medi-kit. He kicked out hard, breaking something within his assailant's body, and then rolled free, slashing with his silver Tanith blade. A man yelped – and then screamed deeper and more fully as his staggering form mis-footed and tumbled into a chasm. But the others had him, striking and pummelling him hard. Three sets of hands, three men.

'Enough! Ebzan, enough! He's mine!'

Dazed, Gaunt was dragged upright by the three Patricians. Through fogged eyes, across the cavern, he saw Flense advancing, pushing Dorden before him, a lasgun to the pale old medic's temple.

'Gaunt.'

'Flense! You fething madman! This isn't the time!'

'On the contrary, colonel-commissar, this is the time. At last the time... for you, for me. A reckoning.'

The three Jantine soldiers muscled Gaunt up to face Flense and his captive.

'If it's the prize you want, Flense, you're too late. It'll be gone by the time you get there,' Gaunt hissed.

'Prize? Prize?' Flense smiled, his scar-tissue twitching. 'I don't care for that. Let Dravere care, or that monster Heldane. I spit upon their prize! You are all I have come for!'

'I'm touched,' Gaunt said and one of the men smacked him hard around the back of the head.

'That's enough, Avranche!' Flense snapped. 'Release him!'

Reluctantly, the three Jantine Patricians set him free and stood back. Head spinning, Gaunt straightened up to face Flense and Dorden.

'Now we settle this matter of honour,' Flense said.

Gaunt grinned disarmingly at Flense, without humour. 'Matter of honour? Are we still on this? The Tanith-Jantine feud? You're a perfect idiot, Flense, you know that?'

Flense grimaced, pushing the pistol tighter into the wincing forehead of Dorden. 'Do you so mock the old debt? Do you want me to shoot this man before your very eyes?'

'Mock on,' Dorden murmured. 'Better he shoot me than I listen to any more of his garbage.'

'Don't pretend you don't know the depth of the old wound, the old treachery,' Flense said spitefully.

Gaunt sighed. 'Dercius. You mean Dercius! Sacred Feth, but isn't that done with? I know the Jantine have never liked admitting they had a coward on their spotless honour role, but this is taking things too far! Dercius, General Dercius, Emperor rot his filthy soul, left my father and his unit to die on Kentaur. He ran away and left them. When I executed Dercius on Khedd all those years ago, it was a battlefield punishment, as is my right to administer as an Imperial commissar!

'He deserted his men, Flense! Throne of Earth, there's not a regiment in the Guard that doesn't have a black sheep, a way-ward son! Dercius was the Jantine's disgrace! That's no reason to prolong a rivalry with me and my Ghosts! This mindless feuding has cost the lives of good men, on both sides! So what if we beat you to the punch on Fortis? So what of Pyrites and aboard the *Absalom*? You jackass Jantine don't know when to stop, do you? You don't know where honour ends and discipline begins!'

Flense shot Dorden in the side of the head and the medic's body crumpled. Gaunt made to leap forward, incandescent with rage, but Flense raised the pistol to block him.

'It's an honour thing, all right,' Flense spat, 'but forget the Jantine and the Tanith. It's an honour thing between you and me.'

'What are you saying, Flense?' growled Gaunt through his fury.

'Your father, my father. I was the son of a dynasty on Jant Normanidus. The heir to a province and a wide estate. You sent my father to hell in disgrace and all my lands and titles were stripped from me. Even my family name. That went too. I was forced to battle my way up and into the service as a footslogger. Prove my worth, make my own name. My life has been one long, hellish struggle against infamy thanks to you.'

'Your father?' Gaunt echoed.

'My father. Aldo Dercius.'

The truth of it resonated in Ibram Gaunt's mind. He saw, truly understood now, how this could end no other way. He launched himself at Flense.

The pistol fired. Gaunt felt a stinging heat across his chest as he barrelled into the Patrician colonel. They rolled over on the rocks, sharp angles cutting into their flesh. Flense smashed the pistol butt into the side of Gaunt's head.

Gaunt mashed his elbow sideways and felt ribs break. Flense yowled and clawed at the commissar, wrenching him over his head in a cartwheel flip. Gaunt landed on his back hard, struggled to rise and met Flense's kick in the face. He slammed back over the rocks and loose pebbles, skittering stone fragments out from under him.

Flense leapt again, encountering Gaunt's up-swinging boot as he dived forward, smashing the wind out of his chest. Flense fell on Gaunt; the Patrician's hands clawed into his throat. Gaunt was aware of the chanting voices of the three Jantine soldiers watching, echoing Flense's name.

As Flense tightened his grip and Gaunt choked, the chant changed from 'Flense!' to that family name that had been stripped from the colonel at the disgrace.

'Dercius! Dercius! Dercius!'

Dercius. Uncle Dercius. Uncle fething Dercius…

Gaunt's punch lifted Flense off him in a reeling spray of mouth blood. He rolled and ploughed into the Patrician colonel, throwing three, four, five well-met punches.

Flense recovered, kicked Gaunt headlong, and the commissar

lay sprawled and helpless for a moment. Flense towered over him, a chunk of rock raised high in both hands to crush Gaunt's head.

'For my father!' screamed Flense.

'For mine!' hissed Gaunt. His Tanith war-knife bit through the air and pinned the Patrician's skull to the blackness for a second. With a mouthful of blood bubbling his scream, Flense teetered away backwards and fell with a slapping splash into a pool of black fluid.

His body shattered and aching, Gaunt lay back on the rock shelf. His men, he thought, they'll…

There was the serial crack of an exotic carbine, a lasrifle and a barb-lance. Gaunt struggled up. Caffran, Rawne, Mkoll, Larkin and Bragg stalked into the cavern. The three Jantine lay dead in the gloom.

'The surface… we've got to… ' Gaunt coughed.

'We're going,' Rawne said, as Bragg lifted the helpless form of Domor.

Gaunt stumbled across to Dorden. The medic was still alive. Drained of power by the cavern, Flense's pistol had only grazed him, as it had only grazed Gaunt's chest when he had thrown himself at Flense. Gaunt lifted Dorden in his arms. Caffran and Mkoll moved to help him, but Gaunt shrugged them off.

'We haven't got much time now. Let's get out of here.'

Twenty-Nine

The subsurface explosion ruptured most of the Target Primaris on Menazoid Epsilon and set it burning incandescently.

Imperial forces pulled away from the vanquished moon and returned to their support ships in high orbit.

Gaunt received a communiqué from Warmaster Macaroth, thanking him for his efforts and applauding his success.

Gaunt screwed the foil up and threw it away. Bandaged and aching, he moved through the medical wing of the frigate *Navarre*, checking on his wounded… Domor, Dorden, Corbec, Larkin, Bragg, a hundred more…

As he passed Corbec's cot, the grizzled colonel called him over in a hoarse, weak whisper.

'Rawne told me you found the thing. Blew it up. How did you know?'

'Corbec?'

'How did you know what to do? Back on Pyrites, you told me the path would be hard. Even when we found out what we were looking for, you never said what you'd do when you found it. How did you decide?'

Gaunt smiled.

'Because it was wrong. You don't know what I saw down there, Colm. Men do insane things. Feth, if I'd been insane enough to try and harness what I found… if I'd succeeded… I could have made myself warmaster. Who knows, even emperor…'

'Emperor Gaunt. Heh. Got a ring to it. Bit fething sacrilegious, though.'

Gaunt smiled. The feeling was unfamiliar. 'The Vermilion secret of Epsilon was heretical and tainted by Chaos. Bad, whichever way you care to gloss it. But that's not what really made me destroy it.'

Corbec hunkered up onto his elbows. 'Kidding me? Why then?'

Ibram Gaunt put his head in his hands and sighed the sigh of someone released from a great burden. 'Someone told me what to do, colonel. It was a long time ago...'

A MEMORY

Darendara, Twenty Years Earlier

Four Hyrkan troopers were splitting fruit in the snowy court-yard, lit by a ring of braziers. They had found some barrels in an undercroft and opened them to discover the great round globe-fruit from a summer crop stored in spiced oil. They were joking and laughing as they set them on a mounting block and hacked them into segments with their bayonets. One had stolen a big gilt serving platter from the kitchens, and they were piling it with slices, ready to carry it through to the main hall where the body of men were carousing and drinking to their victory.

Night was stealing in across the shattered roofs of the Winter Palace, and stars were coming out, frosty points in the cold darkness.

The Boy, the cadet commissar, wandered out across the courtyard, taking in the stillness. Distant voices, laughing and singing, filtered across the stone space. Gaunt smiled. He could make out a barrack-room victory song, harmonised badly by forty or more Hyrkan voices. Someone had substituted his name in the lyric in place of the hero. It didn't scan, but they sang it anyway, rousingly when it came to the bawdy parts.

Gaunt's shoulder blades still throbbed from the countless congratulatory slaps he had taken in the last few hours. Maybe they would stop calling him 'The Boy' now.

He looked up, catching sight of the landing lights of a dozen troop ships ferrying fresh occupation forces down from orbit, their bulks invisible against the darkness of the night. The landing lights reminded him of constellations. He had never been able to make sense of the stars. People drew figures in them: warriors, bulls, serpents, crowns; arbitrary shapes, it seemed to him, imperfect sense made of stellar positions.

Back on Manzipor, back home years ago, the cook Oric would sit him on his knee at nightfall and teach him the names of the star groups. Years ago. He really had been a boy then. Oric knew the names, drew the shapes, linked stars until they made a ram or a lion. Gaunt had never been able to see the shapes without the lines linking the stars.

Here, now, he knew the lines of lights represented drop-ships, but he couldn't imagine their shapes. Just lights. Stars and lights, lights and stars, signifying meanings and purposes he couldn't yet see.

Like the stars, the sweeping ship-lights occasionally went dim as they passed beyond the wreathes of smoke that were streaming, black against the black sky, from the parts of the Winter Palace that still smouldered.

Buttoning his storm-coat, Gaunt crossed the wide expanse of flagstones, his boots slipping in the slush. He passed a great stack of Secessionist helmets, piled in a trophy mound. There was a stink of stale sweat and defeat about them. Someone had painted a crude version of the Hyrkan regimental griffon on each and every one.

The men at the braziers looked up as his figure loomed out of the darkness.

'It's the Boy!' one cried. Gaunt winced and smirked at the same time.

'The Victor of Darendara!' another said with a drunken glee that entirely lacked irony.

'Come and join the feast, sir!' the first said, wiping his juice-stained hands on the front of his tunic. 'The men would like to raise a glass or two with you.'

'Or three!'

'Or five or ten or a hundred!'

Gaunt nodded his appreciation. 'I'll be in shortly. Open a cask for me.'

They jibed and cackled back, returning to their work. As Gaunt moved past, one of them turned and held out a dripping half-moon of fruit.

'Take this at least! Freshest thing we've had in weeks!'

Gaunt took the segment, scooping the cluster of seeds and pith out of its core with a finger. In its smile of husky, oil-wet rind, the fruit was salmon-pink, ripe and heavy with water and juice. He bit into it as he strode away, waving his thanks to the men.

It was sweet. Cool. The fruit flesh disintegrated in his hungry mouth and flooded his throat with rich, sugary fluid. Juice dribbled down his chin. He laughed, like a boy again. It was the sweetest thing he'd tasted on Darendara.

No, not the sweetest.

The sweetest thing he had tasted here was his first triumph. His first victorious command. His first chance to serve the Emperor and the Imperium and the service he had been raised to obey and love.

In a lit doorway ahead, a figure appeared. Gaunt recognised the bulky silhouette immediately. He fumbled with the fruit segment, about to salute.

'At ease, Ibram,' Oktar said. 'Carry on munching. That stuff looks good. Might just have to get myself a piece too.

'Walk with me.'

Gnawing the sweet flesh back to the rind, Gaunt fell in beside Oktar. They passed the men at the brazier again, and Oktar caught a whole fruit as it was tossed to him, splitting it open with his huge thumbs. The pair walked on wordlessly towards the Palace chapel grounds, through a herb-scented garden cast in blue darkness. Both ate, slobbering and spitting pips. Oktar handed a portion of his fruit to Gaunt and they finished it off.

Standing under the stained glass oriel of the chapel, they cast the rinds aside and stood for a long while, swallowing and licking juice from their dripping fingers.

'Tastes good,' Oktar said at last.

'Will it always taste this fine?' Gaunt asked.

'Always, I promise you. Triumph is the endgame we all chase

and desire. When you get it, hang on to it and relish every second.' Oktar wiped his chin, his face a shadow in the gloom.

'But remember this, Ibram. It's not always as obvious as it seems. Winning is everything, but the trick is to know where the winning really is. Hell, killing the enemy is the job of the regular trooper. The task of a commissar is more subtle.'

'Finding how to win?'

'Or what to win. Or what kind of win will really count in the long term. You have to use everything you have, every insight, every angle. Never, ever be a slave to simple tactical directives. The officer cadre are about as sharp as an ork's arse sometimes. We're political animals, Ibram. Through us, if we do our job properly, the black and white of war is tempered. We are the interpreters of combat, the translators. We give meaning to war, subtlety, purpose even. Killing is the most abhorrent, mindless profession known to man. Our role is to fashion the killing machine of the human species into a positive force. For the Emperor's sake. For the sake of our own consciences.'

They paused in reflection for a while. Oktar lit one of his luxuriously fat cigars and kissed big white smoke rings up into the night breeze.

'Before I forget,' he suddenly added, 'there is one last task I have for you before you retire. Retire! What am I saying? Before you join the men in the hall and drink yourself stupid!'

Gaunt laughed.

'There is an interrogation. Inquisitor Defay has arrived to question the captives. You know the usual witch-hunting post mortem High Command insists on. But he's a sound man, known him for years. I spoke to him just now and apparently he wants your help.'

'Me?'

'Specifically you. Asked for you by name. One of his prisoners refuses to speak to anyone else.'

Gaunt blinked. He was confused, but he also knew who the commissar-general was talking about.

'Cut along to see him before you go raising hell with the boys. Okay?'

Gaunt nodded.

Oktar smacked him on the arm. 'You did well today, Ibram. Your father would be proud.'

'I know he is, sir.'

Oktar may have smiled, but it was impossible to tell in the darkness of the chapel garden.

Gaunt turned to go.

'One thing, sir,' he said, turning back.

'Ask it, Gaunt.'

'Could you try and encourage the men to stop referring to me as "The Boy"?'

Gaunt left Oktar laughing raucously in the darkness.

Gaunt's hands were sticky with drying juice. He strode down a long, lamp-lit hallway, straightening his coat and setting his cadet's cap squarely on his head.

Under an archway ahead, Hyrkans in full battledress stood guard, weapons hanging loosely from shoulder slings. There were others, too: robed, hooded beings skulking in candle-shadows, muttering, exchanging data-slates and sealed testimony recordings.

Incense hung in the air. Somewhere, someone was whimpering.

Major Tanhause, supervising the Hyrkan presence, waved him through with a wink and directed him down to the left.

There was a boy in the passage to the left, standing outside a closed door. No older than me, mused Gaunt as he approached. The boy looked up. He was pale and thin, taller than Gaunt, wearing long russet robes, and his eyes were fierce. Lank black hair flopped down one side of his pale face.

'You can't come in here,' he said sullenly.

'I'm Gaunt. Cadet-Commissar Gaunt,'

The lad frowned. He turned, knocked at the door and then opened it slightly as a voice answered. There was an exchange Gaunt could not hear before a large figure emerged from the room, closing the door behind him.

'That will be all for now, Gravier,' the figure told the boy, who retreated into the shadows. The figure was tall and power- ful, bigger even than Oktar. He wore intricate armour draped with a long purple cloak. His face was totally hidden behind a blank cloth hood that terrified Gaunt. Bright eyes glared at him through the hood's eye slits for a moment, appraising him. Then the man peeled the hood off.

His face was handsome and aquiline. Gaunt was surprised to find compassion there, pain, fatigue, understanding. The face was cold white, the flesh pale, but somehow there was a warmth and a light.

'I am Defay,' the inquisitor said in a low, resonating voice. 'You are Cadet Gaunt, I presume.'

'Yes, sir. What would you have me do?'

Defay approached the cadet and placed a hand on his shoulder, turning him before he spoke. 'A girl. You know her.'

It was not a question.

'I know the girl. I... saw her.'

'She is the key, Gaunt. In her mind lie the secrets of whatever turned this world to disorder. It's tiresome, I know, but my task is to unlock such secrets.'

'We all serve the Emperor, my lord.'

'We certainly do, Gaunt. Now look. She says she knows you. A nonsense, I'm sure. But she says you are the only one she will answer to. Gaunt, I've performed my ministry long enough to recognise an opening. I could... extricate the secrets I seek in any number of ways, but the most painless – to me and her both – would be to use you. Are you up to it?'

Gaunt looked round at Defay. His stern yet avuncular manner reminded him of someone. Oktar – no, Uncle Dercius.

'What do you want me to do?'

'Go in there and talk to her. Nothing more. There are no wires to record you, no vista-grams to watch you. I just want you to talk to her. If she says what she wants to say to you, it may provide an opening I can use.'

Gaunt entered the room and the door shut behind him. The small chamber was bare except for a table with a stool on either side. The girl sat on one. A sodium lamp fluttered on the wall.

Gaunt sat down on the other stool, facing her.

Her eyes were as black as her hair. Her dress was as white as her skin. She was beautiful.

'Ibram! At last! There are so many things I need to tell you!'

Her voice was soft yet firm, her High Gothic perfect. Gaunt backed away from her direct stare.

She leaned across the table urgently, gazing into his eyes.

'Don't be afraid, Ibram Gaunt.'

'I'm not.'

'Oh, you are. I don't have to be a mind reader to see that. Though, of course, I am a mind reader.'

Gaunt breathed deeply. 'Then tell me what I want to know.'

'Clever, clever,' she chuckled, sitting back.

Gaunt leaned forward, insistent. 'Look, I don't want to be here either. Let's get this over with. You're a psyker – astound me with your visions or shut the hell up. I have other things I would rather be doing.'

'Drinking with your men. Fruit.'

'What?'

'You crave more of the sweet fruit. You long for it. Sweet, juicy fruit…'

Gaunt shuddered. 'How did you know?'

She grinned impishly. 'The juice is all down your chin and the front of your coat.'

Gaunt couldn't hide his smile. 'Now who's being clever? That was no psyker trick. That was observation.'

'But true enough, wasn't it? Is there a whole lot of difference?'

Gaunt nodded. 'Yes… yes there is. What you said to me earlier. It made no sense, but it had nothing to do with the stains on my coat either. Why did you ask for me?'

She sighed, lowering her head. There was a long pause.

The voice that finally replied to him wasn't hers any more. It was a scratchy, wispy thing that made him start backwards. By the Emperor, but it was suddenly so cold in here!

He saw his own breath steam and realised it wasn't his imagination.

The whisper-dry voice said: 'I don't want to see things, Ibram, but still I do. In my head. Sometimes wonderful things. Sometimes awful things. I see what people show me. Minds are like books.'

Gaunt stammered, sliding back on his seat. 'I... I... like books.'

'I know you do. I read that. You liked Boniface's books. He had so many of them.'

Gaunt froze, tremors of worry plucking at his spine. He felt an ice cold droplet of sweat chase down his brow from his hairline. He felt trapped.

'How could you know about that?'

'You know how.'

The temperature in the room had dropped to freezing. Gaunt saw the ice crystals form across the table top, crackling and causing the wood to creak. Gooseflesh pimpled his body.

He leapt up and backed to the door. 'That's enough! This interview is over!'

He tried the door, making to leave. It was locked. Or at least, it would not open for him. Something held it shut. Gaunt hammered on it. 'Inquisitor! Inquisitor Defay! Let me out!'

His voice sounded blunt and hollow in the tiny confines of the freezing room. He was more terrified than he had ever been in his life.

He looked round. The girl was crawling across the floor towards him, her eyes blank and filmed. Spittle welled out of her lolling mouth. She smiled. It was the most dreadful thing young Ibram Gaunt had ever seen.

When she spoke, her voice did not match her mouth. The utterances came from some other, horrid place. Her lips were just keeping bad time with them.

Cowering in a corner, watching her slow, animalistic approach across the icy floor, Gaunt managed to whisper: 'What do you want from me? What?'

'Your life.' A feathery, inhuman voice.

'Get away from me!' Gaunt murmured, struggling with the door handle, to no avail.

'What do you want to know?' the horror asked, suddenly, calculatingly.

His mind raced. Maybe if he kept it talking, he could slow it down, figure a way out... 'Will I make commissar?' he snapped, hammering on the door, not really caring about his question.

'Of course.'

The lock was straining, starting to give. A few moments more. Keep it talking! 'Tell me the rest,' he urged, hoping she would cease her crawl towards him.

She was silent for a few seconds as she thought. Her eyes went blacker. The tremulous, thin voice spoke again. 'What I told you before. There will be seven. Seven stones of power. Cut them and you will be free. Do not kill them. But first you must find your ghosts.'

Gaunt shrugged, fighting with the lock, still not really listening. 'What the feth does that mean?'

'What does "feth" mean?' she replied plainly.

Gaunt hesitated. He had no idea what the word meant or why he had used it.

'Your future impinges on you, Ibram. Ghosts, ghosts, ghosts.'

Gaunt turned. He'd fight if he had to. The door wasn't giving and the slack-mouthed freak was getting too close. 'In my profession I make plenty of those. Tell me something useful.'

'You're an anroth.'

'A what?'

She hissed and stared up at him. 'I haven't the faintest idea what it means, but I know you are one. Anroth. Anroth. That's you.'

Gaunt scrabbled across the room to the far wall to put more space between them.

She crawled around slowly.

'This is all madness! I'm leaving,' he said.

'So leave. But one thing before you go.'

He looked back and she smiled terrifyingly at him under her veil of loose black hair.

'The warp knows you, Ibram Gaunt.'

'To hell with the warp!' he barked.

'Ibram, there will come a day… far off, far away, when something coloured in vermilion will be the most valuable thing you have ever known. Chase it. Find it. Others will seek it, and you will defend it in blood. The blood of your ghosts.'

'Enough with this!'

She shuffled forward on her knees like an animal. Spit from her mouth splashed the floor.

'Remember this! Ibram! Ibram! Please! So many will die if you don't! So many, so very many!'

'If I don't what?' he snapped, trying to find a way out of this hell.

'Destroy it. You must destroy it. The vermilion thing. Destroy it. It makes iron without souls.'

'You're insane!'

'Iron without souls!'

She clawed at his legs, scratching and pulling at the ice-rimed cloth.

'Get off me!'

'Worlds will die! A warmaster will die! Don't let any of them have it! Any of them! It is not a matter of the wrong hands! All will be wrong hands! No one has the right to use it! Destroy it! Ibram! Please!'

He threw her off and she fell away from him, sprawling on the frozen floor, crying.

He reached the door, his hand on the latch. It was suddenly unlocked. He turned back to her. She rose from the floor, her dark eyes wet with tears. Her voice was her own again now.

'Don't let them, Ibram. Destroy it.'

'I've never heard such rubbish,' Gaunt said diffidently. He took a deep breath. 'If you're truly gifted, why don't you tell me something real? Something I might actually want to know. Like… like how did my father die?'

She pulled herself up onto the stool. The room went cold

again. Fiercely cold. She looked deep into his eyes and Gaunt felt the stare pressing into his brain.

Despite himself, he sat down again on the stool. He looked at her dark eyes. Something told him what was coming.

In her own voice, she began. 'Your father... you were his first and his only son. First and only...'

She fell silent again for a second, then she continued: 'Kentaur. It was on Kentaur. Dercius was commanding the main force and your father was leading the elite strike...'

Dan Abnett is a multiple *New York Times* bestselling author and an award-winning comic book writer. He has written over forty novels, including the acclaimed Gaunt's Ghosts series, and the Eisenhorn and Ravenor trilogies. His Horus Heresy novel *Prospero Burns* topped the SF charts in the UK and the US. In addition to writing for Black Library, Dan scripts audio dramas, movies, games, comics and bestselling novels for major publishers in Britain and America. He lives and works in Maidstone, Kent.

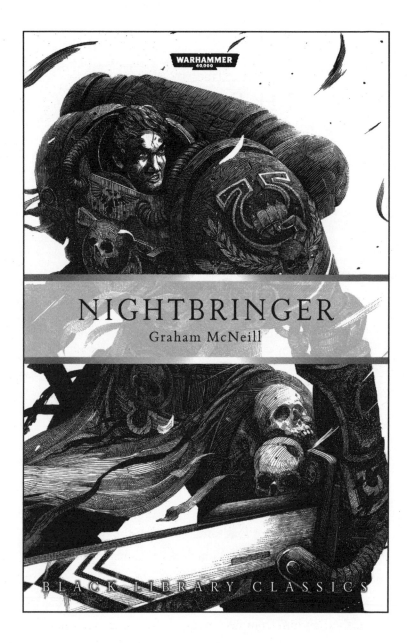

WARHAMMER
40,000

NIGHTBRINGER

Graham McNeill

BLACK LIBRARY CLASSICS

An extract from
NIGHTBRINGER
Graham McNeill

Uriel hit the deck of the alien vessel and rolled aside as the next Ultramarine warrior slammed down behind him. He sprang to his feet and drew his power sword and bolt pistol in one fluid motion. He swept his pistol around the room as he took in his surroundings, a low-ceilinged room stacked with round containers.

He thumbed the activation rune on the hilt of his sword and the blade leapt with eldritch fire just as a pair of crimson-armoured warriors charged through an oval shaped doorway. Their armour was smooth and gleaming, adorned with glittering blades, and they carried long rifles with jagged bayonets.

'Courage and honour!' screamed Uriel, launching himself at the eldar warriors.

He smashed his power sword down on the first alien's collar-bone, shearing him from neck to groin. The other alien stabbed with its bladed rifle and Uriel spun inside its guard. He hammered his elbow into his attacker's face, pulverising its helmet visor and breaking its neck.

He spared a glance behind him as more of the Ultramarines dropped through the hull breach. Pasanius was there, the blue-hot burner of his flamer roaring and ready to incinerate the enemies of the Emperor.

Uriel raised his power sword and yelled, 'The bridge!'

He sprinted through the doorway, finding himself in a narrow, shadowed corridor, with smooth walls that tapered to a point above his head.

A strange, truly alien aroma filled his senses, but he could not identify it. Two curving passages radiated forwards, their ends disappearing from sight.

Uriel picked the left hand corridor, and charged down its length.

He shouted, 'Pasanius with me! Dardino and Venasus take the right.'

Uriel heard the beat of footsteps from up ahead and saw dozens of the armoured warriors charging to intercept him. They carried the same bladed rifles and Uriel could see a number of larger, more dangerous weapons amongst their ranks.

Raising his flamer, Pasanius shouted, 'Get down!'

Uriel dropped and felt the whoosh of superheated promethium as it washed over him down the corridor. Alien screams echoed from the glassy walls as the liquid flames cooked their bodies within their armour and seared the flesh from their bones.

Uriel pushed himself to his feet and charged forwards, hurdling the burning corpses and leaping amongst the eldar. His sword slashed left and right and where he struck, aliens died. With a wild roar, the Ultramarines followed their captain, swords hacking and cutting amongst the aliens. Screaming, chainsaw-edged blades ripped through the flexible armour plates and flesh of the aliens with ease.

Chaplain Clausel bellowed the Canticles of Faith as he smote the aliens with his deadly crozius arcanum.

Uriel felt a close range blast of splinter fire impact on his arm. He ignored it, his armour absorbed the blast. Another blast slammed into his helmet and he snarled, spinning and beheading his attacker.

The last of the eldar died; the corridor had become a stinking charnel house.

None of the Ultramarines had fallen, though several bled from minor wounds. Pasanius fired short bursts of flame along a bend further down the corridor, deterring any counterattack.

Uriel opened a vox-channel to his other squads.

'Dardino, Venasus. What's your status?'

Venasus answered first, his voice steady and controlled despite the sounds of fierce battle raging around him. 'Strong resistance, captain. We have encountered what looks like a major defence point. Dardino is attempting to flank the aliens. I estimate six minutes until we overwhelm them.'

'Make it four! Ventris out.'

Gunfire spat towards the Ultramarines, ricocheting from the walls and filling the air with whickering splinters. The same type of splinters Uriel had dug from the church wall on Caernus IV.

Pasanius was on the ground, a dark, smoking hole punched in his shoulder guard. Uriel could hear the sergeant's cursing over the vox-net as the big man dragged himself away from the bend in the tunnel, never once releasing his grip on his flamer. Uriel could hear the sounds of more aliens moving to intercept them and thumbed a pair of frag grenades from his belt dispenser.

The weight of fire began to intensify and Uriel knew they had to keep pushing on lest the assault be halted in its tracks before it had even begun.

He rolled around the corner and fired two shots from his bolt pistol. The heavy *crack-thump* of bolter ammunition was reassuringly loud compared to the aliens' weaponry. A pair of aliens fell, their chests blown open by the mass-reactive shells as Uriel flipped both frags down the corridor. He fired twice more before diving back into cover as the grenades detonated simultaneously, hurling bodies through the air in the fiery blast.

Uriel leapt to his feet and dragged Pasanius upright.

'You ready for this, old friend?'

'More than ever, captain,' assured Pasanius hefting the flamer.

Uriel nodded and spun around the corridor, bolt pistol extended before him.

'For the Emperor!'

The Ultramarines followed Uriel as he pounded towards a crimson door, embossed with intricate designs of curving spikes and blades. Even from here he saw it was heavily armoured.

Cross-corridors bisected this one and Uriel could hear the sounds of battle from elsewhere in the ship. Red armoured figures dashed along parallel corridors and he shouted to watch the rear. With so many cross-corridors, there was a very real possibility of being outflanked and surrounded.

He slammed into the door and smashed it from its frame.

Uriel charged through the door, battle-hungry Ultramarines hard on his heels. They entered a vast, high-roofed dome and Uriel grinned with feral anticipation as he realised they must be on the command bridge at last. An ornate viewscreen dominated the far wall, with wide, hangar-like gates to either side. Iron tables with black leather restraint harnesses stood in a line, alongside racks of horrendous, multi-bladed weapons.

In the centre of the chamber, standing atop a raised command dais, was a tall, slender alien wearing an elaborately tooled suit of armour, similar to that of his warriors, but coloured a deep jade. He wore no helmet and his violet-streaked white hair spilled around his shoulders like snow. His skin was a lifeless mask, devoid of expression, and a thin line of blood ran from his lips. He carried a gigantic war-axe, its blade stained red.

Dozens of aliens filled the room, heavily armoured warriors, hefting long, halberd-like weapons that pulsed with unnatural energy.

The room reeked of death and terror. How many souls had met their end in this desolate place, wondered Uriel?

He had no time to ponder the question as the wide doors to either side of the viewscreen slid open. A horde of near naked warriors, both male and female, riding bizarre skimming blades and carrying long glaives, swept from each door.

Bolter shots felled half a dozen, but then they were amongst the Ultramarines, slashing and killing with their weapons. Uriel saw Brother Gaius fall, severed at the waist by the bladed wing of one of the flyers. His killer looped overhead as Gaius's body collapsed in a flood of gore.

Uriel put a bolt round through the whooping alien's head, watching with grim satisfaction as his limp body plummeted to the ground. The shrieking blade-skimmers spun high in the air, coming around for another pass.

Bolter rounds exploded amongst them as Dardino and Venasus led their squads into battle. Uriel shot dead another flyer as Venasus moved to stand beside him, his armour slick with alien blood.

'My apologies, captain. It took us five minutes.'

Uriel grinned fiercely beneath his helmet. 'I know you'll do better next time, sergeant.'

A skimmer exploded as Pasanius's flamer gouted a vast stream of liquid fire over its rider and fresh gunshots echoed through the dome. The vox in Uriel's helmet crackled to life as the Thunderhawk pilot patched into his personal link.

'Captain Ventris, we will have to pull back soon. The alien vessel is increasing in speed and we will not be able to maintain the umbilical for much longer. I suggest you begin falling back, before I am forced to disengage the docking clamps.'

Uriel cursed. He had no time to acknowledge the pilot's communication as he smashed a leather-harnessed warrior from his sky-board and rammed his sword through his belly. He saw the jade-armoured, albino warrior cutting a path towards him and wrenched his sword clear.

Some shapeless mass writhed around the warrior's legs, but

Uriel could not discern its nature in the gloom. A trio of the skimming warriors swooped in towards Uriel. He blasted two from their boards with well-placed bolter fire and beheaded the third. The jade warrior cut down two Ultramarine battle-brothers with contemptuous ease as they tried to intercept him.

Uriel shouted at his warriors to stand fast.

'This one is mine!'

From the icons on his helmet visor, Uriel could see that seven of his men were dead, their runic identifiers cold and black. His breathing was heavy, but his stamina was undiminished.

A space cleared around the two warriors as battle continued to rage throughout the bridge. The shapeless forms around the alien's legs resolved into clarity and Uriel was horrified as he clearly saw the heaving mass of creatures that hissed and spat beside the alien leader. A repulsive, horrifying and piteous agglomeration of thrashing, deformed flesh, sewn together in a riot of anatomies, writhed at the alien's feet. Each one was unique in its nauseating form, but all hissed with the same luna-tic malevolence, baring yellowed fangs and jagged talons.

Uriel extended his sword, pointing the tip at the alien leader's chest.

'I am Uriel Ventris of the Ultramarines and I have come to kill you.'

WARHAMMER

TROLLSLAYER

William King

BLACK LIBRARY CLASSICS

An extract from
TROLLSLAYER
William King

Felix thought they had been spotted, and he froze. The smoke of the incense filled his nostrils and seemed to amplify all his senses. He felt even more remote and disconnected from reality. There was a sharp, stabbing pain in his side. He was startled to realise that Gotrek had elbowed him in the ribs. He was pointing to something beyond the stone ring.

Felix struggled to see what loomed in the mist. Then he realised that it was the black coach. In the sudden, shocking silence he heard its door swing open. He held his breath and waited to see what would emerge.

A figure seemed to take shape out of the mist. It was tall and masked, and garbed in layered cloaks of many pastel colours. It moved with calm authority and in its arms it carried something swaddled in brocade cloth. Felix looked at Gotrek but he was watching the unfolding scene with fanatical intensity. Felix wondered if the dwarf had lost his nerve at this late hour.

The newcomer stepped forward into the stone circle.

'Amak tu amat Slaanesh!' it cried, raising its bundle on high. Felix could see that it was a child, though whether living or dead he could not tell.

'Ygrak tu amat Slaanesh! Tzarkol taen amat Slaanesh!' The crowd responded ecstatically.

The cloaked man stared out at the surrounding faces, and it seemed to Felix that the stranger gazed straight at him with calm, brown eyes. He wondered if the coven-master knew they were there and was playing with them.

'Amak tu Slaanesh!' the man cried in a clear voice.

'Amak klessa! Amat Slaanesh!' responded the crowd. It was clear to Felix that some evil ritual had begun. As the rite progressed, the coven-master moved closer to the altar with slow ceremonial steps. Felix felt his mouth go dry. He licked his lips. Gotrek watched the events as if hypnotised.

The child was placed on the altar with a thunderous rumble of drum beats. Now the six dancers each stood beside a pillar, legs astride it, clutching at the stone suggestively. As the ritual progressed they ground themselves against the pillars with slow sinuous movements.

From within his robes the master produced a long wavy-bladed knife. Felix wondered whether the dwarf was going to do something. He could hardly bear to watch.

Slowly the knife was raised, high over the cultist's head. Felix forced himself to look. An ominous presence hovered over the scene. Mist and incense seemed to be clotting together and congealing, and within the cloud Felix thought he could make out a grotesque form writhe and begin to materialise. Felix could bear the tension no longer.

'No!' he shouted.

He and the Trollslayer emerged from the long grass and marched shoulder-to-shoulder towards the stone ring. At first the cultists didn't seem to notice them, but finally the demented drumming stopped and the chanting faded and the cult-master turned to glare at them, astonished.

For a moment everyone stared. No one seemed to understand what was happening. Then the cult-master pointed the knife at them and screamed: 'Kill the interlopers!'

The revellers moved forward in a wave. Felix felt something tug at his leg and then a sharp pain. When he looked down he saw a creature, half woman, half serpent, gnawing at his ankle. He kicked out, pulling his leg free and stabbed down with his sword.

A shock passed up his arm as the blade hit bone. He began to run, following in the wake of Gotrek who was hacking his way towards the altar. The mighty double-bladed axe rose and fell rhythmically and left a trail of red ruin in its path. The cultists seemed drugged and slow to respond but, horrifyingly, they showed no fear. Men and women, tainted and untainted, threw themselves towards the intruders with no thought for their own lives.

Felix hacked and stabbed at anyone who came close. He put his blade under the ribs and into the heart of a dog-faced man who leapt at him. As he tried to tug his blade free a woman with claws and a man with mucous-covered skin leapt on him. Their weight bore him over, knocking the wind from him.

He felt the woman's talons scratch at his face as he put his foot under her stomach and kicked her off. Blood rolled down into his eyes from the cuts. The man had fallen badly, but leapt to grab his throat. Felix fumbled for his dagger with his left hand while he caught the man's throat with his right. The man writhed. He was difficult to grip because of his coating of slime. His own hands tightened inexorably on Felix's throat in return and he rubbed himself against Felix, panting with pleasure.

Blackness threatened to overcome the poet. Little silver points flared before his eyes. He felt an overwhelming urge to relax and fall forward into the darkness. Somewhere far away he heard Gotrek's bellowed war-cry. With an effort of will Felix jerked his dagger clear of its scabbard and plunged it into his assailant's ribs. The creature stiffened and grinned, revealing rows of eel-like teeth. He gave an ecstatic moan even as he died.

'Slaanesh, take me,' the man shrieked. 'Ah, the pain, the lovely pain!'

Felix pulled himself to his feet just as the clawed woman rose to hers. He lashed out with his boot, connected with her jaw. There was a crunch, and she fell backwards. Felix shook his head to clear the blood from his eyes.

The majority of the cultists had concentrated on Gotrek. This had kept Felix alive. The dwarf was trying to hack his way towards the heart of the stone circle. Even as he moved, the press of bodies against him slowed him down. Felix could see that he bled from dozens of small cuts.

The ferocious energy of the dwarf was terrible to see. He frothed at the mouth and ranted as he chopped, sending limbs and heads everywhere. He was covered in a filthy matting of gore, but in spite of his sheer ferocity Felix could tell the fight was going against Gotrek. Even as he watched, a cloaked reveller hit the dwarf with a club and Gotrek went down under a wave of bodies. So he has met his doom, thought Felix, just as he desired.